PAINTING THE TOWN RED

W0114603

LOOK FOR THESE EXCITING WESTERN SERIES
FROM BESTSELLING AUTHORS
WILLIAM W. JOHNSTONE AND J.A. JOHNSTONE

The Mountain Man

Luke Jensen: Bounty Hunter

Brannigan's Land

The Jensen Brand

Smoke Jensen: The Early Years

Preacher and MacCallister

Fort Misery

The Fighting O'Neils

Perley Gates

MacCoole and Boone

Guns of the Vigilantes

Shotgun Johnny

The Chuckwagon Trail

The Jackals

The Slash and Pecos Westerns

The Texas Moonshiners

Stoneface Finnegan Westerns

Ben Savage: Saloon Ranger

The Buck Trammel Westerns

The Death and Texas Westerns

The Hunter Buchanon Westerns

Will Tanner: U.S. Deputy Marshal

Old Cowboys Never Die

Go West, Young Man

Published by Kensington Publishers, Inc.

PAINTING THE TOWN RED

WILLIAM W. JOHNSTONE
AND J. A. JOHNSTONE

PINNACLE BOOKS
Kensington Publishing Corp.
kensingtonbooks.com

PINNACLE BOOKS are published by

Kensington Publishing Corp.
900 Third Avenue
New York, NY 10022

Copyright © 2025 by J.A. Johnstone

All rights reserved. No part of this book may be reproduced in any form or by any means without the prior written consent of the Publisher, excepting brief quotes used in reviews.

Without limiting the author's and publisher's exclusive rights, any unauthorized use of this publication to train generative artificial intelligence (AI) technologies is expressly prohibited.

This book is a work of fiction. Names, characters, businesses, organizations, places, events, and incidents either are the product of the author's imagination or are used fictitiously. Any resemblance to actual persons, living or dead, events, or locales is entirely coincidental.

To the extent that the image or images on the cover of this book depict a person or persons, such person or persons are merely models and are not intended to portray any character or characters featured in the book.

PUBLISHER'S NOTE: Following the death of William W. Johnstone, the Johnstone family is working with a carefully selected writer to organize and complete Mr. Johnstone's outlines and many unfinished manuscripts to create additional novels in all of his series, like The Last Gunfighter, Mountain Man, and Eagles, among others. This novel was inspired by Mr. Johnstone's superb storytelling.

If you purchased this book without a cover, you should be aware that this book is stolen property. It was reported as "unsold and destroyed" to the Publisher, and neither the Author nor the Publisher has received any payment for this "stripped book."

All Kensington titles, imprints, and distributed lines are available at special quantity discounts for bulk purchases for sales promotion, premiums, fundraising, and educational or institutional use.

Special book excerpts or customized printings can also be created to fit specific needs. For details, write or phone the office of the Kensington Sales Manager: Kensington Publishing Corp., 900 Third Avenue, New York, NY 10022. Attn. Sales Department. Phone: 1-800-221-2647.

PINNACLE BOOKS, the Pinnacle logo, and the WWJ steer head logo Reg. U.S. Pat. & TM Off.

First Printing: October 2025
ISBN-13: 978-0-7860-5152-6
ISBN-13: 978-0-7860-5149-6 (eBook)

10 9 8 7 6 5 4 3 2 1

Printed in the United States of America

The authorized representative in the EU for product safety and compliance is eucomply OU, Parnu mnt 139b-14, Apt 123
Tallinn, Berlin 11317, hello@eucompliancepartner.com.

1893

CHAPTER 1

Dead Broke, Colorado, was quiet that September afternoon. Quiet if you compared things to how they had been just a few weeks earlier, when the town had been practically overrun with gunfighters that a crooked gambler had brought in and then tried to steal the silver nugget—weighing, according to legend, a beefy 1,776 pounds—that Mayor Allane Auchinleck, better known as Nugget, had found back in 1885.

No one would argue that the town was much quieter than Dead Broke, located some two miles high up in what was known as This Side Of The Slope, had been during those lawless days. Days? Dead Broke's reputation had grown so much, its lawlessness had lasted years, but eventually had settled down, boomed, prospered, drawn attention as a silver mecca everywhere from San Francisco to New York City—and even overseas. But that had been way back then, during the glory days, when silver was worth the months or years it might take to find. These days, Dead Broke sure had a lot fewer people, now that the silver market had crashed and the Panic of '93 kept painting a grim picture for the future of this, and other, mining towns.

The town had boasted a population of right around ten thousand in the mid-1880s. Now it was down to . . . ?

If Duncan "Mick" MacMicking had to guess, a hundred? Maybe 150? And most of those would take off for lower elevations soon, because this high up, winter came early and held on for a long, cold time.

But Duncan liked things quiet. As Dead Broke's town marshal, he found a certain pleasure in living in a small town, too high up for most snakes, too high up for most people. Sure, the altitude at two miles up would tax a fellow's lungs now and then, especially after the first snow had fallen—just a few inches, not the feet that were sure to dump on these mountains in the coming months.

Only a few hardcore miners remained in town, and they weren't digging for silver or gold, but lead and zinc. Duncan had never heard much about lawlessness and death and murder over zinc and lead.

He sat in Sara Cardiff's Crosscut Saloon, playing penny-ante poker with Ben Usher—like Duncan, a man who had earned a reputation as a top gun and villain (though Usher happened to be a decent fellow) because of those hack writers who kept turning out cheap novels about plenty of wild Westerners—the same scribes that had helped give Mick MacMicking a reputation. Old Syd Jones, like Duncan and Usher, had also become something of a legend across the West.

And here they were, lazing away in a dying Colorado mountain town.

Of course, the way Duncan and Usher saw things, Syd Jones deserved his reputation. He was a stand-up guy, honest to his ramrod straight backbone, and now that he was off the hooch, just as fine a fellow as anyone could find—especially on This Side Of The Slope.

Yawning, Jones left the bar with a coffeepot and

walked over, taking his good, sweet time, and topped off the mugs in front of Duncan, Usher, and Logan Ladron, the only dealer who had gumption enough to stick it out in what was now the only gambling place in Dead Broke. In fact, now that the Lucky Dice Gambling Hall was out of business, it was the only place where a fellow could get a drink of whiskey outside of Percy Stahl's beer mill or—if they wanted to risk their tongues, teeth, throats, stomachs, and souls—buy some homemade hooch from Mayor Nugget.

Coffee, smelling powerfully strong, splashed into the neglected mugs in front of Duncan and Usher, and Jones set his own mug on the table before moving to a faro layout that now served as a good enough place to set coffeepots, hats, woolen scarves, and one sawed-off shotgun. Dragging a chair over, Jones settled into it, picked up his cup, and sipped.

Usher dealt two cards to Duncan, then took three himself. Logan Ladron had folded without taking a draw.

"Your bet," Usher said.

Duncan studied his hand for just a second, then tossed the cards onto a nickel and two pennies—the nickel being the ante, and the pennies being Duncan's bet and Usher's call.

"I fold."

Usher looked at his hand, and, stifling a yawn, threw his cards atop Duncan's.

"Me, too."

"Watch ya mean, you is foldin'?" cried Mayor Nugget, sitting at another table, looking through a mail-order catalog. He closed the big book and pointed a gnarly finger. "'Em fellas done folded. That pot's yours."

Usher left the coins on the table, but gathered the cards, straightened the deck, and passed it to Ladron.

"It wouldn't be respectable to take money with what I was holding." He set the deck in front of Ladron. "Your deal."

The gambler stared at the deck. He had stopped drinking coffee an hour ago and had been spending more time moving his five pennies, two dimes, and one nickel around. He studied the deck and shook his head.

"Never thought I would say this, but I'm just too bored to play poker."

Nugget slammed the catalog shut. "Miss Sara pays you to deal poker, son, or twenty-one or checkers."

Ladron stared at Nugget, then shot glances to Jones, Usher, and Duncan. He shook his head, whispered, "Dealing checkers," and picked up the deck, which he started shuffling.

Usher found his cup and took a swallow. "Nah, Logan, you're right."

"Yeah," Duncan agreed.

"Y'all ain't gonna play poker no more?" the mayor asked.

Duncan looked at the clock above the bar—again. How many times had he checked his watch or that clock? How many times had he looked at a calendar over the past several days? He couldn't even remember how long he had been inside the Crosscut Saloon.

"Want to look at this big book?" Nugget asked. "It's got all sorts of pictures in it."

Ladron shook his head. Usher drank more coffee. Syd Jones had opened a blade on his pocketknife and started cleaning his fingernails.

"They's wagons and stickpins and real perty pocket watches. And pistols. And boots." He turned a page. "And dishes." Another page. "More dishes." Another page. "Lots of dishes." He looked up, sighed, and closed the catalog, pulled on his beard, and looked at Syd Jones.

"Can I have some of your coffee, Syd?"

"Sure." The old lawman rose. "It'll break up the monotony."

"The what?" Nugget asked.

Syd Jones didn't answer. He found the pot and walked over to where the mayor sat.

"Where's your cup?"

The only things in front of Nugget were his jug and the catalog.

"Ain't got one."

With a chuckle, Jones placed the pot on the table and walked toward the bar.

"Nugget," Duncan said, "can't you get your own cup?"

The mayor stared a moment at Jones, who did not stop, and then looked back at his marshal. "Syd's fetchin' it. He's just your depitty. I'm mayor. I've got important things to do."

Duncan shook his head. Syd was already to the bar, moving behind it to find the coffee cups. Then he stared at his old friend.

"This remind you of something?" he asked.

Ben Usher's snort passed as a laugh. "Yeah. Yesterday."

Ladron turned over a card, then put it on the bottom of the deck. "I was . . ." He had to stop in order to stifle a yawn. "I was thinking the day before."

A door squeaked open upstairs, and Duncan turned around to stare up.

Sara had been awake for a while, but now she had taken a bath, and from where Duncan sat, she looked wonderful. She wore a blue dress—a warm blue, like her eyes—and her blond hair looked different, but he couldn't figure out what she had done to it. It didn't matter. She was beautiful. She always looked beautiful.

"Good morning, gentlemen," she called out from the balustrade.

Duncan looked again at the clock behind the bar, and again stared at his watch. Yes, it was still morning. Some hours before noon. He had hoped it would be a bit after twelve, at least. This day was dragging on, just like yesterday and the day before.

Well, folks said winter days passed the longest.

But it was barely autumn.

This year might never end. This day might last for all of eternity.

Sara was moving toward the stairs, and when she started heading down, Duncan decided that if today lasted forever, well, that wouldn't be bad. No. That wouldn't be bad at all.

"Is there any coffee down here?" she asked when she stood on the ground floor. "I thought I smelled some."

Nugget sprang from his chair and pointed at the pot on his table. "It's right here, Miss Sara. Right here. Come on over, and I'll run and fetch ya a cup."

And he took off, moving like a man much younger than his years. "Pull up a chair if you wanna," he said, staggering into an empty table, almost overturning it, and then slid to a stop at the bar. He moved behind it, stopping at a bottle of brandy on the backbar, uncorked it, took a swig, set the bottle back down, but not the cork, and disappeared.

Sucking in a deep breath and holding it, Duncan waited for that dreadful sound of a glass or stoneware breaking, or some other catastrophe, but Nugget came up in a moment, and he held a pewter mug, and then he hurried back.

Duncan turned around. Sara had not moved.

Nugget slammed the mug next to the pot and spun around, trying to smooth his dirty vest and fix the collar of his coat.

Usher stared at the coins before him and shook his head, stifling a laugh.

Sara started moving slowly, smiling as she passed the would-be cardplayers, and stopped at the table.

"Thank you, Mayor Nugget," she said, and reached for the pot.

"Nugget, aren't you—" Ladron started, but stopped at Duncan's *Shhhhhhhhhh*.

Usher whispered: "You want her to get her hand or something scalded by that ol' coot?"

She filled the mug, set the pot down, and raised the mug in a toast toward Dead Broke's mayor, then back at her other friends, and walked to the batwing doors and peered outside.

"Oh, it snowed last night," she said.

"Just a dusting," Ladron said.

"What a beautiful morning." She sipped coffee, breathed in deeply, and, still looking outside, said, "It doesn't feel too cold."

"Sun's up," Usher said.

"Sun's hotter at twelve thousand feet," Duncan added.

"Snow'll be melted." Syd Jones yawned. "By afternoon."

"Oh, it'll be back, that's certain sure," Nugget said. "I been up here long enough to know that. We'll be snowed in by November."

"Cut off from all of civilization," Syd Jones agreed, nodding while reaching for his cup of coffee.

"Snowed in till spring." Duncan looked long at Sara Cardiff. "What a wonderful thought."

"No drunks." Syd Jones nodded.

"No dumb punks wanting a reputation," Ben Usher whispered.

"Lots of snow cream," Nugget said, smacking his lips. "Snow cream. With milk and sugar and sweetened with my special brew."

"And ten degrees below zero feels like summertime," Ladron said, shaking his head. "Good thing I won that buffalo robe off of Dylan Pugh three weeks ago."

Sara drank more coffee and turned back to walk to the only people in her saloon.

"And how are you all doing?"

All answered in unison.

"Other than complaining about the weather."

Syd Jones was the only one who remembered to pull out a chair for the beautiful woman, and she thanked him, then settled down.

The silence fell quickly.

"One good thing about winter," Syd Jones said after a long while.

"What's that?" Ladron asked.

"Well." The old lawman eyed Usher, then Duncan, and said, "Those young toughs looking to get a reputation won't be coming up here to paint the town red."

Usher raised his cup and clinked it against his old mentor's. "That's a fact," he said.

Then came a shout from outside.

"Marshal MacMicking! Marshal MacMicking!"

A moment later, Joey Clarke, a smart twelve-year-old, raced through the batwing doors, which banged behind him. He rushed toward Duncan and pointed out the window.

"There's a man riding into town!" he yelled as he slid to a stop. "A man."

The boy's eyes were wide open, and his face pale.

Everybody was standing now. Sara ran, and stood behind the boy, holding his shoulders. "Easy, Joey," she said. "What is it? What's the matter, honey?"

All of the men formed a semicircle around Little Joey and Sara.

"Easy, Joey," Duncan said.

"Men often ride into Dead Broke, Joey," Nugget said.

But not lately, and not this time of year, Duncan thought.

"It's likely that this hombre just wants to see my Diamond Nugget of Silver. Gosh, we ain't gotten no visitors to see my most wonderfullest discovery—the reason for this city today—in some time. But if he's got money for the tour."

"No, no, no," Joey managed to choke out between breaths.

"I'll go see that feller." Nugget started for the door.

"No, Mayor Nugget!" Little Joey screamed. "Don't step outside. He might shoot you dead."

That stopped Nugget. That stopped everyone.

"Marshal!" Joey stopped, slowed down, and managed to catch his breath. "Marshal. This stranger. He's wearing two pistols! Ain't *No Firearms Allowed* still the rule of law?"

Duncan shot a glance toward Usher, who pushed back his chair.

Usher sighed before he spoke in a tired whisper: *"No dumb punks wanting a reputation . . ."*

Yeah, Duncan thought. That had been a hopeful wish, but an improbable one these days—even with winter coming. As long as there were gunfighters, there would always be challenges like this.

It was enough to make a man who had to wear a gun wish he had never strapped one on. Then again, Duncan could recall those years—before Syd Jones whipped the devil out of him and some brains into his noggin—when he had been a punk with a gun and, till he met Syd Jones, what he thought was a real fast draw.

The next voice came from outside.

"MacMicking. Or you, Usher. I'm callin' you out. I don't care which one. Just step outside . . . and get ready to die."

CHAPTER 2

Ben Usher sighed, shook his head, and slowly pulled the ivory-handled Colt Thunderer from his holster. He checked the cylinder, and said, "I reckon it's my turn," before sliding the double-action revolver into the holster.

"No." Pushing himself out of his chair, Duncan MacMicking tested the heavy Schofield .45 in his holster. "I reckon I'm still marshal of this town, so I guess this is my job."

"Duncan." Sara Cardiff's voice was barely a whisper.

He gave her his most reassuring smile, nodded at the others, and walked toward the batwing doors, but made a detour around the bar, disappeared underneath, and came up with a sawed-off ten-gauge Greener. He opened the breech, pulled out one shell, slipped it back into the barrel, then did the same with the second shell. Once he snapped the barrels back in place, he moved to the doors, looking through the opening to find the latest gunfighter—or what folks might call a gunfighter these days—still sitting in the saddle of a piebald mare.

The kid was, as the saying went, advertising a leather store. Step-in chaps that hadn't a scratch on them, and darn little dust for a fellow who had been climbing up this mountainside. The boy, wanting to look his best, must have stopped at the stream and cleaned himself up. Black hat, with a tie-down string to keep the wind from blowing it to Nebraska. Black shirt. Black ribbon tie. Black gun belt. Black pants. Black boots. Black frock coat. Black spur straps. And the boy was as white as Christmas snow.

But there was that black holster that the tail of the coat had been pushed behind, with the pearl handle of what looked like a single-action Colt reflecting some sunlight.

The kid sported fuzz over his mouth and what he probably fancied as a menacing underlip beard. His face showed recent sunburn, which likely meant he hadn't grown up a bored farm or ranch kid. Probably came from some good family in a city. Denver, maybe, or Colorado Springs. He didn't look like the type that could have ridden much farther than those two towns.

Did I look like that when Syd Jones beat the tar out of me?

Duncan shook his head at that thought.

"Which one is you?" the boy managed to ask.

Duncan couldn't help but blink. Blinking was dangerous when you faced a gunman. The good ones, the *smart* ones, always sought that edge, and a blink gave them a really good advantage. Blinking was a mighty good way to get yourself killed. But the boy was too young to know that.

The question ran through Duncan's head again.

Which one is you?

The kid had spoken loud enough that Ben Usher let out a chuckle, and had Usher been standing here and Duncan was back with his friends, he probably would have done the same thing.

But standing here behind those batwing doors, he felt, well, insulted.

"Does it matter?" he finally said.

The boy shrugged, then tried out his smile of sheer menace. Which did nothing but make him look constipated.

"I like to know who I'm killin'," he said, deliberately dropping the G so he would sound like he was a veteran of these kinds of shootouts.

Duncan gave a slight nod. "I'm MacMicking. Marshal of Dead Broke." He tilted his head at the sign that hadn't blown down yet, the sign that said:

**THE CARRYING OF FIREARMS
BY ANY MAN,
TOWN CITIZEN, OR VISITOR
WITHIN THE CITY LIMITS
OF DEAD BROKE
—CONCEALED OR IN OPEN VIEW—
WITHOUT A PERMIT
IS STRICTLY PROHIBITED
FINE: $75
AND CONFISCATION OF WEAPON**

There was a bullet hole in the center of the D in "Concealed," but that was new. The punk that Ben Usher had wounded in the arm, not a full week ago, had managed to do that. It made the boy happy—happier than he was with the bullet he took in the shoulder for his troubles.

It was something, the kid had said as they carted him to Doctor Aimé Cartier to dig that bullet out and send the boy back to his mama, that he could brag about. He had begged Duncan to keep that sign up. He might want to bring his friends up to see it sometime.

"You're in violation of the law, son," Duncan told this latest punk to come up the mountain. "We don't allow folks to carry firearms within the Dead Broke city limits."

The boy grinned. "I reckon I'll just let you try to take this gun from me, MacMicking."

Slowly, like an actor hogging a scene in some theater, the boy eased out of the saddle, taking his time, and taking his eyes off MacMicking, who figured he could have put twelve bullets in the boy—and that included emptying the .45's cylinder and reloading his revolver—by the time he was on the ground and standing, still in the street, in front of the entrance to Sara Cardiff's saloon.

The horse, ground-reined, walked across the street to a water trough out of the line of fire.

Which meant the horse had some sense. Its owner? Not a lick.

The boy turned a few yards away, pushing back the tail of the dark coat and keeping his right hand just inches above the pearl handle of his revolver.

"I'm glad it's you I'm facing, MacMicking. I would have settled for Ben Usher. But you . . . you're the top dog. Or was. Till I rode into town."

Duncan sighed. The wind was blowing too hard and away from the Crosscut, and Usher was busy talking to Sara, telling her it was all right, that Duncan knew what he was doing, and Syd Jones was stirring something into his coffee and making an awful racket, while Logan Ladron kept shuffling the deck over and over again. No way Usher had heard what that boy had just said—and that was something MacMicking wouldn't have let him ever forget. No luck, though. It didn't matter. He slowly shook his head.

"You comin' out, MacMicking? Or do I have to walk in there and drag you out?"

That stopped the conversation Usher was having with Sara. It stopped Syd Jones from banging that spoon on the side of his coffee cup, and it made Ladron quit messing with that deck of cards that were already worn down. Nugget just smacked his lips.

The wind moaned.

Duncan chanced looks up and down the street. Empty, of course. Like every other street in Dead Broke. There was a cat lying on the busted boardwalk in front of that abandoned general store, and a mouse ran from underneath the boardwalk to a trash bin, but even the cat had no interest in the mouse.

The horse quit drinking, shook its head, turned slightly toward the boy who had brought him up to this out-of-the-way town, snorted, and nuzzled the dead grass at the side of the trough to see if it might be worth chewing on.

"Don't make me come in there after you," the boy said. "Ain't you got any sand in your craw?"

"I'm getting too old for this," Duncan whispered. Then he pushed his way through the batwing doors that bounded behind him as he stepped onto those planks and onto the ground. He kept right on walking toward the boy, whose eyes widened and whose face grew paler than the noonday sun.

"Th-th-tha . . ." He raised his right hand—his gun hand, the stupid punk—and pointed at the Greener that Duncan held, left hand on what remained of the hard wood under the barrels, right hand on the iron, trigger finger in the guard, thumb against the hammers.

He walked straight toward the boy.

"That's a shotgun!" the boy finally managed to call out. "That . . . that . . . ain't . . . fair!"

Duncan powered forward like a bull.

"What's fair in a gunfight?" Duncan roared. "How do you think Jack McCall killed Wild Bill Hickok in Deadwood all those years ago? You think Doc Holliday or the Earps gave any of those Clanton boys a chance down in Tombstone?"

The horse, the cat, and the mouse were looking at the boy and Duncan with curiosity. The boy might have been wetting his pants. His right hand had moved away from the Colt and was pointing, in a terribly shaking hand, as Duncan kept walking.

"John Wesley Hardin wasn't anything but an assassin. And a lot of lawmen I knew weren't any better."

Twenty feet separated them now.

"There's just one rule to a gunfight, kid. Live through it. And you live through a gunfight by the grace of God and luck. If I had any sense, the second I got through those batwing doors, I would have blown you in half."

That's when the boy fell to his knees, bowing his head into his hands and sobbing like a freshly spanked newborn.

"Please," he begged. "P-p-p-p-pl-please . . . don't . . . d-don't . . . k-k-kill me."

Duncan stared down at the pathetic figure. He saw how white his hand and fingers were that gripped the Greener. He realized that he had never cocked the hammers. That, he figured, might have been a good thing. As riled as he was at this green, stupid punk of a kid, Duncan could have easily touched the hair triggers and with the buckshot in those loads, that cat and mouse would have had a bountiful supper—had just one of those double triggers been pulled.

His heart pounded against that tin star pinned to his vest.

"Please don't kill me," the boy begged, sniffling, tears sprinkling the dirt on the street. "Please. Please. Please. My mama. My mama. Oh, Mama, come help me."

The batwing doors banged again, and Duncan felt the saneness return to his head and heart. He shifted the Greener to his left hand, then knelt in front of the aspiring gunfighter. His right hand touched the shoulder of the frock coat, tightened, but he made his voice as friendly as he could.

"Stand up, boy," he said. "Stand up."

The kid raised his head. Duncan had seen livelier faces

on corpses, but he was glad this kid wasn't a corpse. He came close to being one, though.

He helped the boy to his feet, then pushed away the tail of the black coat, and pulled the ivory-handled, nickel-plated Colt from the holster.

"The fine's seventy-five dollars, boy," he said, "and confiscation of the firearm. But I'll just take this Colt."

It was one of Colt's newer models, an 1892 New Army, looked like a .38 caliber. A .41-caliber would likely have been too powerful for this snot-faced little boy. Probably cost him twelve bucks at a gun shop or one of those catalogs that sent anything through the mail. Or maybe he had borrowed, or stolen, it from his pappy. Double action. Duncan always preferred the single-action models. He never trusted those self-cockers. He had been using the same Schofield for . . . well, he didn't feel much like counting those years.

With the kid on his feet, Duncan started steering him toward the saloon, where Logan Ladron, Syd Jones, Ben Usher, Nugget, Little Joey, and Sara stood waiting on the boardwalk. Another figure appeared across the street.

Duncan saw the man and nodded. "No need of your services this time, Doc," he told Aimé Cartier.

The doctor crossed the street, anyway. "I guess I could use a bracer."

You ain't the only one, Duncan thought.

"You . . . you . . . you . . . takin' . . . taking me . . . taking me . . . to jail?" the kid asked.

Duncan almost laughed. His jailer, Winston DeMint, probably would enjoy having someone to talk to these days.

"I think the gun is enough of a fine," he told him. "But"—he nodded at the entrance to Sara's saloon—"I've never run a man out of town without letting him get something to eat."

It was a long ride down the mountain.

"Can I have a whiskey?" the boy asked.

"I said *eat*." Duncan hoped he sounded tough and strong. Though he was thinking that he sure would like a whiskey right now himself.

He looked over the boy's black hat and called out, "Any chance we could get this young man some food in his belly before he rides back to . . ." He leaned closer to the boy. "Where you from?"

"Leadville."

That was closer than Duncan had figured. But it was still a long ride down this mountain, then up another steep one. It was probably easier to get to Denver.

Sara Cardiff was steering Joey Clarke into the Crosscut, and Logan Ladron followed, likely to help find some food.

Duncan handed the double-action Colt to Usher, who studied it for a moment, then shoved it into his waistband and crossed the street to fetch the boy's horse.

"Why didn't ya shoot this punk?" Mayor Nugget said. "Ya had ever' right to."

"I was thinking about the city budget," Duncan said. "We'd have to pay the gravediggers and coffin makers."

Nugget tugged on his beard, thinking a bit, before spitting tobacco into the street.

"He gonna pay the fine?"

"This'll do."

And the mayor liked having that toy in his hand. He probably didn't realize that a New Army Colt was worth a whole lot less than seventy-five bucks. But it would give Nugget something to play with for a while.

They watered down some coffee for the boy, and fed him cold biscuits and some leftover ham, and Sara tried to warm up some fried potatoes.

"What's his name?" Sara whispered while the boy

showed a marvelous appetite for a kid who had come inches away from being buried in an unmarked grave.

"You know we don't ask a fellow his name in these parts," Duncan reminded her.

She snorted, then turned and said, "What's your name, son?"

"Larry," he said while chewing a mouthful of ham. "Larry Tuckness."

"Where do you live?"

He told her.

"Can you get home all right? That's not an easy ride from here."

He swallowed, then washed down the grub with weakened coffee. "I can make it. Even if I have to camp sometime tonight."

"It's getting cold."

He drank more coffee. "I'll be fine."

"She's a worrier," Ladron said with a smile.

The boy finished his food, thanked everyone, and rose, putting on his hat and then noticing his gun belt. He unbuckled it and laid the rig on the seat of his chair. "I don't reckon I'll have need of this anymore."

"I don't know," Ben Usher said. "A fellow who knows when to use a gun and when not to use a gun . . . that's the kind of fellow a man in my business can respect."

Duncan took the boy's pistol from Nugget and set it beside the belt and holster.

The kid looked up.

"What about the fine?" he asked nervously.

Nugget opened his mouth, shut it, then pouted. But he kept quiet.

"Guns," Duncan explained, "are generally returned when visitors leave town."

The kid stared again, then shook his head, and picked up his hat and settled it onto his head.

"I reckon I don't need a gun. Y'all keep it."

Nugget's face brightened again.

They walked him to the boardwalk and watched him step into the saddle. He nodded, thanked them again, and backed the horse up, then started into a walk down the road that led down the high mountain to the low, civilized country.

Nugget was the first one back inside the Crosscut. He picked up the Colt and the gun rig. "This is being constipated into the Dead Broke coffers," he said. "Since the boy was fined for violentin' the ord . . . the ord . . . the laws of this here town of mine. City of mine, I mean." He raised the revolver and studied the shiny nickel finish. "Is I needed for anything else right now?"

"I don't think so, Mayor," Sara said.

"Mighty fine, then. I got lots of city work to do. Gosh." He stamped his boots on the floor. "I shoulda offered that boy a tour. He coulda paid to have seen my wonderful silver nugget. That's probably what he come up here for, anyway. Till y'all distracted him and tried to lead him down a lawless path."

He snorted and hurried out of the saloon.

Little Joey Clarke left, too. The doctor followed. Logan Ladron said he was ready for a nap. And Syd Jones figured he might as well fetch some grub and bring it to the town marshal's office and jail so Winston DeMint didn't starve to death.

So Usher, Cardiff, and Duncan sat down at the table and resumed their game of poker for penny-ante stakes.

They were at it for two long, boring hours. Until the next gunfighter rode into town.

CHAPTER 3

"Ben Usher," the voice called out from the street. "I'm calling you out."

Usher stared at the cards he had been dealt, then sighed and looked across the table at Duncan.

"Reckon this one must have met that boy you sent packing on the trail," Usher said. "And since that one faced you, he must figure it's my turn."

"Want me to take him?" Sara did not even try to hide her sarcasm.

Usher didn't answer. Duncan frowned.

"This has to stop!" Sara slammed down the cards she held and pushed her chair back. She rose and Duncan had to move faster than he had in some time to catch her before she stormed through those doors—and might have caught a bullet from the latest unknown nobody wanting to make a name for himself.

While Sara was shouting and stamping her feet, and Duncan was having a hard time keeping his toes from being squashed and finding an opening so he could tell her to calm down, Usher finished his cup of coffee, checked his Thunderer, tugged down the front brim on his hat, then walked past the arguing couple and stopped behind those batwing doors.

"I hope you ain't yeller enough to walk out of that hog ranch with a shotgun the way your pard done to that young feller I met on the trail," called the boy on a pinto mare.

Which confirmed Usher's theory that this punk had met that other would-be gunfighter.

It also stopped Sara Cardiff from stomping on Duncan's toes.

"Hog ranch?" she thundered, and pushed away from the marshal. "Who's calling my saloon and gambling parlor a *hog ranch?*"

Duncan reached for her, but grasped only air.

Ben Usher figured he had better step out before Sara reached him; otherwise, she might get hurt.

The doors banged as Usher moved fast, letting his right hand stay close to the Thunderer, but not close enough to cause the boy to do something foolish.

This one looked like he had come straight off a farm or ranch. He hadn't spent a small fortune on black duds and a fancy gun rig.

Farm. Not ranch.

The boots the boy wore told Usher that much. The clothes were old, patched here and there with a mother's love, and the kid's shoulders were broad and strong. He might have topped six feet when he stood straight. The shirt was old flannel, but didn't have as many patches as the pants. His hair was yellow, his eyes clear, his face smooth. Duncan couldn't make out a gun belt, and the saddle upon which he sat had no scabbard for a long gun. The hat he wore was straw, battered, but it was tight on his yellow hair, so the wind wasn't taking it off.

"I'm Ben Usher," Usher told him.

"Proud to meet you," the boy said. "Sorry I have to kill you."

"Not as sorry as I am."

"Will you let me step off my hoss?"

Usher nodded.

The kid eased off the pinto, and then Usher saw the pistol—looked like an old Starr revolver, probably from the Civil War—stuck in his waistband. If Usher stood a little closer, he figured he could see the specks of rust on the cylinder and barrel.

The boy nodded his thanks, then eased his right hand toward the grips of that relic of a revolver.

"What made you call me out instead of MacMicking?" Usher asked.

"From what I've read, you're meaner than Mick MacMicking," the boy said.

Usher sighed and shook his head. "I guess I should have shot that first dime novelist who wrote that tripe about me. It would have saved me a lot of grief."

"You ain't gonna get a chance now," the farm kid said. "Because I'm going to shoot you down like the dirty dog you are."

"Then you'll have to shoot me," Duncan called from behind the batwing doors, and Usher heard that numbingly loud banging as his old friend stepped out of the Crosscut and moved a few feet down the boardwalk on Usher's right.

"Because," Duncan said, "I'm the town marshal of Dead Broke, and we don't allow gunfights here."

The next sound was a wild laugh, and though Usher had been taught better—and knew better—his eyes shot off toward the corner of the building across the street, and there came Dead Broke's mayor, Nugget, snorting and then taking a pull from his jug, lowering it, wiping his filthy mustache and beard, and stepped onto the dirt and started walking. All that city work he had to do sure hadn't taken long.

"Dead Broke ain't never allowed no gunfights," Nugget said. "But they happen here more than anywhere else, I reckons. And it ain't good for a town that ought to be respectable. Besides, how is this town—my town—how's it gonna get back to its glorious days when folks had nothin' to do but haul out silver by the tons and visitors come just to see my big nugget." He took another pull, and lowered the jug. "You want to see my silver nugget, boy? Ain't nothin' like it in the whole world. I'll give you my children's rate. It's one of the seventeen wonders of the world."

"I came here to kill Ben Usher," the farm boy said. "And MacMicking if he's in a hurry to die."

"Nobody's in a hurry for that," Sara said.

The kid made another mistake. He looked at Sara—not that Usher blamed him for that. She was a right attractive woman.

The boy pointed at the woman.

Yet another error that would have gotten most gunmen killed.

"Is that a derringer in your hand, lady?" the farmer asked.

"Yes," she said. "A .41 caliber. Four shots. Sometimes just one goes off, sometimes two. Once all four. That made a right mess of that tinhorn who turned out to be a sore loser."

"He's buried in the cemetery." That was Logan Ladron. *This street is getting way too crowded for a gunfight,* Usher thought. And then he thought: *Sara Cardiff hasn't killed any tinhorn in Dead Broke. That's not to say that she hasn't wounded a man or two in her lifetime. And no telling how many hearts she has broken.*

"I've got dibs on that gunman if Sara doesn't leave him dead in the street."

Usher recognized the voice of Syd Jones, and the heavy clomping of his boots on the boardwalk across the street.

About the only person not crowding around the Crosscut Saloon now was . . .

"And if Syd don't kill him, I'll take a crack at that punk myself."

That was Winston DeMint, the jailer. He must have finished his lunch in a hurry.

The boy's head went from one person to another, and then he remembered the person he had called out, and he whirled around and looked into Usher's cold, hard eyes.

"You see how it is, boy?" Usher said. "That's the life of a gunfighter. Once you get a reputation, it follows you to the grave. And for most of us, that grave comes a lot earlier than it does for men with brains. You kill one man, then another, and then it's just a matter of time. Before there's a headstone—maybe—over your grave."

"Not like the storybooks," Duncan said. "And to be honest, most of those dead men no one will ever remember."

"Maybe their mothers," Sara said softly.

Usher nodded. "Maybe. If that good, loving mother hasn't disowned her son for shaming her so."

"Living the life of a gunfighter," Syd Jones said, and shook his head. "It's not what I'd call living. Not living at all."

Usher nodded. "Yep. Once you get that reputation, you stop living. You start dying."

"'Not a day at a time,'" Ladron said. "'You don't count days.'"

Usher sighed. Ladron had read that line from one of those blood-and-thunder tales that had been written about Ben Usher himself. In fact, that hack writer had Usher speaking those words. Usher wondered if he could sue Ladron for stealing. Then he smiled.

The words had done the job. The words and seeing all these men, armed with revolvers or shotguns or rifles . . . or Sara Cardiff's four-shot derringer.

"Boy." Mayor Nugget walked up to the kid and put his hand over the lad's now-slumping shoulders. "The ground up here's gettin' too hard froze to dig no more graves, and I's feelin' gen'rous, so if you just ease that hunk of iron from your britches and hand it to Miss Sara here, I's gonna give you a free tour of my Diamond Nugget of Silver. Free. For only ten cents. You gots ten cents? It usually costs five dollars."

The boy's hand moved, and the Starr came out of the pants. Sara Cardiff walked over and took it by the barrel, and the boy blinked. Color started coming back to his face now, and his hands stopped shaking too hard.

Sara handed the old revolver to Usher, and then Duncan pulled a coin from his vest pocket and handed it to Nugget.

"For the tour, Mayor." He nodded at the boy. "It's worth seeing, son. One of a kind."

"Seventeen hundred and seventy-six pounds," Nugget said.

"Solid silver," DeMint said.

"Where do you live, son?" Duncan asked.

The boy pointed southeast. "Farm off Badger Creek."

Syd Jones whistled. "That's a far piece from here."

"Yes, sir."

"Ya ain't gonna be able to get home afore dark, sonny. Not afore two, maybe three darks."

"Let him sleep in the jail," DeMint said.

And the kid's eyes brightened. "Can I? Really?"

"On the house," Duncan said.

And they watched Nugget and the farm boy walk down the street before turning north past the marshal's office and jail and toward Chasm Park, where Nugget lived in his mansion with that massive chunk of silver.

"Well," Ladron said, lifting his head toward the sinking sun, "two gunfights in one day."

"And nobody died," Sara said.

"That's worth celebrating," Duncan said, and they all walked into the Crosscut Saloon.

CHAPTER 4

"Nobody even worth killing," Ben Usher said in the café, where he and Duncan were sipping coffee. "Just kids whose parents should have taught them better."

Days had passed since they had sent that last aspiring gunman back to his farm on Badger Creek. It took a while for Duncan to figure out what his old partner was talking about.

With a sigh, Duncan set his coffee cup on the table. "Are you missing bullets coming at you?" he asked.

When Usher looked up, Duncan saw a hardness in Usher's eyes, but that passed quickly, and he shook his head. He picked up his fork and touched the potatoes on his plate, then set the fork on the plate and pushed back his chair.

"I'm just not used to being this bored," Usher said, and started rocking his chair, till the feisty waitress told him to stop doing that, that those chair legs weren't made for rocking, and if he wanted to rock himself to sleep, he should go to the hotel that had rocking chairs for boarders on the front porch. He could sit there and watch that little dusting of snow they had gotten last night melt, but he wasn't going to wear holes into the floor in her place.

He stopped rocking and leaned forward. "Her place. Like she owns this joint."

"She does," Duncan told him.

"What's she doing waitressing if she's the boss woman?"

"No one's left in town to do that job."

Usher sighed.

As town marshal and peacekeeper, Duncan gave Betty Lou a smile, and the waitress/ proprietor frowned, then moved to the door to look out the window and stare at the empty streets.

Dead Broke had recovered somewhat from the crash of the silver market, but it was a different kind of recuperation. Several of the abandoned homes had been taken over by miners—some even brought their wives, a few with children, one with a grandmother—to try their luck at mining for lead, zinc, even saltpeter. It must have been easier to find those minerals than it was to dig up silver and gold, and if those mines panned out, well, Dead Broke might just turn into that nice little town that had long occupied Duncan's dreams.

This was turning out to be a pretty autumn. And a quiet one now.

Usher drained his cup of coffee and picked up a copy of a Pueblo newspaper that had made its way up to the high country and had been left behind by a drummer.

"I kind of like not having anyone shooting at me for a change," Duncan said.

"Yeah." Usher nodded. "Don't get me wrong, Mick. I never enjoyed facing down anyone, drunk or punk or both, but I so miss good poker games—last night I was playing spades with Logan. That's right. Spades. And not for money. And remember when those French gals came from the Moulin Rouge to Carson City?"

Duncan turned around to make sure Betty Lou wasn't

lurking around eavesdropping, because Sara ate here, too. Well, it was the only restaurant still operating, though it wouldn't be long now before Betty Lou got some competition—other than the crackers and sausages Percy Stahl brought out when he had some on hand to bring some folks into his beer mill. Oh, yeah, he sure remembered that night. He remembered something else.

"Hey, how about that cancan dancer we saw in Chicago?" Duncan whispered.

"Oh, my goodness. And she was a ballerina with the dangedest French accent you ever heard."

"That's because she was Italian."

"Didn't matter what she was when she was doing the cancan."

"The Peerless Morlacchi!"

They picked up their mugs and toasted.

Which would probably be the most exciting thing they did that entire day. And possibly this week. Maybe this month.

How many more months are left in the year? Duncan thought.

Monotony returned.

Duncan looked at his empty plate. Usher turned the page in the newspaper.

"She married Texas Jack."

Duncan blinked, then looked up. "Huh?"

"That dancer. The Peerless Morlacchi. She married Texas Jack."

"Yeah, but John always was a lucky son of a gun."

"Not that lucky. How long ago did he die?"

Duncan shrugged. "Five years. More. I can't remember. Pneumonia, wasn't it?"

Usher's head bobbed behind the Pueblo paper.

"In Leadville," he added.

"What were we doing in Chicago?" Duncan asked.

The paper's upper half folded, and Usher said, "Chicago? We were talking about Leadville."

"I mean, what were we doing in Chicago when we saw the cancan and met that beautiful dancer?"

"Delivering the Warren boys to the Pinkertons. Wasn't it?"

"Sounds right." He was out of coffee. Betty Lou was nowhere to be found. But he could get plenty of coffee, and better coffee at that, at the marshal's office and jail. Well, not better, but bitter and strong and pretty much awful, just the way Duncan liked it.

He found his pocket watch, but he had forgotten to wind it that morning, and it had stopped. It didn't matter. Time did not matter in Dead Broke. Nothing mattered anymore. He started wondering how long the citizens of this town would be willing to pay a lawman for his services when few laws were being broken. Still, it was a pretty place to live—but that could change when real winter hit.

"Well, I've learned something," Usher said from behind the Pueblo newspaper.

Duncan nodded. "I learn a lot from reading newspapers."

The paper folded again to reveal Usher's face.

"There's no sense for young want-to-be legends to shoot it out with a couple of legends when they can hire on to any Wild West show and earn money and get to shoot blanks or at paper targets to their hearts' content." He pointed his nose at the type that Duncan could not see. "Another one was in Pueblo last week."

"Bill Cody's?" Duncan asked. "I would have liked to have seen that one. When was the last time we saw Buffalo Bill?"

"Five, six years back?" Usher set the newspaper aside. "Not his show, though. Something called the *King Halifax*

Mounted Riders and Sharpshooters of the World with a Full Tribe of Indians and the Legendary Gunfighter, Killer of the Entire Pickle Caster Gang, Hero of the Plains, Captain Bronson 'Wire Sash' Brown."

"Wire Sash," Duncan said.

"Pickle Caster," Usher whispered.

"That's what it's come to," said Betty Lou.

Both men jerked their heads toward the owner of this café. They had forgotten just how quiet on her feet that woman could be.

Or maybe, all this doing nothing since the gunfighters had stopped coming up to Dead Broke had dulled their senses.

"You done eating, boys?" She gave them a stern look that suggested they had better be done eating. "I'd like to take my afternoon nap before the rush for supper."

Rush for supper? Duncan sighed. *That's a dream.*

"Sure," Duncan lied. "Ben and I ought to make our rounds. Make sure no one's doing anything he shouldn't be doing."

"Yeah," Usher said without trying to hide even just a hint of sarcasm.

Duncan fished out a bill and handed it to her. She took the dollar and went back to the money box to get his change.

The page of the newspaper turned. Usher said, "Hmm. Now this is interesting."

"Then you're not reading anything about what's going on in the town of Dead Broke." Duncan didn't try to hide his sarcasm, either.

"Have you heard about this World's Columbine . . . Columbine?" The paper folded to reveal Usher's frown. "I guess good printers are hard to find these days, too."

"Columbian, isn't it?" Duncan said. He looked away,

but couldn't find Betty Lou with his change. Eighty cents was a lot for a tip on two dime meals.

"That's what it said in the Colorado Springs, Cheyenne, and Denver papers."

"It's still going on?" Duncan asked.

"Through October. Unless the tramp printer botched that, too."

Duncan stared at his empty cup, then at the leftover grease on his plate.

"Bill Cody's up there, too," Usher said.

"I think I read something about that when I was still down in Durango. I thought Cody said he wasn't going to be part of that exposition."

The paper dropped to the tabletop, and Usher pointed at the copy, though Duncan wasn't all that fast at reading type upside down, and the headline was pretty small type, too.

"Cody's not with the World's Fair," Usher said.

World's Fair. That's what most folks were calling this celebration of the four hundredth anniversary of old Christopher Columbus discovering America. Even if he hadn't really discovered it. The way Duncan recalled things, that explorer and sailor had wound up on one of those islands south or east or both, unless it was south and west, of Florida.

Florida. Duncan had never been there. That's where some Texas Ranger had caught up and captured John Wesley Hardin, that Texas hard case. He was still down in that big brick prison in Huntsville. Had been for . . . what, pushing fifteen years?

"He set up his Wild West show right next to the exposition's grounds." He tapped the tiny typescript. "Making a fortune there."

"Fortune? Who's making a fortune?"

That wasn't Betty Lou's voice. The two lawmen looked up to see Nugget standing in front of them.

"Bill Cody," Duncan answered. "And the owners of the World's Columbian Exposition." He had remembered the title of that big to-do up in Illinois.

Nugget blinked. He might be the only person in these United States and her territories that had not heard of, or at least remembered, this big to-do of a celebration going on up north.

"Well, it won't be nothin' like if we get a good cold winter and that young painter of ourn gets to put up his city of ice with all 'em perty sculpturners."

Sculpturners. Duncan hoped he could remember that one. It had possibilities. Sounded a lot more rustic than "sculptures," anyway.

Have mercy, Duncan told himself. *That's what my mind has been reduced to.*

Duncan looked over the mayor's shoulders and saw Betty Lou counting pennies. He was glad that only a dusting of snow had fallen. If this woman was going to weigh him down with pennies, he might have sunk to his knees from the weight had several inches of snow been melting.

"Y'all done et?" Nugget asked.

Both men nodded.

Nugget glanced at the plates. Not enough scraps to fill an ant's belly.

"Betty Lou's closing up, Mayor," Duncan said.

"Aww. I ain't hungry," the old skinflint lied. He pointed at the paper. "You done readin' that thing?" he asked Usher.

That got a smile from Duncan's old partner, and he folded the paper and held it to the greasy vagabond of a mayor.

"All yours, Mayor."

The old rapscallion took the paper and hurried outside. Duncan figured he'd find Little Joey Clarke to read the interesting articles in the Pueblo paper. Either that, or the mayor would just look at the illustrations in some of the advertisements.

As soon as Nugget was out the door, Betty Lou returned with Duncan's change in a coffee cup. Duncan thanked her and she went back through the rug that separated the dining area from the kitchen. He counted out five cents, and figured that was a good tip, but she was a nice woman and knew how to cook potatoes.

He and Usher rose, and, once Duncan had managed to get all those coins into his trouser pocket, they walked outside.

A covered farm wagon came creeping down the street.

"Folks are returning," Usher said.

The driver pulled hard on the reins to stop the wagon. He was a wiry man, with a long beard, mostly pepper with streaks of salt, thin for a miner. The woman at his side was bigger than he was, with a deeper tan. He was pale as a ghost. Lot of miners were that way. That's one job Duncan never wanted to have.

"Marshal," the man said when the mules had stopped.

Duncan sometimes forgot he even had a badge pinned to the lapel of his black coat.

"Call me Mick," Duncan said. "Most folks do."

The man nodded. The mules decided this was a good time to empty their bladders.

"My missus," the miner said. "Name's Porter. Colum Porter. She's Francine."

"Welcome to Dead Broke," Duncan said. His head tilted to Usher. "My deputy, Ben Usher."

The name meant nothing to either, which made Duncan

feel better. Not that either one of them looked like a person seeking to earn a reputation as some sort of man-killer.

Usher removed his hat. "Pleasure, ma'am," he said, and Duncan grimaced, knowing that he should have said something like that himself.

"People don't pass through Dead Broke," Duncan said with a smile. "So I take it that you've come this high up to settle down?"

"Hope to make it rich," Colum Porter said.

"I hope you do. You make it rich, the town gets rich." He grinned his best marshal smile. "And I get paid."

"I know a bit about lead and zinc. Mined for both in the Upper Mississippi Valley. In northwestern Illinois mostly."

"And some in southwestern Wisconsin," his wife chimed in.

"Some," the man agreed, nodding. "Ain't never tried it this high up, though."

"You'll have a short season, I'm afraid." Duncan pointed to some of the patches of snow in the shady parts of the street. "We'll see a lot of snow in the coming months. But some of the miners who've come up already have had some luck. The fellow you need to talk to about mining is Dylan Pugh." He could have said Nugget, but the mayor would have charged the newcomers.

Usher cleared his throat as though he had consumption.

Duncan excused himself as he turned around and whispered, "Pugh hasn't salted anything since he married that mail-order gal."

Usher shrugged.

Duncan turned back to the newcomers. He told them where to find Pugh, who was pretty much the fellow in charge of the mines now, and how the café right here was a good place for supper. He didn't look like the type who gambled, and his wife looked like the type who wouldn't tolerate a man who favored cards or roulette, and Duncan wasn't comfortable suggesting Percy Stahl's beer mill or even Sara Cardiff's place.

He did say that some folks were looking for saltpeter, but the man said he knew lead. He might mine here and there for zinc, but he was a lead man.

"We've been called lead men ourselves," Usher said, and smiled at his inside joke.

"Guess we'll be living in a tent for a while, woman," the miner said.

"I figgered," she told him.

"No need for y'all living in a tent," Duncan said. "Not this late in the year. I know it gets cold in Illinois. Ben and I spent a few weeks in Chicago some years back, so we know about cold."

"Have you forgotten that February in Idaho?"

Duncan ignored Usher's whisper.

"There are plenty of cabins that have been abandoned since the Panic hit," Duncan told the couple. "You're welcome to any that aren't already occupied, though you might have to chase some rats and cats out of them."

"That's mighty nice of you," the woman said.

The man was suspicious. "That ain't what I'd expect from a town with this reputation."

Usher nodded. "And in the old days, I'd agree with you. But this isn't the Dead Broke of the 1880s."

"Or the Dead Broke of, oh, a month or two back," Usher whispered.

Again, Duncan managed to ignore that remark. The man in the wagon must not have heard.

"Who do I pay rent to?" he asked. "Or how do I buy one?"

"Dylan Pugh will work all that out."

Again, Usher cleared his throat, but Duncan knew what he meant this time.

"And if a scraggly, wild-looking fellow that calls himself Nugget asks for rent money, don't listen to him."

"Meaning he's a crook?" the miner asked.

"Our mayor," Duncan said.

"Synonymous for 'crook,'" the wife said.

Which impressed Usher and Duncan. Yes, this was the kind of people Duncan wanted to see settling in Dead Broke. The man wore no sidearm, and the long gun that he had spotted leaning next to the stern, strong woman was a single-shot hunting rifle, probably older than Duncan's great-aunt Alyce.

"Yes, ma'am." Duncan smiled and tipped his hat.

The man gathered the reins, called out a handful of unintelligible words that didn't sound like profanity, and the newcomers headed up the street.

"Nice folks," Usher said.

"Seem like," Duncan agreed.

"What do you want to do now?" Usher asked.

They walked toward Sara Cardiff's Crosscut Saloon, and Duncan peered through the batwing doors, but saw no one, not even Ladron playing solitaire, and he knew he ought to get back to his office. Where he would probably play solitaire.

"I hear it's easier to mine for lead and zinc," Usher said.

They started walking down the boardwalk.

"Saltpeter, too," Duncan said.

"Maybe I'll try that," Usher said.

Duncan shot him a sideways glance, then chuckled. "I don't see you mining, Ben."

"I don't, either," Usher agreed.

They crossed the muddy alley, then came to another sorry excuse for a boardwalk.

Duncan had a full stomach and liked the folks he had just met. That sure was a lot better than having punk kids riding into town and challenging him, or Usher, to a gunfight.

"You know, Ben," he said, and he was being genuine, "Dead Broke is finally becoming the nice little town that I've been dreaming of for some years."

"You know, Mick," Usher said, "you can have it."

CHAPTER 5

It was a crisp, cool day in Dead Broke. There hadn't been any kid, or grown man, in town with a gun on his hip and a desire to have a reputation as a gunfighter in better than a week. But it seemed like every other day, a miner, or miners, or a mine speculator, came to town. Even Nugget was forgetting his mayoral duties and was climbing across the hills looking for a new form of pay dirt. Sometimes he was chasing zinc, sometimes lead, and now and then saltpeter, though he wasn't exactly certain what saltpeter looked or smelled like. He had a color illustration of zinc. And anyone who had spent as much time in Dead Broke as Nugget had, had plenty of experience dealing with lead.

That Sunday afternoon, Duncan had spent some time out in the country around the town by himself.

Sundays remained the Sabbath, even two miles up in the Rocky Mountains. Typically, this was Duncan's day off. Which meant he didn't have to sweep the boardwalks that hadn't rotted away, and he wasn't escorting the children from the schoolhouse. He wouldn't have to be doing that in maybe a month, or perhaps just a few weeks. In Dead Broke, at more than eleven thousand feet in elevation, there wasn't much of a summer break for the schoolteacher or the students.

Their long break came during the winter—which arrived pretty fast at this altitude. There were some years, Joey Clarke had explained, when they would already be out of school and shoveling snow this time of year.

He decided to go fishing. That'd be different.

The trout weren't biting, though, at least not in the streams that Duncan tried. He went to that little lake, which wasn't frozen over yet, the one where Sara liked to go for picnics. The trout weren't interested in becoming Duncan's supper there, either. He did get in a good nap, though, and came back to town satisfied—at least until he saw the horse tethered to the hitch rail in front of Duncan's office.

It was Ben Usher's horse. Behind the saddle were stuffed saddlebags and a bedroll, with a heavy coat and an India rubber poncho strapped to it. The stock of a rifle stuck out from the scabbard, and two canteens were hanging from the horn.

Sighing, knowing what that meant, Duncan stepped up on the boardwalk, leaned his fishing pole against the wall, and opened the door.

Inside, Winston DeMint was sipping coffee, and Usher sat reading a week-old Denver newspaper, but he was dressed for riding, spurs strapped to his boots, and the buckle of his gun belt showing beneath his unbuttoned coat and linen duster.

The paper lowered, and then Usher straightened, folded the paper, stuffed it in the bucket of old papers, where he had found it, and nodded.

"Catch anything?"

"Nope."

Closing the door, and putting off the inevitable, Duncan turned to DeMint. "Anything happen while I was fishing?"

"Killed a horsefly." DeMint set his cup on the edge of Usher's desk. "Ben and me were making odds on if that'll be the last horsefly to die before winter sets in."

"Inside or outside?" Duncan asked.

"Huh?"

"The fly. Did you kill it inside or outside?"

DeMint scratched behind his left ear, pondering.

"Outside."

Duncan let his head bob in approval.

"What odds did y'all figure?" he asked.

"Twenty to one," DeMint said. "We usually get a warm spell after the first frost. Then it ain't nothing but miserable cold."

"Are those odds for outside flies, or are you counting the ones trapped inside, too?"

DeMint's stare faded into confusion.

"Outside." Usher broke the silence. "Inside flies live longer."

"Not in my cabin," DeMint boasted.

Duncan moved to the coffeepot, filled a cup, lifted it toward his lips, and then lowered it suddenly.

"'Not in my cabin'?" Duncan walked back to the desk and held the cup out for DeMint's inspection. "Does drowning a fly in my coffee cup count?"

"Well, lookee there," DeMint whispered.

The cup moved toward Usher, who shrugged. "Again, inside flies don't count. And it might have died in that cup of natural causes."

Duncan dipped finger and thumb into the cup, pulled out the fly, and flicked it back toward the stove, then took a long sip and turned back to Usher.

"Pulling out?" he asked, though he already knew the answer.

Usher shrugged. "I guess I'm just not ready for a life of leisure."

"Well, like they say, 'It's calmest before the storm.'"

"Who says that?" DeMint asked.

"Everybody," Duncan barked.

"I ain't never said it," DeMint said.

"Said what?" Duncan asked, staring hard at Usher.

"'It's calmest before the storm.'"

Usher laughed. "You just said it," he told the jailer.

"Said what?" DeMint asked.

"'It's calmest before the storm,'" Usher told him, and looked back up at Duncan. "Now we've all said it."

"Just like I said."

The two lawmen laughed, and DeMint ran his hands through his hair before catching on to the joke.

"You guys should be up in Chicago with Buffalo Bill. Or performing at the opera house in Leadville."

"Used to be an opera house here," Duncan said. "It got burned down during all the troubles."

They were prolonging things. Duncan knew he couldn't keep it up, and he took another swallow of coffee. "Fly gives it some flavor," he said, and set the cup on the desk.

"You tell Sara?" Duncan asked.

Usher's head shook. "I figured I didn't have to. She's known it—I could tell by the look in her eyes—for almost a week."

"Syd Jones?"

Usher shook his head. "Syd rode out Friday. You know that. To escort that wagon company up this mountain. I'll see Syd on the ride down, I expect. And he probably knew I'd be leaving before even I did."

That made sense to Duncan.

"Logan?"

"He asked me yesterday how long I'd stick it out."

"Nugget?"

Usher chuckled. "He'd forget five minutes after I'd tell him."

"Joey Clarke?"

Usher stood. "He's your pard. He won't miss me."

"I don't know about that," Duncan said. "Drift Carver?"

"You plan on going through the entire population of Dead Broke, pal? There's a lot more folks here than they were a month ago, but even if you name them all, you'll be done fairly quick. You tell them I said, 'So long,' and that maybe I'll see y'all down the trail again sometime. And I paid my tab at Percy Stahl's and collected the three dollars Bryn Bunner owed me."

"You still owe me a dollar and fifteen cents."

Usher nodded toward the desk.

"It's right here," Winston DeMint said. "All in pennies."

That caused Duncan to smile, which he followed with a soft curse, and then shook his head.

Usher held out his right hand.

Duncan stared at it, sighed, and gripped it hard and fast. He tried to smile. Usher just gave him a quick nod.

"What are your plans?" Duncan asked, and picked up the cup to sip more coffee.

"Denver for a bit. See if I can find anything enticing in the newspapers there. I'm thinking of finding a town that's a lot warmer than it is on This Side Of The Slope."

Duncan nodded in understanding. "Warmer should be easier to find."

"And livelier."

"That might be a bit harder," Duncan said.

"That duck race Wednesday was a good one," Usher agreed.

"Better for me," Duncan said.

Usher nodded at the desk. "Like Winston said, your buck-fifteen is right there."

"In pennies," DeMint reminded them.

The two friends smiled and shook hands again.

"I'll let you know where I wind up," Usher said, moved past Duncan, and shook hands with the jailer before crossing to the door, which he pulled open, stepped back, and softly whispered a curse.

Sara Cardiff blocked the opening.

"You've got some nerve, mister," she said, hands on her hips, face flushed. Behind her stood Little Joey Clarke and Mayor Nugget.

"Joey saw your horse saddled, and Percy Stahl said you paid the tab you owed him." Usher retreated as Sara moved toward him like an angry bull. "Running out!"

"Riding out," he corrected. "To see the elephant."

"Running out," she repeated. "Without even a goodbye."

"It's not goodbye, Sara," he said softly. "It's just, 'Till I see you next time.'" He put his arms on her shoulders, pulled her to him, and enveloped her in a long hug, then pushed back just a little, smiling, and leaned forward and kissed her gently.

But it was a long kiss.

Duncan cleared his throat.

The couple parted, and Usher managed to turn toward his friend and wink—without letting Sara see his mischievous grin.

"Like I said, I'll let you know where I land." He turned, moved to the door, and shook the mayor's hand, saying, "I wish you all the luck in the world with your mining enterprises, Mayor. If I had more capital, I'd invest it all in you, sir, because I've never met a miner like you."

Then he dropped to a knee and held out his right hand toward the young schoolboy.

"You're leaving us?" the boy said, his voice cracking while he desperately tried to keep the tears from rolling down his cheeks.

"You've read enough of those dime novels, Joey, to know that heroes don't stay in one place anywhere. You know that saying about seeing the elephant."

He nodded, then shook his head. "I've never seen any elephant."

"I have."

"Really?"

"At a circus in Philadelphia."

"Was it big?"

"Mighty big. Gray. With yellow tusks. But you've lived out here long enough, and read too many dime novels, so you know what 'Seeing the elephant' means."

Joey nodded. "See what's over the next hill, across the next river, to see adventure and wonders and new folks."

Usher smiled.

"I've been all across the West. I've seen plenty of good towns and good folks, and, yeah, as a lawman, I've seen a lot of owlhoots and bad folks that I've had to put away—and sometimes, when they gave me no choice, put in a grave. But in all the towns where I've been—Deadwood, Tucson, Abilene, Wichita, gold camps whose names I've already forgotten—I've never felt as home as I have in Dead Broke, Colorado."

Joey perked up.

"Does that mean you'll be back, Mr. Usher?" he half-shouted.

"Well, I sure hope so, Joey. This is a wonderful town."

"Maybe it'll be in the next novel that gets wrote up 'bout you," Nugget said, "and Joey'll read it to me, won't you, Joey?"

The boy nodded.

"Maybe so," Usher said. He shook the boy's hand, then again shook hands with the mayor. Once outside, he gathered the reins to his horse and looked back at his friends.

"Like I said," he said, and swung into the saddle, "this isn't a sad farewell. It's just a brief parting. Y'all take care."

Clucking his tongue, he turned the horse around and rode away.

Nobody went back into the marshal's office and jail until he was out of sight. And when they did move, they moved slowly.

And sadly.

Dead Broke just didn't seem the same, and Ben Usher had been out of sight for just two minutes.

CHAPTER 6

With his left hand, Duncan MacMicking withdrew one of the six nails he had stuck between his lips, placed it on the new piece of pine planking, and, with his right hand, pulled the Schofield from his holster. Index finger in the trigger guard, he spun the .45 around so that the bottom of the butt was facing him, finger still in the trigger guard, middle finger behind the hammer, ring and pinky fingers over the cylinder and barrel and touching the tip of his thumb. With a quick movement, he reversed the revolver so that now he had the barrel in his hand.

That was the easy part. Anyone who lived with revolvers could do that trick. The next part could be dicey. And painful. Even though, as a man experienced in using firearms, he had unloaded all bullets from the cylinder and stuck those in the pockets of his jeans.

Now he fished a rusty nail from the pile on the ground, saw it was too bent to work, tossed it toward the empty Arbuckles' Coffee can—missed, but close enough—and found a straighter nail, which he pressed against the wooden plank. His left hand, gloved, moved up the long plank to the end, and pressed down firmly against the wooden brace. He drew a breath, eased the Schofield's butt to the head of the nail, and then, satisfied, he raised the revolver again and started tapping until the nail was maybe a quarter of an inch into the plank.

Now came the hard part. He raised the .45 higher and brought it down hard.

The sound made him smile. It was the sound of wood against metal, not wood against finger.

Again, he hammered the nail, which was in deep enough for him to remove his left hand, and just blasted that nail until the head was driven all the way into the wood.

Finding another nail good enough to use, he tried his carpentry skills again with the same success. One more nail on this end of the plank, and he could move to the middle brace, then the end brace and he would . . .

He glanced down the boardwalk. The rotting planks had been removed. Turning, he saw the stack of planks on the side of the street. He looked at the pile of nails. Three nails on both ends, three nails in the center. Nine nails per plank. His gaze moved back to the boardwalk being repaired. The planks were about four inches wide. He measured the distance. Thirty feet? Thirty-five? Three planks per foot. Three times thirty is . . . ?

His heavy sigh turned into a curse, but he made himself focus, buckle down, get back to work. He and the Schofield became a regular machine, like one of those steam- or water-powered engines moving a mill's saw or a riverboat. He finished that plank, and though he thought he felt sweat forming on his forehead, he did not bother to wipe it off. He grabbed a new plank, butted it against the one he had just nailed in place, sorted through the pile of nails and pulled out three that would work, and returned to carpentry. One nail in. Then another. The final one on the end nearest the building. Then he was hammering the center portion. Done. The end near the streetside. One nail. *Piece of cake.* Middle nail. *He's no match for me.* Last nail. Set. Tapped in. *Now for the finish.* Bang! Bang! . . .

And then the yelp, followed by that echo of profanity, with the Schofield rattling on the boardwalk, and Duncan shaking his left hand, and spitting out saliva and then sucking in a deep breath, bending his thumb, cringing at the pain, then lifting that arm, and sticking the grieving digit into his mouth.

The throbbing had hardly lessened when the voices across the street reached his consciousness.

"What time you got?"

"'Round half past nine."

"None of that round stuff, Bryn. Exactly what time?"

"Nine twenty-seven."

"Seconds?"

"Seconds? Are you serious?"

"Well, is it closer to twenty-seven or twenty-six or twenty-eight?"

"It's nine twenty-seven!"

"But that's now. When he smacked his thumb with that big hogleg of his'n. That's the time we need."

Duncan rose from his knees, and let his hand fall from his mouth, though he still shook it in the cold air. He stared across the street.

Bryn Bunner and Syd Jones kept arguing.

"Will you two shut up!" Joey Clarke's father demanded. "I'm trying to count." Five other men stood across the boardwalk, including Winston DeMint and Logan Ladron.

"Make it nine twenty-six," Jones said.

Ladron held up a notebook. "Nobody had nine thirty. So the winner is nine twenty." He cursed softly and shook his head. "I knew I should have taken nine twenty-five."

"I had nine twenty-five," Syd Jones said.

Sara Cardiff's dealer nodded. "Yep." He brought the book up, then turned, smiling, and held it up for Duncan's view, but he still wasn't seeing clearly, with the tears in his eyes and his thumb still throbbing.

He watched as the paper currency and change was handed to Syd Jones, who thanked them and slid his winnings into his pockets.

"Good show, Mick," the old lawman called out, giving a slight wave to Duncan, and he moved down the boardwalk. "I'm buying when Percy Stahl opens up later today." He shot Duncan a long glance. "Goes for you, too, Marshal. If you think you can hold a glass of lager in that hand of yours."

"He's gonna be a finishing carpenter one day," Joe Clarke, Little Joey's father, said, and laughed at his joke.

"If he ever finishes that boardwalk," Bryn Bunner said, "it'll be a miracle."

Those spectators went on about his business. Duncan checked his thumb. It didn't look as bad as it felt, but he still worried that he might lose that thumbnail.

"You poor thing," Sara told him inside the Crosscut Saloon.

Duncan studied her face, but conceding that Sara had made a living as a gambler for some time, he could not tell if she happened to be serious or condescending.

Their eyes met and held.

"What got into you?" she asked.

He was thinking the same thing.

Finally, he shrugged. "It was something to do."

"It was nice of you, too," she said, and rose, leaving him for the bar, but returning with a bottle of bourbon and three shot glasses.

Duncan looked around. They were the only ones in the saloon—at least out here on the main floor. She set the glasses down, and filled each shot, then slid two toward him. Sara picked up the remaining one and looked at him.

"The shorter pour is medicine. Go ahead and stick your poor, ugly thumb in that glass." She raised the glass in toast, and Duncan picked up the fuller glass in front of him. He nodded, then brought the glass to his lips and sent it down. She did the same. Then she sat down.

"I'm serious about the other glass," she told him.

His hesitation caused her to laugh aloud.

"You're such a baby sometimes," she said.

Frowning he raised his left hand and moved the thumb toward the glass.

"Yes," she told him without him having to ask, "it will sting. But it'll also cut down on the chances of infection. Do you know how much mud and filth have been on those rotted old wooden things?"

"Planks," he said.

"Plunk," she said, and made the motion with her left hand, thumb down, heading toward her empty glass.

He obeyed. She was right. It did burn. More than he expected, but the fire didn't last long. But that could have been because the batwing doors started banging and in came Mayor Nugget.

"How you doin', pardner," he said as he made his way to the couple.

Duncan withdrew his injured thumb from the glass, and dropped his hand underneath the table, shaking off the drops of bourbon and waiting for that fire to cool down.

Once he reached the table, Nugget saw the shot glass, smiled, and nodded at Sara. "Nice of you to be thinkin' of your pardner," he said, picked up the glass, and downed it before Sara could even raise her hand in warning.

The old coot smacked his lips, turned the glass upside down, and placed it back on the table.

"Somethin' dif'rent 'bout that brand," he said, and then walked back to the nearest table and dragged a chair over to sit with the couple.

"Well, pardner," Nugget said, "we's makin' us some good progress." He stared at Sara.

"That's good," she said.

"Maybe. This is new ter'tory for ol' Nugget, you know. Now, I could find gold sometimes, and ever'body knows 'bout how good I was at findin' silver. Ain't nobody but ol' Nugget ever found hisself a nugget like that one I gots me. The one that brung us all to this part of This Side Of The Slope." He smacked his lips.

With a sigh, Sara slid the bottle toward him.

As was his custom, Nugget did not bother using the glass. He took a long pull from the bottle, wiped his mouth, took another swallow, and, after a belch, set the bottle on the table, and wiped what one could see of his mouth underneath that thick, greasy mustache and beard, then nodded.

"I brung us in another partner," he told Sara.

"Partner?" Duncan stared at Sara.

"You did what?" Sara asked.

"Partner. Not fifty-fifty like us'n's. Bryn Bunner knows more about silver, but he ain't no idiot when it comes to zinc and lead. And he says he don't know much 'bout saltpeter, just a few things, but that ain't his speculatin'est."

"You brought in Bryn Bunner—without talking it over with me?" Sara poured herself a shot of whiskey and killed it in an instant.

Duncan was glad those hard eyes weren't boring through him right now. He had seen that look enough over the years.

"No." Nugget turned, spit on the floor, and looked

back at Sara, then wiped his beard. "I ain't hirin' Bryn for nothin'. But I ain't stupid enough not to listens to him."

Sara relaxed, but just a little.

"Go on," she said in a quiet voice.

"Well, Bunner tol' me to look up this feller, Silas Drury. Called him an expert miner. He's from Arkansas. Silas Drury. Not Bryn Bunner." He pursed his lips, looked across the empty saloon, then asked, "You know where Bryn Bunner comes from?"

"No," Sara barked. "Silas Drury?"

"Uh-huh." Nugget reached for the bottle, but Sara moved faster than a hammer swinging for a nail. She jerked it back.

"Arkansas is a long way from Colorado," she told him. "I've seen Arkansas. And the mountains there are nothing like the ones on This Side Of The Slope."

"There was a gold strike in Georgia," Duncan said, just so he wouldn't be sitting like that knot on a log. "From what I read. I think there are diamonds in Arkansas."

"Shut up," Sara said.

Now Duncan wished he had more bourbon in his glass. He brought his left hand up to study his thumb.

"Nugget," Sara said, "just what are you trying to tell me?"

"Partner," Nugget said. He stopped to breathe in, then out, and sighed. "I sent a telegraph off to Denver. That's where Bryn said Silas Dreary—"

"Drury," Duncan corrected.

"Like I said. That's where he be. Imbibed him up to come see my wonderfullest nugget of silver and maybe tell us what he thinks about findin' the best by-thunder lead or zinc mine up here and make Dead Broke famouser again."

He waited, staring at the bottle. Sara started looking

more like herself, and slowly slid the bottle of bourbon back toward the mayor.

"And?" Her question was so soft, Duncan wasn't sure the mayor had heard.

"Ain't heard back," he answered. "Like I said, I just sent it. And it got through. Line wasn't down. I expect we'll get an answer tomorrow. Maybe sooner. Can't tell. But then maybe he'll help us. Get us off on the right path. See, your Nugget ain't the idiot folks think he is." He took another long pull from the bottle, set it down, and wiped his mouth again.

"All right. Now I gots to get backs to my mayorin' duties. All this lead and zinc minin' is takin' up lot more of my time than I figgered it would. So . . ."

He turned quickly and looked at Duncan's left hand.

"What in blazes did you do to your thumb?" he demanded. "Hoss step on it?"

"It's nothing," Duncan said, and the left arm quickly disappeared under the tabletop again.

"Well, I'll lets you knows iffen I hears back from that Arkansas dude. Good meetin'. If that Silas Derby is as good as Bryn Bunner says he be, we might get this town crankin' to what it was in the eighties."

"I hope not," Duncan whispered.

Mayor Nugget left the Crosscut, and Duncan stared across at Sara. When she finally met his eyes, he said:

"Partner?"

CHAPTER 7

She waited until the doors stopped banging.

Finally, Sara shrugged her shoulders. "A girl has to make a living, same as a man. You're getting paid for being town marshal, but I can't stay in business with you and Logan playing penny-ante poker and praying that some miner will come inside to buy more than one shot of rye."

She sighed. "I thought all miners drank like Nugget and played poker as bad as Grandma Ramona."

"I thought you said your grandmother helped teach you how to mark a deck," Duncan said.

"That was Grandma Mary. On my mother's side. Grandma Ramona was a staunch Baptist, from her hair that only came out of a bun when she washed it once a month to her ancient shoes that only came off her feet when she took a bath."

He sighed and shook his head. She reached over and let her right hand fall atop his left hand.

"I like it here," she whispered. "Especially since you came to Dead Broke."

He moved his right hand over hers.

"The only reason I came was because Drift Carver said you were here."

She smiled. "That's nice of you to say, but you would have come, anyway, because of Syd Jones."

He shrugged. "Maybe."

"You know it's more than maybe."

"All right," he said. "But the only reason I stayed . . ."

He didn't have to finish that sentence.

Sighing, she withdrew her hand and looked around the empty saloon. "If something doesn't happen soon, I'll have to find a new town."

"Well," Duncan said, pausing, then sighed and shook his head. "I don't know of any mining town doing well."

"Then I'll find a cattle town. Fort Worth. Dodge City isn't doing the business it was six or seven years ago, but I hear it's still growing."

Duncan nodded. "Yeah, it's growing. But it's not the same Dodge City. Just like it's not the same Fort Worth. I know. The U.S. marshal in Denver hired me, while I was marshaling in Durango, to haul a prisoner to Dodge City, and the marshal in Dodge hired me to take a prisoner to Waco, and I had to pass through Fort Worth on the way there. I couldn't find a decent poker game in Texas, and I couldn't find anything other than bad beer in Dodge."

"Alaska?" she asked.

He shook his head. "Dead Broke's cold enough for me." So he tried one.

"Sandwich Islands?"

"You'd get seasick," she told him.

A minute passed. Then another. Both felt like hours.

"You think Laurent Dubois's ice sculptures will bring folks up here?" he asked.

"He said it's still not cold enough. After what happened earlier, with that warm front melting all his sculptures—"

He cut her off. "We should have waited. Should have known better. That cool summer just fooled us."

She sighed. "I thought I'd like a quiet place to live."

"Me, too."

Their eyes met, and both smiled.

"We're hopeless," they said at the same time—and they laughed together.

She stood, looked toward the entrance, and found him again. "Let's take a walk around town."

He shrugged. "I ought to make my rounds." He rose from his chair, which he slid back under the table, and glanced at the empty saloon. "But who'll mind the place?"

"Whoever comes in," she said, "can have it."

The following day mirrored the one before—and dozens before that. So did the next day.

But two days later—or Duncan thought, though it was hard to tell a Wednesday from a Thursday or a Saturday from a Monday by then, though Sundays were easy enough because the pastor and the priest rang the church bells. Anyway, it wasn't a Sunday. So . . . two days later, unless it was three or four, or just one, Duncan was disturbed from reading a month-old newspaper from Nashville, Tennessee, by Little Joey Clarke.

The boy barged through the door so fast and yelled so loud he woke Winston DeMint, who was sleeping in one of the empty cells, and caused Duncan to rip the page he was reading—not that he remembered anything he had read.

"Marshal! Marshal! You gotta come quick. Quick, she says. C'mon!"

"Whoa." Duncan stood. "Slow down, Joey. Slow down. Who says?"

"Miss Sara. Miss Sara."

The door opened to the cells, and DeMint stared hard. "What . . ." He stopped to yawn. "What—"

"Miss Sara wants the marshal. A man has come to town. A stranger."

Duncan found the gun belt and holster hanging on a peg. Now, this was more like it. A stranger in town. He hoped it wasn't another one of those punks looking for a fight and something upon which one could build a reputation, but if it was, well, maybe Duncan wouldn't be so generous and merciful this time.

DeMint walked toward the gunrack for a shotgun.

"Hold on, Winston," Duncan told his jailer. "You best wait here. But keep the door open, and if shooting starts, come fast."

"You seen Syd?" DeMint asked.

"Not this morning. He said something about wetting a fishing line last night."

The jailer nodded, but moved to the rack and pulled out a Greener. "All right," he said. "I'll be ready if you need me."

Joey's head was darting back and forth between the marshal and the jailer.

"You see that stranger?" Duncan asked as he checked the bullets in the .45's cylinder.

"No, sir," the boy answered. He wet his lips. "I was just walking by on my way to the schoolhouse, and she must have seen me, on account she come through the doorway and called out my name, and asked me—she even said 'pretty please'—to tell you that 'that man's in town' and for you to come to the saloon quick as you can."

"'That man.' 'That man.'" He blinked and let the Schofield slide into the leather. "What man?"

"'That man,'" Joey said. "That's all she said, Marshal. I run as quick as I could."

"'Ran,'" DeMint corrected.

"All right," Duncan said. He did not bother finding his coat, though it was chilly that morning, but pulled the hat off the peg and set it on his head. "You run along to school, Joey. And thank you for telling me about that man."

The boy had that look in his eyes, and Duncan wasn't going to risk him getting hurt. "I said *to school,* Joey, and that's an order. Don't worry about me. This is probably nothing at all. Just a visitor. Maybe a newspaper scribe who wants to write about me."

"Yeah," DeMint said. "Yeah. A newspaperman."

Little Joey Clarke pouted, but when Duncan opened the door, the boy walked out, head down, and Duncan made sure he started for the schoolhouse and not the Crosscut Saloon.

"Leave the door open," DeMint reminded him. "So I'll hear the gunshots and know to come help you."

Duncan stared at him a long second. "Thanks," he said, and turned, feeling the sound of his boots thumping on the boardwalk he had repaired and thinking that if he got himself killed in the next few minutes, the citizens of Dead Broke would think fondly of him for his carpentry skills, at least.

The streets were empty, but, these recent weeks, it was hard to find anyone on the streets at this time of morning. The miners were already up in the mountains, looking for any ore that wasn't silver, the kids would be at the schoolhouse—Joey Clarke must have been running late—and the few businesses that remained in town would be open, praying for someone to come in and buy something. The stagecoach would have come in and gone. That reminded Duncan that he had not bothered to walk to the hotel, where the stagecoach stopped, turned around, and left—not even to change the team of mules. That would happen at the station at the bottom of the mountain. He had stopped checking on the stages weeks ago, because he wasn't seeing anyone get off a coach, but quite a few kept getting on, moving away, permanently.

His mind worked sharply. That's how he had managed to stay alive all these years. The street was empty. The man in the Crosscut Saloon likely knew the location of the marshal's office, so that stranger knew Duncan would be walking down this boardwalk—right past those windows. He'd make an inviting target.

So, ever the fox, Duncan turned the corner, picked up his pace, and jogged to the alley that ran behind Sara's place. No windows there. He stopped at the back door, which led to the storeroom. That was worth a try, so he gripped the knob with his left hand, his right resting on the Schofield. He turned and swore softly. Locked.

He moved on to the street, bit his bottom lip, and peered around the corner. Nothing. This side of town was as dead as any other.

Stepping off the ground onto the boardwalk, he moved slowly. No windows here. This was where that long mahogany bar was, then he was at the corner. He could hear liquid being poured, a soft cough—maybe the gunman was a lunger.

Doc Holliday? No, you idiot. Doc died five years ago—more than five. Think, fool, think.

Pressing his back against the wood, he inched his way toward the batwing doors. The main doors were open, hooked to the walls so they wouldn't bang. This street remained empty, but he heard voices inside. A man and a woman were having a conversation, but he couldn't identify the man. It didn't sound like Logan Ladron.

Most certainly, it wasn't Nugget. If this man came to Dead Broke to kill Duncan, he wouldn't have ridden in on a stagecoach. Unless he planned on stealing Duncan's horse as a further insult after he had shot the legendary lawman down.

You are thinking like one of those wretches who pens those dime novels.

He stopped against one of the doors hooked to the wall. The voices were easier to hear now.

"Thank you. That's very kind of you to say, sir." That was Sara.

She's distracting him. That's my girl.

He eased the revolver from his holster, put his thumb over the hammer, and made his move.

Duncan barged through the batwing doors, ready for action. Sara, standing behind the bar, turned. So did the man in a checkered suit and bowler hat. Sara's eyes widened. The man, portly with long graying whiskers and a porkpie hat, held a glass of whiskey in his right hand.

The only noise came, not from a Schofield .45 or any other brand of revolver, but the batwing doors—and that .45 felt like a steamboat's anchor in Duncan's right hand.

"Duncan," Sara said in a startled voice. "What are you doing with that pistol?"

Duncan blinked. The man smiled and raised his glass in toast.

"Marshal MacMicking," the man said. "Good morning to you, sir. You have a fine city here, sir, and a most gracious hostess. Yes, sir. Most gracious, indeed. Where is that grand mayor of yours, sir? I am Silas Drury, sir. Of Drury and Cervelli Mining Enterprises of Galena, Arkansas."

Somehow, he stopped his face from flushing with

embarrassment. He remembered the Schofield. And Sara's question. But Duncan had been a lawman and a gambler for a long, long time, and he quickly came up with a lie.

"Oh." He laughed and raised the .45 carefully. "I was nailing some planks—fixing a boardwalk in town, sir. Yeah. That's what I was doing when Little Joey found me." The gun slid back into the holster. "Forgot I even had it."

He told himself that he needed to keep Little Joey Clarke away from Sara Cardiff for a few days, till no one remembered what had just happened, and where Joey had found Duncan to deliver Sara's message.

When they were seated at an empty poker table, with Mr. Silas Drury of Drury and Cervelli Mining Enterprises of Galena, Arkansas, sipping rye, Sara enjoying coffee, and Duncan supporting his chin with his left hand and his right elbow resting on the table, Duncan listened to the mining expert talk about his business.

"I didn't know Arkansas had mines," Duncan said when the man stopped talking.

Drury grinned. "Do you know what 'Galena' means, sir?"

Duncan shook his head.

"Lead ore," he answered. "That was probably what most of the early settlers, back when Arkansas was just a territory, found. Galena. But yes, Marshal MacMicking, Arkansas is rich in minerals. Coal is probably the most common, but saltpeter is common—for which you must be thankful."

"Saltpeter," Duncan said blandly.

The big man laughed. "It is key to making gunpowder, and from what I've heard about you, gunpowder and lead are most precious to a man of your—shall I say—talents?"

Duncan stifled a grunt and just nodded.

"We've also mined for goethite and hematite." He didn't explain what those things were used for. "Salt, of course." He didn't have to explain salt. "And someone asked me recently about diamonds, but I just laughed as, while that would be a wonderful gift to my home state, I'm not sure diamonds are a good investment for a mining operation. But . . . who knows?"

He paused long enough to sip his whiskey.

"Granted, many mining operations have played out, but Galena is home; however, I rarely am home."

"And what brings you to Colorado?" Duncan asked.

"Prospecting." He laughed. "I am, after all, a miner."

Duncan sipped coffee. "Bryn Bunner," he said, but the man laughed again.

"Yes, I have talked to Mr. Bunner. A giant of a man, with a giant heart, too. And he loves this area." Drury nodded in appreciation. "And I can see why."

"Bryn's found lead," Duncan said.

"Indeed, and the ore sample he showed me is of good quality. Good quality. Not great."

"What's the difference between good and great?" Duncan asked.

"For me, ten dollars a ton." He smiled at the look on Duncan's and Sara's faces. "Lead is not gold, my dear companions. But it can be profitable. And less dangerous."

"Meaning cave-ins?" Sara asked.

"Meaning murders." The miner finished his whiskey. "People kill over gold and silver. Even diamonds, or so I've been told by miners in Africa and places like that. Zinc? Lead? Things like that? Not so much. But a good mine can make a profit."

Sara cleared her throat, and when both men looked at

her, she spoke softly. "Bryn said the lead he found was of good quality. But what can a lead mine support?"

The miner shrugged. "That will depend on what I find. But this area—what is that quaint phrase you call it?"

"This Side Of The Slope?" Sara guessed.

"Yes. This Side Of The Slope. I love this far west. Arkansas is Western in some ways, but Southern in many others, and Midwestern in other ways. This Side Of The Slope. What a grand name." He cleared his throat.

This guy sure likes to talk, Duncan thought.

"Many towns in Arkansas—and other states and territories—do well with lead, zinc, saltpeter. Those don't bring in the hordes the way gold and silver can, but that isn't a bad thing, as you know. The biggest problem with a mine at this elevation is . . . this elevation. Hauling seventy-five thousand pounds of pig lead to the railroad could be costly. But we shall see. I first need to look for myself. Bryn Bunner is a good man, yes, and a wise miner, but he has been digging for silver most of his life. I have made a small fortune by working those less nefarious minerals."

"Would you invest?" Sara asked.

"That depends." He covered a yawn and shook his head. "My apologies. But all this traveling from Denver in that rugged and most uncomfortable stagecoach has worn me out. With your permission, I should like to take my leave and catch up on my sleep. Is there a good restaurant in town where I could take you two and Mr. Bunner and that mayor, of whom I've heard so much about, to supper?"

Duncan was trying to think of a place this side of Denver that might meet this Arkansan's idea of good. Sara had the right answer, though.

"Of course," she said. "You come right here at six this evening and you'll have the best meal you've had in ages."

"Splendid." He clapped his hands. "Now, where is the best place for lodging?"

Obviously, he had seen the hotel, or what was called one in Dead Broke, where the stagecoach had stopped—and it didn't pass muster.

Duncan was thinking about the bunks in the jail. Sara was thinking of the upstairs rooms that no one was using. Neither thought their thoughts would be appreciated by this dandy.

But the batwing doors banged open, and in barged Nugget, and his appearance excited Silas Drury so much that he ordered another round of refreshments. Then another—though by then, Sara and Duncan had switched to coffee.

Nugget told him about his Hope Diamond of Silver and that he had moved away from silver mining and now was sniffing his way to another fortune.

"I always thought that large nugget was nothing more than a fairy tale," Drury said.

"Well, you won't think nothin' like that never ag'in oncet you sees what me and my late pard—good ol' Sluagdach found ourselves back in '85. C'mon, Mr. Dreary. You's gonna get to see this for just half off what I customarily gets. Ten dollars."

"I'll be delighted."

"And wait till you get a taste of my brew."

"Even better."

The two departed, merrily singing—if one could call that singing—leaving Sara and Duncan alone.

"Well?" Sara finally asked when the doors stopped making that infernal racket.

"Well, what?" Duncan asked.

"Do you think there's a chance he can help save Dead Broke?"

Duncan shrugged. "Bryn Bunner said he liked what he saw when he found that lead and zinc. I know Bryn Bunner. I don't know this character, but I can send some telegrams out and—"

"He's the real thing," Sara said.

Duncan waited.

"I've been in Dead Broke a long time, pardner," she said. "Before you came up here, I had all sorts of mining visitors who liked to gamble. And some of those gentlemen mentioned Silas Drury of Arkansas. And I found his name in a mining journal and quite a few newspapers. And who do you think suggested his name to Nugget?"

Duncan just shook his head and grinned. "You're a wonder."

Her face brightened. "I like when you say that."

He thought that might be a good opportunity to steal a kiss, but her face suddenly paled and she stiffened. "Oh, my," she finally whispered.

Duncan came to her. "What's the matter?"

"He . . . he . . . he . . ." She managed to raise her right hand and point at the entrance. "He's coming back here for supper and—"

Duncan hugged her gently. "Don't worry," he whispered.

"But he'll be back."

"No, he won't," Duncan told her. "Not today, anyhow. Maybe tomorrow. Tomorrow afternoon."

"But he said—"

Duncan stopped her with his laugh. She stared up at him, and he patted her arms.

"When Nugget serves him his brew, Mr. Silas Drury is

going to be out cold for a long, long time. If he's down here by three o'clock tomorrow afternoon, I'll pay you five dollars."

She considered that, but, being a professional gambler, said: "No bet."

CHAPTER 8

Silas Drury survived his first taste of Nugget's brew, and the two men, accompanied by Bryn Bunner and a curious Syd Jones, went off the next day to check out the mountainside. Duncan would have gone along, but Mrs. Klann came over to say that her son had cut school again and was likely fishing in one of the creeks, and would the marshal have time to go find him and bring him back so she could tan his hide so that the little rascal would not sit comfortably for a month of Sundays.

So Duncan found Drift Carver, tolerably sober, in his cabin, and after pouring six cups of coffee down the old man's throat, the two of them set off looking for young Gary Klann.

They climbed up alongside the creek bed.

"Lake's a lot easier to get to." Drift Carver was already heaving.

"Lucile said he didn't go to the lake. You know how boys are, Drift. They want to get into the woods. And this is where all those kids go fishing."

"Which is why"—Drift had to pause, straighten, cough, and wheeze—"nobody's caught a . . . fish . . . in this stream . . . in . . ." He gave up trying to complete the sentence and moved the last ten yards to where the country started to level off into gentle rolls and not rugged, hard climbing country.

Duncan was thankful for easier climbing, too. Carver had slung two canteens over his shoulder. He pulled one off, unscrewed the cap, and took a long pull, then held it out toward Duncan.

"Why'd you bring canteens?" He pointed at the stream that flowed three feet from them. "This water's pure as anything around here."

"That ain't sayin' much." Carver still held out the canteen.

Duncan shook his head.

"It ain't water, pardner," Carver told him. "It's whiskey. You can chase it with crick water, if you wanna, though."

"No, thanks." Duncan shook his head.

With a shrug, Carver secured the cap and put the strap over his shoulder again, then found his plug of tobacco and was about to bite off a chunk when something caught Drift's eye, and he moved to a well-worn trail, then squatted.

Walking over, Duncan saw Carver pick up a turd, break it open, raise it to his nose, and then sniff.

"Bear scat," Duncan whispered.

Carver nodded, pitched the remnants away, and rubbed his hand on old leaves.

"Fresh?" Duncan hoped most of the bears would be heading into dens to sleep, but he knew it hadn't gotten that cold yet.

"'T'ain't old." Carver pushed himself up. "You didn't bring no rifle."

That was obvious. Duncan pointed to the Henry that Carver carried, strapped over his back. "That's loaded, I hope," Duncan said.

"Of course." The old-timer wiped his mouth. "Aw." He shrugged and waved his hand. "Bear's likely hunting a place to sleep."

"Yeah."

Neither sounded like they were convinced.

They walked slowly, keeping about twenty paces between them.

"See any tracks?" Duncan asked.

"Just the bear's. Kid's too puny to make no tracks."

"We know where the boy's going," Duncan said.

"Yeah. Likely the bear's got the same notion."

They listened, but the only noise came from the gurgling stream and the wind in the trees. By Duncan's guess, they were fifteen minutes from the little lake. He studied the trail that gradually sloped up another six hundred feet before a hard fifty yards more. Then it would level out for a quarter mile. That's where the lake was, feeding this stream and two others. It was one of the best places to fish.

Bears knew that, too.

They listened in the silence of the wilderness, but again heard only wind, water, and their own pounding hearts.

"Let's pick up the pace," Duncan said, and he moved ahead of Carver.

They were sweating and panting by the time they covered the last of the easy rise, stopping to take a cupful of water in their hands from the creek. The next part was the hardest. Before they started the climb, Carver pointed at the claw marks.

Duncan saw something else.

He picked up a shiny button and pulled out a small string of thread.

Carver sighed. "Red coat. That's what his mama said."

Nodding, Duncan slipped the button into the watch

pocket of his trousers. His hand found a hold, and he started pulling himself up the mountain.

It wasn't that hard of a climb. Not really. At least, not during summer and autumn. Kids did it all the time. So did miners when they were off, and Duncan enjoyed the peacefulness of it. Why, he and Sara had brought a picnic lunch up here two weeks back. This wasn't a sheer cliff. It was just not what one would call a hiking trail. You had to climb it, but it was still angling and now it was slippery. Duncan could see marks made by Gary Klann's fingers and boots.

Keep going up, he told himself. *Keep going up. Remember, it'll be much easier going down.*

He could see the top now and stopped to look back down. Old as he was, Drift Carver was still part mountain goat. Duncan needn't worry about him.

Inching forward, sweating despite the chill in the air, using his right hand, he grabbed the old tree root that had been there for ages. Kids called it "the Elevator"—and those boys hadn't seen an elevator except, maybe, in illustrated magazines. Duncan had seen one—at the New York Life Building in Kansas City two years ago. He hadn't ridden on it, though. He considered those things no better than coffins.

But that root would pull a man up. It had pulled him up with Sara squeezing the life out of him on that silly picnic.

His right hand grabbed the thickest part of the uncovered root, then his left, and that's when he heard the scream of a boy.

The echo that followed wasn't a boy's. It wasn't even an echo. It was the roar of a bear.

"Go," Drift Carver managed to cough out. "Go. I'm"—he stopped to suck in oxygen—"behin' ya."

Duncan pulled and felt himself lifted. His left hand let

go of the root and grabbed the top of that chunk of granite. Then his right followed and he pulled, grunting and praying simultaneously, until his upper torso was on hard rock. He heard the rushing of the stream and the wind. Coming to his knees, he wiped the sweat off his forehead and heard the boy screaming.

"Get away. Get away! Shoo! Shoo, bear, shoo."

Duncan rose to his feet. He didn't wait to help Drift Carver, even if the scout had the long gun they'd need. That was another mistake they had made. The fellow with the rifle should have taken point on the climb.

The boy trembled in a tree, but it wasn't that tall of a tree, and the bear—a big mama grizzly—stood underneath, roaring and reaching, but the kid was out of reach.

Duncan drew the Schofield and charged. He cocked the hammer and squeezed the trigger. The bullet kicked bark off the tree, and the bear turned around and saw Duncan.

Dropping to all four feet, the bear snarled and charged. Duncan was running, his lungs heaving—"staggering" would be a better description—but when he realized the bear was abandoning the boy in the tree and coming for him, he stopped running.

The bear likely weighed 550 pounds, maybe six hundred. But it moved like a thoroughbred.

At least the boy is safe, Duncan thought. *For now.*

He stopped and aimed the Schofield, but the bear was practically on him. He hardly had the .45 out of the holster when he dived as hard and as far as he could to his left, feeling the bear rush past him, then feeling the trunk of the fallen tree that he met. He flipped over the trunk, landed on pinecones and hard rocks, and came up leveling his right hand, only to see that his hand no longer held that revolver. The bear had turned and was coming back.

Duncan found a piece of a limb from the lightning-struck pine and leaped over the trunk.

The bear slowed now, savvy, sniffing, growling, sizing up this puny little man in the woods.

"Joey," Duncan called. "I want you to run to the creek. Then run as hard as you can back to the Elevator and get down as quick as you can."

How he managed to say all that with his lungs working harder than a steam engine, he couldn't say. He didn't even know if the kid heard him, until the boy's voice reached him.

"My name's not Joey. It's Gary. Gary Klann."

"Just run, you—"

The grizzly charged and drowned out the foul word that had slipped out of Duncan's mouth.

The bear stopped before it met Duncan and rose, towering over him. Its head lowered. That beast's breath stank worse than Nugget's, and Duncan shoved the limb he held into the mammoth's open mouth.

The heavy limb snapped like a toothpick.

Duncan bounced back. His lungs burned. Sweat poured down his face. Somehow, he managed to unbuckle his gun belt, and he began swinging it, picturing in his mind young David and his slingshot, but the holster held no stone to slay old Goliath. When it struck the bear's left forefoot, it had the same effect as a gnat.

He whirled the belt and holster again, and lashed out, but the bear fended off the leather and the next thing Duncan knew was that his right hand was empty and the gun belt was flying toward the lake. It splashed on the edge.

More than once, he had seen men fighting bears in circus acts, but those were old bears, and he remembered the show he had run out of Durango with Colossus the

Giant Grizzly He-Bear, which turned out to be a she-bear that was nowhere near as big as the grizzly Duncan now faced. And this bear had not had its teeth and claws removed.

He reached for a stone, but that was a mistake, because the bear was quick, and swung a massive front paw that caught Duncan by the side and sent him sailing over the fallen tree and onto hard granite that ripped shirtsleeve and skin.

Rolling over, he came up to his knees, trying to find a stick or stone or anything that might help him. The bear again stood on its hind legs and roared, its breath stinking and massive drops of bear saliva pounding Duncan's face.

He saw those red eyes and yellow teeth and sharp claws and knew he was done for.

But a shot rang out.

The bear dropped to all fours and turned. Another shot fired, sparks flying off granite where the bullet had struck. Duncan heard the echoes of the two reports, and the bear must have thought the cavalry had ridden to the rescue.

It turned around and ran off, past the lake, into the dark forest.

The echoes of the shots faded away, and all Duncan heard now was neither the stream nor the wind, but rather the pounding of his heart.

He managed to catch his breath, and coughed out, "Thank you, Drift Carver."

There was no echo, but a snort, and then a kid's voice.

"Drift Carver ain't here. You can thank Gary Klann, Marshal."

Duncan turned. At first, he thought he was hallucinating. Maybe this was a dream. Maybe he was dead.

But then, Gary Klann stood before him, holding a smoking Schofield .45 in his right hand.

* * *

They found Drift Carver not at the Elevator, but at the bottom of the drop-off, where he had fallen and busted his left ankle.

Duncan let him sip whiskey from one of those canteens.

"Can I have some water, too?" young Gary asked. "I'm parched."

"Drink from the creek," Drift told him.

"Can I go back and fetch my fishing pole?" the boy asked.

"No!"

The boy pouted, then walked to the stream. Drift watched him for a moment, then took the canteen from Carver and had a hard pull himself.

He wiped his lips and returned the canteen to the old scout.

"Tell me you can walk," he said.

"Not hardly." Drift pointed to the other canteen. "I drunk that one waitin' for you two to come back." Seeing the marshal's face, the old-timer explained why. "Hey, a busted ankle hurts like blazes. I drunk only fer the medicinal purposes."

The boy returned, and Duncan corked the canteen, and slung it over his shoulder.

"What time you reckon?" Carver asked.

Duncan looked up, but shrugged after a minute. "Can't tell. Not up here."

"Why don't y'all leave me and—"

"Shut up," Duncan snapped. He turned to Gary Klann. "I hope you get the paddling of your life."

"Hey," the boy said, "I saved your life. You'd be et up by that ol' she-bear iffen it wasn't for me."

"He-bear," Duncan said.

The boy snorted. "Yeah. Right."

He rose stiffly and nodded at the boy. "Help Mr. Carver up. Then, Drift, you'll be ridin' piggyback on me. Boy, you take the point. Watch your step, and if I fall, get out of our way 'cause we'll be rolling like a rockslide."

"Will you deputize me?"

"You're deputized."

"I want a badge."

"You're about to get a beating."

"Joey Clarke's got a badge."

He sighed. "I'll give you a deputy's badge when we get back to Dead Broke."

"Promise."

"Or I could stake you out the way we did LeRoy Blackhawk in New Mexico Territory that time."

"All right. All right. As long as I get a deputy's badge."

And so they started, moving gingerly, picking the easiest paths, stopping fairly often to drink water or whiskey and catch their breath. It was late in the day when they limped back into Dead Broke. Duncan located an old badge and handed it to Gary Klann, who ran off to show his mother; and Winston DeMint went to fetch Doc Cartier, who wrapped up Drift Carver's busted ankle, and patched up Duncan's cuts and bruises, then gave them his instructions.

"Stay away from grizzly bears for a while."

CHAPTER 9

A few days later, a Denver newspaper reporter showed up in the Dead Broke marshal's office, asking Duncan to retell the story of his fight with the grizzly bear and not to leave out any of the juicy tidbits.

And that visit came about just when Duncan was moving around better. His brain wasn't as fogged over as it had been, either, which was how he remembered the press some—*most*—of the Denver papers had been heaping on Duncan's town.

"Which paper are you with?" he asked.

"The *Times of the Rockies,*" the bald-headed man, with the big belly, answered.

Duncan frowned. "Are you the reporter who called this town 'Dread Broke'?"

The bald head shook. "That was the *Gazette.* And I know that reporter. She's a good gal. She told me that was just a mistake by the tramp printer. If it makes you feel any better, that printer moved on last week. Got a job down in Albuquerque."

After refilling his coffee and trying to guess if this

inkslinger was lying, another thought popped in Duncan's brain.

"How'd you hear about that fight down in Denver already?"

News didn't travel that fast, especially with the unpredictability of the telegraph line that ran down the mountain to the railroad.

"The Sutters told me."

The Sutters. Duncan sighed.

"I was at the stagecoach station checking on new arrivals," the reporter said.

Duncan shot Syd Jones a glance. The old lawman looked just as sad as Duncan felt, and shook his head, and then both men turned to DeMint.

"Hadn't heard about them leaving Dead Broke," he said.

"Looks like everybody'll be doing their own laundry for a while," Jones said. "Or sending it down to Denver."

"Not Denver," the reporter said. "San Diego, California. Mr. Sutter said they wanted to get as far away from This Side Of The Slope as possible."

Duncan considered opening the door and throwing the man out, but then he thought that maybe a write-up in the Denver paper about grizzly bear fights could bring some folks to town. Fighting a bear had to be a gamble, and maybe some of those boys would try their luck at Sara's saloon.

He looked at the business card the reporter had given him: CARL WOODWARD. It sounded like the name of an honest man.

"What do you want to know?" he asked after letting out another long sigh.

Syd Jones stood to drag his chair closer to Duncan's desk, and Duncan gave his mentor a hard stare.

"Just want to hear how you tell it this time," Jones said.

Duncan gave him his most menacing look.

"Been telling the story often, Marshal?" Woodward asked.

"Oh, to schoolchildren mostly," Duncan said. "To warn them about the dangers in bear country."

He frowned. Woodward didn't write that down in his notebook.

Duncan was about halfway finished with his narrative, and he had been keeping the tale an honest account, when the door opened and in rushed Bryn Bunner and the Arkansas mineral man, Silas Drury. Both men were out of breath—as if they had been chased down the mountain by a she-bear. He hadn't seen either of those two since his last talk with them. They spoke so fast, Duncan finally held up his right hand. That didn't stop them at all, and only managed to make them talk faster, simultaneously, so that his ears and head started aching.

He reached for his Schofield, but the revolver was in the holster on the belt that was hanging on the rack, so he found his empty coffee mug and slammed it on the desk like a judge's gavel. That sounded just as loud as a .45, and it stopped both men's jaws from moving.

Taking advantage of the moment of silence, Duncan ordered, "One at a time." He motioned toward Mr. Woodward. "We have another newspaperman with us." He nodded at Bryn Bunner, since he knew that miner better than he knew the expert from Arkansas. Bunner stared at the reporter.

"Tell him," Silas Drury said. "This town could use some favorable newspaper articles for a change."

"Silas got excited by some flickers he saw in that cave

Nugget was in last week," Bunner said. "Thought it might be silver."

Duncan sighed, shook his head, and couldn't hold in the chuckle.

"Silver," he said flatly. Those two miners were talking about silver when that market had gone bust a while back. Silver had gotten Dead Broke into this mess.

"Thought it was silver," Bunner said. "But turns out . . . it wasn't."

The wry grin straightened, and Duncan leaned forward. The expert started: "Mr. Bunner and I—"

"Bryn," Bunner said, "call me Bryn."

"Bryn," Drury corrected, making Duncan wonder if this conversation would go on till Christmas.

"The two of us quickly began to build a furnace," Drury said.

Mr. Woodward's pencil moved furiously.

It was easier, he realized, when he was the lawman in a cattle town. Cattle were easy to figure out. The market might change, as all markets do—going up, going down, leveling out—but cattle were cattle. Gold, silver, and any other minerals all had their individual characteristics and quirks. Just like the miners themselves. Cowboys, well, they were all the same—no matter what brand they rode for, no matter the color of their skin. Cattlemen weren't any different, either. At least, not to a lawman.

"Well," Drury said, "once we had the furnace going, I tossed in some ore from the cave. It didn't melt. Just disappeared. And you should have seen the rainbow of colors."

"That's all there was," Bryn Bunner said. "A beautiful rainbow."

The two men fell silent. Duncan cleared his throat.

"A rainbow?" he said, and waited.

"Zinc," Drury said.

"Zinc," Duncan echoed.

"Zinc?" the newspaperman asked.

"Zinc," Bunner said, and grinned like he was holding four aces.

Reaching for the knob on the bottom drawer of his desk, Duncan studied the faces of the miners, then pulled open the drawer. He glanced at the bottle, sizing up how much rye whiskey remained.

"How much is zinc selling for?" Woodward asked.

"Sixteen dollars a ton," Silas Drury said.

Sara Cardiff opened the door just in time to hear the mining expert's answer. She stopped.

"And lead?" Syd Jones asked.

"Fourteen," Drury said, but raised his hand. "Understand, gentlemen . . ." He paused and bowed toward Sara. "And you, the most charming lady in all of Colorado."

Sara curtseyed and came inside, shutting the door, and setting a basket from which emanated the most delicious odors of baked bread and what smelled like roast beef.

"You have to deduct the cost of hauling ore to market."

"How much?" Duncan asked.

Bunner shrugged. "Forty cents."

Duncan found himself wondering why he ever thought becoming a lawman was a good path to take.

"Now," Drury warned again, "just so you know the facts, the price for zinc is way down. It was twenty-eight a ton back in '89, and thirty-one dollars and seventy-five cents two years ago."

But silver was below seventy cents an ounce. And nobody was investing in silver mines these days.

"Does Dead Broke have a royalty?" Drury asked.

"Royalty?" Woodward asked.

Bunner answered both questions. "No. No royalty." He looked at the lawmen and reporter. "Some mining districts take a royalty, usually fifteen percent. Twenty-five percent is about as high as I've ever found. That's charged by the landowners. But up here, most of the claims aren't leased. Nobody ever thought land up this high was worth buying—even after the big silver strike in '85."

Syd Jones just shook his head. "All these years, I was marshaling here. I could have owned a lot of land, had I sense enough to spend my wages on property and not lead and gunpowder."

Silas Drury cleared his throat. "Now, don't get your hopes up quite yet. Those flakes that led us to believe there might be some pay dirt in lead and zinc here . . . could be a fluke, though I think we have a strong possibility of finding valuable ore."

"And," Bryn Bunner added, looking directly at Duncan and Syd Jones, "zinc and lead doesn't bring in the parasites the way gold and silver do."

"Plus," Drury added, "a town this high up in the mountains, with no railroad here and none likely to come, well, we need investors. Men—or women—who have money to spare and can help us fund our enterprises. I still am amazed that towns like Dead Broke and Leadville have managed to survive during the silver boo—"

He didn't finish, because a tremendous boom shook the building, and Duncan was glad he hadn't pulled out that bottle of liquor, because he likely would have dropped it and smashed it on the floor.

As it was, Sara Cardiff fell, but Syd Jones caught the basket of food she had brought in, and Silas Drury managed to catch Sara before she hit the floor.

"Someone's robbing the bank!" the newspaperman yelled. "They've blown open the vault!"

"What vault?" said Syd Jones.

"What bank?" Duncan said. He moved toward the door

and retrieved his gun belt, then stepped outside into the chill and onto the empty street. The others followed. He saw no smoke. That was the good news. He had lost track of the number of towns he had seen almost wiped out by fires, and two or three that had never recovered from them.

"I think it came from the mountains," Syd Jones said. He shielded his eyes with the palm of his left hand and looked above the building tops.

Clouds hid the tallest peaks. Duncan thought they could be dumping some snow, but he couldn't find any smoke, and the echoes of the explosion had faded away. Still, he walked down the street toward the Crosscut Saloon. Sara caught up with him first. The others followed several paces behind.

Logan Ladron stood on the street by the time Duncan and Sara reached the saloon. He was looking up at the mountains, too.

"Any idea where that came from?" Duncan asked.

The gambler shook his head. "It woke me up from a mighty good dream," he said.

Percy Stahl had wandered from his little saloon. A few heads appeared in the doorways, one from an upstairs window, and Duncan could hear the voice of the schoolmarm, and while he couldn't make out the words over the begging and pleading of her students, he figured he knew what they were saying. They wanted to see for themselves.

The problem was, Duncan knew, they couldn't see anything. The echoes had died now. The ground wasn't shaking, so it wasn't an earthquake.

Has Colorado ever had an earthquake? Duncan wondered.

Doc Cartier emerged with his black bag.

"Well?" he asked.

Duncan shook his head. "Beats the devil out of me," he said. "We all heard it. But what was it?"

"I thought some punk kid had come into town and instead of trying to outdraw you, Mick, he just thought to blow you to kingdom come."

"That's great." Woodward pulled out his notebook and started writing.

"You're not putting that in your newspaper, Mr. Woodward," Duncan told him.

"Marshal," the man said as he kept writing, "we have a free press in this country."

"That might be the case, but I just survived weeks of punks coming up here with six-shooters, and I am not going to have a bunch of idiots come up here throwing sticks of dynamite at me." He pulled the Schofield out of the holster and eared back the hammer as an exclamation point to his reasoning.

Woodward's face paled. He closed the notebook, stuck it inside a coat pocket, and returned the pencil above his ear.

Duncan nodded and returned his gaze to the high country.

"That wasn't dynamite," Silas Drury said.

"It certainly wasn't a rifle," Syd Jones said.

"Or a cannon," Logan Ladron said.

"Maybe," Bunner suggested, "one of the new miners."

Percy Stahl cleared his throat. "That noise sounded like just one thing."

All eyes turned to the saloonkeeper.

"Nugget," Stahl said.

"Lord have mercy," Sara whispered.

Duncan felt like seconding that.

"Nugget," Syd Jones said with a heavy sigh.

"It wasn't from his place," Ladron said.

"No." Duncan pointed at the towering peaks. "It wasn't that close. I'm certain it came from somewhere higher up."

"Anybody seen Nugget today?" Syd asked.

No heads bobbed in the affirmative.

"Come to think of it," Sara said, "I haven't seen Nugget in some time."

Still, Duncan saw no trace of smoke from the mountains, or in town, or even heading down the trail toward the railroad. It certainly wasn't thunder, and Percy Stahl was right. That noise had all the trademarks of Allane Auchinleck. Drunk or sober.

When have you ever seen Nugget sober? he thought.

"I tell you what," Bryn Bunner said. "I'll take a hike up the mountain a ways. I have a good idea where Nugget has been prospecting of late. I'll see if I can turn up anything."

"Just make sure you're back well before sunset," Duncan told him. "And stay out of the way of any bears."

Bunner smiled.

"I'll join you," Silas Drury said, but Duncan's head was shaking before he finished the sentence.

"No, sir, I think you ought to stay in town. You're a newcomer to these hills, and a visitor—an important visitor. We don't want you getting lost in those woods. It's not too early for a dumping of snow."

"I'll go."

Duncan cringed and he turned to Sara.

She was ready for him. "I *am* his partner. I'll go."

He wouldn't win that argument. Not in a million years.

Sighing, he nodded. "Get some grub first." He looked at Doc Cartier. "No need you taking a long walk uphill, since we don't know if anybody's hurt, but if you've got—"

The doctor quickly handed him his black bag.

"The rye," he said, "is for medicinal purposes only."

"All right." Duncan took the bag. "Get some coats. Bryn, get that mule of yours in case we need to carry somebody out. We'll meet right here in fifteen minutes."

"Can I come along?" the Denver inkslinger asked. "This would make a fantastic story for the *Times of the Rockies*."

"No," Duncan told him, but Carl Woodward was standing right between Sara Cardiff and Bryn Bunner when Duncan came back, and he was too tired to argue with the man.

"You pull the mule," Duncan told the reporter.

They started toward the high country.

"I hear there are giant grizzly bears in this country," Woodward said. He was smiling at his joke.

"Shut up," Duncan told him.

CHAPTER 10

Bryn Bunner took point, with Duncan and Sara following, while the reporter and the mule he led brought up the rear.

They entered the woods, trees that somehow had survived those wild and roaring rush days of 1885 and after, and Duncan realized how smart those old-timers, like Nugget, who had platted the town had been. Dead Broke was, by no means, flat, and the hills one had to climb on certain streets often tired even a healthy, young miner—or lawman—right quick-like. But they had chosen wisely because once you hit the woods, flat ground was hard to find.

Duncan saw Sara pull up the collar of her coat, and he turned his head to make sure Carl Woodward was doing what he was supposed to be doing. He was, head bent, right hand gripping the reins to the mule.

The temperature dropped substantially, and the trail wasn't much of a trail. Low brush crowded both sides, but they moved on and up.

Ten minutes later, Duncan felt himself leaning forward, and breathing hard, as they started climbing up the mountain. He found a branch on the side of the path, and stopped, stooped, and picked it up. He needed the big stick to push himself upright, shook his head, and handed it to Sara.

"This will help," he said, and felt his lungs burn.

"Thanks," she answered in a dry whisper.

Woodward breathed heavily, too, when he stopped behind them.

"You all right?" Duncan asked.

The man smiled. "Rather be . . . riding . . . this mule."

Duncan replied with a grin, "We'll take a breather when we reach the first clearing."

On and up, they climbed.

They must have moved that first clearing, Duncan thought fifteen minutes later—though it felt like fifteen hours.

But the forest thinned out, and once they eased past a wall of sheer granite, Duncan remembered his last trip up this way, and felt his heartbeat lessen. Staying close to the rock wall, they moved to the edge, then around the corner. Duncan let Sara go first, then headed back to the struggling newspaperman.

"Here," he said, extending his right hand.

Carl Woodward reached with his right hand.

"No." Duncan almost laughed. He wasn't going to pull this city slicker around that turn. "The reins."

"Oh." The man let out a quick chuckle, and raised his hand, from which Duncan took the reins.

"Grab hold to the pack," Duncan said. "Let the mule pull you for a change. It's not far."

It sure felt like far, though.

But once they rounded the granite, Sara and Bunner were waiting at the clearing, staring below at Dead Broke, which looked like it was fifty miles away.

"My goodness," the reporter said. "What a view." He turned to Bunner. "How far have we come?"

"Five hundred feet," the miner answered.

"Five hundred feet!" Woodward exclaimed. "It feels like five hundred miles."

Duncan and Sara echoed Bunner's chuckle. It was Sara who explained.

"Five hundred feet . . . in elevation."

"Welcome to This Side Of The Slope," Bunner said as he walked to the mule and removed a canteen.

They all drank.

"How high does this mountain get?" Woodward asked.

"This one goes all the way to fourteen thousand and some. Not quite as tall as Mount Elbert. That's in the Sawatch Range. And not the tallest in this range, either, but it's right close."

After wiping his lips with the back of his hand, Duncan asked, "How far to Nugget's—"

But he didn't get to finish the question because a wiry, redheaded young man, wearing a red-and-black plaid mackinaw and a porkpie hat, came running into the camp from uphill.

He seemed as surprised to find this party as Duncan was to see him.

"You's the marshal? Ain't ya?" the kid said.

"Yes." Duncan had seen the boy before, but just knew he was one of the miners who had come in maybe a week or two before that mess with Conner Boyle and his gunmen had been cleaned up.

"I thought so. You heard the cave-in?"

"Cave-in!" Duncan said.

"Yes, sir. We was a good mile away, digging for lead. Ground rumbled like it was the end of days."

"Son," Bryn Bunner said, "what we heard down in Dead Broke didn't sound like a cave-in. It sounded like four cannons going off at the same time."

"Well," the boy said, "reckon that coulda caused that cave-in. Can you help?"

Duncan stepped forward. "Lead the way."

Around the side of the mountain, they moved; Duncan wanting to ask questions, but also knowing the need to save one's breath. The trail forked and the boy took the left path.

"That's . . . where . . . Nugget had been digging," Bunner whispered, pointing at the lad's back.

Moving with urgency, they covered a half mile in distance and four hundred feet in elevation, and there the terrain flattened. Duncan saw the side of the mountain, surrounded by fallen rocks, and perhaps as many as fifteen other miners, who had formed a line and were moving rocks like a bucket brigade during a fire in town. But even two hundred yards away, Duncan could tell they wouldn't be able to move most of those rocks.

Sara sprinted ahead, but she wouldn't catch up with Bryn Bunner, who must have mountain goat blood in his body. Duncan hurried after them, but quickly gave up and slowed to a walk. He was still far ahead of Carl Woodward.

"Marshal!"

Duncan recognized the miner, but couldn't place the name. The big man, with a massive beard and chest about the size of that mule Carl Woodward was bringing along, stepped out of the line, swatting dust off his clothes and acting like he was at sea level.

"We were working our claim over yonder way." The wave of his hand was about as descriptive as the man's words. "Came here and found half the mountainside blocking the entrance."

That was an exaggeration, but whatever had happened had brought a load of rock down.

"This is the mine Mayor Nugget has been working," the miner said.

"Is Nugget in there?" Sara asked.

"We don't know."

"What we heard in Dead Broke," Duncan said, "couldn't have been a rockslide. Not on this side of this mountain."

"Didn't sound like a rockslide to us, either. It sounded like the world coming to an end."

Duncan turned to Sara, whose face startled Duncan. He had never seen her that pale.

"Are you all right?" He feared the altitude was about to make her faint.

"Nugget's in there," she said. "I know he is."

"We don't know that for sure." But Duncan figured she was right.

"All right." Duncan turned to Bryn Bunner's voice.

"We need ropes," Bunner said, taking charge—and Duncan, a lowly lawman whose tool was a revolver, was happy to have him giving orders. "We need shovels. We need pickaxes. And we need a lot more men than we have here. And mules. Plenty of mules. To haul those big boulders away, or at least get them away from the mine's entrance."

They sent the kid down to Dead Broke. Duncan thought about sending the Denver reporter, but realized that the boy was a much better choice. Three men took off for mules. One went to fetch a wagon and all the tools he could scrounge up.

In forty minutes, this part of This Side Of The Slope was busier than the town of Dead Broke had been since folks realized that the silver crash was for real—and was going to stay real for a long time.

The wagon turned out to be just a cart, but Duncan

certainly didn't see any way anything larger could have ever made it up here, up the current path—unless they disassembled the rig and brought it up by mules to be put back together.

Everyone worked, including Sara, and two women Duncan couldn't remember seeing. Which could be a good thing, since the way they dressed, had Duncan known them, it might have been a hard thing to explain to Sara.

The strongest mules pulled away the larger boulders, and Bryn Bunner stood on a flat-topped chunk of granite, directing orders like a big-city policeman.

"Abstreiter, you dunce. Those rocks can stay right where they are. Over there. Over there. That's where the entrance to Nugget's mine is. Work over there, you dumb oaf!"

"How do we know Nugget was in there when that mountain came down?" someone bellowed. "He could be in Dead Broke."

"He wasn't in Dead Broke," Sara barked back.

"How do you know?" the angry miner snapped.

"Because he hasn't come inside the Crosscut Saloon since yesterday."

No one argued with Sara's logic.

Duncan stepped out of the way to avoid being trampled by the two unfamiliar women carrying heavy buckets with both hands, and moved closer to the makeshift podium where Bunner had set up his command.

"Is there another way into this cave?" he asked.

Bunner stopped just long enough to pick up a canteen and take a long swallow. He shook his head as he laid the canteen back atop the rock.

"Not that I know of."

"He'd have air shafts, wouldn't he?" Duncan knew he was grasping for anything hopeful.

"If he was smart, he would. But we're talking about Nugget."

The big man stooped to pick up the canteen, which he tossed to Duncan.

Catching it, Duncan nodded his thanks to Bunner and took a small swallow.

"He'd have to drill a long way to vent this mine," Bunner explained, "and you know how that old codger is. And that's a long way to drill through granite, anyway."

Nothing looked good. Nothing sounded good.

Bunner must have read Duncan's face.

"It's a big cave, Mick," he said. "Well, Nugget said it was huge. You know how he is. He wouldn't let me inside." He turned to bark instructions to the two working girls, who had dumped their loads and were returning to help. When they came closer, Bunner handed the closest one the canteen.

"You're doing fine work, ladies," he told them.

He yelled something at someone, then reached down to take the canteen back, thanked them both, and shot Duncan a glance.

That glance said, *Get to work. This conversation is over.*

Duncan obeyed. He might be marshal of Dead Broke, but this was outside his jurisdiction.

He moved to the debris that blocked the entrance, filling buckets, or the back of the cart, with smaller stones. . . . Getting out of the way when a mule or team of mules dragged massive chunks far enough.

His hands were scraped, raw, the knuckles and fingers bleeding, and if there was one thing a lawman with a reputation like Duncan's always took care of, it was his gun hand.

Too late for that. As long as he didn't break a bone in his trigger finger or lose his thumb, he was all right.

The next break he took was when he stopped and looked for the sun. He couldn't see it. He found his watch, but it had stopped, and when the fatter of the two women stumbled, he went to her and took the pail she was carrying.

"Rest," he said, or at least mouthed the word. He squatted, picked up some of the stones that had fallen out, and returned them to the pail. He pointed to a spot where people were drinking water or coffee or shoveling something into their mouths to give them strength to keep up this brutal pace. She nodded, then moved in that direction, while Duncan carried the pail, emptied it, and found a good rock to place his watch, hat, and the gun belt and Schofield, which he didn't think he would need for a while.

He wasn't worried about someone stealing the .45 or the watch.

And that made him feel a lot better about miners.

He felt the chill now, and realized the sun was sinking behind the mountain. That's when he finally smelled woodsmoke, and turning, he saw the fires. Sara and the reporter stood near one of them, Woodward scribbling in his notebook as he talked to Bryn Bunner, who was sipping coffee.

Duncan was on the pile, much smaller than it had been hours earlier, but still a mountain in and of itself.

He picked up stone after stone and tossed them aside. He was the headman for the moment, at least until that burly Scot was finished with his break and food and coffee.

After wiping his face with a dirty handkerchief, he shoved the rag into a pants pocket and went back to work.

Ben Usher would be laughing his head off if he saw me now.

He moved another rock, heavier than most he had been removing, and let it fall to the earth.

That's not true. He reached for another large blackish stone. *Ben Usher would be right here, working just as hard as everyone else is.*

This rock he gripped was troublesome. It didn't want to move. Duncan did not know where he found the strength, but his aching fingers dug through the muck and pebbles, and managed to get a grip. He tugged. Nothing. Tried it again. The rock wanted to win this fight. Grinding his teeth, closing his eyes, Duncan groaned and felt the resistance ease. Then, with a savage growl, he jerked. The rock came free, and the weight of it almost carried him off the top of this hill. He slid a few feet down, then swung his arms away from his body. The rock came with it, and he let it go.

"Falling rock!" he yelled, but that was wasted breath. No one was below. The rock pounded on other stones. Few people even heard him, or heard the rock, but someone said something.

Duncan looked around. The nearest miners were on the far side of the rubble, digging lower.

He looked back at where the troublesome rock had been. Streams of gravelly sand and small stones were pouring down—like a waterfall. But not down the side of rubble and rocks and blood and bits and pieces of men's clothes and their own skin. It was going . . . into the mountain.

Duncan jumped toward the hole. He peered through it, just maybe four inches by three, but a hole. He could feel air moving through it, and after blinking away much dust, he thought he saw a light. A torch.

He pressed his face as close to the hole as possible.

"Hello, in the cave?" he sang out, asking a question, he realized, instead of just an announcement.

The light seemed to move. It must have been away from the hole. It didn't seem that bright, but his eyes were so strained, so dirty, it hurt to even blink.

The light vanished.

Maybe Duncan had imagined it.

But he knew he wasn't dreaming when the voice sang out.

CHAPTER 11

"MacMickin'! Is that you? Good gracious, it's 'bout time you gots here. You's gotta help me."

Relief swept over Duncan. Nugget was outrageous, corrupt, drunk more often than sober, and not to be trusted with anything important, but he had a kind heart—mostly—loved children, and was, when Duncan really thought about it, better than some of the mayors in many of the towns where Duncan had served as a lawman. Well, maybe not many. But certainly a few.

"We're digging you out now," Duncan said, then turned, cupped his mouth, and shouted, "I've busted through! Nugget's in here. He's alive. He's alive!"

The cheers erupted like it was Independence Day, and Duncan smiled, watching as men and women, including Sara, sprinted to the massive slide of rocks and dirt. He heard something else, too, and turned back and leaned closer to the hole.

"Did you say something, Nugget?" Duncan asked.

"Don't gets me out of here yet. Not yet."

Duncan thought he had misheard.

"What?"

"I ain't ready to get out of this mine. I need you to do something. Something important for me. Real important."

Duncan couldn't stop his response. "Are you crazy?" Of course, he had known the answer to that question—a resounding *yes*—since arriving in Dead Broke.

"I knows—" the mayor began, but Duncan cut him off.

"Nugget. Mister Mayor. This cave-in was pretty bad. It's a miracle we punched through. But you can't stay in there. Even with this air hole. That whole ceiling could fall down on you anytime."

Nugget fired up some unflattering descriptions of Duncan, laced with several bits of profane language that made Duncan glad the people were still cheering and applauding and running to the bottom of the pile of rocks. They couldn't hear what Duncan was hearing.

He wasn't sure he understood the last part himself.

Dumbfounded, he asked: "You want to stay in there?"

"I gots all I needs," Nugget said. "Gots a jug of my brew down here. Rocks didn't smash it. Now I gots some light."

Duncan shook his head. "Anyone down there with you?"

"Just me and my jug."

"Well—"

Nugget cut him off. "All I needs for you to do is get down to town and file a claim—in my name. You try to put this in your name and not only will I fire you as town marshal, I'll . . . Listen, old pard, you do me right. File the claim in my name. You know how I make my mark. Even Little Joey has signed some papers for me when I . . . well . . . when I wasn't . . . ummmmm."

"When you were drunk," Duncan said. He thought that old coot was drunk right then.

"Just file the claim for me, in my name, and I'll put you down for five percent of the first month's haul. Six-and-a-quarter percent. For two months. But that's my best offer."

"I don't want your money, Mayor. I just want you out of there."

"I don't come out till I gots that paper that says this part of this mountain be all mine."

"And Sara Cardiff's," Duncan reminded him.

The man coughed. He kicked something, probably a stone. "Yeah. But she ain't a half pard. But, yeah, she's in for—"

"I'll ask her what her percentage is," Duncan told him. "She's smart enough to have kept those documents."

Men and a few women—Sara included—were starting to climb up.

"I just can't come out of here—"

"Mayor," Duncan said, "it'll be days, long days, maybe weeks, before we can get you out of here and even longer still till you—this is your problem, once we've got you out—can open up this mine."

"That's fine with me. Now, then, here's what you need to put down in the claim. *My* claim. Remember that."

For a crazy old fool, Nugget knew exactly what he wanted logged in the claim. Duncan didn't have a sheet of paper or a pencil, but he had always been blessed with a rock-solid good memory. Still, when the first helpers arrived, Duncan slipped down to the newspaper reporter and got a piece of paper from him, then borrowed Woodward's pencil and wrote down everything Nugget had told him.

At the hole, Bryn Bunner started barking orders. He needed a rope and a canteen and a small pail so they could lower food and water to the mayor. Nugget shouted something, but this far down that ridge of rocks, Duncan couldn't make out the mayor's orders.

He handed back the pencil to Woodward and stuck the note in his vest pocket.

"I have to go to town," Duncan said.

The reporter's eyes turned suspicious.

"Won't be for long. I'll be back as soon as I can. If you could tell Sara and Bunner that I'll be back . . ." He thought of a lie. "I need to let Doc Cartier know that Nugget's all right. And get some more ropes to bring back up." That was pretty good, he thought. Even Sara might believe him. And ropes and more supplies were going to be needed. "Be back as quick as I can."

Though, he thought, it would be mighty tempting when he got into Dead Broke, to pack his traps, saddle his horse, and hightail it for some part of the country that wasn't this crazy. He might have done it, too, he thought, when he was halfway down the mountain, if it weren't for Sara Cardiff.

"He wants to talk to you," Bryn Bunner told Sara.

She stood above the hole, on a flatter part of the slide. Bunner was on his knees, but pushed himself to his feet and walked over to where she was, while the Denver newspaper reporter quit jotting down notes and beat Bunner to her.

"Let me assist you, ma'am," Woodward said. "These rocks are loose as a goose."

She gave him a smile and a thank-you, and he helped her down and past Bunner to the rock. Woodward eyed that hole and could not hide his envy. She knew why he had assisted her here. So did Bryn Bunner.

"Nugget said he wanted to talk to the widow Cardiff," Bunner said evenly, without a trace of sarcasm. "Not you."

Nugget's voice rose out of the hole.

"But you tell that newspaper fellow that I'll give him lots more stories when I has the time. But not right now. Not till . . . Never mind."

Bunner and Woodward steadied Sara as she knelt, then lowered herself onto the bedrolls they had placed over the rocks near the small hole. Duncan had been on his belly, with just rocks, not bedrolls, for a cushion.

"Nugget," she called out, and heard the strange echo.

The crazy old coot came into view, banging his left ear with his hand and shaking his head.

"Don't yell, pretty Sara, my partner."

Hearing Nugget's words, Sara sighed and felt like a fool.

"I can hear you fine if you just whisper. Can you hear me?"

"Yes," she said, softer this time.

The ragged head nodded.

"Partner," he whispered.

She smiled. "Partner," Sara said.

"Can anyone hear me 'sides you?"

Sara could barely hear him and told him that much in a low whisper.

"Sure?"

She pushed herself up slightly to look around. Bryn Bunner had gone down the slope and was at a makeshift table with the newspaperman and several miners she had known from Dead Broke and two or three of the newcomers who were after zinc and lead, now that silver wasn't worth mining.

That boy who had walked up the mountain with Sara and the others, and two miners she knew from town, and knew that one of those didn't speak anything but German and a few English words: "yes," "no," "whiskey," "maybe," "son of a . . ."

Well, she thought they were safe, and let herself down closer to the hole.

"It's all right, Nugget," she said softly. "Nobody's

paying much attention to me right now." She thought to add something hopeful. "They're looking at a way to get you out of here as quickly as they can."

He grunted, cursed, and pulled the jug to his lips, which smacked as he lowered the jug and wiped his beard, if not the lips, with his shirtsleeve.

"As long as I ain't out of here till MacMickin' gets back."

Her head shook in confusion. "Where is Dunc . . . Where did Mick go—and why?"

The man smiled for a second, then let out a wild cry that had Sara raising her head; the boy and the miners stopped their palaver to see if Sara or Nugget, or possibly both, had lost their sanity.

"It's all right," she told them, smiled, and waited till those eardrum-busting echoes faded away.

Then she returned to the hole and peered inside.

A long pull of the jug helped Nugget's ears. He smacked his lips and smiled up at Sara.

"I done this myself," Nugget told her.

"Done what? You did what yourself?"

"Caved in this mine."

Her head raised. She figured she had misheard. When she looked back down, Nugget was dancing around the jug he had set on the dirt, singing some miner's song that she never quite understood.

She waited till the song ended, and Nugget clapped his hands, stopped dancing, and looked back up. "I outsmarted anyone tryin' to steal this mine afore I could claim it all legal."

"You didn't file a claim before?" she said, and it took all her willpower not to scream.

"That's right." He spit onto the dirt and looked back up. "File a claim, and folks start lookin' 'round. Or they'll try to claim somethin' next door so they can drill in, secret-like, and get ore that's rightfully, and legally, mine. I know that's a fact. Folks tried to do that with my silver mine. And I done it five or six or, no . . ." He stopped, cleared his throat, mumbled something, and looked up again with a broad smile.

"Just jestin' 'bouts me doin' somethin' not proper."

Sara's head shook. "I don't know what you're talking about, Nugget."

He chuckled, burped, and grinned.

"I blowed myself up in here so nobody could take what's rightfully mine." He smiled. "Mine. Mine mine. Ha! Hey, is that newspaperman still around? He might like that for his story. Mine mine. Get it?"

Her answer was a hard frown.

Then she whispered, "You did this? You trapped yourself in this mine?"

His head bobbed rapidly. "Uh-huh." He tapped his temple with his right forefinger. "Pretty smart, huh?"

Sara's head shook. "No," she whispered. "Not smart, Nugget. Not smart at all."

He laughed. "That's what you think, pardner. That's what you think. But you ain't seen what I found in this cave, darlin'. No, sir—I mean, no, ma'am, you ain't seen it at all. But you will. You will for sure. 'Cause me and you is pards."

Her head ached. She thought:

Sara Cardiff, you've made some boneheaded moves in your time. Played some hands you should have folded early. Let Duncan MacMicking slip away one time. And there was that filly you bet on in that race down in Bisbee. But . . . why ever did you go into partnership with this crazy old drunken fool?

"You know my Diamond Nugget of Silver?" he asked.

That got her attention, but she was worn out.

"Yes, Nugget," she said. "I've seen it. But—"

He cut her off. "That seventeen-hundred-and-seventy-six-pound chunk of solid silver that men have died tryin' to steal, and that brung lots of good folks, kids and adults, and old-timers that make me look like, well, Mick MacMicking. Made this town I founded—and I mean no disrespect to my gone-to-Glory pard, good ol' Sluagdach—the envy of towns 'cross this state, and even these entire United States of America."

And that gave her pause. She realized she was holding her breath, and slowly she exhaled.

Nugget turned around as though he thought he heard someone. If he had, he realized it was just a rat, more than likely, so he raised his head to Sara and chuckled for several seconds. Then he danced a quick jig in a circle, let out a war cry, and when the echoes had stopped, he looked up at Sara gain.

"Pardner," he said in a soft whisper, "what I's found here is gonna, make no mistake 'bout this, put that silver nugget of mine to shame."

CHAPTER 12

"This is highly irregular, Marshal."

Jawbone Stewart had been working at the U.S. Land Office in Dead Broke for three years. He was a wiry man, with a thick graying mustache and long sideburns. More hair on his face than on the top of his head. He looked at the paper Duncan had given him, then turned and stared at Syd Jones.

It had been luck—maybe fate—that Duncan had run into his old mentor as soon as he got to town. After explaining what had happened, Jones had cleared his throat, shook his head, stared up the mountain, then turned and said, "Let's go."

And here they stood, in the small office, one of the solid stone structures in Dead Broke, staring at a man who believed that anything filed in his office had to be beyond question.

And Duncan himself had plenty of questions he wanted to pound Nugget and Sara with. But here he stood.

The things a man did for the love of a woman.

"It's legit, Anton," Syd Jones said.

Duncan realized he had never known Jawbone's real name.

The agent frowned. Duncan really couldn't blame him.

With a sigh, he said, "Well, this is all according to the Mining Act of 1872. I know Nugget's a citizen of our United States, so he's eligible. And Miss Cardiff?"

"She's a citizen." *This might take forever.*

"Well, does she know that once a mining claim has been made, the owners must perform a hundred dollars' worth of labor each year?"

"There's going to be probably a thousand dollars' worth of work done in the next day or week," Duncan barked.

"If Mrs. Cardiff or if Nugget doesn't contribute to the claim's annual improvements, the stake of that co-owner will revert to the other co-owner. That's just the way the law reads, Marshal."

"That's fine, that's fine," Duncan said. He would go bald, and maybe grind all his teeth to the roots, the way this was going.

Shaking his head, Jawbone looked at the paper and then pulled out one of the forms. He spoke as he read and wrote, but didn't get far before he stopped and looked up at the two lawmen.

"Notice is hereby given that . . . Can you spell Mayor Nugget's real name?"

Duncan turned to Jones, who shrugged. Sighing heavily, Jawbone mumbled something, then turned around and went to some cabinets, groaned as he knelt to open the bottom drawer, riffled through some papers, and called out to Jones, "Can you write this down for me?"

Jones approached the counter, grabbed a pencil, and turned over a piece of paper.

"A-L-L-A-N-E. Then, A-U-C-H-I-N-L-E-C-K. Got that?"

Jones spelled it out again. The agent nodded, slipped the paper back into a file, closed the drawer, and used the handles to pull himself back to his feet.

Once he had copied Nugget's given name onto the form, he went back to work. Duncan spelled Sara's name for him, and then the agent asked, "Any other partners?"

Duncan shook his head.

The man read from the form. "'. . . have made an application for a United States Patent for the . . .'"

He stopped.

"What's Nugget calling this one?" He spoke with weary exasperation.

Duncan shrugged.

"It's gotta have a name."

Duncan looked at Jones, who just shook his head.

"The Crosscut," Duncan said. He figured Sara would like that.

"The Crosscut Mining Claim," the agent said as he printed slowly.

Then he took the paper from Duncan, the one Duncan had written from memory after Nugget's dictation from down in that hole. Jawbone read aloud as he wrote.

> "'. . . situated in the Dead Broke Mining District,
> Dead Broke County, Colorado, consisting of
> sixteen hundred and fifty-nine linear . . .'"

This was going to take forever.

"Jawbone," Duncan said.

The man finished writing down some figures, then looked up.

"How much is this going to cost?" He tried to give his

most pleading look. "I really need to get back up that mountain."

"I'll pay him," Jones said. "And I'll forge Sara's and Nugget's names." He grinned. "Nugget's is easy enough, anyway."

"I could get fired for this," Jawbone complained.

Syd Jones shook his head. "You won't. Because if this claim is like the one Nugget filed after he found his silver nugget, you're going to be the busiest Land Office agent in the state of Colorado."

The man sighed. "Busy enough already. All these miners coming in looking for all these newfangled things. Sure was easier when it was just silver and gold."

Duncan's left hand was on the doorknob when the land agent called out, "You know this has to be published in the newspaper nearest the claim, and it has to run for sixty days."

With a heavy sigh, Duncan turned around. "What's the nearest newspaper?"

"Leadville as the crow flies," Jawbone said, "but . . ." He shrugged.

"Georgetown?"

"I think that one stopped publishing some years back," Jawbone said.

"Central City?"

"Most pick a newspaper in Denver," Jawbone said.

This conversation could go on for years. Too bad the newspaper in Dead Broke shut down.

Duncan smiled when the thought came to him. "We'll give it to Carl Woodward. I'd never heard of that paper he's writing for in Denver till he got here." He turned to Syd Jones. "How about you?"

"Nope."

With that, Duncan was out the door.

* * *

Then he went to work. His first stop was at the Crosscut Saloon, where Logan Ladron was sipping coffee at the bar with the bartender and Winston DeMint. Luck was starting to favor Duncan. He wouldn't have to go to the marshal's office and jail to give DeMint some orders.

He sent the gambler to get as many mules as he could find, and as many men who seemed strong enough to swing a pickax or haul rocks away from a mine. DeMint would be going to the liveries now in business and the one general store to get every rope, bucket, shovel, and tool that was in stock.

When he came out of the Crosscut, he saw Percy Stahl and called him over.

When Percy heard what was going on, he said he'd be glad to help. Why, he wouldn't have a roof over his head if it weren't for Nugget. He'd take his own horse and bring up two kegs of beer for the boys. Duncan went to the stable, where he kept his horse, saddled it, and was riding toward Nugget's place when Joey Clarke's mother flagged him down.

"I heard what happened, Marshal," she said.

He wasn't in the mood for conversation, but when she started talking, he listened. He didn't have to say a word.

"I'll get every woman I know—the best cooks, anyway—and some who have boys a lot more raucous than my Little Joey. We'll bring up food to cook and coffee to drink."

Duncan's mouth tried to open, but Mrs. Gloria Clarke cut him off.

"Don't tell me it's a long way up to those mines. It's a much longer way up just to get to Dead Broke. This town wouldn't exist if not for Nugget, scoundrel that he is, so we're going to help. Whether you like it or not."

Duncan felt the smile forming on his face.

"I like it just fine, Mrs. Clarke," he told her, then kicked his horse into a trot, turned left at his office, and kept the trot up to the trail that led to Nugget's place.

His guards numbered only three these days. Duncan had heard stories of the days when Nugget had a dozen or more—and in those years, he probably needed that many. But things were calmer now, though they had been pretty wild up till fairly recently.

One of the guards met him with a cocked Greener, its barrels sawed off almost to the forestock.

"Your boss is trapped in a cave-in," he said.

The man's eyes narrowed. "Where?"

"Up yonder." Duncan nodded. "He's alive. We're digging him out. But we could use some help."

"We ain't much good for movin' dirt, Marshal."

Duncan thought about telling him that none of these gunmen weren't good for much of anything, but he didn't want these men to shovel dirt or haul rocks away from the mine's opening.

"We've got enough miners to do that part of the job."

The man didn't relax, or lower the scattergun, but his eyes became something a bit larger than the slits they had been.

"Speak your piece, Marshal."

Duncan relaxed. The man lowered the barrels of that Greener so they pointed at the wooden porch, but he didn't lower the hammers.

"One of you stay here. Nugget would throw a temper tantrum if there wasn't at least one gun protecting his silver nugget. And most of the men in Dead Broke will be working up that mountain, because that's the kind of people they are. But I want one of you to stay in my office. I'll deputize that one—"

"How much does a deputy get paid?"

The Greener was now pointed straight down.

"Five dollars." He added: "A day."

The guard's thumb was lowering both hammers. "I'm your man."

Duncan nodded. "We'll fill out the paperwork when this is all over."

"All right."

"The other man I need to bring a gallon of your boss's brew—better make it two gallons—up that hill to the cave-in site."

A smile now appeared on the guard's face. Duncan might have even heard a chortle.

Shaking his head, the gunfighter said, "I suppose all that diggin' works up a man's thirst."

"Nugget's brew won't be used for whiskey." Duncan reined his horse around. "That stuff is more powerful than nitro. We might need it to get your boss out of that mine."

He started back up the trail.

"He'll need a mule to carry that whiskey up the hill. I'll have one sent—"

"No need, Marshal. We got plenty of mules and horses here."

"All right. Much obliged."

He spurred the horse back to his office, checked with Percy Stahl, Winston DeMint, and Syd Jones, then headed up the mountain.

Bryn Bunner took the gelding's reins, and listened as Duncan told him who was coming up and what they were bringing.

"How's Nugget?" Duncan then asked.

"He was singing right before I came down." The miner smiled. "If that didn't cause another cave-in, nothing will."

Duncan started looking around. This place had become the proverbial beehive.

"Why don't you get yourself a cup of coffee and a bite to eat?" Bunner suggested.

"No." Duncan shook his head. "I—"

"Coffee," Bunner said, and pointed at a fire, around which some makeshift tables had been set up, and the wives of miners were serving hot food and hot coffee to the volunteers. It was an impressive sight. "And food. Good grub. You need it, Marshal. We've got a long ways to go."

Duncan was tempted, but he had more than a healthy stubborn streak.

"Sara Cardiff's down there now," Bunner said with a laugh. Then he headed back toward the cave-in.

And Duncan decided that he could use some hot coffee and good food.

Torches, lanterns and bonfires provided heat and light as the skies darkened. Sara rose, walked to him, and gave him a hug, and while they embraced, she whispered, "You could have told me where you were going."

"I know," he said. His mouth opened, but she closed it with her index finger, took his hand into hers, and led him to a camp table. "Sit down," she ordered. "I'll bring you coffee and your choice, elk stew or mule stew."

"Elk," Duncan said.

She waited till Duncan finished the second helping of stew, and slid back, sipping coffee, and staring at her.

She just looked at him, and saw a smile slowly form on his handsome face. But she was also looking behind him, and didn't move closer till that crew had dropped their cups, plates, and utensils—including the one who ate stew with his fingers—and were walking away.

Most of the men had finished eating by now, and the women were cleaning up. When they had gone to wash the dirty dishes, she leaned closer to him.

"It's been a long time since I've been at a cave-in," he said. "Forgot how that can bring a community together."

"Duncan," she whispered.

He turned to her.

"It wasn't exactly a cave-in."

His face hardened.

"Well," she said. "I guess it's still a cave-in. But . . . Nugget did that on purpose."

"He did what?"

She brought her finger to her lips and shushed him.

"Why on earth—" Duncan started, but Sara finished.

"Because this is Nugget we're talking about. He says he has found something that'll make his giant silver nugget pale in comparison."

Duncan rolled his eyes.

"I know," she said.

"He dynamited the cave?" Duncan said. "Himself? While he was still in it?"

"Yes," she answered.

That would explain the explosion they had heard down in Dead Broke. The rumbles from a normal cave-in would not have likely been heard in town.

"Was he drunk?" Duncan asked.

"Most likely," Sara said. "What he told me was that he wanted to make sure no one else put in a claim before he did."

"Which," Duncan said, now full of knowledge from Jawbone in town about the operations and procedures of

filing a mining claim in the state of Colorado, "he has—
both of you have, I mean—and Syd will be bringing up the
paperwork. It just has to go through the usual process.
Sixty days to make sure no one challenges your claim."

"I know," she said.

"Nugget tell you all that?" Duncan asked between
swallows of hot, reviving coffee.

Her head shook. "Like I'd believe anything he said."
Her head tilted toward the pile of rocks. "Bryn Bunner.
Though I visited Jawbone after Nugget first approached
me. Picked his brain." Her face paled. "You don't think
he's going to want to wait sixty days before he comes out
of that awful cave? Mine, I mean. Awful mine. Do you?"

Duncan wiped his mouth with one end of his bandanna.

"He's crazy," he said, "but he's not *that* crazy. Nobody's
going to be working in any mine up this high in sixty
days—and maybe not after thirty. Let's go up there and
tell him that his claim is legitimate, at least."

CHAPTER 13

"I ain't a-comin' out!"

Nugget said that loud enough early that morning for those standing around Duncan—Carl Woodward, Bryn Bunner, Sara Cardiff, now joined by Syd Jones and Silas Drury—to hear. And they heard it again as Nugget's echoes carried through the hole in the mine's roof.

Raising his head away from the opening and rolling over to his side, Duncan stared at the reporter's shocked face. Syd Jones, wearing a wan smile, just shook his head and chuckled. Duncan still didn't see anything funny about this. Bryn Bunner just shrugged.

"Jus' sends me grub and beer and hot coffee. I'll be fine."

Nugget's words came out of the opening and bounced around inside the mine.

That led to Nugget yelling: "Darn 'em echoes. Quit repeatin' what I's sayin'."

Which also reverberated.

Duncan rolled back and waited till silence returned down below.

"Mayor"—Duncan figured that maybe Nugget would be a bit more pliable if he called him that rather than the stupid fool that Nugget was—"you're needed in town. You're the mayor."

"I's makin' you's the vice mayor. Like a vice president. You handle things for me whilst I stays in my new mine."

Duncan snapped. He was usually calm under pressure, but now he called Nugget every dirty name he could think of, and he didn't care how many times those curses bounced off the cavern's walls and came out of the hole so that people down below, and maybe halfway up the trail from Dead Broke, could hear.

"In two or three weeks, nobody's going to be coming up here because there will be six feet of snow covering this place!"

Place . . . Place . . . Place . . . Place . . .

That might have been a stretch. In two months, certainly no one would be coming up here. But there would be snow—that was certain—here in three weeks. Probably six inches at least, manageable, but the snow and sleet that would follow would keep accumulating, and even if the winter proved to be incredibly dry, the temperatures would drop below zero. Well below zero.

"It'll be freezing. Deadly freezing!" Duncan yelled when the echoes faded.

Freezing . . . Freezing . . . zing . . . zing . . . zing . . . zing . . .

That was an undeniable fact.

"We won't haul your frozen carcass out of this hole till May!"

May . . . May . . . May . . . May . . .

"You stupid—"

That epithet echoed, too.

"I'll take my chances!" Nugget called back.

Duncan sighed, shook his head, and looked back to his friends for help.

"Let me talk to him," Sara said.

After pushing himself to his feet, Duncan swung his right arm toward the hole. "Have at it," he told her, and helped her lie down on the blankets covering the rubble.

She didn't yell. She spoke in a hushed, pleasant voice. She didn't lie. She said that winter would protect whatever it was he had found in the Crosscut Mining Claim.

"Crosscut?" Nugget's question, and some profanity that followed, also came through the hole loud enough so that everyone below could hear. "Who in blazes come up with that stupid name?"

"I did," Sara lied.

"Well, it's all right, I reckons. Names don't matter none. What matters is what's I's discovered."

"Nugget," Sara said, "if you don't come out of there, I'll . . . I'll just cry." She let out a wail of despair.

"What an actress," Silas Drury whispered. "Haven't seen a performance that grand since watching Lillian Russell in *La Cigale.*"

"You come down here, pardner," Nugget called back, "and you'll see for your ownself what's keepin' me here."

Sara pushed herself up, shot a quick glance toward Duncan, then called out to Nugget: "No way I'm going down there. I don't like caves, mines, whatever you want to call them, and I've never been part of any trapeze act. What do you want me to do? Climb down on a rope? Let someone lower me down there and then pull me back up. No. No, sir. Not for anything!"

"Then give somebody your pixie!"

Drury whispered, "I do believe he means 'proxy.'"

Duncan sighed. "I'll go."

"No," Syd Jones said softly, but with authority in his whisper.

"He's right," Silas Drury said. "Mr. Nugget has made a

discovery of some sort. I respect you as a lawman, Marshal MacMicking, but this visit requires someone with knowledge of mines and minerals." He waited.

Duncan understood. He was also relieved. He couldn't shimmy through that hole, and he wasn't too crazy about having anyone lower him into that dark pit with a rope. Right now, though, no one, not even Sara, would be going down that small opening in this mountain.

"That," Drury said, "leaves it up to our good man Mr. Bunner and myself."

"I don't mind going, sir," Bryn Bunner said, "but I'm on the heavy side."

"Then the duty falls to me." Drury cleared his throat. "But we'll need to widen this hole."

"And," Bunner said, "hope the whole roof doesn't fall in and bury Nugget and whatever he has—or *thinks*—he has found."

They informed Nugget of the plan and he agreed. They told him to step as far back from the hole because dirt, debris, and rocks—some of them large and heavy—would be falling and no one wanted the mayor of Dead Broke to be hurt. Nugget picked up his jug and walked out of sight, calling out when he said he was safe and sound and ready, but sure could use some more whiskey, and that maybe a chunk of ham with some mashed potatoes. Corn bread would be welcome, too.

Ignoring the mayor's request, the men went to work, bringing up some muscular miners to help with the digging.

It was late afternoon when the hole had been widened, and ropes tied together to lower Silas Drury down.

"We could wait till tomorrow," Sara suggested. "When the light's better."

Drury shook his head. "It could rain or snow tomorrow. The clouds now are clear, and this shouldn't take me long." He chuckled. "I wonder what has so impressed our good man and mayor, Mr. Nugget."

"So do I," Bunner whispered.

"Then let's get to it," Drury said.

Drury was experienced at this sort of work—much more than Syd, Duncan, or Sara—and Bunner and Duncan handled the thick rope as they lowered the mining expert into the hole, while Jones lay on his belly and watched, telling Duncan and Bunner when to slow down or letting them know that everything was going fine.

"A few feet more," Syd Jones said. "That's it. Good. Good. Just a bit more. He's on the floor!"

Bunner let go of the rope, which Duncan secured by wrapping it around a large boulder and tying it off. Sara moved to the edge and looked down. Duncan fell beside her. They all peered as Nugget ran to Drury, helped him out of the makeshift harness the miners had put together. Drury looked up and smiled and waved.

"All's well that ends well!" he called.

"Come on," Nugget said, grabbing the man's forearm and dragging him out of view. "You ain't never seen nothin' likes what I's 'bouts to show you."

"Tallyho!" the mining expert said, faking an English accent.

In an instant, both men were out of view. But on top of the mine, the others did not budge, staring into the darkening hole, scarcely breathing, waiting for Drury or Nugget to reappear.

Then came a shout and a wild curse from Drury.

The barnyard curse echoed, too.

"This is absolutely fantastic!" Drury screamed.

"It's the greatest discovery in the world."

* * *

Silas Drury came back below the opening, but Duncan couldn't really make out the man's face as the Arkansas miner started telling them what to do. Bunner and Duncan should come down. The reporter wanted to go, wanted to see for himself, but Drury shook his head.

"In good time, sir," he said softly. "In good time. Right now, we need some engineers, and Mr. Bunner is capable of seeing what must be done. And I think the local law should get an idea of what we are dealing with."

Duncan looked at Syd, and Syd looked at Duncan. Sara looked at them both. None said a word.

"Do you want to come up?" Duncan asked the Arkansas mining expert.

"No, Marshal. I shall stay here for an hour or more to get measurements and sketches. If you can bring down some paper and pencils, that would be helpful."

"And whiskey and food," Nugget said. "Ain't gotta be ham and potatoes. I's so hungry I could fry up this feller down with me . . . iffen I had a fryin' pan and some bacon grease. And maybe some thicker blankets. And whiskey. And can I get a cake? And a pie? And don't forget that whiskey."

Duncan ground his teeth.

Silas Drury said: "Give this man anything he wants."

The work began. Bunner set out to recruit the strongest-looking miners he could find. Sara found some food, no pies, but managed to procure a couple of slices of pound cake. And a boy—he couldn't have been much older than Joey Clarke—gave Sara two pieces of hard candy for the mayor. She tried to refuse, but the kid insisted. She found an empty bottle with no label, and had it filled with tea. She wasn't sending Nugget any whiskey, but she figured that reprobate would get some, anyway. You couldn't keep Nugget and whiskey apart for long.

Bunner went down first, carrying a sack containing all that Sara had managed to scrounge. Duncan came next, with a canvas sack filled with lanterns, candles, and a pint of pilsner, which Sara had not seen.

When Duncan's boots touched bottom, he waited for the miners to give him some slack, and then he slipped off the rope, which dangled there. He thought about telling them to bring it up, but killed that idea before his mouth opened. Having that rope—the only way out of this pit—gave him at least some hope of security.

Once Duncan stepped away, blankets, coats, and even a pillow dropped through the hole.

It was much darker down here than Duncan imagined. The candles and two lanterns that Nugget had going did not provide much light, and he found a match and lit one of the lanterns.

Bunner had not waited for Duncan. Neither had Nugget nor Drury.

He could see lights from their lantern and candles in the darkened distance.

Lantern in hand, Duncan moved to the lights and the men.

It got colder the farther he moved from the hole above. Bunner was talking in excited whispers, but Duncan could not make out what the miner was saying. As he neared the men, he saw something behind them, tucked away in what must have been some kind of antechamber of rock. Light reflected off it. Duncan blinked. He cleared his throat and Bunner's head turned around.

The miner smiled.

"You've never seen anything like this, Marshal," Bunner said, and raised his lantern toward that chamber. Holding a candle, Silas Drury walked toward it.

Nugget guffawed. "You folks figgered me to be crazy. Or lyin'. But I ain't neither of 'em things."

"This is the greatest discovery since Sutter's Mill," Silas Drury whispered.

"No!" Nugget spat. "My Diamond Nugget of Silver was greater than that one. But this is the greatest one since 1885."

They held up their lights toward the chamber, and Duncan saw it for the first time.

Only . . . he didn't really know what stood before him.

It was a huge boulder, sort of shaped like a bell. Like the Liberty Bell that Duncan had seen in Philadelphia that time when he was appearing as himself to give shooting lessons and teach children not to break the law, consort with bad influences, or drink intoxicating beverages—and to mind their mothers and fathers and not pick on their sisters. All of which Duncan figured he had done more than those two dozen Philadelphia boys.

And this was much larger than the Liberty Bell. But this was no bell. It was rugged, misshapen. The flickering light from the candles and lanterns reflected off this large chunk, the color a mix of blue and white. At first, he thought it was silver, but tarnished silver, while knowing that even a piece of silver this size wouldn't be causing miners to smile and giggle and look all too greedy. Not these days.

"Zinc?" he guessed.

"Yes," Silas Drury said. "But not just zinc. This is the greatest specimen of zinc I have ever seen."

"It sort of looks like the Liberty Bell," Duncan conceded.

Nugget clapped his hand. "That's a crackerjack name for what I done discovered."

Duncan turned to Dead Broke's mayor. "Liberty Bell?"

"No," Nugget said. "What Bryn here just whispered to me. The Zinc of Zion." His head bobbed, but then he frowned. "What exactly do 'Zion' mean?"

"It's a hill in Jerusalem," Drury whispered. "Upon which the city of David was built."

"David who?" Nugget asked.

Duncan didn't want this conversation to go off track. "How much do you think it weighs?"

Bunner shrugged, but whispered, "Tons."

Drury's head moved in agreement. "Six tons. Maybe seven."

"Eight tons." Nugget clapped his hands. Duncan didn't know where that old coot got *eight* out of six or seven. "That's more than even my diamond nugget. That just weighed seventeen hundred and seventy-six pounds. That ain't even a ton." He frowned. "Ain't it?"

"Not quite a ton," Silas Drury whispered. "But this is."

"Don't touch it too much, Nugget," Bunner called out when Nugget walked closer to his discovery. "Zinc is brittle, you know."

"I ain't no dummy, Bunner. I was in these mountains lookin' for ever'thin' under the sun whilst you was soilin' your diapers. Found gold. Found silver. Found ever'thin' worth findin'. And now I's found the greatest zinc discovery ever knowed to mankind. Ain't that right?"

Duncan waited for Silas Drury to correct the crazy old coot. Instead, the mining expert's head moved up and down in awed respect.

"It's not going to fit up that hole we come down from," Bunner said.

"No." Drury cleared his throat. "We're going to have to shore up this cavern."

"Mine," Nugget said.

Drury nodded. "Yours."

"No, mine. This ain't no cavern. It's a mine. I gots the claim. Filed it proper." He nodded at Duncan. "It's all mine."

"It's all yours," Drury agreed. "But this is something special. We must do something special with it. That will bring a boom to your town, Mayor, that will replicate what happened after you discovered your . . . your . . ."

"Nugget of Silver," Nugget said. "Diamond Nugget of Silver. On accounts that it's shaped like a diamond. Like this one's shaped like that there Liberty Bell."

"Right."

"What are you thinking, Mr. Drury?" Bunner asked.

"I don't rightly know yet. We must consider our options. But first, we have to get this mine secured." He pointed. "That I believe is the nearest place to start. We make an opening there. After this place is shored up."

"It's pretty shored up its ownself," Nugget said.

The miners started debating about the needed precautions, where they should put the entrance, ruling out Nugget's original, which wasn't that much larger, Nugget said, than the hole Duncan had punched into the ceiling.

"What I come through was so small a rattlesnake or a gopher couldn't hardly gets through," he said. "Had to do lots of shimmyin' and a-twistin', but I's gotten to be real good at 'em kinds of things."

Eventually, they all agreed on Drury's selection.

"Let's get busy," Bunner said.

Duncan nodded. He took one more look at Nugget's discovery, and shook his head as he walked back to the ropes and the way out—the only way out for the time being—thinking:

How in the devil can a man like Nugget find maybe the largest chunk of silver in Colorado and now the largest piece of zinc? Isn't there a thing in this world called justice?

On the other hand, if this bell-shaped chunk of zinc

would bring in more miners, he might be able to keep his job as town marshal before Dead Broke became a ghost town. And Sara would be staying here, too.

Plus, zinc miners, so far, had been nowhere near as troublesome as those who sought silver and gold.

CHAPTER 14

These United States of America were a mighty fine place to live and work, Duncan thought. And Colorado had to be the finest—no offense to Arkansas. As a lawman, at least before he pinned on a badge in Durango, he had worked mostly cattle towns. But cow towns were different than mining camps. Cow towns brought in cowboys, mostly young Texans, far from their homes, and, after spending four to six months on a trail, following smelly beef and sitting in a saddle twelve to eighteen hours a day, they wanted to blow off some steam. If that meant shooting up the town, raising Cain, busting streetlamps or windows, or racing their horses up and down dusty streets—or riding them into saloons—that was just part of the cost of being a cow town. Those cowpunchers would sleep off their drunks in jail or what had to be converted to a jail when the cells got too full; the foremen or ramrods or ranchers would pay the fines, and they'd be gone till the next herd came in or the next cattle season started.

But miners lived in mining towns. They were citizens, maybe temporary if they didn't find pay dirt, but citizens. They had a stake in not just their claim, or the mine in which they worked, but in the town. It was their home.

Most of them would protect their mine, their family (if they had one), their house, their fellow miners.

Sure, Duncan had had to arrest some when they got full of ardent spirits. And he had to whip Bryn Bunner when Duncan first pinned on the badge in Dead Broke—just to prove who would be the true boss of this town. And there certainly had been a lot of friction between the working miners and the mine owners, or those so-called conglomerates, when this Panic of '93 kept going on and on. But most of that had settled down.

Besides, the miners hadn't caused the violence when Duncan first arrived. That had been some rotten, corrupt villains. But those vermin were dead or run out of town now.

Mining towns weren't cattle towns. Cattle towns were often divided—one part of town for the respectable citizens, the barbers, the storekeepers, the hotels for the cattle buyers and the railroad officials, the druggists, the milliners, doctors—maybe even a dentist—and folks like that. And the other side for the whiskey peddlers, the gambling halls, the dance-hall girls, and those types of folks. That's why Duncan's jobs in cattle towns had never lasted all that long. The respectable citizens drove off the prostitutes and the gamblers, and the cowboys and their bosses found another cow towns, while the former cow town either became a fine community that welcomed farmers and factories—or it faded quickly into a ghost town.

In a mining town, everyone was in this together. They all worked for one purpose. Sure, that purpose was for profit—but that was true for any business, any enterprise, and any town or city. Miners might disagree—and often did—with mining owners, but the miners needed those owners, and the owners sure couldn't make a living without the men who went into those holes in the ground, or—not in Dead Broke, but in placer mines—panning streams, creeks, and rivers for gold.

That's what Duncan told Syd Jones, anyway.

"Have you been dipping into Nugget's brew?" the old lawman said incredulously.

Duncan turned and stared at his old mentor.

"You weren't here during the boom in the mid-eighties, son. This place was worse than the fiery pit. Newspapers all across the state—and the country, from San Francisco to Kansas City to New York City, from the Dakotas to Texas, across the Atlantic, and, as far as I know, from Alaska to the Sandwich Isles to the Far East, and all the way down to that Australia island—said Dead Broke had a man for breakfast every morning. And that wasn't a lie. Because I was carrying out dead men, buryin' them, or killin' them myself."

Jones had to wipe his face. He wasn't sweating. But he must have felt like he was. Shaking his head, Jones let out a long sigh. "Apologies for blowing my top, but I'm getting too long in the tooth for these kinds of headaches."

"Sixteen dollars a ton," Duncan said.

"How's that?" Syd Jones asked.

"That"—Duncan motioned toward the caved-in mine—"that Liberty Bell of Zinc, or whatever name Nugget's going to give it. Five. Six tons. That whole thing isn't worth more than a hundred dollars."

Jones stared in silence, then started rubbing the beard stubble on his face.

"Men have been killed for a whole lot less," he finally said, but that came out in a whisper.

Duncan nodded in agreement. "That's a fact," he said. "But Nugget's diamond-shaped chunk of silver is worth, even with the collapse, around twenty thousand dollars.

I think that Diamond Nugget of Silver would bring more trouble than this . . . zinc rock."

Jones cocked his head. "You did that math right there like that, that quick, in your head?"

With a grin, Duncan shook his head. "Sara did it. A couple of nights ago. We were just talking, and she did it. With a pencil and paper."

"Makes me feel better then," the old lawman said. "A tad better. Not a whole lot, though. I got a feeling down deep in my bones and in my gut that this Liberty Bell of Zinc is going to cause you and me and all of Dead Broke a whole lot of trouble."

Duncan wouldn't say it, but he had similar feelings. Misgivings. Something like that.

"They haven't gotten it out of the mine yet," he said.

Jones nodded, then let out a soft chuckle. "You thinking about caving it in?" The chuckle became a laugh. "Blowing it up. They say, I hear, that zinc isn't strong rock."

"I couldn't do that," Duncan said. "Not to Nugget. Not to anyone."

"Couldn't—wouldn't—do it myself," Jones said. He sighed. "But trust me on this. That thing inside that mountain is going to bring us lots of headaches and grief."

"Part of being a lawman, I reckon," Duncan said.

"Well." The old man shook his head. "Guess we'll see what happens." He stared at the whirlwind of activity as the men kept working. "It might take them a long time to get that place dug out and that big chunk of metal out so folks can see it."

But, to their surprise—and to the envy of mining towns across the nation—it didn't take men like Bryn Bunner and Silas Drury and even that old rapscallion Nugget himself to work wonders.

Which was . . . THE WAY OF WESTERNERS.

That was the headline that appeared over Carl Woodward's claptrap in the *Times of the Rockies* toward the end of September.

Yet even before that article appeared in the Denver newspaper and was quickly reprinted in papers across the United States, the word of Nugget's latest—and fantastic—discovery on This Side Of The Slope brought more and more people—mostly men, but at least a score of women—into Dead Broke.

A few businesses reopened, even though it was getting late in the year and winter would be coming in hard soon. A French woman opened a bakery. A big gent from Colorado Springs took over one of the abandoned livery stables. A drummer came in with a wagonload of supplies and started up a new hardware store.

Winston DeMint was standing in front of his office one morning when Duncan walked up. The jailer was talking to a puny fellow with a waxed mustache, who was sitting in the saddle of a fine, but hard-blowing, chestnut mare. Another stranger in town. The man turned toward Duncan and nodded.

"Howdy, Marshal," he said.

Duncan nodded at the pasty-looking gent. Gambler, Duncan thought. Or something like that. The heavy jacket he wore made him look bigger than he actually was. Duncan didn't see a scabbard on the saddle, and the man didn't sit in the saddle like he was carrying a firearm, but he didn't look . . . well . . . respectable.

"New in town?" Duncan asked.

The man shook his head. "Just passing through, Marshal. Came up to see if this town is worth setting up a shop."

"We welcome legitimate businesses." Duncan stressed *legitimate.*

"I am sure you do."

DeMint found a cigar in his pocket, put it in his mouth, and fished out a match.

He was lighting it when the newcomer looked down the street. "Can I get to that new zinc mine on horseback?"

"If you're careful." Duncan stepped back and studied the sky. "Doesn't look like rain or snow. It can be messy when it gets wet." He stared at the man again. "You in the mining business?"

"In a way." The man's smile had an ugliness to it.

Duncan knew what that man meant, and the man figured that out quickly.

"But you're right about the snow. The mines will close down for the winter, I take it."

Duncan nodded. "Most of them. Those higher up. There are a few closer to town that might stay open, but the winters here can be pretty hard, and very long."

"That's what I was thinking." He nodded and found the reins he had laid across the front of his saddle. "But you have many vacant buildings. Maybe that old saloon will still be for rent or sale come spring."

That might be the old Lucky Dice, the late, lousy Conner Boyle's place.

"That would take some fixing up," Duncan said.

"Imagine so," the stranger said.

In silence, they studied each other for a long while.

"Nice visiting with you, sir," the man said after turning toward DeMint. When he looked back at Duncan, he nodded. "Guess I'll ride back to Denver. Was a pleasure to make your acquaintance, Marshal. I've heard much about you."

Duncan just nodded.

He watched the man turn his horse around and ride slowly out of town. The stranger did not look back. Duncan stared until the man was out of view.

"He didn't go up to see Nugget's mine," DeMint said, tapping the ash off his cigar. "That's what he had been talking about doing before you rode up."

"No," Duncan said. "He didn't."

"He wasn't a miner. I could tell that much about him. Too puny. Might be a lunger."

"He didn't cough," Duncan said.

"No." DeMint took another pull on his cigar, exhaled, then tapped the stogie out on the hitch rail in front of the marshal's office and jail. "What do you think he meant when he said, 'In a way,' after you asked if he was in the mining business. That wasn't an answer."

Duncan turned and stared at DeMint.

DeMint cocked his head for just a moment, then straightened. "Oh."

With a smile, Duncan headed for the door, opened it, and moved a brick with his foot to keep the door open, to let some of the stuffiness—and DeMint's cigar smoke— out. A marshal's office needed a good airing out fairly often, and the weather was cooperating on this fine autumn day. DeMint followed him into the messy office.

"Women," DeMint said. "He's one of them—"

The sound of footsteps stopped him, and both men turned to the door as Sara Cardiff stopped at the doorway.

"One of them what?" she asked.

"Nothing," DeMint said.

She stared at Duncan, who shrugged.

"Who was that stranger you were talking to?" she asked.

Duncan started for the coffeepot. "Want some of Winston's brew?" he asked her.

"No. I've had my fill of coffee for this morning."

Duncan took his time filling his cup. When he turned around, she was staring at him.

"Who was that stranger?" She put a hardness to the question this time.

"He didn't say."

She turned to the jailer for confirmation.

"Didn't give his name," DeMint said. And that was all DeMint had to say. But that wasn't all the jailer said. "Just said he was in the mining business . . . *in a way.*"

The coffee Duncan swallowed almost went down the wrong way. Instead, most of it went onto his shirtfront.

Not that Sara or DeMint noticed.

"Oh." Sara's frown was hard. She turned to Duncan, but didn't ask if he was all right, didn't look at the coffee stain on his freshly washed white shirt. She just stared at him, waiting on Duncan to say something.

"Expressed some interest in the old Lucky Dice," Duncan said.

"We should have burned that down," Sara said.

"It is an eyesore. And would take a lot of fixing up." Duncan sipped more coffee.

"Funny," DeMint said.

Still staring at Sara, Duncan didn't even hear him.

"What's funny?" Sara asked.

Duncan turned toward his jailer now.

"That fellow. I was throwing the coffee grounds onto the street and he come riding up. I reckon he could have been in town earlier, but he sure looked like he'd just come up the hill."

Duncan ran his hands over his face. He said nothing.

Finally, Sara gave up. She sighed and said, "I was thinking about walking up to see how that mine's going."

That stopped Duncan. Well, the man could have rounded the block or something. And he was gone now. And Sara . . . well . . . was here.

"It's partly yours," he told her, and grinned.

She didn't see any humor in his comment. Her eyes burned through him, and he set the coffee on the stovetop. "Would it be all right if I accompanied you?"

"That would be nice," she said.

He walked to the gun case and pulled out a Winchester, grabbed some extra shells, and shoved them in his coat pocket.

"Are you expecting trouble?" Sara asked.

"A grizzly might be eating whatever it can find before going to sleep for the winter," he said. "I doubt if we'll run into one," he added quickly, "but I'm always on the careful side."

Once he turned back around, he gave her his most comforting smile.

"You're in charge, Winston," Duncan said. He held out his arm, grinned again when Sara took it, and they walked back into the crisp, clear morning.

CHAPTER 15

They stopped inside the Crosscut Saloon, where Logan Ladron was sweeping out the place.

"I'll be right back," Sara said, and she started for the staircase to her office, and sometimes home, to fetch a jacket. It would be colder higher up.

Ladron leaned his broom against the bar and asked Duncan if he'd like a morning bracer.

"No, thanks." Duncan watched Sara until the door closed behind her upstairs. Then he turned around and nodded at the broom. "Busy?"

Logan grinned. "Actually, a couple of those zinc miners dropped in last night for some poker. We had some nice conversations about zinc, good whiskey, why faro isn't as popular as it used to be."

"Because too many faro dealers cheat," Duncan said. He set his Winchester atop the bar.

"Which is why I stick to poker."

They both looked upstairs again.

"She's prettying herself up again," Duncan said with a sigh.

"She doesn't need to," Ladron said.

"I know that." He smiled. "She probably knows it herself."

Duncan cleared his throat, and the dealer turned to face him.

"Fellow rode into town this morning and was talking to Winston when I walked up. Said he was in the mining business *in a way.*"

"In what way?"

Duncan shrugged. "I took it to mean prostitution."

Ladron nodded, but made no comment.

"He said, 'Maybe that old saloon will still be for rent or sale come spring.' Then he rode out of town."

Ladron shook his head. "He could do a whole lot better than that place. Lots of old houses of ill repute are still standing, back from the olden, bloody times. In much better shape. You going to let him set up shop?" He laughed. "Well, you'd be run out of town if you didn't, knowing miners."

"I didn't have to," Duncan said. "Like I said. He rode out of town. He said with winter coming on, he wouldn't have much business. That's true enough for running a brothel or a gambling hall. So down the mountain he went."

Ladron nodded, suddenly stopped, and looked hard at Duncan. "You mean to tell me he rode all the way up here, looked around town a bit, then rode back to wherever home is?"

"I'm not sure he rode around town," Duncan said. "Winston said he was riding up the road when he walked outside. The fellow rode up, started a conversation. Then I walked up."

"Recognize his face?"

Duncan shook his head. "I'll go through the dodgers in

the office when I get back from our hike up to Nugget's new mine."

"What did he look like?"

"Pale. Winter jacket. Chestnut mare. That was mighty tired. No rifle. I couldn't tell if he was packing a sidearm. That jacket was a size or two too big for him."

"Give a name?"

Duncan's head shook. "He didn't give one. Being a friendly Westerner, I didn't ask."

Logan glanced through the open doors and windows, shook his head, and looked back at Duncan.

"I didn't see anyone ride past here all day. But I wasn't paying that much attention, trying to get the place ready for a booming business tonight."

The upstairs door opened, and they watched Sara come out in a heavier coat and a short-brimmed hat, scarf over her neck. She looked happy as a young gal on her birthday.

"I'll keep an eye out," Logan said. "Is Syd around?"

"He's still up at the Crosscut Mining Claim." He smiled after saying the name of Sara and Nugget's mine.

"Who's still up at the mine?" she asked from the foot of the stairs.

"Syd." Duncan turned around, removed his hat, and bowed. "Well, you sure look lovely."

"Thank you." She curtseyed.

Duncan took one step toward the batwing doors, frowned, and turned around.

"Do you mind if we go out the back way?" he asked.

She gave him a hard stare. "What on earth for?"

"Well," he said, "it's a long walk up to your mine and all." He danced around a little. "You know. What's . . . in the back of . . . you know?"

Sara let out a long breath. "You mean . . . the privy?"

"Why, Sara Cardiff!" He gave a look of mock surprise.

"Such indecent language." But he took her arm, picked up the long gun, and led her toward the rear door.

Both Duncan and Sara were stunned by all the progress those miners, carpenters, and engineers had managed in such a short while. The Crosscut Mining Claim—no, it had to be the Crosscut Mine by now—was booming.

Scaffolding surrounded much of the front of the mountain, and carpenters were busy putting up other buildings. No one would call it a separate town. Not yet, anyway. But it was getting mighty close to that. Smoke came out of the top openings of several tents, and a man was plucking on a banjo while a skinny redheaded woman worked a jaw harp. The aroma of strong coffee and fried ham—even that especially pleasing smell of sourdough biscuits—made Duncan's mouth water. He realized he hadn't eaten any breakfast, and that walk up the mountain with Sara wasn't exactly a stroll down those new board-walks in Dead Broke.

"Come to see your claim, ma'am?"

Both turned to find Syd Jones walking toward them, his eyes bright—though a lot of beard stubble on his cheeks— and a double-barrel scattergun in his right hand. He wore a linen duster, unbuttoned, over a red-and-black plaid mackinaw.

"No." Sara walked up to the old lawman, hugged him, and gave him a kiss on his cheek. "We came to see you."

"Well." When Sara stepped back, Syd looked over her shoulder at Duncan, but just for a moment. Then he looked down at Sara and said again. "Well. You're most welcome up here anytime."

Another voice came out from behind them.

They all looked at Nugget.

"Howdy, pardner!" He strolled up and beamed at Sara. He wasn't as dirty as he had been back when he was in the mine, but he certainly had not had a bath recently. "We's 'bouts to get the new entrance all shorn up. They's fellas inside already putting up supports so we won't have to worry 'bout no cave-ins no more."

Duncan noticed another miner, not as tall but heftier than that rail-thin rapscallion Nugget, standing maybe fifteen yards behind and off to Nugget's left. He held a pitchfork over his shoulder and was sipping from a big tin cup near a bucket of water.

"Then we'll be able to get my Liberty Bell of Zinc. I like that better'n the Zinc of Zion. We'll get it out of here and down the trail and soon it'll be rights besides my Diamond Nugget of Silver—and no tellin' how many folks is gonna be comin' up here to see it."

The man finished his water and knelt to refill his cup. Mining is a thirsty business, Duncan told himself, but something about this man just didn't seem right. But Nugget kept talking and then began calling for Duncan, so he turned away from the miner and looked back at the mayor of Dead Broke.

"And y'all's comes up here rights in the knack of time."

Knack? Duncan sighed.

"We's 'bouts ready to bring that masterpiece of zinc out of my mine." He coughed. "Our mine. *Our* mine." He smiled down at Sara, but his eyes seemed to be filled with fear until she gave him a pat on his arm and a short grin.

"Nugget!"

Duncan recognized Bryn Bunner's voice. All turned around toward the mine, and Duncan made out the Arkansas zinc expert standing beside him.

"We're bringing her out!" Bunner yelled. Two armed

guards came up past Bunner, and Silas Drury started motioning the crowd to make room.

Nugget was already running toward the mine.

Sara let out a childlike squeal and clapped her hands. She didn't seem anything like a gambler at that moment, and it made Duncan smile. She walked rapidly after Nugget, and as more people—miners, wives, women who weren't wives, children, cooks, dogs, cats—everyone was gathering around to get their first look—in daylight, at least—of the largest chunk of zinc ever found.

Syd Jones moved slowly, which was a smart thing to do. A body in front of this stampede might find himself trampled. Duncan caught up with him, but something made him stop.

"Syd," he said. "Something's not right." He turned around and saw the man in the duster. He wasn't holding a pickax anymore, but was returning something to the pocket of his duster. That something caught the sun's reflection, and Duncan knew it was a mirror.

"Hey, mister!" Duncan yelled. "Hands up! I'm the law here."

He brought up the Winchester as the mirror the man was trying to shove into the pocket caught the corner, slipped out of his hand as he stepped back and saw Duncan and his .44-40. The mirror fell on a chunk of rock, shattering. The man's hand found the butt of a Smith & Wesson.

A gunshot boomed—but not from Syd and not from the man in the duster. The whine of a ricochet screamed. Then women started shrieking as more bullets came from the mountainside, and others from a bunch of small wagons and carts about 150 yards away.

The man who had signaled those gunmen up that hill had pulled his revolver, but then came another cannonade, and it wasn't from Duncan's repeater, but behind him.

The man dropped his .32, spun around, and dropped to his knees, and tried to extend his arms as he fell forward. But the arms didn't work anymore, and he couldn't break his fall.

Not that it mattered. Because from the size of the bloody hole in the back of that duster, he was dead before he hit the ground.

Duncan dropped to the stony dirt, feeling a bullet tear a hole in the side of his hat. He rolled over to see Syd Jones on a knee, holding the shotgun in his left and his smoking Peacemaker in his right. After a quick nod, he jumped behind a large boulder near the side of the mountain. Duncan rapidly began crawling toward his mentor, but he kept his eyes on where Sara and Nugget had taken shelter. She was all right. Both of them crouched behind another water barrel.

Once he reached Syd, Duncan realized how hard his heart kept beating. He pressed his back against the rock, and felt the old lawman take the Winchester from his hand.. He had holstered his Colt. Duncan didn't know where Syd had left the shotgun.

"Catch your breath, son." The stock came to his shoulder, and Syd eared back the trigger, raised the rifle, and waited.

"Thanks," Duncan said. He barely got that word out. His throat felt like he had been walking through the Mojave for three days, not in a green forest with ample water on a crisp, clear day.

"What made you suspicion that hombre?" Jones asked without moving the Winchester an inch.

"Too clean for a miner," Duncan said slowly, cleared his throat. "And then . . . his shoes."

"Shoes?" Jones was still focused on the mountainside. The gunfire had faded, at least, for the moment.

"Never seen a . . . miner . . . wearing . . . dancing slippers," Duncan said.

Now the rifle came down, not to the ground, but level, and Syd Jones shot the dead man a glance. "Oh, yeah. Blue leather. Saw him at the show last night this troupe brought in." The rifle came up and he focused again on the high ground.

"Wasn't much of a dancer, either," Jones said.

"They have the high ground," Duncan said a moment later.

To his surprise, he saw his old friend smile wryly.

"Well, they think they do."

Duncan sat up now, wishing he had a long gun. Syd's sawed-off shotgun and the lawmen's two revolvers weren't going to be of much help from men with rifles up in that high country. And then he saw a flash of light. It came higher than where he had seen a few muzzle flashes.

"You see that?" he whispered dryly.

"Yeah." Syd's smile grew larger. "But that ain't coming from some greenhorn who wears blue shoes."

The smoke came first, then more smoke and flashes, followed by the roar of rifle fire up in that rugged, rocky country.

"Hold your fire!" Bryn Bunner called out just as Syd was yelling the same thing.

The figures looked like toys from where Duncan crouched. One twisted and fell and lay still. Another rolled halfway down the incline. A third flew back and then dropped off the side and landed with a sickening crunch in the rock pile a few feet from the entrance to Nugget's—and Sara's—zinc mine.

Two others quickly tossed away their rifles and were screaming as they raised their hands.

"We give up!"

"Reckon it's over," Syd said, finally lowering the hammer on Duncan's Winchester.

Duncan holstered his useless Schofield and took the rifle. "Here maybe," he said, though his voice sounded soft, doubtful—not the way he usually talked. "But I'm heading back to town." He cleared his throat. "Tell Sara where I've gone. You can make out up here."

"Yeah."

"And keep those fellows who gave up from getting themselves lynched."

Even that doesn't sound like myself, Duncan thought, but tried to explain that away by blaming his eardrums after all that shooting.

"These are good folks," Syd said. "They aren't gold and silver miners."

Duncan was already walking toward the trail that led downhill.

"Maybe. But gold and silver thieves aren't as crazy as any fool who'd go to all this trouble for a big rock of zinc. It's not even as pretty as gold or silver."

Now, that sounded like the old Duncan. In command. Strong.

CHAPTER 16

Duncan turned the corner to walk to his office, but stopped when he saw a dead man in the street.

Well, he had to assume the man was dead. Winston DeMint and Logan Ladron stood over him in front of the town marshal's office, both of them holding guns at their sides, DeMint a Sharps carbine and Ladron his revolver. A few folks stood in the doorways of their shops. He saw no sign of Doctor Aimé Cartier.

As he resumed his walk, Ladron and DeMint turned and saw him, and Ladron slid his pistol into a holster and the jailer butted the carbine in the street. Before reaching the office, Duncan had a good guess at who that corpse was.

The heavy jacket he had worn was gone, and there was a big hole and a lot of blood in the center of his chest, and so much more blood spreading from both sides Duncan knew there was an even bigger hole in his back. The waxed mustache didn't look so neat now, and he was even paler in death than he was when Duncan had last seen him.

Duncan stopped and stared down at the corpse. A Henry rifle lay at the dead man's side.

"He didn't go back to Denver after all," DeMint said.

Duncan nodded.

"Bet he wished he had," Ladron said. He turned to Duncan. "Sounded like the Fourth of July up in those hills."

"Yeah. Nobody's bad hurt—on our side." He looked at DeMint. "You'll have some boarders later today, but I want to get them out to Denver as soon as we can. I'll telegraph Marshal Newton."

"We got plenty of room in the jail," DeMint said.

"I know." Duncan nodded. "But I'm not keeping them locked up till the judge gets here—and that might not be till spring or summer."

He sighed and shook his head. "We'll probably have more folks locked up than we can hold once the gawkers start coming up here till the first hard snow."

"Nugget's zinc is out of the mine?" Ladron asked.

Duncan nodded. "What happened here?" he asked DeMint, though he had a pretty good idea.

But it was Ladron who answered.

"I was on my way to the jail, when we first heard the ruction up in the hills." He pointed at the dead man. "This gent comes out of nowhere and takes a shot at me." He touched his ear. "Almost lost this."

DeMint picked up the story. "I just happened to be loading this Big Fifty. Cracked the door a bit, saw him, and whilst he was cocking his piece, I let him have it."

Which was just how Duncan figured it.

DeMint toed the stock of the Henry with his left boot. "I don't recollect him having a long gun whilst he was talking to us."

"Drift Carver came up right after this was all over," Ladron said. "He went down the mountain a ways to see if anybody else was with this assassin."

"Drift walking okay?" Duncan asked.

"Got a limp," Ladron said. "But he said he's fine."

"He was using a .44-40 for a walking stick," DeMint added. "What happened at Nugget's mine?"

Duncan kept it short. He was thinking that he might want a few more deputies till he could get those surviving outlaws out of town. He would add that in his telegram to Denver's marshal. Preventing a lynching was a good reason for transferring prisoners to another jurisdiction these days. Of course, back when Duncan first pinned on a badge, lynching prisoners was considered a good idea. He sure could use Ben Usher right about now.

He was wrapping up his story when hoofbeats sounded, and a moment later, Drift Carver came trotting up on the chestnut horse that the corpse at Duncan's feet had left somewhere.

The old scout reined up and gave Duncan a quick nod.

"There was another one," Carver said. "But I reckon he musta lost his nerve when the gunshots started, and the tracks showed that he was at a full gallop out of this high country."

That would explain where the dead man got the rifle, anyway.

"Can I keep his horse?" Carver asked.

Duncan let out a sigh. "Get something to carry this luckless idiot to the undertaker," he said. Then he squatted by the dead man to look for some sort of identification. Carver trotted off, DeMint said he would heat up some coffee and food, and Ladron squatted on the other side of the corpse.

"How you figure it?" the gambler asked.

"He and his pardner were left here to keep us pinned up in my office, I suspect," Duncan said. There was a silver watch, but no engraved name or anything. Some paper money, coins, and lots of rounds for his .44 long gun.

"That's why you went out the back door with Sara," Ladron said, nodding his understanding.

"Just in case he was keeping an eye on things here." Duncan found a rabbit's foot and held it up, shaking his head.

"Never believed in such superstitions," Ladron said. He changed the subject. "But you were right about him."

"Sometimes it works that way. Sometimes it doesn't. Pays to be careful."

Which, he knew, was one reason he had lived so long as a lawman with a national reputation.

By then, Germaine was riding up in his wagon. Duncan stood and the two men exchanged nods after the undertaker reined up.

"This is getting to be busier than it was in the old days, Mick," Germaine said.

Duncan tilted his jaw toward the mountains. "There are more up near the Crosscut Mine," he said. "I imagine they'll be bringing some bodies down."

As he climbed down from the rig, Germaine pulled out his tape measure and said, "Well, this town's name has always been about half right. It's never stayed broke, but there has always been a wealth of *dead* around here."

He squatted by the body and started unwinding the rolled-up measuring tape. "For the life of me, I don't know why all those other men of my profession ever left this town."

Sara Cardiff said she could handle things fine. Things were busier than they had been, but not like those rip-roaring days and, as had often been pointed out, zinc miners and lead miners didn't gamble or drink like those who sought, and sometimes found, silver and gold. So

Duncan was able to deputize Logan Ladron, Drift Carver, and a zinc miner who had gotten a flesh wound through his upper left arm during that badly planned robbery at the Crosscut Mine, and they took the prisoners down the mountain to Denver.

It took another day before Nugget and some freighters managed to get his Liberty Bell of Zinc off the mountain and into town.

Nugget, who had once promised that his Diamond Nugget of Silver would stand as a statue in Dead Broke, swore that he would put that big stone of zinc next to it one day—in his guarded three-story home. But for the time being, it would just stay in the barn in the big wagon—at least until he figured out how to get six tons of rock into his magnificent home. He announced that tours would begin for both his great mineral discoveries, for a dollar a head, fifty cents for children under twelve years old. But the Panic that had set in across the country changed his mind when he only got a few takers, so he reduced the price to forty-five cents for everyone. He was holding it there, he vowed.

Carl Woodward said goodbye and took the next stage to Denver, saying he wanted to make sure the printers didn't butcher the articles about Nugget's Liberty Bell of Zinc, adding that he thought his article would be picked up by newspapers across the globe and that people would be flocking from as far away as London, Paris, and Sucre.

It took only three days before the first visitors came to Dead Broke and asked to see Nugget's new discovery. Well, they didn't actually ask to see it. The four men came armed with a wagon to haul the big boulder down the mountain, and one of them put a gun to Nugget's head.

They might have gotten away with it, too, because they had oiled the wheels of the wagon so it didn't make much noise, and one man drove the wagon. The three others had ridden in earlier, one at a time, so they wouldn't arouse suspicion.

Of course, they didn't need to bring a wagon, since the boulder was already in the wagon in Nugget's barn. Apparently, they had not conceived just how heavy six tons was.

The man with the black hat rode up to Percy Stahl's and drank a few beers, chatting that he was looking for work and hoping to find something. He even said he hadn't heard one thing about Nugget's latest great mineral discovery and, in fact, he hadn't even heard of Nugget. Turns out, it was later learned, that he had some experience on the stage, having traveled once with a Shakespearean troupe.

The man in the black-and-tan checkered britches went to Mize's barbershop, and even though Jim Mize was closing up—he wasn't nicknamed Mizer Mize without reason—he sharpened his straight razor and tried out some new jokes on the fellow, who wanted to know who might be hiring up here, but not for mining work, as that was too hard.

Pyle Condon drove the wagon. He told Winston DeMint, who was walking back to the jail after eating his supper, that he was delivering some canned peaches to Nugget's place and needed directions. DeMint didn't think anything about that at first, since Nugget was the sort of fellow who would order a wagonload of peaches on a whim, so he just pointed up the road and told Condon where to drive.

The fourth man nobody saw—not then, anyway—as it was growing dark and most of the townsfolk were either drinking a whiskey or trying their luck against Sara Cardiff or Logan Ladron in the Crosscut Saloon, sipping a beer at Percy Stahl's, or eating supper with their wives and children, like the Clarkes would have been doing if Little Joey hadn't asked his mama if he could take a slice of her peach pie to Nugget, knowing how fond Nugget was of peaches.

And it was Little Joey who ran to the marshal's office and reported what he had seen outside of Nugget's home.

"Slow down, Joey," Duncan said, and asked DeMint to bring a dipper of water to the boy.

"There was a man with a shotgun—I think it was a shotgun—and he was aiming it at Mayor Nugget's two guards. You know, the fellas who guard his famous silver and zinc discoveries."

Duncan tilted his head.

"Are you sure?"

The boy didn't pout. His lips flattened and he looked like he had just been insulted.

"The double front doors were open—and you know how big those doors are. And you know how many lanterns and candles the mayor has in that house, so the sun might not be high, but there's enough light in that house so I can make out four men with guns and a wagon backed up to the mayor's front porch."

(That wagon was found still in front of Nugget's porch.)

Duncan tried to think of another approach, but heard the splash in the water bucket and looked up to see DeMint moving to the gun rack.

"Fellow rode past me an hour or more ago and said he was delivering a bunch of peaches to Nugget's." He grabbed a Winchester repeater.

Straightening as he rose, Duncan said without looking back at the youth: "Joey, I need you to do me a favor."

"Yes, sir." The boy's voice had turned timid.

"Run by the Crosscut Saloon and tell Mr. Ladron that Mr. DeMint and I need him. Tell him to hurry over here."

"You mean *here*?"

"That's right. Hurry." He drew his Schofield and found a shell in his belt. Most men kept the chamber under a revolver's hammer empty. It was a safety mechanism to prevent even an experienced gunfighter like Duncan from accidentally shooting himself in the foot. But when he was facing robbers and thieves, and possibly killers, a man wanted to shoot as many times as he could before having to reload.

"But shouldn't you go to the mayor's house?"

Duncan had to fight off that curse he wanted to bellow.

"They have to ride right past us to get out of town, son," he said. "Now hurry."

"But what if they *murder* Mayor Nugget?"

The .45 shell almost slipped out of Duncan's finger and thumb.

How have you been able to keep a job as marshal for so long? went through his mind.

And that's why Pyle Condon stopped the wagon he was driving—not the wagon he had driven to Dead Broke—when he and his three companions came out of Chasm Park and found themselves staring down Winston DeMint's rifle barrel, the twelve-gauge Greener double-barreled shotgun that Duncan had borrowed from his jailer, and a .45 Colt held steadily in Logan Ladron's right hand.

"There's only three of you and four of us," said the fourth man, who gave his name later as John Smith, and was said to be the brains behind the conspiracy.

"No." That was Mr. Clarke's voice, and he came down the street with a Marlin rifle in his hand, and he was followed by Percy Stahl, undertaker Germaine, and Doc Cartier, the latter who was holding a .44 Remington in his right hand and his black satchel in his left.

Footsteps sounded down the other street that came up from Duncan's office, and the first voice from that crowd made Duncan cringe.

"If you've harmed Nugget in any way, we're going to string all four of you up and leave you for the buzzards."

Duncan wasn't a greenhorn, and neither was Ladron or DeMint. They kept their eyes on the four men, but Duncan told himself he needed to have a word with Sara when this was all over and remind her that she was a lady—even if she ran a gambling hall and saloon—and that she didn't need to be risking her life in affairs like this.

He never had that conversation, of course, having realized all that would do would make her madder than a hornet.

"This doesn't have to end ugly, mister," Duncan said. "But . . ." He had learned all about those long pauses during his career. They could be so effective. "It's your play."

Pyle Condon heard more footsteps, and a few unmistakable metallic clicks of the hammers of six-shooters being cocked and levers working on repeating rifles. The streets were soon full of people—armed men, young boys shouting, and their mothers screaming at them to get home or their fannies would be tanned something good. And to the man's credit, Condon slowly reached and pulled the brake lever, then raised his hands over his head.

So did the man wearing the black hat and the fellow in the checkered britches. The one folks finally saw, even though it was fairly dark by then, who turned out to be one of the Crosscut Mine's crew, and who had actually conceived the plan that he had brought to Pyle Condon, tried to race his horse through the crowd, but a blast from one barrel of the Greener Duncan aimed at the horse's forefeet made the horse rear, tossing the rider hard into the street. By the time he rolled over and got his lungs working regular-like, Winston DeMint had him covered with the muzzle of his rifle aimed less than an inch from the badman's nose.

It was pushing midnight before all the statements had been written down, the four men were locked up, and Nugget finally realized that no one in Dead Broke would let him lynch the four scoundrels. No one was hurt. The Liberty Bell of Zinc was returned to its proper place— the fool thieves gave up on trying to move that Diamond Nugget of Silver.

Nugget kept the wagon the bandits brought and the oxen, which he sold a few days later for a good price.

When most of the citizens had gone home, Duncan poured some coffee and handed the cup to Sara before pouring one for himself.

"Well," she said after taking a sip. "At least this won't wind up in a newspaper."

But it did, two days later in the *Times of the Rockies.* It was Nugget's own account, as told to Nugget's guard (the one known to read and write, so his stringing together of words actually made sense). The article might not have been completely accurate, but at least it was not overtly exaggerated. Following Nugget's orders, that guard rode out of Denver with ten copies of the newspapers, five for Nugget, and the rest sold by Nugget for two dollars, except the one he donated to the school library—but that was Little Joey Clarke's idea.

CHAPTER 17

Amos Filmore arrived in Dead Broke about the same time that Nugget's guard rode out carrying that newspaper article for the *Times of the Rockies*. He came in a heavy wagon with trunks and furniture and a vault, which even Bryn Bunner couldn't lift by himself. He had lots of papers, too, and showed them to Nugget, but since Nugget's literate guard was on the way to Denver, Nugget brought Mr. Filmore to the Crosscut Saloon, where Sara Cardiff read the letter of introduction and then asked Logan Ladron to run and fetch Duncan.

After the exchange of handshakes and brief introductions, Sara said, "Mr. Filmore wants to open a bank."

"Here?"

It was a little early in the day for a joke that good, Duncan thought, but when he took the letter that Sara held out, he read it and then looked up over the paper—Filmore had the prettiest handwriting Duncan had ever seen from a man's hand—and said, "A lot of banks are failing these days. Especially in mining towns."

"That's a fact."

Duncan couldn't place Amos Filmore's accent. Back

east maybe, probably in the States, but there might have been a bit of England or Wales mixed in it.

"I do not have the capital of the big boys, Marshal. And the banking business has always been a risky enterprise, but I have had some success. . . . Not enough to make me one of the major players, but I think I can stay open."

Not playing poker, Duncan didn't mind that his face showed skepticism.

"Marshal." Filmore smiled softly. "This summer was rough. I thought I was going to go broke. Even I had to withdraw funds that I kept in New York City. And, by my guess, I bet more than three hundred banks shut their doors. A good friend of mine in New York had to sell assets. Another colleague from Chicago jumped in front of a train. We've seen a massive reduction of currency."

Then he smiled.

"However, interest rates are starting to go down. Banks are reopening. I think Dead Broke, with its zinc and lead operations, has a golden opportunity to shine again. Bright—but not as bloody—as it was in the eighties."

"Why Dead Broke?" Duncan asked.

"Why not?" The man chuckled. "You are fairly removed—this high up—from the rest of this state. Even Leadville is easier to get to than here, and I considered Leadville, but it is hurting much more than this fair—and somewhat charming—city."

"How's that?" Sara inquired.

"Oh, Leadville will recover in time. It has a strong backbone, hard workers, sharp-minded leaders."

Duncan frowned. Nugget had been called a lot of things as mayor of Dead Broke, but nobody had ever even jokingly called him sharp-minded. And Duncan didn't consider himself a leader of this town. He just wore a badge.

And when it came to economics, the numbers Duncan was most familiar with were six—as in six-shooter—.45—as in caliber—and fifty-two—as in the number of cards in a poker deck.

"Marshal," Filmore said. "I don't expect to make my fortune here, but I think I can help Dead Broke. Having a bank is a key to a town or city's survival. Now, when was the last time there was a bank in Dead Broke?"

The man had a point.

"You have miners coming in by the score," Filmore said, and went on to name some businesses he had seen while driving into and around town. "That discovery of that great piece of zinc has been carried in newspapers around the continent and perhaps across the Atlantic Ocean. This won't be like the California or the Pikes Peak rushes. Zinc and lead don't cause major booms, at least in my experience, but that's because those who mine for zinc, lead, and less glorified minerals are the backbone of our society."

"You really think you'll have success?" Duncan asked.

The banker shrugged. "It's a gamble. We don't know if this slight turn upward will last. The opening of my bank, like the banks that are starting to reopen, and the resumption of the flow of cash and the return of credit, might last. But it might collapse, too. And how people react is never easy to guess. The American economy is not out of the woods yet. We might not fall into a deeper level of distress, but there is the chance that this downturn will worsen. I'm just willing to bet that I can make out—and help Dead Broke recover."

With a shrug, Duncan handed the letter back to Mr. Filmore. "Well, it's your money, I guess." He turned to Sara. "Any ideas for a suitable location?"

"Not Gyp Jansen's," she said. "What the dynamite they

used didn't blow apart, the fire they set did. Pretty much burned it to the ground."

Jansen was a banker, Duncan recalled, who had skipped town with all the deposited cash before Duncan left Durango to take the marshal's job here. The depositors hadn't taken that very well.

"How about Rich Lewis's old place, next to the Joyful Mine headquarters, which they burned down?" Logan Ladron suggested.

Sara nodded. "It's made of stone."

"Which is why it didn't burn down, too," Ladron said.

It sounded all right to Duncan, and Ladron rose when no one objected and volunteered to show the newcomer to the site. Mr. Filmore thanked him, and they walked out of the saloon and climbed into the big wagon.

After the wagon had gone down the street, Sara poured Duncan a cup of coffee at the bar, and they stood there, in silence for a while, till Duncan drank most of the cup and wiped his mouth.

"What do you think?" Sara asked him.

Duncan shrugged. "I guess it would be good to have a bank in town." Though he was thinking the exact opposite. The best thing about not having a bank in Dead Broke was that it kept the bank robbers out of town. Looking over his cup, he tried to read Sara's face. But that was hard to do, since she was a pretty good gambler.

"Do you think it's a good idea?" she asked.

He set the cup on the bar. "Well, it's your money."

She laughed. "Not mine. I bank in Denver."

In his office the next day, Duncan wrote a letter to the city marshal in Trinidad, the Colorado town in which Mr. Filmore had previously set up his bank. He also wrote to the U.S. marshal in Denver, just asking to let him know if there was something on this Filmore that he ought to know—or if there's nothing about any banker named Amos Filmore. One of the references was a merchant in Fort Davis, Texas, where Filmore said he had also banked, so he wrote the local lawman there, too, just to make sure Filmore wasn't some confidence man. The citizens of Dead Broke had worked hard, and Duncan didn't want them to be fleeced.

He took those to the hotel and had the clerk, after paying him for the stamps, drop them in the mail bag. Of course, there was no guarantee that anyone would write him back with good news or bad news. But that was the way things went sometimes.

It wasn't until Nugget's rider came back with all those copies of that Denver newspaper days later that Dead Broke's mayor came barging into Duncan's office.

"What's this here banker doin' in my town?"

Duncan looked up from the mail he was going through.

"Banking," he said.

"Can he do that?"

"If he has money. And if people start getting accounts, making deposits, he can."

"But I been doin' bankin' business. A bit."

Duncan smiled. "Well, you can still do your business . . . but I seriously doubt if Mr. Filmore is going to charge the interest you charge. So you might have to, well, either get out of your so-called banking business, or start lowering the interest."

"I don't charge for interest or any other kinds of thinkin'. Folks pay me to keep their cash or minerals from gettin' stole."

"I know. And you pay your guards for protecting that money."

Nugget stared as if Duncan had lost his mind.

"I pay my guards to protect my Diamond Nugget of Silver and my Liberty Bell of Zinc and my own money. I don't pay 'em for nothin' else."

Duncan just shook his head and tried not to laugh.

The mayor tugged his beard. He glanced at Winston DeMint and asked, "Is you bankin' with that Filmore dude?"

DeMint was poking an oily rag through one barrel of his shotgun with a long steel rod. The rag fell into a pile of newspapers he had placed to keep the oil and mess off the floor, and he turned the shotgun toward the window and stared into the barrel for a second before setting the big weapon on his desk.

"I've kept out of banks since the Panic of '73," he said. He picked up the rag and stuck it in the shotgun's second barrel, running it through with the rod, and watching the rag land on the papers again. "No banks for me. Especially with what I've been reading in the papers."

Nugget glanced at the oil-stained papers on the floor, shook his head, and looked back at Duncan. "Don't see how he can read nothin' with all that grease on 'em papers. But I ain't changin' no subject, Marshal, so you . . ."

His voice trailed off. He wet his lips, turned his head toward the door, and then leaned forward and shook his finger at Duncan. "How come he took over the Lewis house?"

Duncan shrugged. "Because the old bank got burned to the ground during the troubles earlier this year."

Nugget's head moved up and down. "Yeah. But that was Jansen's bank. We had more'n one bank here before things turned sour on us. There was the First Bank of

Dead Broke. Then the Denver Banking House. And, of course, Percy Stahl took lots of folks' money and kept it for them whilst they was drinking so they didn't drink all their money after they just got paid."

"That was mighty nice of Percy," Duncan said.

"Oh, he took out some looking-after fees hisself. Same as I do for those folks who needs some money." Now the old miner leaned forward and lowered his voice to a whisper. "He don't own that stone house now, do he?"

Duncan leaned back in his chair. He hadn't thought about who owned the place. Some kind of lawman he was turning out to be, but that's what can happen when a man gets lazy. "There could be a squatter's rights claim to that house," he guessed.

"Could be." Nugget's head bobbed up and down. "But there ain't. This is my town. You knowed that since you gots here. So maybe I oughts to go an' visit this bankin' dude and see if he's got enough money to pay me the rent he owes me." He stood up and headed out.

Duncan shot a glance toward DeMint, who laid the shotgun on the desk and leaned over to wrap up his oily rag in the newspaper and throw it into the stove.

"Do you know who owns that place?" Duncan asked.

DeMint's head shook. "No idea, but it wouldn't surprise me if Nugget did."

With a frown, Duncan rose from his seat and found his hat and coat, then walked out of the office and made a beeline for Dead Broke's newest bank.

He got waylaid while walking to the newest business in Dead Broke when Percy Stahl showed him one of the newspapers Nugget's guard had brought in and sold to him for an outrageous sum.

But the money the saloonkeeper had paid for a two-cent

paper wasn't anywhere near as ridiculous as the article Duncan skimmed through.

"This article makes like that big chunk of lead is worth a fortune," Stahl said, "and you and I—even Nugget—knows it's not worth much. It's just a crazy thing that happens now and then."

"I know," Duncan said, and moved down the boardwalk. He had seen men steal for less money, and, despite what the banker had told him, things were still tough for most folks—and a lot of them had no money and no job, but they still had mouths to feed.

He got stopped two more times before he finally made it to the new banking institution. He had to stop when he stepped into the stone building. It was hard for him to believe that this was just one of many abandoned structures in town when he had first arrived in Dead Broke. And it had been an empty building up until Mr. Filmore started moving in.

Duncan figured he'd hear Nugget yelling up a storm and waving a crooked digit in the banker's face, but instead he heard laughter.

A bell rang when he opened the door, but he barely heard that because Nugget was bent over in front of Mr. Filmore's desk, slapping his knee and hooting and snorting. He laughed so hard he dropped on the floor the cigar he had been smoking. Behind the desk, Filmore's head tilted back and his right hand pounded the desktop. He looked like he was crying, since he had been laughing so hard.

"Can I help you, Marshal?"

Duncan barely heard the soft voice. He turned to find Landace Purington to his left. Quickly, he removed his hat. He tried to remember his vocabulary, but that outrageous laughter distracted him.

The widow smiled. "They sure get along, don't they?" she said.

"I reckon so," Duncan whispered, and shot the two men a glance before turning back to Widow Purington.

"I was walking by when he was moving in," she said. "We started talking and he asked me if I would like a job." She shrugged. "Money being what it is these days, I said I'd sure give it a whirl. I'd been a teller in Silverton before Harold and I came to Dead Broke. So this isn't new to me."

The laughter faded into something less raucous and Nugget and Filmore started talking again, neither one of them noticing Duncan.

"I believe," the widow said, "they have just about reached an agreement."

"For rent?" Duncan asked.

"Oh, no. They settled that in three minutes when the mayor stormed in here, wagging his finger and saying this and that. Mr. Filmore sure knows how to handle an angry customer."

Duncan shot a quick glance. Filmore was standing now, leaning over the desk, relighting Nugget's cigar.

"The mayor has agreed to let his latest discovery be displayed in the bank window for a week, maybe two, as a promotion for not only our institution, but for Nugget and the city of Dead Broke. Instead of having Nugget charging fees for himself, this will be free."

The last word stopped Duncan. *"Free?"* He added: *"Nugget?"*

The kind woman grinned. "As I say, Mr. Filmore can be quite charming."

He turned at the sound of footsteps on the boardwalk and saw two women walk by. Then he noticed people on the other side of the street. A buckboard was parked in front of the hardware store. A man wearing black sleeve garters stood talking to Mrs. Clarke. Someone was painting the old saloon that had been empty since Duncan first arrived, and two freighters were unloading a fine barber's chair into the building.

There had been two barbershops in Dead Broke when Duncan first arrived.

"Looks like Jim Mize and Lou Jacobsen are going to have competition," Duncan said.

"Yes, indeed," the widow said. "You wouldn't even guess that Dead Broke was in a serious economic panic," she said.

She was right. Duncan turned around and saw the banker leaning forward and Nugget puffing on his cigar, while Filmore pointed at a paper on the desk as though Nugget could read. Nugget said something, and the laughter started again.

"Would you like to open an account, Marshal?" the kind lady asked.

Duncan shook his head. "No. Not yet, anyway. Besides, I wouldn't want to interrupt that conversation."

He nodded, thanked her again, stepped out onto the boardwalk, put on his hat, and decided that it wasn't too early for a drink at the Crosscut Saloon. He sure could use one and wondered if Ladron and Sara—or anyone else in Dead Broke—would believe him when he told them what he had just witnessed.

CHAPTER 18

"I wouldn't call it a gold rush," Sara said, and when Logan Ladron opened his mouth, with that gleam in his eye, she quickly added: "Zinc rush. Lead run. Whatever you want to call it. Or not call it."

Ladron closed his mouth, but it remained curve upward and she could read laughter in his eyes.

"But," Sara conceded, "it is busier than it has been."

That's the conversation Duncan caught as he walked up to Ladron's table.

Ladron gave him a nod, and Sara stared at him in silence. He knew she was looking at the satchel he carried in his left hand.

"And how busy are you?" Ladron asked.

He shrugged. "I don't mind not being busy," he answered after giving the question a moment's thought. "Nobody has come in to steal anything or shoot at anybody. Hope it stays that way."

She nodded at the leather bag. "Going somewhere?"

He nodded and waited. When neither asked where he was going, he frowned. "You're not curious about where I'm going."

After failing to stifle a yawn, Ladron reached for his

half-filled cup of cold coffee. He sipped it, uninterested, and Sara grabbed a deck of cards and started shuffling.

Duncan frowned.

That's all it took for Sara to giggle, and Ladron set down the cup and laughed aloud. He turned so he could look directly into the marshal's face.

Sara pushed aside the deck and laughed with Logan.

"What's so funny?" he asked.

It took a moment, but between some guffaws, Sara finally managed to nod at Duncan and, unladylike, snort out, "You."

"Me?" Duncan said.

"You," Ladron said, and laughed harder.

Duncan shook his head, and Sara finally said, "We know where you're going."

He stiffened. "Well, just where am I going?"

Ladron pointed at the satchel. "To open an account at our new bank."

Duncan lost his poker face. Sara would later say—a mild exaggeration—that he lost a good bit of color. He wanted to ask just how they knew that, but he wasn't about to. And he didn't have to, because just a few seconds later, Sara was pointing at his satchel.

"That . . ." But she couldn't get another word out because she kept giggling.

"Well!" Duncan demanded, but turned at the sound of the doors banging. Sara and Ladron tried to stop guffawing, but Syd Jones just kept walking toward them, as though they were acting normal.

"Syd," Duncan said. "Will you . . . ?" His voice trailed off as he raised the satchel, and stopped, staring at the leather bag and feeling his face redden. On came Syd, finally stopping by the coffeepot and pouring a cup for himself. Then he turned toward Duncan.

"What you carrying in that bag, sonny? Jacks? Pennies?" The bag jingled as he lowered it.

"He's . . . off . . . to . . ." Sara couldn't finish.

"The bank," Logan said, and laughed hard again.

"That a fact?" Syd sipped coffee.

Duncan tossed the satchel onto the table, almost knocking the cup out of Ladron's hand, and the melodic sound of coins bouncing this way and that rang loud and clear. That just made Sara laugh harder.

When a modicum of gravity returned to the Crosscut Saloon, Duncan mumbled, "Most of them are twenty-dollar gold coins."

Well, a few of them were.

"How are things up the slope?" Duncan asked, hoping the conversation could be steered in a new direction.

"Not bad."

"You did hear about the new bank opening, didn't you?" Sara asked.

"Oh, yeah." He took another drink. "Drift Carver came up with some mail yesterday."

"Are you going to deposit in the bank?" Duncan asked. He hoped the query didn't sound overly hopeful, but he wasn't sure he wanted to put his savings in any bank—at least until he heard back from some of those to whom he had mailed queries about Mr. Filmore.

The old-timer snorted, then said, "The mines don't pay that much."

"How about the miners?" Duncan asked. "Think any of them will bring some of their money to the bank?"

His head shook. "We have a sorta banker up yonder. Mostly loans some of the miners who don't do too well at the faro bank that has been set up there. Or they come down here and lose to a most charming and gracious lady." He gave Sara a quick wink.

She smiled.

"So what brings you down here?" Duncan asked.

Syd Jones ran the back of his left hand over the white stubble that covered his face. "The lady up the slope who charges four bits for a shaving doesn't have the steadiest hand, so I thought I'd come down here. Maybe treat some folks I know to a good supper—after I'm all cleaned up."

"They must be paying you pretty good, Syd," Ladron said with a smile.

"Better than a certain town marshal I know paid me." Winking at Sara and Ladron, he stepped over and pushed the black satchel about six inches. There wasn't that much jingling inside, but that could have been drowned out by Sara's cackling.

"All right," Duncan said. "All right." He moved over and picked up his bag. Sighing, he looked at Sara and Ladron and shook his head before turning back to his mentor.

"You trying Mize or Jacobsen's today?" he asked. "I could use a good shave myself." He was looking directly at Sara when he said that. She had been known to give Duncan a good shave now and then.

She stuck her tongue out at him, then grinned.

"Heard y'all have a new barber in town," the old lawman said.

Duncan snapped his fingers. "That's right. Ready?"

"Sure." Syd Jones finished his coffee, set the cup down, and nodded his thanks to the two gamblers. "I wasn't joking about some food. My treat. How 'bout if the marshal here and I stop by after we get ourselves all prettied up? I'll get y'all back here before it's dark and you get busy with folks wanting to make a fortune."

Sara nodded. "Oh, it has been busier than it was, Syd,

but I wouldn't call it busy. And I think I'd enjoy eating something I didn't cook."

"Good enough. You ready?"

Duncan took the satchel. This time, he heard just how loud those jangling coins were when he walked.

When they reached the batwing doors, Sara called out, "Don't worry, Syd. Duncan knows where that new barbershop is. It's right across from the new bank."

"You see a copy of the *Times of the Rockies* with all of Nugget's swagger, exaggeration, and lies?" Duncan asked after they had crossed the street.

"Yeah. One of his guards brought it up. You know. The one who knows how to read." Syd Jones's head shook as he chuckled. "He read it aloud. Before the miners went into the Crosscut Mine to start their day. Reckon, Nugget wanted to know just how famous he made them all— though he's the only one mentioned in that article. Didn't even mention Sara."

"Oh," Duncan said, "she didn't mind."

Confound it, he thought, *this satchel is louder than an orchestra in a Denver saloon.*

"That Liberty Bell of Zinc is getting to be a lot more of a bother than I ever thought it would be," Jones said.

Duncan didn't bother replying or expanding on that. He didn't have to. Syd Jones filled the void.

"Some folks just go a little mad when the world stops working the way they thought for a long time it was going to work. But that usually doesn't last too long. That craziness, I mean. Not that there won't be some other things— good and bad—that'll come along."

He tipped his hat at Dylan Pugh's wife as she walked down the boardwalk, twirling a parasol and holding a small, wrapped package. She started to smile, but the jingling in Duncan's satchel distracted her—and then she was past them. He thought her face looked like she was completely bewildered by all that noise his bag made.

"Things been quiet here in town?" Jones asked.

"It's been all right," Duncan said. "But I don't know what that *Times* story will do."

The old veteran chuckled. "You've been a lawman long enough to know that you never know what anything will do to get things off track or straighten things out."

They turned the corner and kept walking. *It's always a good feeling,* Duncan thought. *Walking with Syd Jones. Talking with Syd Jones.*

He could see the new bank on the other side of the street. The front door was open, but no one was standing in front of the building, looking through the big window at Nugget's Liberty Bell of Zinc. Maybe the curiosity had faded. And perhaps no one would be coming up to see— or try to steal—that big chunk of mineral.

He nodded ahead and slowed down.

"Here we are," Duncan said, and stopped in front of the building.

"This used to be a saloon," Syd Jones remembered.

It still looked like one—at least from the outside. A pole had been placed next to the double doors, but who-ever was doing the painting had just gotten the white coat down. The diagonal stripes of blue and red hadn't been painted yet. And the bullet hole through the big glass window was still there. The signage had faded over the years, so no one could hardly read it, and curtains now hung from the inside.

That fancy chair sat right in the middle. And a skinny man with black hair, and a comb in one hand and a whisk brush in the other, stood over a fellow wearing old cavalry boots and tan trousers, who leaned way back in that chair as the barber worked on his hair.

The man—the barber—was singing as he worked. It sounded like something foreign.

"Reckon it ain't a saloon now," Syd said. "Sings a lot prettier than your black bag."

They stopped at the doors. A hand-painted sign hung over the right-side knob.

Lu Barbieri di Dead Broke

"What do you think?" Duncan's confidence had begun to wane.

"Well, if he cuts as pretty as he sings, I reckon it's worth risking getting our throats slit." Jones stepped back and looked through the glass again. "Let's wait till this gent gets up. Looks like he's paying the barber right now." He motioned Duncan toward the door, and Duncan stepped up and put his hand on the knob.

"All right," Jones whispered. "He's coming. Open—"

"I can see him." Duncan opened the door, and the man—another newcomer to Dead Broke—and Duncan didn't have a name, so he just nodded and said, "Howdy."

"Marshal," the man said. He nodded at Syd, turned right, and walked up the boardwalk. He held his hat at his side, and he was whistling.

"Didn't see blood," Jones said as he stepped toward Duncan.

"Whistling's a good sign," Duncan said.

"And he's holding that bowler like he wants folks to see how good his hair looks," Jones said.

"We could try Lou's," Duncan suggested, but it was too late.

"Entrate, entrate," the little barber said as he pulled

open the door and pulled Duncan in first. *"Benvenuto. Benvenuto."* With his left hand, he signaled Syd Jones. He said some other words neither man could understand.

Syd Jones stepped into what had been a bucket-of-blood saloon back in the day—but he didn't feel all that comfortable about it.

CHAPTER 19

Syd Jones went first. His stubble was a lot thicker, and the barber—whose name, first or last (neither Duncan nor Syd could tell)—was Gaudenzio. Or something like that. He didn't speak more than a handful of words, but Duncan figured out that the price for a shave was ten cents.

The place was small—but Syd Jones told Duncan that the saloon that had been here before was small, too, and the whiskey had to be about as foul as anything ever called whiskey.

In that case, *Lu Barbieri di Dead Broke* was an improvement.

The barber motioned Syd to the chair first. Since there were no waiting chairs, Duncan started to leave, but the man called out to him in that musical voice of beautiful but incomprehensible words and Duncan looked back. The little barber motioned with the straight razor and then pointed to a corner.

"Your satchel," Jones said. "I think he's saying you can leave it here."

Duncan waited for Jones to finish the joke, but the little man's head went up and down, and it did look like he was pointing at the satchel and then motioning to the corner.

Well, Duncan told himself, *it beats having to hold that outside and have all those passers-by staring at me or, Lord forbid, hearing that money.*

So he walked to the corner, set the satchel on the floor, smiled at the barber and his new customer, and went outside.

He leaned against the hitch rail while Gaudenzio went to work on Jones. He sure was efficient, and the door opening surprised Duncan. Moving off the hitch rail, Duncan stared as Syd ran his right hand easily over that side of his face.

Duncan stepped closer. He sniffed.

"You smell nice," he said.

"Ain't bad," Jones agreed.

"You aren't bleeding," Duncan said.

"Never felt a thing." He jerked his thumb toward the building. "He just hummed and sang a bit. Don't know what he was singing. Then he slapped some sweet-smelling stuff on my face and said that would be ten cents."

"Well," Duncan said.

"Your turn, my boy."

With a smile, Duncan stepped toward the door that the little barber was holding open.

"By the way," Syd called out, "I told him you'd pay for both of us. I mean . . . all that money you're carrying, I figured I ought to lighten your load before we crossed the street."

Duncan sighed. He would sure be glad when this day was over.

The barber turned pale when Duncan took off his coat. Duncan looked around him before he noticed the badge pinned to his vest.

"Oh," he said. "This."

"You . . . ?" the little man whispered.

"Town marshal. Newly hired." He unpinned the badge and stuck it inside the pocket of the coat now hanging on a rack.

"Mar-shal," the barber repeated.

"That's right." He looked, and quickly realized that the man was afraid.

So Duncan laughed, trying to put the newcomer to the West—and likely to these United States and territories— at ease.

"Don't worry, mister. I've never arrested anyone for bad shaving. And from the looks of what I saw on that old hoss you just tended to, I'm certain that I'll be bragging about you to all the men in Dead Broke."

He didn't think Gaudenzio understood most of those words, but the man seemed to be steadying now. That pleased Duncan. No fellow wants an unsteady barber holding a razor to his throat.

And, truthfully, Duncan was always nervous when it came to new or strange barbers.

But the little tonsorial artist worked like an angel. Whatever had triggered those nerves in Gaudenzio had vanished. Almost instantly, as soon as Duncan was sitting in that fancy chair, and Gaudenzio had tilted him back and covered him with a fresh sheet, Duncan knew what Syd Jones had meant when he said he didn't feel anything. The man sang or hummed with a soothing tenor voice, and that razor glided so smoothly, Duncan felt relaxed. And he had never felt relaxed in a barbershop.

His name was Gaudenzio Giuffrida. Duncan got that much. He had come to Colorado from Chicago. Or maybe he was in Colorado on his way to Chicago. There was a brother somewhere. Chicago, Duncan thought. The brother's name was Gennaro. Both names start with a G. Duncan could remember that much.

And then, the small, melodic man was slapping some cool balm over Duncan's cheeks. Gaudenzio even brushed the dust off Duncan's hat and handed it to him. Duncan reached inside his trousers pocket and pulled out two bits. The man told him to wait and headed for his money box, but Duncan told him not to worry about it. Then he had to explain what a tip was. The man looked shocked. Then honored. And he bowed and backed up, bowed and backed up, and nodded and kept whispering, *"Grazzi. Grazzi. Grazzi. Grazzi."* That had to be *"thank you,"* Duncan figured.

The little barber helped Duncan into his coat, but when he pulled out the badge to pin it on his vest, he saw the fear returning and the swarthy man's face lightening a few shades.

Duncan tapped the badge. "Señor Gaudenzio." He hoped he got the name close. "This"—he tapped the badge again—"isn't anything to fear. This just means that I am here to help you whenever you need help. To protect you . . . or any law-abiding citizen. This doesn't mean I'm bad. It means I'm a helper. I'm paid to help people— businessmen like yourself. I'm here to protect people, too. You savvy any of that?"

The man blinked.

Duncan tried again. "This badge," he said, tapping it with his index finger, "means that I am your friend."

"Friend," Gaudenzio tried.

Duncan smiled. "That's right." And they shook hands again, with the barber's face now beaming again, and him whispering over and over again: "Friend. *Amicu.* Friend. *Amicu.*"

Amicu. Sorta like amigo, Duncan thought.

"Amicu," Duncan said aloud. And tapped his chest. "I am your *amicu* . . . amigo."

"*Amicu,*" Gaudenzio said, and tapped his chest. "Amigo. Friend." "Amigo" came out a lot better than "friend." Then he went on for about half a minute, but he was speaking his native tongue way too fast and way too authentic for Duncan to catch anything.

They shook hands again, and Duncan was getting to like this little guy, but he also knew that if he didn't get out of here in a hurry, he'd never hear the end of it from Syd Jones.

Duncan was about to pull open the door when the man called out, "*Signuri Amicu.*"

Duncan turned around.

Smiling, Dead Broke's new barber pointed his razor toward the corner.

Duncan turned and barked out a laugh. He walked to the corner and picked up his satchel. It sang out its own song—which wasn't nearly as pretty as the barber's voice—and walked over to shake the little man's hand.

"Thank you," he said, and then remembered *grazzi.* Which, now that he thought about it, was like gracias. He said, "*Grazzi.* Gracias. *Grazzi.* Thank you."

The barber was a quick learner. "*Grazzi,*" he whispered. "Thank . . . you."

"That's right. We'll be having ourselves a good talk one of these days. And I'll tell everyone in town just how good you are at shaving a fellow."

Everyone, he thought, *except Jim Mize and Lou Jacobsen—Gaudenzio's competition.*

They shook hands again.

Outside, he looked for Syd Jones, who wasn't leaning on the hitch rail or standing near the barbershop. Duncan glanced up the street and saw his old teacher standing in front of the millinery shop, and he walked toward him.

What the Sam Hill is Syd doing? Shopping for a woman's hat?

Then he realized what had Syd's attention—and it wasn't hats.

Duncan hadn't stepped past the old saloon's large window when he spotted the five men riding down the street. The singing of his coins in his satchel stopped him. He stopped and knelt as if he were tightening the straps on his spurs—if he had been wearing spurs—and pushed the leather satchel against the wood frame building. Then he unpinned the badge and stuck it in his vest pocket and rose.

He didn't see many people on the boardwalk. That was a good thing.

Up the street, Syd Jones had stopped by the hardware store and picked up a card that explained how something worked, but he wasn't reading that at all. Duncan knew that. He was reading the way those men were riding, spaced apart, and he was getting a good look at the scabbards on their saddles, and what might those long linen dusters be hiding on their persons.

Duncan was close now. "Hey, you old tinhorn!" he called out, and increased his pace.

Jones looked up, snorted, and said, "I'll be a lame mule."

Duncan pounded Jones's shoulder. Jones pulled off his hat and slapped it against his thighs.

"Been a long time, pardner," Jones said.

"Too long," Duncan said. "How 'bout a snort?"

"You speak the language of my tribe."

Duncan pointed down the street.

"We can get a drink right down the street."

So they turned around, ahead of the five riders, and headed back to Gaudenzio's. The barber's pole wasn't complete. The sign on the false front still read, though the paint was long faded, SALOON. The five riders might not notice the barber's chair through that big window. They would—if Duncan and Syd Jones were reading this right—be focusing on the new bank.

Duncan didn't even glance at his black bag.

He stopped at what had been a furniture store. Most of the building was in ruins, windows broken, rats running around inside, and the big mirror was mostly broken, too, but there was just enough glass left for them to look in the mirror as Syd Jones began pretending to be rolling a cigarette.

"They've stopped," Jones whispered.

"Yeah."

"Maybe changing their mind."

Jones kept miming his act as a cigarette-roller.

"Or maybe they're reading us as a couple of dumb lawmen."

"No luck."

"Yeah." Duncan saw that the men were coming up the street again . . . slowly.

"We need to get them in something like a cross fire," Jones whispered.

"I've got an idea," Duncan said. "I go into the bank. You take cover here."

"You go into that bank, it might scare them off."

Duncan nodded. "I sure hope it does." He stepped off the boardwalk.

"I know you, you horse thief!" he called out while waving at Syd. "You won't have a nickel to spend on rye whiskey. Let me get some cash from the bank and I'll meet up with you at Percy's place."

The five were riding right to Dead Broke's newest—and only—bank.

He hoped his coat, and the angle at which he was heading, would prevent those riders from realizing that he was entering the bank with a Schofield .45.

Through the door he went and breathed out a sigh of relief. Except for Amos Filmore and Landace Purington, the bank's lobby was empty.

He closed the door behind him and looked around.

Filmore looked up and rose from his desk. The widow started to smile, but Duncan wasn't playing poker and she quickly understood something wasn't right.

"There's a back door here, I hope," Duncan said.

The widow's face paled.

The banker might have understood. He pointed at a door. "Private office," Filmore said. "The door's locked." He bent to open a desk drawer. "I'll give you the keys."

"You can take the keys yourself, sir," Duncan said. "And take Mrs. Purington with you."

Duncan pulled out the Schofield, and fished out an extra .45 shell, explaining as he put a sixth bullet into the cylinder. "Five men are riding down the street, and Syd and I didn't like the looks of them."

"I see." Filmore put a small chain of keys into his coat pocket.

"I could be wrong," Duncan said.

The widow found her coat. "You usually aren't," she said.

She started for the door. The banker walked to Duncan and said, "I'd like to stay here. This is my bank."

Duncan smiled. "But it's my job." He tilted his head toward the widow. "Please, sir. We don't have much time."

Filmore nodded, but his left hand went inside his coat

pocket and pulled out a .41-caliber Remington derringer. "It's not much, Marshal," the banker said, "but it's loaded."

Duncan took it and slid it into his pants pocket.

The banker opened the door, and once Landace Purington was through it, he walked into the room, turned, gave Duncan a final nod, and closed the door behind him.

Duncan started moving now, removing his hat, deciding that the counter where the tellers would be working probably was his best place. He leaped onto the counter, swung his legs to the other side, and dropped to the floor, letting his hat fall to the floor, then kicking it aside. He straightened his tie.

He kept his focus on the big front window, but right in front of it was that stupid, big, bell-shaped piece of zinc. What he wouldn't give for a sledgehammer instead of a .45 and he could just reduce that piece of trouble to dust.

Just then, the door swung open, and Duncan almost dropped the derringer he had started to pull out of his pocket. He hadn't seen any of those five riders come into view and wondered how they could have slickered him so.

But they hadn't.

It was Gaudenzio, and he was carrying that black satchel that sang out louder than all the church bells in the state of Colorado on an Easter Sunday.

Out of the corner of his eye, he saw the first rider come into view.

"Amicu!" the barber called out, and, using both hands, raised the black bag with both hands.

Then another rider stopped and swung out of the saddle.

"Amicu Marshal!" Gaudenzio sang, his eyes bright, his voice melodic but powerful. He needed both hands to lift the black satchel up to his waist.

"Well, ain't this interestin'." The first rider had entered the bank.

He pulled out the sawed-off shotgun that the linen duster was hiding.

"Marshal, eh. Marshal. You musta thought you could catch us Haden brothers with our pants down." The shotgun started coming up, and the second rider was already stepping inside the bank.

CHAPTER 20

The Haden Gang.

That changed this game completely. The descriptions of the three brothers and two first cousins fit, but there were probably fifty men in Dead Broke who also fit those vague descriptions. The outlaws came from good stock—but didn't most outlaws? The Hadens were prosperous ranchers up around Turkey Roost in Larimer County on the Wyoming border. They had started out just doing the things stupid teenagers did—sort of like what Duncan himself was doing at that age—causing mischief after drinking too much ale around Virginia Dale or across the border at Colorado Junction.

But then they took to robbing banks, first in Greeley, then over in Akron. It was the railroad holdup at The Siding, west of Cheyenne, that got the Pinkertons and bounty hunters chasing them.

Dead Broke was pretty far south of their range.

"How you want to play this, lawdog?" the shotgun-toter asked.

The barber was whispering something in his native tongue. He kept crossing himself as he prayed.

With a great show of peaceful nonresistance, Duncan

lowered the hammer of the Schofield, then held the revolver out, butt forward.

"That's a good start," the Haden brother said. "But why don't you take your finger out of the trigger guard. You don't want me to think you're gonna try a border roll on me? Do you?"

He grinned.

Duncan hadn't even thought about spinning the revolver around and starting a shootout. But he did as he was told. Now he held the .45 by the barrel, and kept his left hand raised high.

"That's better." The shotgun didn't lower, and the man holding it walked up slowly, bracing the stock against his stomach, keeping his finger on one of the triggers, and then slowly taking the Schofield. Duncan showed nothing even remotely similar to resistance.

The man backed away, and shoved Duncan's pistol into his waistband.

"All right," he said.

The other Haden stepped outside and waved his hand, then came back into the bank and walked to the Liberty Bell of Zinc.

"That sure looks perty," he said.

That would be one of the cousins, Duncan guessed. The brothers were the smart ones, it was said. The two cousins were typically the killers. At least that's what the Pinkerton reports always said—especially after that bloodbath at The Siding.

"That's why we came here," the brother with the shotgun said.

Duncan dropped his poker face. He looked out the window again. One of the riders had dismounted and was pretending to be tying his horse to the hitch rail. The two others sat in their saddles and pretended to be talking, but they were watching. One looking down the street, the other up the street.

He wondered what Syd Jones was thinking. Or doing. Wise as Syd was, he would be crouched out of view. There was nothing to do at the moment. Well, he could start the ball by blowing apart one of the men with his rifle, then shooting as many as he could. But Syd knew that would likely lead to one dead town marshal and one dead new barber.

The cousin touched the chunk of zinc. "Perty," he said again. He put a big hand on the gem and gave it a shove. "But heavy. Mighty heavy."

"That's right," the shotgunner said. He didn't look away from Duncan. The little barber kept praying in his own language.

"Wait a minute, fellows," Duncan said. The cousin turned around and glowered. The Haden brother just smiled. "You came for that zinc? Not the bank money?"

The brother's laugh was just a snort. "Why would us Hadens waste our time on a bank in a crummy town like this? Maybe a thousand dollars? Two? When we could have the greatest treasure in all the West."

The cousin's head nodded. "That's what that paper said, ain't it? Ain't it?"

Sighing, Duncan shook his head.

"Boys," he said after a moment, and then pointed at the zinc. "That rock weighs six tons."

"Yep." The brother's face did not change. "It sure does."

That's when a massive freight wagon pulled up in front of the other hitch rail. The outlaws still on horseback moved out of the wagon's way. Four oxen pulled the wagon.

How the brothers and cousins figured they would get

away in that rig, with the weight they'd be carrying, and not get caught—or stuck—was beyond anything Duncan could imagine.

"What are you going to do?" Duncan asked. "Bust it into a thousand pieces?"

The cousin looked shocked. His eyes narrowed and his fingers tightened into fists so hard that his lower arms trembled.

"And ruin this . . . art . . . this creation . . . of God's?"

"Easy, Rufus," the Haden brother told his cousin. "He's just a poor, ignorant lawman. Can't help himself."

Duncan looked out the door again. He drew a deep breath when the driver stepped down from the wagon.

That was the biggest man Duncan had ever seen—and he had paid money to go to lots of circuses that came to towns like Durango. The fellow who rode shotgun stepped down, too, and that man made the driver look like a spindly teenager.

He didn't know where the two other behemoths came from, but they followed the two giants into the bank.

Another of the Hadens came in behind the muscular men. The brother who had Duncan's Schofield nodded at Nugget's discovery, and the big men went to it. Surrounding the stone, they squatted and let their massive hands feel around the lip of the bell-shaped rock.

The barber stopped praying. Gaudenzio's head tilted a bit as he looked in disbelief at those giants.

One of the big men's head nodded.

The one facing Duncan, more or less, said, *"Yksi . . . kaksi . . . kolme . . ."*

Duncan didn't recognize the language, but the savage grunts and groans belonged to a universal tongue. Out of the corner of his eye, he saw Gaudenzio. The barber had stopped shivering and mixing his prayers with songs. Instead of looking like a frightened kid, he looked like someone stunned to disbelief.

The giants grunted and strained—one of them cut loose with a rippling fart—and cursed. And stopped. Then they tried again with the same results, but sans the fart.

The outlaws with the guns resembled shocked school-children.

That's when Duncan laughed out loud.

The leader raised his shotgun, his face returning to that menacing glare, but Duncan could not help himself. He pointed at the ridiculous sight in front of the big window. If those other outlaws hadn't been blocking the view, prob-ably the passers-by on the other side of the street would have been howling with riotous laughter themselves.

Duncan's body finally stopped trembling, and while he caught his breath, he heard the little barber trying, but fail-ing, to stop giggling.

"Shut up!" the Haden brother said.

Duncan sucked in a breath, exhaled, and managed to steady himself. "I'm sorry," he said, "but it took upward of twenty miners up the slope to get that rock onto the back of a wagon. Big miners. The strongest men they had." He almost laughed again. "Those four giants from whatever carnival or dime museum you found them at are going to hurt themselves."

The Liberty Bell of Zinc had not budged.

Swearing savagely, the Haden brother barked to the brutes, "Stop it. Before you rip your arms out of the shoulder sockets." He turned to the cousin. "Keep an eye on them."

Then he came outside. "Marcus! Bust out that big glass. Then all of you—except Nick—get in here. That rock's too heavy for even our strongmen to budge."

"But you said—"

"Forget what I said. Now get in here before we start attracting too much attention."

From the look of things across the street, the Hadens were already getting lots of looks.

When most of the gang came inside the bank, the brother pointed at the rock.

The glass began shattering as Marcus Haden started smashing the window with the stock of his Winchester. The big brutes got out of the way and rubbed their shoulders or backs. Glass shards rained onto the floor. Then the bandit ran the barrel up and down the sides, knocking out the remnants of shards. He started to come through the window.

"Give me that gun," the Haden with Duncan's .45 said, and he took the Winchester in his left hand. Still holding the shotgun in his right, he whirled toward Duncan.

"You get in there with them," he said. "And you better do your best lifting, because if I don't like what I see, I'll blow you apart."

Then he trained the sawed-off at the barber. "You, too, little . . ." He sighed and lowered the shotgun. "Never mind. You'd just get in the way."

Duncan felt like the tiniest man in the world—he had seen one of those at Doris's Big Dime Museum when he was in New York City some years back, though he had liked the trained polar seals better. The monster sea serpent and the leopard boy had looked fake to him.

It was a tight fit. The two giants beside him almost pushed his own arms out of the shoulder sockets. After bending their knees, the biggest of the brutes counted again, slower this time, as though that would give them more strength.

"Yksi . . .

"Kaksi . . .

"Kolme!"

Duncan tried. Tried hard. He never considered himself a weakling, but he sure didn't have the muscles of most of the men who tried to budge Nugget's heavy discovery.

If the Liberty Bell of Zinc moved a fraction of an inch off the rug upon which it sat on the floor, that would have been something.

They gave up after maybe ten seconds of straining, grunting, and sweating.

By now, Duncan figured, the widow Purington and the banker Filmore would have alerted Winston DeMint about the ongoing attempt to rob the bank. DeMint would have been smart enough not to tell Nugget, but he would have found Logan Ladron. Maybe Percy Stahl. Dylan Pugh if he was around. They wouldn't have had time to send someone on horseback up the slope to the mining camp and bring back the best of the lot. They'd give up on trying to find Syd Jones.

They would have enough men who knew how to shoot and were probably throwing barricades in the street to cut off the gang's escape route.

He looked through what had been an expensive and large window.

But if that was the case, why were there so many people standing across the street? He couldn't blame Syd Jones, still likely somewhere in that abandoned, falling-apart building. Jones was waiting for the right time to make his play. Or was he?

"Again!" the Haden brother barked. "You help, too, this time, Marcus!"

The extra pair of hands did nothing to change the fact that the Haden boys were about a dozen or more men short of ever getting this big rock out of the bank and into that big wagon's bed.

The straining, grunting, cussing, and farting stopped again. The lifters tried to catch their breath.

"This . . . stupid!" one of the leviathans grumbled.

Nick Haden eased his horse up close to the boardwalk. "What's stupid is us waitin' around here. We should've been out of this dung heap of a town ten minutes ago."

"We're not leaving," the young Haden leader snapped, "till we've got that fortune in zinc on that wagon."

The rider spat, then swore. He vaguely pointed down the street. "Well, maybe you can get this stampede of kids to help you." The horse started to buck, but one of the Hadens stopped that, and backed the animal up, snapping, "Watch out, lady!"

That's when the face of the milliner appeared.

"Marshal," she said, "what on earth is going on here?"

Two of the brutes straightened and removed their hats.

Duncan also stopped trying to massage his creaking spine. He cleared his throat. The lie came to him quickly— maybe too fast—but he wanted to get rid of her before things got ugly. *Uglier,* he corrected. This situation was getting to feel more like that job he had hauling nitro-glycerin after that cave-in in Durango some years back.

Constance Turner made great hats. At least that's what Sara kept telling him. Duncan got his hats straight from the John B. Stetson operation—as did most of the men he knew. Miss Turner's hats looked great on Sara, though. She was an artist when it came to design. Well, Sara thought so, anyway, and Miss Turner had remained loyal to Dead Broke. After a fire burned down Jansen's bank before Duncan had arrived in Dead Broke, the flames destroyed Constance Turner's shop, too—and all those hats she had created, putting her own spin on hats she had seen from as far away as London and Paris.

He swept his battered old hat off his head and thought up the first lie that came to him.

"I'm sorry, Miss Turner. We're just following the mayor's orders. He wants his nugget—I mean, his zinc bell . . . ummmmm . . . right beside his Diamond Nugget of Silver again. Pair them up. You see."

She didn't see. She asked: "But what about the children?"

Duncan blinked. He wanted this lovely lady to get out of here quickly. He knew this was a keg of dynamite awaiting that one little spark.

"Children?" he asked in almost a whisper.

She pointed down the street.

"Yes. The schoolchildren. Miss Hereford is bringing them down the street right this very minute—just as Mayor Nugget told her to do."

Miss Hereford. The schoolmarm. She had replaced that old man who had gotten fed up with Dead Broke and miners' children and living way up in the middle of nowhere a while back.

Nick Haden yelled, "That's what I've been tellin' y'all! There's a stampede of kids about halfway down the street—comin' right at us."

The Haden in charge snarled, then let a wicked grin crease his face.

"Those kids. They'll get us out of town. Forget that shiny rock, boys. We'll rob this town of everything else. And those kids will be the key to us making this trip uphill pay us what we came for." He snorted out a laugh. "And them kids will get us off this mountain safe."

Constance Turner's face paled.

"Grab her, Fin!" the Haden leader barked.

The big brute—the one who did the counting before the lifting—moved fast, and pulled Constance Turner through the opening, his thick shoes cracking the shards of glass on the floor. She tried to scream, but his rough hand clamped hard and covered almost the woman's entire face.

Duncan now figured that this punk who was barking all the orders had to be Jim Bob Haden, though he had always thought the boss of this outlaw gang was older and nowhere near as ruthless as this savage little piece of swine.

"And you, Mister Marshal, are gonna make sure nothin' goes wrong. Ain't that right?"

CHAPTER 21

There wasn't much Duncan could do. Not at that moment, anyway.

Jim Bob Haden took Constance Turner from the big brute, put his arm around her waist, and pulled her tightly against his body. He braced the double-barreled shotgun's stock against her slim waist and pointed those two cavernous barrels right at Duncan's midsection. Haden held the shotgun with his right hand, but his left had pulled Duncan's Schofield, and he managed to cock the pistol without much effort. That weapon he pointed just a few inches from the hatmaker's temple.

"How much blood gets spilt, lawman, is gonna be on your hands," the swine snorted.

"All right." Duncan didn't hesitate. "But the first thing that needs to be done—"

"I'm giving the orders, lawdog!"

Duncan drew in a deep breath, exhaled slowly, and put his hands on his hips. "Then give them. Go ahead. Kill me." He nodded at the pretty woman before him. "Kill her." His head tilted toward the little barber. "And go ahead and carve another notch into your pistol's handle and shoot down that little barber."

He straightened. "And see just how far any of you boys make it out of Dead Broke."

The seconds slowed to what felt like hours, but Duncan saw how Jim Bob's face had paled.

Duncan let out a soft chuckle. "I don't think any of you will live long enough to get off that boardwalk."

"Jim Bob," Marcus Haden whispered slowly, pleadingly.

The outlaw didn't have much time to spare. His head nodded quickly, but he tried to sound tough, like he remained in command, when he said, "All right. You just get that street cleared. Or you are out of a fine-looking little thing of a dressmaker."

"Hatmaker," Duncan corrected, turned, and walked through the bank's doors.

"You," he said to one of the men with a shotgun. "Fire a round from that cannon. In the air."

The man frowned.

"Do it!"

The man obeyed. The shotgun roared, and moments later, the pellets rained down on the roofs of nearby buildings. But that peal of thunder got the crowd's attention.

He cupped his hands over his mouth. "Everybody!" He repeated that three or four times. "Stop what you're doing and stand still." He sighed and glanced at the outlaw with the smoking scattergun.

"Again!" he ordered.

"Again?" the man asked with suspicion.

"Do what he says!" Nick Haden bellowed before his brother could approve or reject Duncan's order.

The second barrel boomed.

That weapon, Duncan logged in his brain, was now empty. He had to keep it that way.

"All right," he told the outlaws on the street, in the

doorway to the bank, and those standing in front of that Liberty Bell of Zinc, which Duncan wished he had never seen. He pointed in the direction of the schoolchildren.

"Kids. There has been a bit of confusion. So I want you to follow your sweet teacher and go back to the school-house."

He heard a mix of whining and crying and saw a lot of pouting.

"Wait a minute!" the Haden leader shouted. "That ain't—"

Duncan kept barking out orders.

"Don't worry, children! Mayor Nugget is going to bring his Liberty Bell of Zinc to the schoolhouse later this week or early next week. Maybe even tomorrow."

He wondered if tomorrow was a school day. For the life of him, he couldn't remember what day it was. Well, it wasn't Sunday. He knew that much.

The schoolteacher must have sensed the imminent danger, as did a couple of the parents of kids who had been coaxed by her to come help her herd those little scamps. Duncan thought he saw Little Joey Clarke helping the adults get the kids turned around. They were marching— reluctantly, not singing, not shouting—back toward the schoolhouse. But at least they were getting farther out of range for any bullets that were likely to be flying at any moment.

So that was one good mark in Duncan's favor when he found himself standing at those pearly gates.

"We need those kids as hostages!" the punk shouted.

The rest of the crowd—the adults—might prove to be a little harder to persuade. But Duncan was ready.

"Gents," he said, "I've got some good news for you fel-lows." He pointed down the street. "Percy Stahl says for the next thirty minutes, the beer is on the house at his place."

That got rid of half the men. The rest—most of them, anyway—weren't exactly teetotalers, but they were good men, and they had been in Dead Broke through the glory days, the bloody days, and now the big depression. And they knew something was bad wrong on this part of town, on this particular day.

His eyes stopped on Max McClintock.

"Max," he said softly.

"Marshal," the peddler said, nodding his head.

"Think you can do a big favor for me?"

The man nodded in silence.

"Take the rest of these men up to the mayor's house." That was about as safe a place as any Duncan could think of at the moment. He now wished he had thought to send the students, their teacher, and the chaperones to Chasm Park.

McClintock stared, wet his lips, eyed the ruffians in front of the busted-up bank, and then looked back at Duncan.

"That what you want?" he asked.

Duncan nodded. "That's what I want."

"All right." He sighed and turned around. "Come on, boys. The first round of Nugget's brew will be my treat."

And now they were walking away. Duncan couldn't believe how well his luck had held. Well, luck for those innocent citizens. He still hadn't figured out a way that he could get out of this pickle alive.

But all that remained—on the side of innocent lives— were a few stragglers on the boardwalks.

He cupped his hands over his mouth again and started shouting: "Folks! Folks! You good citizens, I need you to follow these orders without question or pause. It's for your own safety. I want you to go inside the nearest building, whichever one's the closest. When the last person is inside, I want someone to close the door, and then everyone should lie flat on the floor and cover your heads."

The women were quick to obey. The men hesitated.

Arnie Stillman yelled back: "What on earth for, Marshal?"

Duncan decided to give him an honest answer.

"So you'll have a better chance of living to see tomorrow."

That seemed to work. In fact, the people cleared the streets quicker than he had thought they would. Doors shut. Some of the shades were pulled down, but most of the folks followed his orders just the way he had given them. They didn't mess with any shades or curtains. They closed the door and hit the floor.

Suddenly, the street was empty—except for the ruffians standing in front of the new bank. Slowly, Duncan turned around and saw Jim Bob Haden, who was grinning the biggest smile that didn't hold an ounce of humor. Constance Turner still stood in front of him. The brutes remained near the Liberty Bell of Zinc. The outlaws hadn't climbed aboard the horses. They were waiting for the leader to bark the next order. The little barber was pushed out of the bank by Marcus Haden, who pressed a revolver barrel against the frightened man's temple.

"What about the zinc?" Rufus Haden called out.

"Leave it," Jim Bob said. He lowered the shotgun and Duncan's Schofield.

"Mount up, boys," he said. "We'll ride out fast and furious." He shoved the hatmaker toward the hitch rail. "I'm afraid, little darlin', that you'll have to come along with us. But don't worry. We'll be gentle. And we'll likely turn you loose when we're a mile lower."

"Take her, Fin. Put her in the back of the wagon. At least we'll have something of value to take out of this dead broke town." He laughed. "It's sure earned its name this fine day."

One of the cousins was guarding the little bartender.

"What about this one, Jim Bob?" he called out.

"Squash him like a bug." Jim Bob Haden was walking toward Duncan. "But not until I send this big lawdog to shake hands with the devil . . . with his own pistol."

Shoving the shotgun into his left hand and pulling the .45 from his waistband with his right, the leader of the outlaws kept walking.

Sighing, Duncan slid his hands into the pockets of his coat.

"No hard feelings, lawman," Jim Bob Haden said as he walked toward Duncan. Then called out, "Rivers, fetch me my hoss. And get ready to ride hard. Hard and fast. Shoot anyone that shows his head. Or her head."

He kept walking, his smile widening as he neared Duncan. Ten yards. Nine. Eight.

"Got any last words, Marshal?" Jim Bob asked.

Flame and smoke erupted from the right-side pocket of Duncan's coat, and Jim Bob Haden dropped to his knees, the Schofield slipping from his fingers, the shotgun falling into the dirt. Duncan pulled out the derringer—the .41-caliber Remington—the banker had given him.

The words Mr. Filmore had said earlier came back to Duncan clearly—or as clear as they could with gunfire resuming on this street in Dead Broke.

"It's not much, Marshal, but it's loaded."

He bolted forward. He had to get that Schofield. He didn't think he could hit the cousin who was about to slice the little barber's throat with the derringer, but that .45 would do the job.

But as he ran, as Jim Bob Haden, blood gushing from the center of his chest and leaking from a corner of his mouth, fell facedown into the street, he saw Gaudenzio spin quickly, and the barber had been hiding a weapon himself. The razor slashed forward, the cousin dropped his weapon and reached for his throat, as blood sprayed like a geyser.

The little fellow dropped his razor and swiped the weapon from the dying cousin's hand.

A rifle roared, and another outlaw went flying from his saddle. Syd Jones had been waiting for what had to feel like eternity for a man like him, but now his rifle kept roaring, and the old man's skill with a repeating rifle was as sharp as it had been back in those cow town days.

Duncan had his Schofield now. The big brute Fin was charging. Duncan knelt, pressing a knee on Jim Bob Haden's back—not that the punk could feel anything now, except Lucifer's hot breath.

He aimed at the charging behemoth, but didn't get to pull the trigger. Syd Jones had fired again, and, big as he was, tough as he was, Fin was no match for a .44 slug into his forehead.

Suddenly, Duncan saw men rising from the bank's roof. His Schofield came up, but quickly lowered. It was the banker himself—and even the widow Purington—and two or three other men. Duncan recognized Logan Ladron and Winston DeMint. He would have to compliment all of them later, because no one had heard them on the roof while they were inside that bank.

It was over in a minute. Most of the fight, anyway. Or would be, as soon as Duncan and Syd Jones stopped

Constance Turner from kicking the other Haden cousin in front of the big wagon the outlaws had backed up to Dead Broke's new bank.

This street was filled again with the citizens of Dead Broke. The merchants brought plenty of ropes to tie up the surviving outlaws, who had been captured. Doc Aimé Cartier came by to declare the dead and to work, somewhat leisurely, on the wounded outlaws.

Gaudenzio became Doc Cartier's assistant, and he was so busy, Duncan could not thank the little barber for all of his help. But he would make sure he did tomorrow morning. No, that might have to wait until tomorrow afternoon. He had some business he needed to get straightened out—but even that pressing emergency would have to wait.

That was the problem with gunfights. A lawman had to make careful reports on what he had witnessed, and he had witnessed a lot—and this was one gunfight that was a lot more complicated than . . . well . . . practically any other fight Duncan had been in.

"Nugget!" he yelled.

People looked around like he was crazy.

He found Syd Jones, asking one of those Goliaths questions about where they came from, how long they had known the Haden Gang, how much was supposed to be their cut.

"Where's Nugget?" Duncan demanded.

Syd Jones looked up with a heavy frown. "I haven't seen him."

Duncan turned, cupped his hands, and yelled, "Where's Nugget?"

"He's probably at his mine," someone suggested.

"Percy!" Duncan had found someone else.

Percy Stahl was tightening some rope around another

one of those strongmen's hands. He pulled the ends of the rope tighter and looked around the giant's side.

"Yeah?"

"Have you seen Nugget?"

"Not today." He nodded toward the mountains. "Likely at his mine."

Which is what everybody had been telling Duncan since he started asking about the mayor.

"All right," Duncan said. "Leave that owlhoot alone. I want you to ride up the slope and you find that scoundrel and you bring his butt down that mountain and to me."

Percy Stahl wasn't much of a brawler, and he had a modicum of respect for a marshal's badge, but he wasn't an idiot.

"Ain't no way I am bringing anybody—not even myself—down that hill in the dead of night."

The sun was sinking now, and the dark came quickly and blacker than pitch at this time of year.

Syd Jones cleared his throat. That was a warning to Duncan that he still remembered. Maybe Duncan realized how crazy he was acting now.

He nodded. His voice softened, but only in volume. The tension, the tightness, the explosiveness, remained.

"All right. First thing in the morning."

Stahl nodded.

Some semblance of peace returned to Dead Broke—for that moment.

To Duncan's surprise, none of Dead Broke's citizens came away with any serious injuries.

That, he knew, was pure luck.

Duncan himself just had a few scratches, though later that evening, Sara would poke holes through his coat where bullets had gone through.

"You're the luckiest man I've ever known," she told him.

He shrugged. "In gunfights, maybe. But you beat me in cards often enough."

She didn't want to, but she couldn't stop the sly smile.

"Well," she said, "it's over. And nobody in Dead Broke was badly injured."

Duncan reached over for a bottle of bourbon and poured himself a shot.

"Oh, it's not over," he said. "Not until I have a few words with our good mayor."

Sara did not like that look in her lover's eyes.

CHAPTER 22

When word came up the slope about the attempted robbery, Nugget rushed down—at least as fast as the burro could carry him over that rough trail. Fearing the worst, he was relieved to see that his Liberty Bell of Zinc was, for the most part, unharmed. A few pieces of zinc might have been chipped off by bullets and some rough handling, but it still looked like a bell, and those bullet creases would add, the mayor figured, to the stone's overall value.

He thought of a new promotion: *The Liberty Bell of Zinc That Ended the Reign of the Haden Gang.*

That had to increase his treasure's value.

Why, folks from all over town—and even several independent miners from up the slope—were coming by to see the carnage and that massive yet beautiful discovery of Nugget's. Free, no less, and that made Nugget a trifle mad, but someone said it was free publicity, which couldn't hurt. It would likely bring in more folks to see what all the fuss was about. Nugget sure liked publicity. He'd have to figure something out.

The new banker told him what had happened, and apologized, as if the Haden bunch was all his fault, and Nugget tried to be gentle with the newcomer to his town, but said he would likely have to end the public viewing of the Liberty Bell of Zinc, since anyone could come by now and steal or ruin his monumental discovery.

But, at least for the moment, the treasure was safe. The banker had hired six men to stand guard over the zinc masterpiece, two per eight-hour shifts.

"Shoot on sight?" Nugget asked.

After a long hesitation, the banker just said that the stone would be protected at all costs.

All costs. Nugget nodded. "That's mighty fine," he said, thinking, but not saying, *As long as all those costs is comin' out of your pocket.* Nugget's own guards could remain protecting his Diamond Nugget of Silver.

Word quickly reached him that Duncan was looking for him, and Nugget started for the marshal's office, but all that worrying about his fortune made him thirsty, so he stopped to quench his thirst at Percy Stahl's grog shop—and after all that stress worrying over his newest, greatest discovery, and that rough ride on a burro with a hard gait, he needed a couple of beers after that first one.

Unfortunately for Nugget, word also reached Duncan MacMicking that Nugget was not only in town, but was drinking at Percy Stahl's place. Duncan made a beeline for the groggery and found Dead Broke's mayor reaching for his third pilsner. Nugget's right hand didn't quite reach the stein when Duncan jerked him away from the bar.

His left hand gripped the thin man's beard—and Percy and a small-time miner, who was having a late breakfast of beer, groaned at how much that must have hurt, yanking a man by the beard a good two or three feet. The miner, of course, was quite happy because Nugget did not spill the beer, and the stein, which hadn't even been touched, was in easy reach.

"Put those on Nugget's tab, Percy!"

That's all the marshal said before he started out of the building, pulling the rail-thin man behind him, and Percy and the miner cringed. *That has to hurt.*

Pushing through the batwing doors, Duncan pulled Nugget right behind him. They crossed the street at an angle, found the boardwalk, Duncan moving like a freight train and Nugget stumbling along behind like the caboose.

The streets weren't that crowded at this time of day—and most of the folks were still gazing at the bank a few blocks down—but those that saw this spectacle stared with open mouths, but no words. Not even whispers (at least until they were sure that the marshal couldn't hear them).

It is doubtful that Duncan could have heard anything because of Nugget's pitiful cries. He yelped like a kicked puppy dog.

A few people gasped. Widow McClurg burst into tears. Little Hamilton Eslinger, playing hooky again, started singing a ditty he made up on the spot.

> *Shave! Shave!*
> *Mayor gets a shave.*
> *He sure will look different.*
> *When the marshal puts him in his grave.*

Outside of his new hardware store, Walter Steckmesser told Doc Cartier that the Eslinger boy sure had talent. The good doctor nodded in agreement, though he was just being polite to the newcomer to Dead Broke.

Had Nugget stumbled and fallen, there was a better than middling chance that a handful of beard and some skin on the chin would have been torn off. And that probably would have happened had Duncan pulled the wiry little mayor all the way to the town marshal's office, but Duncan wasn't that mean—or, more than likely, he just didn't want to go that far before giving Nugget a tongue-lashing.

So the two men disappeared through the doors of the Crosscut Saloon—and that early in the day, even Logan Ladron hadn't shown up, because he had been dealing till three in the morning. Nothing like a bank robbery attempt to send working folks from all walks of life into a saloon to drink and try their luck.

As Dylan Pugh had astutely observed: "After seeing a bunch of dead bank robbers, folks figure their luck has to be better than that of any of the Haden Gang's."

Pugh, at least, broke even in Sara's poker game, and got to bed before midnight.

Duncan stopped a few feet from the bar, then, still gripping Nugget's beard, flung the skinny fellow against the bar. The mayor's yelp and the crashing of a couple of glasses that remained on the bar—neither broke—caused Sara to rush out of her upstairs room.

The cook, who was sweeping near the far wall, calmly stopped her chores, leaned the broom against a table, and walked into the back room, closing the door behind her.

Nugget turned around, pushing up his beard as if to keep his chin from falling to the floor. Tears were in his eyes, and he stood there, trembling all the way up his body.

Sara stopped at the balustrade, caught her breath, and somehow managed to choke back the curse on her tongue, then ran down the stairs. She might have realized that she was still wearing just her nightgown and hadn't even put on slippers. If so, she just didn't care.

"Duncan!" she yelled. "What on earth—"

But the lawman didn't hear a thing. He took four steps

toward the cowering mayor and raised his right hand. It was balled into a fist, and Sara, now on the floor, and coming around the tables and chairs toward the only two other people in the saloon, feared the worst.

"I am sick and tired," Duncan began, "of that zinc ball of trouble." He waved his fist at the mayor.

"Ain't my fault. . . ." Nugget was pleading. "Didn't expect no bank robbers comin' for my great discovery."

That wasn't exactly what Nugget said. No one could really understand anything he mumbled and sobbed and gasped, but if those words aren't exactly accurate, it was what the mayor meant to say.

"Duncan . . ." Sara tried the peaceful approach.

If he heard her, which she doubted, he didn't look her way.

"It's 'em bank robbers' fault," Nugget said, and this time, the words came out clearer.

"It's not the Hadens that have me ready to stomp you till you look like a cockroach run over by a herd of wild mustangs," Duncan said. His face was redder than that silk dress he liked so much to see on Sara.

"I get paid to stop men like those punks. I don't like it. But it's part of my job."

He paused, and Sara thought he might be about to calm himself.

No luck.

"It was bad enough that all those punk kids started coming to Dead Broke. Trying to match Ben's and my so-called prowess with a six-shooter. You don't have any idea what it's like to go face down some fool who thinks he's greased lightning with a .45. You don't know what that's like at all. Yeah, I know. I look like I'm all brave and strong and not worried about a thing, but that's a front. To put fear into whoever it is I'm facing. Give me just a bit of an edge. And, well, here I am. Still alive. Not too many holes in my body."

He stopped long enough to catch his breath and shake his head.

"But it sure drove Ben Usher out of town. And that's a loss for Dead Broke. For you. For me." He even gestured toward Sara. "And for her."

Which meant that he knew she was here. That was something.

"And somehow—by the grace of God—we got through that. Ben's alive. I'm alive. And we didn't even have to kill some kid with a chip on his shoulder or wanting to prove to himself that he was a man. A miracle."

He stepped closer to the cowering mayor, lowering his fists now, and his voice, his chest heaving. He didn't stop until he stood inches from Nugget.

"And then you go and discover another freak of the mining business." His head shook. "A giant six-ton chunk of zinc. And, of course, some men figure they can steal it." His right hand touched the butt of his Schofield. "And I didn't even mind stopping those fools who tried to take that big rock from you up near the mine. Because that was my job, too. But . . ."

His left hand flashed toward the doors that had stopped flapping back and forth.

"But . . . but . . . but what happened at the bank. That's what has riled me, pardner. That's why I'm trying to stop myself from stomping you into something no one will recognize."

Nugget had started to sob. Sara even felt tears beginning to well in her own eyes.

"Those schoolchildren, and their teacher, and some mothers who came to help out. They were walking right toward that bank. All those boys and girls. All those fine folks—not to mention the other innocent bystanders. Walking right into a ring of fire." His voice dropped into something that was part whisper, part plea for help.

"They could've been killed, Nugget. Don't you realize that? They could've been killed. Badly wounded. Scarred for the rest of their lives." He stopped, wet his lips, and shook his head.

"Is that what you want? Little Joey Clarke. Your buddy. The boy who reads you those storybooks. The kid who worships you. He was walking with his schoolmates, his friends. Joey, Nugget. Little Joey. He could have been hit by a bullet. Wounded. Or shot dead in the streets before his thirteenth birthday."

His head shook again.

The next words Sara had to strain to hear.

"Is that what you want, Nugget? Is it? Because it came this close . . ." He held his thumb and forefinger up with just a bit of air between the tips. "This close . . . from happening."

Nugget started bawling then, like a newborn just spanked by the midwife. Sara moved again, straight for that skinny old reprobate, giving Duncan a glaring look, and then grabbing Nugget's left arm and steering him toward her table.

"There, there, Nugget. It's all right."

"I didn't . . ." He choked, snorted, bawled a bit more.

"It's all right, Nugget. It's all right." She used her left foot to drag out a chair, and then eased the mayor into the seat.

"Wouldn't do . . . nothin' . . . to get . . . Little Joey . . . hurt. Or any of 'em sweet little kiddos." He rubbed his eyes, cried hard again, and shook his head. "That boy . . . is special. . . ." The tears flowed like spring runoff.

"Who'd read to me if he got hisself hurt. He reads . . . He reads . . . just fine."

"I know." Sara found the chair beside him and put her arm over his shoulder. "It's all right."

"Poor Little Joey," Nugget said.

"Joey's all right." And, knowing that boy, Duncan figured the kid and all those other boys were still talking, exaggerating, telling each other how close to danger they had been, what they had seen, what they hadn't seen, but wished they had seen. Maybe even pouting that they hadn't gotten a chance to get even closer before the shooting—the real shooting—started. And what they would have done had they been there.

Sara raised her head just high enough to give Duncan that look.

Then she pulled the crazy old coot close and let him sob on her shoulder as she patted the mayor's back.

Duncan held his hands still, and looked at them shaking. He sighed then, and let his fingers ball into fists. That didn't help him much, so he shoved them into his pants pockets, and moved down the bar, to the opening, and he went behind the big, expensive, ornate piece of mahogany. He dipped below, found the jug of Nugget's favorite, and rose. He fetched a bottle of Irish whiskey off the back-bar—it was the closest one to him—and came around the bar and walked to the table, setting Nugget's jug in front of him, then putting the bottle on the table near Sara.

He hadn't gotten any glasses. Well, he had only two hands, and they were still shaking so hard he wasn't sure how he had even managed to get the liquor to the table. He thought about walking back to the bar and bringing back the glassware. But the way he felt, he wasn't sure he could make it there and back without collapsing. He did manage to drag out another chair and drop into it.

Sara kept stroking the mayor's hair.

Sitting on the other side of Nugget, Duncan pulled the cork from the jug and nodded.

"Have a drink, Mayor," he said in a voice he couldn't recognize as his own. "Go ahead. It's all right."

He set the cork on the table and took the bottle of whiskey, removing that cork, too. But he just left the bottle on the table. He wasn't a man to drink at this time of morning. Then he jammed his elbows atop the fine felt, and let his chin fall into his palms and his fingers touched the stubble on both sides of his face. He hadn't gotten a wink of sleep last night. Too busy writing up statements from witnesses, signing papers, sending telegrams to the U.S. marshal in Denver, hoping the messages would get to him, and looking over the bodies of the dead men.

He wondered if the Haden family up in Larimer County would come down to claim the bodies. Or had they disowned their children? He knew he should stand up, walk out. There was plenty to do. There was always a ton of work, and a lot of mess to clean up, after a bank robbery. After a gunfight in the streets.

His head shook. The newspaper reporters would be flocking to Dead Broke again. More writings about the town known for violence—and the town marshal who seemed to know nothing but gunplay—would spread across the state, the country, the world.

What he wouldn't give to get out of Dead Broke for a month of Sundays.

CHAPTER 23

Duncan didn't hear the batwing doors creak open, then stop. He just stared at the table now. He didn't even hear the doors banging, or the footsteps, and he wasn't sure how long Logan Ladron was standing at the table before he noticed the gambler.

Their eyes held, then Logan shot a glance at the mayor. The stare returned to Duncan, then moved to Logan's boss lady.

Finally, he looked away and whispered, "Let me make us all some good, strong coffee." He disappeared, and Duncan just sat there until the smell of coffee—strong coffee—brought him out of this trance he had fallen into.

Ladron poured four cups and put the pot on a board he had brought over to keep it off the felt table, though there were plenty of stains, coffee, whiskey, blood, on it already.

Duncan didn't remember drinking the first two cups. But halfway through his third, he returned to becoming a living, productive member of society.

"Thanks," he told Sara. He then looked at Ladron. "Thanks."

At length, he looked at Nugget, who was drinking

coffee, not liquor, himself. Once the mayor had set the cup down and wiped his mouth, Duncan pushed back his chair, rose, and stood over Nugget.

The mayor looked up. The whites of his eyes seemed completely red.

Duncan held out his right hand—and it wasn't holding his Schofield.

"I'm sorry, Mayor," Duncan said. "I blew my temper. You didn't bring the Haden Gang to Dead Broke. They came on their own. I just . . . well . . . I guess I reached a point where I just broke. If you want to fire me, I'll understand."

Nugget sniffled. "Can't fire you, Marshal. You does too good of a job."

They shook hands. Duncan sat back in the chair. His eyes met Sara's gaze.

"Apologies to you, too."

"Accepted," she said.

They emptied that pot, and Ladron made another. They all visited the privy—not at the same time, but not very far apart—and Ladron asked if he should make another pot. Every head nodded. So they sat there for ten minutes in silence.

Finally, the mayor said, "So what is it that we oughts to do?"

Sara shook her head, and her voice was nothing but a whisper. "I don't know."

"I could taken me a sledgehammer and bust that Liberty Bell of Zinc into nothin' but dust," Nugget suggested.

"No," Duncan said, "don't do that."

That troublesome chunk of color was bringing new life to what had been a dying mountain town. Well, it had brought its share of death, too. The Diamond Nugget of Silver had done the same thing over the years, but if Duncan remembered correctly, that had started early— when that huge but beautiful piece of silver was being written about in newspapers around the world. Outlaws came riding in, got shot down, and the rare statue of silver eventually became more of a tourist attraction. Oh, outlaws or idiots came in every now and then to try to steal it. And the late Conner Boyle had tried to make off with it— with fatal consequences.

"I'm glad you've cooled off," Sara said softly.

Duncan looked at her. He tried to smile, but wasn't certain if he had pulled it off. "So am I. Been a long time since I lost my temper that much."

"Town's still standing," Ladron said.

Sara reached over and squeezed Nugget's nearest hand. "It's all right, Nugget. We'll figure something out."

"Maybe folks will start coming to Dead Broke for a new reason," Ladron attempted.

"Like what?"

The silence lasted half a minute.

"Well," the dealer tried, "I guess some will want to see where the Haden Gang's reign of terror ended."

The way Duncan figured things, the first reporters would arrive on the next stage. The Haden Gang wasn't anywhere near as well known—or feared—as the Wild Bunch. They didn't have the same value as the old James-Younger Gang or the Reno brothers. And the Daltons had met their end—except for one brother now in prison—a year ago in Coffeyville, Kansas. Duncan wondered if people flocked to Coffeyville to see the bullet holes in the bank and the spots where bank robbers had died.

"What we need," Sara said, "is a . . . I don't know

how to call it . . . but a break. A time so that things could cool off."

"That's out of our hands," Duncan said, but thought on that a bit. "Isn't it?"

Sara shrugged.

They thought some more, drank more coffee. Somehow, plates of food wound up on the table, and they all ate—though hardly any of them remembered eating, and certainly none of them could recollect what they had for lunch.

It being in the afternoon, they soon realized they were sipping whiskey, still thinking, still sitting for the most part, though one or two of them would stand and walk around and almost come up with an idea that might work, but rejecting it before even saying what they had been thinking.

They had come to another impasse, though, and had been silently waiting for someone to come up with a crackerjack of an idea when Little Joey Clarke raced inside the saloon.

"Joey!" Nugget shouted, and Duncan felt like a real human being again when he saw the childlike glee in the mayor's eyes.

Sara started to push herself out of her chair. "Joseph Clarke! Why aren't you in school, young man?"

"'Cause school's over for the day," the boy said.

Sara looked at the clock.

"Oh." She sank back into her chair. "Glory . . . where has the time gone?"

"You shouldn't be in a saloon," Duncan said.

"I ain't gonna drink no whiskey," the boy whined.

"Don't say 'ain't,'" Nugget told him. "It ain't proper."

"You ought to go home," Ladron suggested.

"I am. Well, I was. First me and Artie and Malcolm and even Cindy Lou was—were—going to go touch the Liberty Bell of Zinc." He glanced at Nugget. "Not hard. Not gonna leave a scratch or nothing on it. Just to see it. But Artie, all he wanted to do was keep talking about yesterday, you know, telling us how close he had been to danger. That's a lie. That Artie can tell some whoppers. And even Cindy Lou was saying what all she'd seen. But Malcolm said that he saw even more—and sure wished he hadn't seen what he did. And Artie said he wished all of us had gotten a chance to get closer before the shooting—you know, the real shooting started. And then they were all bragging about what they would have done had you"— he nodded at Duncan—"not made us all turn around and run like we was cowards." He sighed. "Well, I reckon I was just a little scared when all that shooting started."

Duncan scratched his head. He seemed to recall most of what the Clarke boy had said. Somewhere. Sometime.

"But, anyway, before we could get to the bank—I found this." He held up a newspaper. "Have y'all seen it?"

He slapped the paper on the poker table.

It was a Chicago newspaper. Two weeks old.

"Where'd you find that?" Ladron asked.

"It was blowing across the street. It's not the whole paper. The wind took two of the pages with it over that new barbershop. I thought I'd bring it to our teacher. You know, she collects papers from the stagecoach drivers now and then. Makes us read some of the articles so we'll know how to read better and know what's happening in some civilized part of the country. She likes to say 'civilized' lots."

"Probably misses it," Sara whispered.

"I thought she might not make me wash the chalkboard after school if I brung her a good newspaper that had something interesting for her to read us—and maybe not make us read it ourselves."

Duncan sighed. "Don't tell me it has something about the Liberty Bell of Zinc in it."

"No. But it's got our good friend Mr. Usher in it," the boy said.

He tapped a small headline at the far upper right.

Duncan slid the newspaper to him, turned it around, and started reading. He started to read it to himself, but Nugget said, "Read it to me. I'm pards with Ben Usher, too." He nodded around the room. "We all is."

Fair enough, Duncan thought. He slid the newspaper back to Little Joey.

"You do us the honors, Joey," Duncan said.

The kid frowned. "Do I have to?" he said with a pout.

"Yes," Sara told him.

So Joey read.

Our trusty correspondent has returned to see what's new at the World's Columbian Exposition—or as more people call it, the Chicago World's Fair—as it enters its last month of an extraordinary run.

Some of the buildings are in as fine a shape as they were in May—still fresh—while others have the bite and look of winter, especially when the mists of autumn rise off of Lake Michigan and bring that foreboding chill and dampness. Yet the Administration Building still showcases its grandness, rivaling—nay, topping—the Pantheon in Athens..

"Isn't the Panthéon in Paris?" Logan Ladron whispered.

"I think they're all over," Duncan said.

"There're two," Sara said. "But neither is in Athens."

"Shhhhh." Nugget glared. "Don't interrupt the boy."

Nodding, Little Joey resumed his reading. *He reads quite well,* Duncan thought.

Nugget, of course, knew that already.

I marvel at towering Illinois Hall.

The crowd is like nothing I have seen, or ever could have imagined.

Seven hundred thousand people—from all of our states and territories, and visitors from too many countries to name—have paid half a dollar and moved through the exhibition's turnstiles. I have seen the villages of the Natives near the Midway Plaisance. I have seen remarkable sights—and not one drunken Illinoisian—jewels of exquisite beauty . . . precious stones—gold, silver, wonderful jewels, treasures from Paris, the best of good, English china—treasures that would have even been the envy of the mighty Aladdin.

A change can be seen each and every hour. Glorious marvels are seen on every corner, in every exhibit. What you shan't see anywhere in this exhibition is dust. It is all glorious. Statues of bronze. Of stone. Wonders of food that never has an American tasted. Glittering pinnacles. Gold and silk.

But the biggest, greatest, and most wonderful exhibit I find is . . . yes, I speak the truth—outside of the gates of this magnificent exhibition. For I have paid another admission fee and stepped into the marvelous world of the Wild West of that grand American hero, William F. Cody—known to the world—and the World's Fair—as "Buffalo Bill."

*And it is here that I have the great fortune to
witness the shooting ability of that heroic lawman
who tamed most of our Wild West, including most
recently in a Colorado mining town called Dead
Broke—what wit, what life, what a joyful name for
a great city of immense wealth.*

*Most likely you know the name. It instills fear
and respect for the law.*

*He is faster than Wild Bill Hickok—he is also,
unlike, that great gunfighter . . . ALIVE—and his
hair is not as long as his employee, the magnificent
Buffalo Bill—and he is handsome and courageous,
but not as brave as I.*

His name is . . . Ben Usher.

"Let me see that," Duncan said.

Joey turned the paper and slid it toward Duncan, the
pointer finger saving his place.

Duncan chuckled. "That old sharper." His head bobbed.
"Ben Usher. Glory be. In a Wild West show competing
with the World's Fair."

"Not just any Wild Hoss thing," Nugget said. "Buffalo
Bill's. That's a good one. Never seen it. But if it's Buffalo Bill's, it has to be top-notch."

Joey kept reading. There wasn't much more.

*For it is I who lights a cigarette and stands
twenty-five paces from the deadly Mr. Usher.*

*"It's harder to hit the cigarette and not your lip
if you shake too much," Mr. Usher tells me.*

*That does not make me feel any better. He
puts his left hand on my shoulder, and gives it a
firm squeeze.*

"I'm just joshing, my friend." He walks away.
"Haven't hit a man's jaw since yesterday."

Everyone laughs. Everyone, I mean, except me.

"One," a beautiful woman in fine silk calls out.
"Two."

And the "Three" and the massive BOOM sound
as one, and the light at the tip of my hand-rolled
smoke disappears.

The applause could have drowned out all the
noise from the World's Fair just across the street.
Or so I am told. For my ears ring from the
thunderous explosion for Ben Usher's revolver and
my own pounding heart and perhaps even my
prayer of thanks to the benevolent God who made
Ben Usher's aim as true as all those dime novelists
and newspapermen, such as myself, have bragged
about.

"You're a good man, Henry," Marshal Usher
tells me, and shakes my unsteady hand with his—
thank goodness—firm, steady hand.

Duncan couldn't help but laugh, and laughing felt good after a long day that followed a long, stressful day and a hard night.

"Thanks, Little Joey," Logan Ladron said.

The kid straightened and smiled.

"You're welcome."

"You better run along," Ladron told the boy. "If your mama finds you in here, she'll wear herself out tanning all of our hides."

The boy didn't move.

"Joey," Sara said softly.

He cleared his throat, and gave a tentative nod toward the newspaper, still lying on the poker table. "Can I have my paper back? I mean . . . so I can give it to my school-teacher?"

Duncan grinned. He picked up the paper, folded it in half, and held it out for the boy.

"Sure, Joey. Take it with you. And thanks for bringing that to our attention."

"And," Sara interjected, "for reading it to us."

"Especially for the fine reading job," Ladron said.

"Yup. But it woulda been better," Nugget said, "had you read some stuff about me."

CHAPTER 24

Ben Usher climbed the steps to the back of the big wagon and, while waiting, remembered those wads of cotton he had stuck in his ears. He reckoned they helped a bit. Well, he certainly could hear all the noise around him. Horses. Cattle. Indians. What felt like a million people carrying on in about a thousand different languages. And the wind whipping off Lake Michigan felt like pure ice.

He shoved the cotton into his vest pocket, hearing some change rattle. Change and a couple of empty bass cartridges for his Thunderer. He had started giving away the empties to some of the children he saw during his bit at this . . .

Well, he couldn't call it a dog-and-pony show, but it sure wasn't the same as the real West.

He looked at the white painting over the red paint of the wagon:

BUFFALO BILL'S WILD WEST
&
CONGRESS OF ROUGH RIDERS OF THE WORLD

Usher shook his head at the painting, a pretty good likeness of William F. Cody himself, flowing hair, neat mustache and goatee, a white hat bigger than anything Usher had ever seen on any man.

It was amazing that Usher could see. The last show started at eight thirty, but a man couldn't tell it was dark. Not in Chicago, Illinois. Lights shined from all around, and not just from the World's Fair, which was just across the row. The wagon started to shake as another train pulled out of the station. The tracks were maybe twenty feet from the entrance to *Buffalo Bill's Wild West.*

And it sure had been wild.

The door opened.

"Oh," the money counter said, "come on in, Mr. Usher."

He had given up on getting the little fellow to call him Ben.

Lanterns lit up the inside, and the open door managed to take most of the cigar smoke outside before it closed.

"Two-hundred and sixty-"—the last digits were lost as a cannonade roared somewhere, which rocked the wagon. When that passed, Cody sighed and said, "You'd think that those two hundred soldier boys from Fort Sheridan would learn they don't have to fire a volley all at the same time. And they come to watch the show. They ain't taking part in it."

Cody sat behind the desk, wearing spectacles as he read. His press agent stood over him, pointing to words and asking for approval. Cody looked bored with all this and focused most of his attention on the fellow counting the day's take.

Usher shrugged. "They just like to shoot."

Cody copied Usher's shrug, then motioned to a chair, and bent below the desk. When he came up, he was smiling and sliding a bottle of good bourbon toward Usher, who sat down.

There wasn't a glass in sight.

"No, thanks, Bill."

The bottle did not move.

So Usher took it and held it back to Cody. "You first, Colonel."

Cody slapped his hands together and exclaimed, "That's why I like you, Ben. You got good manners. Your mammy raised you right." He took the bottle, removed the cork, which fell to the floor. Nobody made any attempt to find it. Cody guzzled down more bourbon in one take than Usher had ever seen since . . . well . . . since last night after the final show. And the night before. And the night before that. And the night . . .

That man could drink from breakfast to bedtime and never even seem drunk.

"Ahhhhhhhhhh." Cody slid the bottle back toward Usher, who took a much smaller sip.

The bourbon wasn't bad. Usher pushed the bottle toward the money counter.

Cody intercepted that and had another snort, then put the bottle far from the moneyman's reach.

"Pretty fair shooting today, Ben," Cody said.

"Thanks, Colonel," Usher said without much feeling.

"But you didn't smile as much today, Ben. Remember, you might be a gunfighter with nerves of steel, but it helps if you smile. At least at the young'uns. And pretty girls, as long as their daddies ain't watching you too hard."

"I'll try to remember that, Colonel."

"Bill. Call me Bill. Or Will. 'Colonel' makes me feel . . . old. You've known me long enough, back when the West was really wild."

Usher didn't think he'd known Cody that well. They had met a few times across the West, shared a campfire now and then, and a bottle of whiskey a few other times.

"It's good to have you with us," the showman went on.

"My last gunfighter couldn't work without whiskey. And then he couldn't work because he couldn't stop drinking whiskey. And shooting that kid in the arm didn't help matters none. Luckily, it just nicked the boy, barely even a scratch, and he felt like he was worth a million bucks, having been wounded by a famous gunman."

The moneyman frowned. "If his dad wasn't so dirt poor, he might have realized that he could have gotten a million bucks rather than two thousand."

"Hush," Cody snapped. He had another short pull from the bottle, which he held out toward Usher.

The money counter said, "The grandstand was full again today, Colonel, and from my tally, not one person got in without paying."

Fifty cents for adults, twenty-five cents for children—but those kids had to be under ten years old, and some of the ticket-takers had been known to question some of the taller, fatter kids—almost always boys—about what year they were born. But these boys weren't Kansas or Iowa kids, most of the children were locals, Chicago-born and bred, and they knew how to answer like a good Chicago lad:

"I dunno. Ask my mama."

And that was just for those who didn't care where they sat. Lots of people paid two bits or even four bits extra to sit in the reserved section.

What that added up to was one big fat purse to be hauling in every day. Two shows: three in the afternoon and then eight thirty in the evening. And Usher could not complain. Not a bit. Cody was generous with what he paid his employees, especially one with the skills Ben Usher had—and a name that wasn't that far down the list of Western heroes than Buffalo Bill Cody's.

Usher was lucky to have a job like this one.

The advertisements in the Chicago newspapers—at

least those Usher had seen—bragged that *Buffalo Bill's Wild West* was the place to be whenever it rained. The grounds were clean. No spectators would come away dusty or muddy. Shows would be performed under the big tent, rain or shine, and the canvas was so sturdy, it never leaked.

There was also a restaurant on the grounds, and the food better than anything you'd find at the World's Fair.

Usher wasn't sure about that, though. Between shows, he had gone to the fair, tasted a banana that he liked a lot, and had better coffee than he had found anywhere at Bill Cody's venue—though, unlike that fine exhibition, the coffee at *Buffalo Bill's Wild West* often tasted like it was made with rye whiskey, not water.

Cody had another snort, shook his head, and leaned forward. "You want to know who you remind me of, bub?"

That was a question Usher hadn't expected. His poker face vanished. "Who?"

"Jim Hickok."

Usher went from slouching in the chair to sitting up straight. "You mean Wild Bill?"

"In the flesh, Lord may he rest in peace." Cody shook his head and sighed. "Now, you're not quite as quick as Jim. But I've never seen anyone who was. And Jim could shoot without missing ninety-nine times out of a hundred. Right-handed or left-handed, he was just as good. But what Jim wasn't—and never could be—was a showman. He hated those lights to shine on him—and I mean that literally. He once shot out a light that was shining on him when we tried a disaster of a play ol' Buntline had us doing and then we done it ourselves. Till I come up with something better, grander, greater than anything in the world. That's why all these people from all over the world are coming to see us, Jim—I mean, Ben—coming to see my Wild West. They want to see us re-create ol' Custer's last charge at the Little Bighorn. They want to see Indians—real Indians—and cowboys, and they want to see legends. Like you, Ben. Like you. But they'd like you a lot better if you wasn't so . . ." He turned to the moneyman.

"Dour," the moneyman said without looking up.

"I see," Usher said. So he was about to get fired. Fired by Buffalo Bill Cody. Well, that would be a story he could tell someone back at Dead Broke. They'd laugh a lot. He almost smiled at the thought.

He waited for Cody to tell him to pack up his stuff, and for the moneyman to slide over some cash. Cody, always generous, would probably pay him more than he was owed. He felt almost like he was back in the Crosscut Saloon.

That's when he suddenly understood that he felt homesick. He had never felt like that before, maybe because he had been moving around most of his life. Could Dead Broke, Colorado, be . . . *home*?

He could smell the perfume Sara was wearing. He could hear Nugget's laugh. He could feel the felt on one of Sara's poker tables. It always felt different than the tables at other saloons and gambling dens. It felt like home.

"But I know how to fix you up just right," Cody said.

"Huh?" Ben had almost toppled over backward in his chair.

The great showman made a vague wave toward the moneyman.

"Show him," Colonel Cody ordered.

The man made a mark on his ledger, stuck pencils over both ears, and bent below the desk. When he returned to view, he held a newspaper in his left hand.

"Third page. Above the *Ali Baba* advertisement for the Chicago Opera House."

Usher found the ad. He might like to see that play. Above it was a short article. There was no telling where the *Chicago Afternoon Daily Press* had picked up this article, and he wasn't sure he believed it, but he read it from beginning to end.

Then he read it again. Finally, he looked up at his boss.

"Do you think this . . . ?" Usher tapped the paper with his trigger finger, looked at it again, and read the first long paragraph one more time. "Do you think it's true?"

"I was hoping you'd tell me."

The moneyman cleared his throat. "There are articles that say the same thing—some of them not, at least obviously, written by the same correspondent. The *Globe,* the *Herald,* the *Record,* the *Tribune,* and the *Daily Inter Ocean.*"

Disappearing behind the desk again, then rattling papers, he reappeared and laid some other newspapers on the desk. He sighed and recited from memory. "The *Pantagraph* in Bloomington had something much shorter. The *Morning Herald-Dispatch* in Decatur had a few sentences, but it cited a Denver newspaper—alas, I forget which one. The *Weekly Leader* in Bloomington even put it on its front page, but nothing ever exciting has happened in Bloomington. Alas, I did not keep those newspapers, as those foolish editors had nothing in them about our Wild West here, and all the records we have been breaking, and how the public just adores Colonel Cody."

Cody cleared his throat and leaned forward. "There even was a mention of it in the *Daily Columbian.*"

That was the newspaper of the World's Columbian Exposition, but from what little Usher had read in that paper, most of the articles had been picked up from Chicago's other dailies. Still . . . he shook his head and re-read the article.

"The Haden boys." His head shook. "They usually hid out in their home county, but that's certainly riding distance to Dead Broke. And if this write-up is anything close to the actual truth, that does sound like the way Duncan— *Mick*—MacMicking would have tried to handle things."

Cody nodded, took another pull from his bottle, which now was practically empty, and leaned closer.

"Is MacMicking as good as . . ." He waved his hands at the papers. "Is he as good as these papers claim he is?"

Usher smiled. He felt something like life returning to his body. "He's better than I am," he said, and was thankful that Duncan MacMicking was not around to hear him say those words.

Colonel Cody and the moneyman exchanged looks. Cody turned and leaned forward. "What about this . . . ?" He frowned, but the moneyman came to his rescue.

"Liberty Bell of Zinc."

Usher shook his head. "I can't say one way or the other. Nugget"—he tapped the paper—"That's what everyone calls the mayor."

"I've heard his name," Cody said. "He was one of the greats in the Colorado mining business. I even spent a few days in Dead Broke back in . . ." He looked at the ceiling for help, and finally said, "In '88, I believe. But I did not have the pleasure of making Mayor Nugget's acquaintance. I don't recall seeing MacMicking there, though."

"He wasn't there in '88," Usher said. "He . . . We . . ." He smiled at the memory. "We were moving around lots, back in those years."

Cody laughed. "Weren't we all! When was the last time we were together, Ben?"

"In '87, maybe, or '86?"

"Sounds right," Cody said. He snapped his fingers.

"Leavenworth, by grab. I was doing that stupid playacting then."

"And Duncan and I were bringing Clay Pitts to prison."

"I tried to get you to come take part in that evening's performance." He slapped his thigh. "And you two galloped off in opposite directions." His laugh was musical.

The moneyman picked up one of the papers and read a few sentences that described the Liberty Bell of Zinc, then looked at Usher for some kind of response.

What the moneyman got was a shrug.

"That's one heavy chunk of zinc," he said.

"There's a museum in this big city that would like to put that big thing on display," Cody said. "But before he does—if he does—I'd like to have it in a tent—not my tent. Not the big tent. But maybe near our restaurant. So folks could come see it. Then it goes to the museum."

Usher let out a short chuckle. "Well, I'm not sure how they'd ever get that to Chicago."

"By train," the moneyman said.

Well, Usher knew that much.

Cody cleared his throat. "Listen, Ben. I want that stone here, and I want our old pard, the marshal, here. That'll give us lots of reasons for folks to catch us for the last weeks we'll be here. Because the day after that confab over yonder"—he waved in the general direction of the big fair—"that's our last day in Chicago and I can get back to the West, the real West, the West that is my home. And if I could have that Liberty Bell of Zinc—and you and Marshal MacMicking, I'd be bringing in more money than I ever thought possible. You and MacMicking, showing off your fancy shooting. That big rock, bringing in all the ladies who love such jewelry."

"Six tons is a lot of jewelry," the moneyman said.

Cody reached into the moneyman's cashbox and pulled

out a wad of bills. The moneyman gasped as his face drained of color—and he was a pale man, to begin with.

"Can you get MacMicking and that big stone—"

"Liberty Bell," the moneyman asserted, but Cody waved him off.

"Can you get them here? We'll pay top dollar, and, again, you'll get a fine bonus."

Usher thought for a moment. "Can you use a card dealer?"

"I've got—"

Usher cut him off. "You don't have anyone as pretty as this one."

"A lady gambler?" Cody looked quite lecherous.

Usher nodded. "She'd probably come with Duncan." He cleared his throat and shook his head. "No, forget that. She'd definitely come."

Cody clapped his hand, and then slapped the moneyman so hard he almost knocked him over the desk and into Usher.

Said the great showman: "Get it done, hoss. Just get it done."

Usher said, "I'll ask. That's all I can do."

CHAPTER 25

Quick Schmid knocked on the door to the marshal's office. Winston DeMint knew it had to be Schmid because the telegraph operator in Dead Broke was the only person in town who would knock at a marshal's office. Most folks stormed inside, demanding one person be arrested, if not hanged by the neck until dead, or wanting to file a complaint against so-and-so. But not Quick Schmid.

His real given name was Rutherford—like one of the recent presidents of these United States—but everyone called him Quick, because if Rutherford Arnfried Schmid was anything, it wasn't quick.

As Duncan's mother might have said of the telegraph operator: *He was anything but quick.*

In fact, he was trying to stifle a yawn in front of the marshal's office when the door opened, and the poor man was almost soaked with ancient coffee that Winston DeMint was about to throw onto the street.

"Whoa!" DeMint said, and managed to turn to his left and send the old brew elsewhere.

Schmid yawned, as if barely avoiding a coffee bath was an everyday occurrence. He nodded at the jailer and held out the slip of paper. "This just came in for the marshal," he said.

"Important?" DeMint lowered the pot in his right hand and extended his left for the telegram.

The telegrapher shrugged. "From Chicago," he said.

That piqued DeMint's interest. He took the paper and glanced at it while asking, "Do I owe you anything?"

"Not a penny."

But Schmid could have told him that he owed ten thousand dollars and DeMint would not have noticed. In fact, he didn't even notice that the telegrapher had already turned around and was walking down the boardwalk. He read the telegram again. And again. Then his mouth opened and he called out Schmid's name, but got no reply, and looked up and saw Schmid was moving down the boardwalk. So he called out to the slow-moving gentleman and Schmid stopped and walked back.

"Could you stop in at the Crosscut Saloon and tell the marshal that he best get back here because he is surely gonna want to read this wire you just gave me."

Schmid yawned. "He's in the Crosscut?"

"Should be. Having his morning coffee."

The telegrapher looked at the empty pot DeMint held in his left hand. "I reckon I know why." Then he turned, said something that might have been "I'll tell him," and moved like a lame mule, but he was moving, and heading in the direction of Sara Cardiff's saloon.

DeMint hated to do it, but he stopped him again. Schmid moseyed back.

"Before you take off, Schmid, I need you to do something for me."

He told the telegrapher what he needed, what to do, what not to say to Marshal MacMicking. He paid him to do it and watched him walk away. Even if Schmid moved faster than he had ever moved in his life, that would give DeMint time to read the wire again. He shook his head, and went back inside, put the paper on the marshal's desk and then a box of .45 cartridges atop the paper so it wouldn't blow away when someone opened the door.

Duncan lowered the telegram back to the desk. "Hmm," he said, not looking at the slip of paper or at Winston DeMint or at anything.

"You think that actually came from Ben Usher?" the jailer asked.

That got the marshal's attention. He looked at DeMint with curiosity. "You think it didn't?"

"Well, it could be an attempt to lure you—and Nugget's big zinc rock—out into the open country. Get you in an ambush. You know how many gangs have taken to robbing trains the past thirty years."

Duncan smiled. "How many?"

"Confound it!" DeMint snapped. "I'm just saying that anybody could have sent that wire, to get you and Nugget and that six-ton pack of trouble off this infernal mountain. Get you on a train in the middle of the Kansas plains and ambush you. Steal that zinc. Kill you. Kill Nugget."

"Seems like a lot of trouble when most of them have ridden up here to try to steal that rock."

"And look where that got them." DeMint glared. "I'm just saying—"

"I know what you're saying, Winston, and I appreciate it. But we could take a riverboat instead of a train. Fool those owlhoots waiting for us in Kansas."

"No, you couldn't. Boats travel too slow. That big circus up in Chicago ends at the end of October. And stop mocking me."

Duncan nodded. "I appreciate your concern, Winston. Honest. But all I have to do to verify this"—he picked up the telegram and waved it—"is to send a wire right back to Chicago."

"You ain't got to do that, Marshal, because I did that for you. Told ol' Schmid to send it straightaway and to get back here with a reply."

Duncan sank back into his chair, studying his jailer as though he had never seen him before.

"You did that?"

"Yep."

"Well, you didn't have to do that."

The former gambler frowned.

"When Ben gets that, he'll laugh his head off. No telling what he'll say in his next telegram. Wondering if I've lost what little nerve I had left." He shook his head as he sighed. "'Does the mayor know you are wasting city funds by sending urgent telegrams like this? STOP. You caught me, Marshal, and I will surrender myself to you when you arrive in Chicago to make your arrest. STOP.'"

"You don't even know that Buffalo Bill Cody has hired Ben Usher as some trick-shot artist," DeMint barked.

"But I do know, Winston. That's what Sara and I were talking about over coffee."

The jailer's face revealed surprise.

"Huh?"

"Sara and I were talking about Ben Usher joining up with Buffalo Bill," Duncan said again.

"Well, why didn't you tell me that before?"

"Because we didn't know it until yesterday." He laughed and shook his head. "After school, Joey Clarke brought in a newspaper he found, and he showed us— *Buffalo Bill's Wild West.* And Ben Usher's name was down at the bottom, world-famous gunfighter, and the man who brought Billy the Kid, Jesse James, the Daltons, and Belle Starr to justice. None of whom neither Ben nor myself ever ran into."

"Newspaper," DeMint whispered.

"From Chicago. Guess Ben started a week or two back. Maybe he had that lined up before he pulled out of here. That would be just like Ben. Sneak off saying he's bored or tired, when he just got an offer to make a whole lot more money than he'd ever make in Dead Broke—no matter what Nugget found next."

"Newspaper," DeMint said even softer than he had the first time. He sank back in his chair, shaking his head.

"Guess we can't stop your telegram," Duncan said.

"No. Reckon not. But you can take the costs out of my salary."

Now the marshal laughed. "No need for that. I appreciate it, Winston. Honest. And we'll see what Ben says in his reply to yours."

The jailer's face changed quickly.

"Are you going?" he shouted. "To join up with *Buffalo Bill's Wild West*?"

Duncan had turned around, rubbing his lips with the thumb on his right hand, back and forth, back and forth. He didn't answer for the longest while.

"It has possibilities," he said. "And not just on the money side of things."

There had been no mention of a salary in Usher's wire, but Duncan figured it would be lots more than he was making here in Dead Broke. But this wasn't about money. This was about having a safe town. Winston DeMint might not have been so far off thinking that some outlaws might think taking six tons of zinc off a train would be a whole lot easier in some far-from-civilization siding on a railroad track than in two miles up a mountain.

No Liberty Bell of Zinc. Outlaws wouldn't likely come to this town without that luring them. Nugget's Diamond Nugget of Silver had lost most of its allure, now considered more of a novelty than some fortune. And the fact that anyone who ever tried to take that silver had died or been imprisoned kept most outlaws seeking easier targets. Besides, just getting to Dead Broke was challenging. And Nugget had his own guards to keep anyone from hauling that down the slope.

The telegram said a museum would like to have the large zinc boulder for a permanent display: *and its* donors *would be happy to make an adequate financial contribution to the brave miner who risked all to bring that zinc from the darkness to the light of the world.*

That was some wire. It must have cost Ben Usher—or Buffalo Bill Cody—a good chunk of change to send a telegram that wordy.

No monster rock of zinc. No outlaws coming to town. Peace could eventually come to Dead Broke. And even Nugget, as greedy as he was, could come to appreciate "an adequate financial contribution."

"Do you know where Nugget is?" Duncan asked.

"I heard he went up to the mine."

Duncan pushed himself out of the chair. "Good. I'll be up there. You're in charge while I'm gone. But don't send any more wires—no matter what Ben Usher says in his reply. You don't want to bankrupt the city."

He stopped at the Crosscut Saloon first and told Sara everything. She told Logan Ladron that he was in charge and that she'd be back as soon as she could; she then raced upstairs to put on something better suited for the mining camps and easier to ride, double, up the incline with Duncan.

They reached the camp quickly. Duncan showed the telegram he had brought to Syd Jones, who read it, and looked at Duncan.

"You plan on taking this job?" he asked.

"Yes," Duncan said, and told him why.

"That's a lot of work—not playacting in one of these Wild West ventures. You know what that's like. But procuring that big, beautiful, but troublesome, rock will take a lot of doing. Do you think Nugget will be interested?"

Duncan pointed at the telegram. "You read that part about salary, didn't you? And 'adequate financial contribution'?"

Jones nodded. "That show's closing in just a few weeks."

"I know. I'm not interested in living that life again. It's good enough for Bill Cody, but it's not what I want out of this world. But that museum wants that stone, will pay Nugget for it, and if we can get that out of Dead Broke, this town might grow into something that people respect, where people want to live—at least in the summer."

The old lawman shook his head. "Who do you have in mind to act as temporary marshal while you're gone?"

"I'm looking at him."

Syd Jones took a step back. "These miners pay me pretty good."

"I know. But with that big rock gone with us to Chicago, I think you'd be good enough—with Winston DeMint and Logan Ladron acting as your special deputies—to do both jobs. Marshal of Dead Broke. The fellow nobody wants to mess with up the slope."

Jones rubbed his chin.

"It'll only be for a few weeks."

"Unless," Jones said, "you get bitten the way that show latched on to ol' Will Cody."

"That's not going to happen, Syd, and you know it."

Jones nodded. "Just wanted to make sure you knew it, son." He looked over at Sara. "You going with them, I'm guessing."

She smiled. "I've always wondered what it would be like to have someone shoot a lit cigarette out of my mouth."

"I never have," Syd Jones said.

"Well," she said, "I really would like to see Chicago. And I've always wanted to meet the great Buffalo Bill. Besides, Ben wrote that I might be a useful attraction."

Jones laughed hard. "And knowing Will the way I know him, and for as long as I've known him, he'll sure be *attracted* to you."

He laughed at the sudden change in Duncan's face.

Duncan found Nugget at his house in Chasm Park late that afternoon. Little Joey Clarke was reading a dime novel to him, and the guards let Duncan look at the Diamond Nugget of Silver until the boy finished the story. The guards always had orders not to interrupt their boss when he was being read a story.

That piece of silver—of history, really—was certainly impressive. He could see why wealthy men and bandits desired to have something like this. It was much prettier, too, than that massive rock of zinc. Oh, the zinc was colorful, but coarse, and outweighed this towering gem by tons.

He heard Nugget raving about the amazing tale Little Joey had just finished, and when Duncan heard the name "Buffalo Bill Cody," he smiled. What good fortune. The boy said he'd be back whenever he had a new book and walked out without seeing Duncan. Then came a few whispers from a guard, a grunt from Nugget, followed by a belch, and the old miner came into the grand room.

"Did he pay his dollar?"

Duncan sighed, fished out a bill, and handed it to the nearest guard.

"No," Nugget said. "You don't pay him. It's my nugget."

The guard handed the bill to Nugget, who stuffed it into the greasy pocket of his jeans.

"You need to see me, eh? Something important? Ain't nobody tried to steal my Liberty Bell of Zinc again?" The last sentence came out almost as a cry.

"No, Mayor. But that's what I've come to talk to you about. Buffalo Bill Cody and a museum in Chicago have made an interesting proposition."

Nugget straightened. He was a right tall fellow when he wanted to be, despite all those years of squeezing through tunnels—"holes" would be a better word—that a gopher would have trouble maneuvering through.

"Buffalo Bill!" Nugget cried. "I just finished readin' a crackerjack story 'bout him." His head tilted, and he eyed Duncan curiously. "You know Buffalo Bill? *The* Buffalo Bill. Bill Cody?"

"Our paths crossed a few times," Duncan said.

"Golly. I thought Ben Usher was the most famous fella you knowed."

Duncan smiled. This might be easier than he thought. "How would you like to spend time with both Ben Usher and Buffalo Bill? And get paid to do it?"

CHAPTER 26

Amos Filmore's bank was looking almost like a bank—except for the heavy tarp that covered the missing large window. He stood outside, instructing the carpenters, when Duncan and Nugget walked up.

"No," Filmore was saying. "Leave the bullet holes. Leave the bullets in those holes. You're not to dig any out as souvenirs. This will be a national monument one of these days. We now have a symbol of history, of justice, of the spirit of America. Of the American West."

"You might have a rival for mayor, Mayor," Duncan whispered with a smile.

Nugget spit out tobacco juice and snorted. "He can't win. My guards count the ballots."

Filmore noticed the two men and gave the head carpenter a few more instructions before walking over to the pair and shaking hands.

"It'll be two weeks, I'm told, before I can get the new window in, and I sure hope the weather holds out till then so we can showcase the legendary Liberty Bell of Zinc again," he said.

"That's what we come to talk to you for," Nugget said.

He walked past the banker and the men with hammers, saws, and screwdrivers, and went inside the building.

The banker glanced at Duncan, who said, "You've been busy of late. I've seen a line out the door some days."

Filmore chuckled. "You'd never think that a bank robbery attempt that left men dead and wounded would be the best advertising for a bank. Suddenly, folks from all over—a lady came up yesterday from Cañon City—all want to have their money in the bank where the Haden Gang paid for their crimes. It's like no one here ever heard of the Panic of '93."

That was a promising start, Duncan thought. He might not need that big rock to keep people pouring into his business.

It didn't take long, either.

Nugget started telling Filmore what needed to happen, and why, and patted the top of the zinc treasure and what all he had gone through to find that national wonder, and how it was like his child, and all those waifs—he must have picked up that word from one of the novels Little Joey had read to him—in Chicago who would be blessed to see this masterpiece.

Then Duncan told the truth.

"I think that's a terrific idea," Filmore said.

This was the American West at its best.

The people of Dead Broke—the newcomers seeking new starts or small fortunes; the miners, who worked in darkness, hoping to find the light of riches, like Nugget often had done; even those who set up businesses that many citizens frowned upon; and others who supported those entrepreneurs till they had spent their last cent of their month's wages—came together.

Most of them would have loved to have the opportunity to go to Chicago to see *Buffalo Bill's Wild West* show or the World's Fair—or both. Some would have loved just to be able to tell a neighbor or family member that they had seen Chicago. Some would have enjoyed riding a train for the first time. And practically everyone in Dead Broke would have marveled at what it was like to breathe in oxygen without a struggle. To remember what humidity felt like.

But they weren't going to Chicago. They wouldn't be part of *Buffalo Bill's Wild West*. They would be running their saloons . . . or the new bank in town . . . or listening to lies at Percy Stahl's place . . . or trying to figure out if Logan Ladron was bluffing or if that hole card completed an ace-high flush.

Yet they all wanted to help. They all believed that this would be great for Dead Broke. It would make those who had read about the violence, the bloodshed, the lawlessness of the past, learn that there was more to this high Colorado town. And that here, even a rough, illiterate miner could strike a fortune. It was the dream of many an American. It was the way of the West.

Duncan stood across from the bank—in front of the ruins of that building where Syd Jones had waited with unbelievable pressure before opening fire on that belligerent Haden bunch. Syd Jones stood with him, as did Sara Cardiff, Joey Clarke's father, Amos Filmore, Landace Purington, and Winston DeMint. The boardwalks were filled with people. Even the schoolchildren were there with their teacher and many parents. Miners—those who drilled in holes for dynamite, those who were in charge of lighting the dynamite, those who had well-paying jobs, and those who struggled to survive—had come down the slope to see this historic event. Their bosses came, too, and did not seem to regret their generosity of giving those humble, rough, hardworking men the day off. Well, some of them were working. Working with other men of the mountains, with carpenters and engineers.

A tower had been erected, stretching higher than the bank's false front. A massive wagon—maybe the biggest Duncan could recall seeing—had been parked in front of the bank, and beneath the tower.

Thirty men had managed to move the Liberty Bell of Zinc out of the bank, through the window opening, past the boardwalk, and under the giant tower, where they set it on a strong platform, thick and sturdy enough to hold up those six tons and sinking only $7\,1/16$ inches into the dirt, which was the exact depth predicted.

"I coulda told you that," Syd Jones whispered, "and I ain't never even been inside a university."

"It's bedrock after that," Mr. Clarke said with a smile.

"Colorado bedrock," Winston DeMint added.

After that, cables hanging from the top of the tower were fastened to the chain-and-rope harness.

Logan Ladron walked toward them, weaving through the immense crowd, before stopping near Sara.

"I locked the doors," he said. "Not that I needed to."

"No business?" Sara said with a smile.

He waved. "I think everyone on This Side Of The Slope is right here."

That wasn't that big of an exaggeration, Duncan realized. He wondered how the dealer had managed to squeeze his way through the masses that crowded Dead Broke. Special stagecoaches had made it up the mountain from Denver and other cities. He had even seen Carl Woodward of the *Times of the Rockies* earlier that morning, but Duncan had managed to avoid getting caught by the reporter or any other newspaper journalist. Someone had told him about an artist doing sketches for one of the illustrated publications, and he had been told—by men who typically did not fabricate or embellish—that reporters had come from cities outside of Colorado—Kansas City, New York City, San Francisco, Cheyenne, Tucson, Fort Worth, Wichita, Sacramento, Laramie, Boise, Nashville—even a correspondent for the *Daily Inter Ocean* of Chicago. Most of the members of the press watched from the roof of the very building where Duncan stood with his friends, and lots of people he barely knew or didn't know at all.

"Well," DeMint said, "care to make a wager?"

Ladron shrugged. "What kind of wager?"

"Three to one that the rock goes right through that wagon bed."

The gambler shook his head and turned to Duncan. "You let your employees gamble?"

"It's his money."

"Well, I'm not taking that bet. Wouldn't seem right."

Led by Dead Broke's most experienced bullwhackers, powerfully strong oxen, from the same man who supplied the beasts pulling the wagon, began walking down the street. There was a sigh of relief from most of the spectators when the harness tightened, and the giant stone lifted an inch off that platform.

The foreman barked orders—but, mindful of the presence of ladies, children, preachers, a priest, and two nuns, he kept his swear words at a lower volume or made them unintelligible—and the stone kept rising. Men moved to the sides, holding up thick poles to keep the zinc from swinging one way or the other, to protect the frame from being knocked over by the big rock.

"Whoa!" the foreman barked.

Duncan realized he had been holding his breath the

whole time. Now he exhaled, as did probably everyone else on the entire block.

"All right!" The foreman soon forgot that he was in the presence of ladies and children and began peppering his orders with rough language, but that did not compare to what the men who had to get those oxen to back up were shouting.

"Back haw!" the headman yelled. And the oxen spun slightly left. "Back!" That was how the *Inter Ocean* would report the event, but that's because the editor of that newspaper would not allow any reporter to use the exact words of that particular, or any, bullwhacker.

"Whoa!"

The wagon stopped moving. Its bed had stopped exactly where it was supposed to, underneath the tower and the giant boulder.

A thunderous ovation sounded from the rooftops, from the boardwalks, and some men on the rooftops turned, cupping their hands over their mouths, and yelled what they had seen to those far back in the crowd, or lining the streets hundreds of yards away, to the unfortunate ones who couldn't see anything but the top of the tower and the backs of those hundreds of men and women and children standing in front of them.

"All right!" the foreman bellowed. "Let 'er down. Gently. Gently."

Men moved closer to the team of oxen pulling the wagon, comforting them, talking in gentle whispers. Some of them put their coats over the animals' eyes, though the oxen were all facing away from the tower and that behemoth rock that was inching its way to the wagon bed. The men working the beasts that were lowering those tons of precious cargo did not mind their language. They used every curse Duncan had heard, and some of them mixed that profanity to create new, foul words.

Yet no one blushed, no one complained. They stood as if entranced, watching the boulder inch its way to the big wagon.

"That wagon looks new," Ladron said.

"It is," Syd Jones whispered.

Those mining engineers had taken the largest freight wagon in Dead Broke and reinforced it, widening the bed so it was big enough to hold the Liberty Bell of Zinc, going over their figures to determine the exact dimensions needed. "There's a science to this, Marshal," the foreman had told Duncan during the construction.

"Science," Duncan had said.

He would never forget the foreman's grin. "You know what science is, Marshal?" He hadn't waited for an answer. "It's what most folks call . . . a wild guess."

Duncan realized how quiet the street had become. Snorting beasts of burden, squeaking ropes and pulleys and chains, the heavy clomping of hooves. That was about all a person could hear, except maybe some slow, unsure breaths and rapidly beating hearts.

When the bottom of the stone had disappeared behind the wagon's walls, the lead bullwhacker called out, "Whoa," and the oxen stopped. Two men jumped into the back of the wagon, and brought out their rulers, measuring the distance between the zinc's edges and the reinforced walls, and also the distance before the boulder would be resting atop a mountain of canvas and blankets to cushion the great gem for its long journey to Chicago.

The men sang out their measurements, which men wrote down in notebooks. Then they took the same measurements and repeated the numbers three times more. Duncan wasn't sure he had ever seen anything like this in all his years. And he had seen all the figuring, all the time and effort it had taken to get this Liberty Bell of Zinc out of Nugget's mine. He had seen how much thought and arithmetic and muscle it had taken to get the giant gem down the slope to town. He had never thought of mining as a science, but it sure was. These men were a whole lot smarter than any dumb oaf who made his living with a badge and a gun.

"All right," the lead engineer said. "Fourteen and three-sixteenths of an inch to go."

The foreman's hand raised. "Ready."

A long second passed. "Go."

"Back!" the bullwhacker screamed. "Back!"

The oxen obeyed.

Two brave men stood on the back of the wagon, one dropping to his knees, then lying on his side, his left hand raising high, as he watched.

The bed of the wagon groaned. It sank and sank and sank underneath the enormous weight.

"That's it!" the man on his side yelled.

"Whoa!" the bullwhacker shouted.

One "whoa" was all that was needed. These oxen were not new to this kind of job. That's why they had been handpicked.

The ore did not crash through the bed.

Applause rang all across the block. Duncan realized that he was clapping with them. And then Sara, her face brighter than he could remember, leaped onto him, wrapping her arms around his neck, and he pulled her closer and kissed her.

"We did it!" she squealed. "We did it! We did it!"

"Yes," he said when he finally let her down. "We did it. *You* did it!"

"We," she told him, and then ran to the first bullwhacker she could see and kissed him.

Duncan lost her in the crowd.

The bands started playing all over. People on the roofs began singing.

> *Should auld acquaintance be forgot,*
> *And never brought to mind?*
> *Should auld acquaintance be forgot,*
> *And days o' auld lang syne!*
> *For auld lang syne, my dear,*
> *For auld lang syne,*
> *We'll take a cup o' kindness yet,*
> *For auld lang syne.*

"This," a voice sounded next to him, "will be a much-remembered day in Dead Broke."

He was pushed toward the voice. He almost thought he was going to be shoved into the dirt and trampled by hundreds of people, but a hand stopped him and pulled him toward the boardwalk.

"What a day," the voice said. "What a day! I've never seen anything like this since we got word of Lee's surrender to Grant."

Duncan saw the face of Carl Woodward.

The man pulled a pencil from his pocket and brought out a notebook.

"Are you ready for the journey to Chicago?"

He sighed. He hoped his shrug would suffice for an answer.

Luck was on Duncan's side. The lead engineer had to dodge a man with a tuba and stopped in front of Duncan and the reporter. The engineer, who had been all business for the past several days, had a flask in his left hand. He held it out to Duncan, who shook his head, but Carl Woodward took it and had himself a good swallow.

"You're a genius, sir," Woodward told him as he returned the flask. "What do you have to say—to the *Times of the Rockies*—about this grand day for mining, for engineering, for the wonders of nature, and for the glory of Colorado?"

They had to back up, turn around, and move into the ruins of the abandoned building to finish that interview. Duncan watched people jump off the roofs and onto the street.

"It's bedlam!" Syd Jones yelled.

He recognized his mentor's voice, but couldn't see him. "What do we do?"

Duncan turned to see Winston DeMint. His nose was bleeding, and the knees of his britches had been ripped.

"You all right?" Duncan yelled above the thundering crowd.

The jailer shrugged, then laughed. "What a day, eh?"

"What a day." Duncan nodded. He looked for Sara, but couldn't see anything but indistinguishable bodies.

"What do we do?" DeMint asked again.

Duncan laughed. "Let them celebrate." He put his right arm around the jailer. "Let them celebrate," he repeated. "They all deserve it."

CHAPTER 27

The party lasted two more days.

Duncan had to send a telegram to Ben Usher and Buffalo Bill that their arrival in Chicago would be delayed a couple of days. The reply came quickly—from none other than Cody himself.

DELAY WILL BE GREAT FOR BUSINESS
STOP ALREADY MUCH PRESS
ANNOUNCING YOUR JOURNEY TO MEET
UP WITH BUFFALO BILL'S WILD WEST AND
WHAT WILL BECOME BIGELOW'S MUSEUM
OF AMERICA'S NATURAL WONDERS
TREASURES AND LEGENDS GREATEST
EXHIBIT STOP FIRST ROUND OF WHISKEY
WILL BE ON ME STOP
I CAN STILL DRINK YOU UNDER THE
TABLE OL HOSS STOP

Wm F Cody
Buffalo Bill
Chicago

But the stagecoach that arrived on the day that hundreds of hangovers began dampened Duncan's enthusiasm.

The jehu on the run had stopped at the marshal's office first and tossed DeMint a sack filled with newspapers. The jailer laid the papers on Duncan's desk, and he read them while sipping coffee that morning—and wishing that it were late enough in the day for him to be sipping some good whiskey. Or bad whiskey. Even some of Nugget's blinding brew.

When Syd Jones stepped inside ninety minutes later, he removed his hat and coat and saw the look on Duncan's face.

"Somebody dead?" he asked.

"Not yet," Duncan said.

Jones hung up the coat and hat and found his cup and filled it with coffee. He turned, pulled up a chair toward the desk, and sat down. Duncan folded one of the papers and held it out for the old lawman to take.

The article was easy enough to find. It wasn't even very long. The newspaper was from Denver—not the *Times of the Rockies*—although the original article had first appeared in the *Laramie Lariat*.

Jones sipped and read, then put the paper atop some lawbooks on the edge of Duncan's desk.

"Pretty much tells exactly where you're going, to get to Cody's show," he said.

"Yeah." Duncan shook his head and sighed. "To the letter."

"Somebody has a mighty big mouth," Jones said.

Duncan nodded. "Somebody named Nugget."

Jones chuckled while shaking his head. "I don't think so, pardner. Nugget ain't got the brains to remember all those details."

"Yeah." After letting out a long sigh, Duncan waved his

right hand toward the stack of newspapers he had already skimmed. "Not all of the papers get into all those specifics. Most of them just praise the engineering geniuses and the excitement of the day. And how lucky the people in Chicago will be when we arrive. And not much about Buffalo Bill at all."

The old lawman grinned. "That'll get Will's dander up for sure."

Duncan found another paper and held it out.

"This one's just as bad," he said.

Syd Jones read it, nodded, and tossed it back on the desk. "You can always change your route. Or just call the whole thing off."

Duncan shook his head. "Can't do that. The idea was to get that zinc away from here. And if we can get it to that museum, that'll do wonders for Dead Broke."

Jones grinned. "Make us part of history. Sorta like you and me are getting into that museum ourselves." He shrugged and sipped more coffee. "In a way, I reckon we are."

"If we can get there." Duncan shook his head.

"Still worried about some highwaymen holding up the train in Kansas?" Jones asked.

Duncan let out a mirthless laugh. "I'm worried about getting down this hill. Then I'm worried about getting that big wagon to Denver. Then I'm worried about getting that big rock onto a train. Then I'm worried about getting that rock all the way to Chicago."

"You used to not worry so much," Jones said. He took another sip from his cup and frowned. "The only thing about you that hasn't changed is that you still can't make coffee."

"Winston made it."

"You ought to fire him."

Something tapped on the door. Syd Jones set the coffee atop a newspaper and looked at it. The tapping sounded again. Jones looked at Duncan, who was staring at the door. Duncan then eyed Jones. The tapping had stopped, then resumed. A muffled voice came behind the thick wood.

Jones whispered, "Is that somebody . . . knocking?"

"Must be a telegram." But Duncan pulled out his Schofield and laid it atop the nearest newspapers. Then he called out, "Come in?" It came out more like a question.

The door squeaked open, and a slight man slipped inside, hat in his hand, head bowed.

"Why," Jones said, "it's our new little barber."

Gaudenzio nodded slightly after he closed the door. When he turned around, he began speaking.

"Whoa." Duncan held up his hand. "Gaudenzio, you're talking too fast and we don't understand your tongue." The man held out an envelope, and Duncan stood, took it from the little man, and looked at the writing. He didn't understand it, either.

"Wait a minute," Duncan said. He looked at the barber and tried, *"Un momento."*

"Sì." The little man smiled. *"Sì. Sì. Sì."*

"How good's your Spanish?" Jones asked.

"About as good as Nugget's English," Duncan replied. "And that's not quite Spanish. Close, but not quite. I thought it was Italian, but Esposito, who works at the Rossi Mine, says it's Sicilian."

He couldn't catch but a fraction of what Gaudenzio said. The man spoke so fast, and his accent was so strong, and he didn't know anything about sign language.

"Wait," he said. *"Un momento."* Duncan shot Jones a glance. "Pour him some coffee. I'll be back in a minute or two."

He looked back at the barber. *"Un momento,"* he repeated. "I'll be back soon. *Un momento,* por favor."

The barber's head bobbed, and Duncan walked out. At least he understood Spanish. Some Spanish, anyway. But Duncan knew that even the Mexicans who worked in the mines, and the Italians, often didn't understand much of Syd Jones's Spanish.

He was back in less than five minutes, bringing Carlos Alcaraz, who ran one of Dead Broke's liveries. Even Alcaraz had trouble understanding Gaudenzio at first because of how fast the fellow spoke—and Alcaraz had been among the English-speaking folks for far too many years. But once he coaxed the barber to slowing down his speech, it came much easier.

"First," Alcaraz said, "he thanks you for all of your help, and he would like to repay you."

"No." Duncan's head shook. "We've gone through that. If there's money in that envelope—"

"No money," Alcaraz said. "It's a letter of introduction to his brother."

"Oh." Duncan looked at Jones, who just shrugged.

"His brother," Alcaraz said, "is named Gennaro. Apparently, Gennaro is a big man in Chicago. If you need anything, just ask to see Gennaro and say that Gaudenzio is your friend. You'll be taken care of."

The barber started talking in rapid-fire Sicilian again. And once again, Alcaraz had him repeat what he had said, but much, much slower. After a second try, Alcaraz said, "The best place to find him is in the letter. It's an address. You can ask anyone in town where it is."

Duncan nodded and Gaudenzio walked over and held out the letter, which Duncan took with a smile and shook the barber's hand.

"Thank you," Duncan said. "Gracias."

"E' n'onuri miu, amici mei."

They shook hands, and the barber walked out the door.

Duncan opened his coat and stuck the envelope into the inside pocket. Then he looked at the clock.

"That all you need, Marshal?" Alcaraz asked.

"That's it. Appreciate your help." They shook hands.

"I'll take good care of your horse, Marshal. Enjoy your trip," and the liveryman walked out.

"You packed?" Jones asked.

Duncan tilted his head toward the wall, where two grips were on the floor.

"Well." Jones rose. So did Duncan. They shook hands. "I'll be reading about you in the newspapers, I reckon. See you in November—unless you get hoodwinked into all that glory and all that money Cody will be giving you."

"You know me, Syd," Duncan said. "I'm all for quiet."

"And you ain't gonna find nothing quiet in Chicago."

Duncan grinned. "It's not like I found anything quiet in Dead Broke, either."

They moved out that afternoon.

Bullwhackers led the heavy wagon carrying the enormous zinc, with one of Nugget's guards riding in the wagon. Four riders, with bandoliers crisscrossing their chests, took the point.

Then came the surrey, Drift Carver driving and Duncan riding shotgun—with a sawed-off Greener in his lap. Nugget rode in the back with Sara.

The wagon following carried luggage and two more guards.

Four guards rode drag.

Snails move faster, Duncan thought. A stagecoach passed them two miles out of town, bound for Denver.

"You two could've traveled in style," Duncan told the mayor and the gambler. "Been in Denver a few days before to relax, before we ever came in sight of the city."

"I ain't lettin' my Liberty Bell gets out of my sight no more," Nugget said. "'Sides, oncet that fella in Chicago pays me what he owes me. . . ." He sniffled and wiped his eyes. "Wells, then I won'ts never ever see my greatest discovery ever ag'in."

Duncan, on the other hand, was looking forward to seeing that big rock one final time.

But, he knew, it would be a long journey just to get to Denver—let alone make it all the way to Chicago, Illinois.

Sometimes they had to climb out of the big rig and walk ahead of the oxen. Duncan told Nugget and Sara that was to rest the oxen. Those big animals had a hard enough time pulling six tons, so losing a little weight would help them, even if only slightly.

There was, Duncan knew, some truth to that—but not much.

The real reason was that the road down the mountain was treacherous in the best conditions, and while the sun was out on that first afternoon, the turns along the rim were tight for a normal freight wagon. With this leviathan, it was, as the driver had told Duncan, "on the tricky side."

Worse, Duncan thought, were the crossings.

"It'd be a lot worse in spring," Nugget said.

Which was true enough. Spring runoffs would have made the roads so muddy, Nugget's big piece of zinc might have sunk the wagon—heavy enough without hauling six tons—all the way to the bed. The wheels sometimes sank half a foot into the ground as it was. But those oxen knew their business—and the men working those animals were considered the best in the state.

Still, they weren't even halfway down the mountain when they made camp that first night.

And it took another two full days before they were off the mountain and on the main road to Denver.

But being off This Side Of The Slope didn't mean the rest of the trip was a quick, fun journey.

They were in Colorado's Front Range. Loveland Pass was just a mite under twelve thousand feet. They had to crawl through Silver Plume. It rained on them, though just a drizzle, for one full day. They went through a mild, but biting, snowstorm for three hours the next morning. By the time they stopped in Idaho Springs—only 7,500 feet high—a fresh team of oxen waited for them, one of the bullwhackers had a mild case of frostbite and another had a broken right forearm. Nugget, to his credit, left the sawbones in Idaho Springs with a wad of greenbacks, and let him touch the Liberty Bell of Zinc after he donned a good pair of gloves.

By the time they had climbed down to Golden, they were below six thousand feet in elevation. Most newcomers from the plains had trouble breathing here, but Duncan felt like he was below sea level. He always shook his head when he reached Denver, the city that bragged about being one full mile high. A mile: 5,280 feet. Dead Broke was twice that high up the mountains.

Nugget paid off the bullwhackers in Denver. They left the wagon in front of the hotel next to the Denver City, Ellsworth & Kansas City Kansas (Not Missouri) Railway station. The shotguns the guards carried kept most people away. The two guards with the repeating rifles made most of the men stay on the boardwalk on the other side of the street, where they kept their hands far from their sides and their coats buttoned.

Carl Woodward was waiting for Duncan, Nugget, and Sara in the hotel lobby. He had copies of the latest issue of the *Times of the Rockies* for the entire party, even the guards, even though only half of the guards could read.

Nugget asked Sara if she'd read him the good stuff, but Sara said she wanted to go to her room and soak in a tub for hours before going to sleep and sleeping till—

"Five thirty in the morning," Duncan told her. "If you want to make it to Kansas City."

"Five thirty?" She looked at him, waiting for a smile that wasn't coming.

"That's later than those boys will be getting up to move that Liberty Bell of Zinc onto the DCE and KCK flatcar. Train leaves the station at five fifty-two in the morning."

How Duncan hated to break Sara's heart.

"Sorry," he said, and he meant it.

She gave him a warm smile. "I can't complain," she said. "I'll get some sleep." She sighed. "I don't think you will at all. Will you?"

He shook his head and watched her go to the front desk to get the key to her room. Nugget led the reporter to the hotel bar. Duncan saw that this fine hotel had a restaurant, so he walked into it, got a cup of coffee, and took it with him outside. He'd be up the rest of the night, but one of the hotel staff said they'd keep the coffee hot all night for the guards, and they had bribed the city police chief to let the hotel saloon remain open all night because lots of folks would want to come by and see that big rock that had caused so much bloodshed in the mountains, in that lawless city called Dead Broke.

Duncan climbed into the back of the wagon, nodding at

the four guards pulling that first four hours of duty. Duncan took a sip of coffee—it tasted too good for his liking—and told two of the guards to get some shut-eye.

"You think you and Burt and Oliver can handle things?" the younger of the two youngest guards asked.

Duncan pointed his chin toward the streets. It was filled with men—businessmen mostly, but some cowhands—none carrying a firearm in view—women, proper ladies—children. They passed the big wagon with the giant stone, gawking, silent or whispering. The parade seemed to stretch all the way back to Golden.

"This isn't Dead Broke, boys."

He nodded at the rooftops, where the police chief had assigned other guards to keep a watch on the big zinc rock.

Denver, Duncan knew, could be as wild and woolly as the most notorious cow towns. But it wouldn't be on this night. This would be peaceful—a chance to rest. But then it would be one long train ride on the DCE and KCK.

Get through Kansas, he figured, and the next train to Chicago would likely be uneventful.

But they had to get through Kansas first.

And Kansas worried him.

CHAPTER 28

Railroad employees knew what they were doing at the Denver City, Ellsworth & Kansas City Kansas Railway. The giant chunk of zinc was put on the flatcar like it weighed sixty pounds and not six tons. Even Nugget was impressed.

"I don't think they even scratched it none," he said, nodding his approval.

Nugget's guards climbed on the flatcar, and Duncan sure pitied those men. He hoped that Nugget was paying them good wages, for they'd be riding in the wind—all four of them—and that wind was going to be blowing hard and cold all the way to the Kansas-Missouri border. And Duncan knew from experience just how cold a Kansas wind could be.

Four other guards went into the passenger car in front of the flatcar, and another four went into the passenger car that was hooked behind the flatcar. The twelve men would take turns freezing in the open. Maybe, Duncan hoped, none would be frostbitten by the time they reached the end of track in Kansas City.

Nugget went to the back passenger car. Duncan looked at Sara. "Any preference?" he asked.

She pointed ahead, so Duncan took her arm and they walked down the platform. A porter took their bags, and another one helped Sara to that first step. The coach wasn't crowded, but this was a special run. There were two deputy U.S. marshals on board, both carrying shotguns and two revolvers. Word must have gotten out about how this special cargo seemed to attract all sorts of bandits.

Duncan had been told about them.

But no one had told him anything about the boy sitting on his knees on a seat, his head sticking out the window, watching the commotion around the flatcar behind them. When he pulled himself back in, he smiled widely and waved.

Duncan did not return the wave.

Instead, he bellowed, "Joey Clarke! What the he . . . What the devil are you doing here?"

"Hi, Marshal MacMicking! Isn't this fun?"

"Fun" wasn't the word Duncan had in mind.

He stared at Sara and was about to give her a piece of what he was thinking, but she looked just as shocked as Duncan.

The front door to the coach opened, and Mrs. Clarke stepped inside, carrying a small valise and an umbrella.

That didn't make Duncan any happier, but at least it meant that the boy hadn't run away from home.

"Someone better start explaining to me—and it better sound good."

Mrs. Clarke set her valise in a seat and walked down the aisle, stopping beside Sara.

"Get your head inside, Joey," she told her son. "The conductor says we'll be pulling out in two minutes."

The coach jerked forward, and everyone had to grab hold of the nearest seat. The two locomotives in front grunted. Steam hissed. A band tried to play something. The four guards sat down. So did Mrs. Clarke.

Duncan choked back the curse he wanted to yell and grabbed hold of the back of the seat in front of him.

The front door opened again, and the conductor came in.

"Leaving Denver City, folks," he said. "Next stop is for water at Cowle's Crossroads."

The train was moving, slowly at first, and the station was behind them.

"Can you stop this thing?" Duncan called out.

The conductor laughed. "Sure. At Cowle's Crossroads." He did a head count. There were no tickets to be punched, as this was a special run—paid for by *Buffalo Bill's Wild West* and Bigelow's Museum of America's Natural Wonders, Treasures, and Legends.

"I'd sit down, Marshal," the conductor said. "Getting out of Denver is the worst part of the ride. But once we're clear, we'll be moving fast. Till we stop. At Cowle's Crossroads. But that's just for coal and water."

He spoke as he walked, nodding at Mrs. Clarke, smiling at Sara, telling Little Joey not to stick anything out of the window—unless he wanted to risk losing a hand or arm. He called one of the deputies by name, stared at Nugget's four guards with displeasure. He opened the door and closed it behind him as he moved to the flatcar.

Little Joey sat down. His mother told him to close the window. She didn't want those nice-looking guards to get frostbite. They'd be cold enough when they had to go onto the flatcar for four hours. Joey reluctantly did as he was told.

"What about school?" Duncan said.

The train stopped suddenly, almost sending Duncan over the back of the chair. He had just straightened when the train lurched again. Sara patted the empty spot next to her, and he sat down. At least he was across from Joey, and he could hear his mother, though she had to raise her voice more than usual just to be heard.

The teacher had excused Little Joey for the rest of the school term.

"It ain't—" Joey started.

"'Isn't,'" his mother said.

"Isn't," Joey corrected. "Isn't like I'm gonna miss much. And my reading is good. Teacher says so. Real good. But I gots to write down what I saw and learnt."

"'Learned.'"

"Learned." Joey said, though his face told Duncan that he wished his mother would quit interrupting him. "Learned at Buffalo Bill's show and that museum. Mostly about the museum, but I'm much more interested in seeing Buffalo Bill come to Custer's rescue at the Little Bighorn, though he ain't—isn't—gonna do Custer much good."

The whistle on the big engine screamed.

Little Joey grinned at the noise.

"Teacher says I have to do a good job on my report. Though I ain't"—he sighed—"I am not so sure Teacher will be back for the next term."

That was always the case. There was no need, Duncan knew, for a teacher to have a name. Old man or young woman, schoolteachers usually left after one winter in Dead Broke. And back in the wild days, some of them left after two weeks in the spring or summer.

Duncan turned to Mrs. Clarke. "Joe didn't come along?"

Her head shook. She had to yell—and Mrs. Clarke was not used to yelling. "Joe had to work. And Nugget . . . well . . . he said two tickets were enough. Even though he didn't pay for them."

That made sense. Nugget figured Cody and the museum would deduct expenses from whatever amount they had agreed upon, even though Duncan was pretty sure neither Cody nor the museum was that cheap.

Sara patted Duncan's thigh.

"Well," he said. "I reckon that's that." He made himself smile. "This should be a nice trip."

The sudden stop almost threw everyone to the next coach.

That conductor hadn't lied about how rough the ride was out of the city. But that was Duncan's fault. He had let Nugget and Cody agree on the railroad they'd use. And that's why the Denver City, Ellsworth & Kansas City Kansas Railway was known for moving freight, not passengers. Well, they sure had done a good job of getting that six-ton jewel onto the flatcar.

Duncan felt Sara's arm wrap around his shoulder and neck. He pulled off his hat and set it on his lap. Then he looked out the window and watched Denver buildings roll on by.

Twenty hours. That's what the conductor said. Twenty hours, barring weather or hitting a cow or running head-on into a westbound train.

He laughed at the westbound-train joke. Duncan didn't. But twenty hours. That was right. If there were no problems, they could be in Kansas City in twenty hours. Just like Duncan had been told in Dead Broke. Just like he had been told in Denver. Twenty hours. That hadn't changed.

But it changed at Cowle's Crossroads. They had to pull onto the siding and let a westbound run through, and the westbound was having trouble, trudging along at twenty-four miles per hour instead of forty or fifty.

"We might be able to make it up," the conductor said. "Those two 280s pulling us can really move like lightning."

The weather held, though, and by Duncan's pocket watch, they had reached the Kansas border by two forty-seven that afternoon. That was even after they had spent an extra forty minutes in Cheyenne Wells so Nugget could remove the tarp and let four ranchers, six cowboys, two ranch wives and six children, plus the three DCE and KCK employees see his Liberty Bell of Zinc. They had to pay, of course: fifty cents for adults and two bits for the kids.

The next delay was at one of the crossings over the Smoky Hill River, to let a massive herd of pronghorn cross. Nugget wanted one of his guards to shoot a couple so they could eat something other than the stale crackers that came with the bad coffee on the railroad. But Little Joey, Mrs. Clarke, and Sara wouldn't hear of such a thing.

They stood on the flatcar, watching, and Duncan ignored his grouchy temperament when Sara put her arm around his waist.

"They're beautiful, aren't they?" she whispered.

"Yeah." He had to agree, but then he sighed. "But I remember . . ." His head shook.

"What do you remember?" she whispered.

"I remember a time, back when I was a young'un, when trains had to stop for a thousand buffalo."

Nugget sighed. "I sure could go for a pickled buffler tongue right now." He spit out a piece of a stale cracker. "'Em crackers hurt my wooden teeth."

At Dead Skunk Springs, Sara was playing blackjack with the two young deputy marshals, Albert Hitschmann and Peter Webster. Not for money. Not with Mrs. Clarke and Little Joey watching. Just to pass the time. After those hundreds of pronghorns, about the only scenery they saw was blowing dust—and wisps of coal smoke from the two locomotives.

"How far to Ellsworth?" Duncan asked the conductor when he made another pass.

The man stopped, holding the back of a seat to steady himself while fishing out his watch.

"Four hours. Probably a bit less."

It turned out to be a bit more. But that was because of the ambush at the next stop at Worst Water Station.

The first bullet smashed through the right-side window and punched a hole in the crown of Deputy Hitschmann's Stetson. Too bad. He hit the ground and dropped the ace and jack he was about to turn over.

Mrs. Clarke let out a scream. She reached over and jerked her son off his seat and fell into the aisle, covering him with her body.

Then everyone was on the floor, but no other gunfire sounded. The engines hissed.

Holding the Schofield, cocked but the barrel aimed at the ceiling, Duncan looked down the aisle.

"You all right?" he asked.

The deputy nodded and sighed. "That's a new hat."

"Better'n a hole in your noggin," one of Nugget's guards said.

"Mr. Nugget?" a high-pitched voice called out.

Nugget spit tobacco juice onto the floor.

"Yeah?" he said, and wiped his mouth.

"Have I got y'all's attention?"

"I reckon."

"Well, I've got a Greener ten-gauge and a Remington .44 on the drivers of your boys in those two engines."

"That's fine," Nugget said, "but I gots twelve of my best men . . . and I gots Mick MacMickin', too, and two other lawdogs—one of who is a mite sore on account you ruint his new hat. You reckon you can top that?"

"Ain't got to."

"What do you want?" Duncan yelled, but he figured he knew the answer.

Only he didn't.

"We wants to see that shiny big rock of yourn."

He had to have misheard. Looking at Sara, though, and seeing her face, he realized he hadn't.

"See?" Duncan asked.

"Yeah. My girl—she can read—she says you was chargin' fifty cents for grownups and twenty-five for littler ones. That still hold?"

"It's a trick," one of Nugget's gunmen whispered.

Duncan thought the same.

"Mister, there are two federal marshals in this car," Duncan called out.

"I ain't payin' for 'em to see it. I got my four sons and two cousins, my old lady, and my oldest boy's third wife. I gots three grandkids, six, nine, and three years old. And I gots my neighbor. He ain't as old as me, but he's in the fifty-cent age, too. And I gots five dollars and seventy-five cents. My old lady figured that out herself, and my nine-year-old granddaughter said it's the same as her cipherin' said it was. Can we see that thing of beauty my old lady has read us about?"

"You're holding up a train to pay to see that rock?" Hitschmann yelled.

"We ain't held up nothin', mister. 'Em train drivers stopped here. We just had to get y'all's attention."

"You coulda blown my head off!" Hitschmann yelled.

"Naw. Not the way my oldest boy's third wife shoots."

Duncan tried to get a decent look at the station. The water tower was on the other side. He could make out a dugout, but couldn't see any of the men—or the three kids. Or the speaker's wife. Or his daughter-in-law with a great aim.

"What about the mama of 'em grandkids of yourn?" Nugget yelled.

"Left her at the place," the voice replied. "So we'd have vittles when we come back. 'Sides, she didn't have no wish to see nothin'—except to see us gone for a few hours."

"It's gotta be a trick," Deputy Webster whispered.

"Holding engineers at gunpoint is a felony," Mrs. Clarke pointed out.

"Ain't just engineers, lady, it's the coal shovelers, too. But I'll pay for 'em to see that pretty rock. I'll pay for all y'all to get a good view."

"You can't touch it!" Nugget said.

"Wouldn't want to," the voice called back. "Shouldn't touch somethin' that wonderful."

"They'll gun us all down the moment we step outside," one of Nugget's men whispered.

"No," Little Joey said, "they won't. He sounds like a nice fellow."

"Who just fired a bullet through this car," Hitschmann whispered, "and parted what little hair's still atop my head."

Duncan's finger tightened on the trigger, and slowly he lowered the hammer.

"Mister," he said, "I'm stepping outside. I'm MacMicking. Mick MacMicking." He never liked that handle, but it generally got some attention—and respect.

"Come ahead. Your conductor and brakeman appear to be doing a good job of coverin' you from the caboose. And I figure y'all got us outnumbered. All we wants to do is see that rock. Can't afford to go to Chicago."

Duncan kept the Schofield in his right hand and crawled on the floor to the rear door before rising. Once outside, he stepped onto the ground and felt the icy blast of the Kansas wind.

"Mister?" Duncan recognized the voice from the other passenger car behind the flatcar.

"Yeah?" the unnamed interloper called back.

"My name is Woodward. Carl Woodward. I'm a reporter for the *Times of the Rockies.*"

Duncan had almost forgotten that the newspaperman was on the train.

"I'd like to step outside. Talk to you."

"The dickens you say!"

"Yes, sir. This will make an interesting story for our readers."

"You mean you'd write about me in your paper?"

"Exactly."

"Can you mention my ol' lady, too? She'd get a kick outta that."

"I'll even spell her name right."

"Oh, you don't have to do that. She don't read no better than I do."

Duncan saw them, all armed, but the weapons now pointing at the dirt. He felt silly all of a sudden, holding that Schofield, the wind freezing. He glanced at the guards on the flatcar, what he could see of them, anyway, since they were all hiding behind the zinc boulder.

The unnamed man handed a muzzle-loading musket to a wiry but thick-shouldered young man. He started walking toward the train, away from the station, and stopped a few feet from Duncan. Woodward came out of the other car, and hustled over fast, trying to keep his hat from tearing off his head.

The man stopped and held out his right hand.

"You be the real Mick MacMickin'?" he asked.

"Yes, sir." Duncan studied the man's eyes, his face, and then he smiled. "But call me Duncan."

The grip was firm. And honest. And while they shook, Duncan holstered the Schofield.

"Name's Hoisington," the man said. "Hoyt Hoisington. But I ain't got nothin' to do with the town over in Barton County. Ain't never been there. Ain't never had no desire to see it. Ain't much to see in Kansas nohow."

It was dark when they left Worst Water Station, but everybody seemed happy. Nugget had even let the little ones touch his Liberty Bell of Zinc. No charge. He let the others touch it, too, but that cost them a nickel. They passed a jug around for a couple of minutes, chatting about the weather.

Carl Woodward asked if it was always this windy.

One of the sons laughed and told him this wasn't even windy.

The sons helped the guards and the brakeman put the tarps back over the big rock. Then they shook hands again.

"That's a real pretty rock, Mr. Nugget," Hoyt Hoisington said. "Real pretty. It sure was worth the trouble of gettin' here." He handed the conductor a bag of beans. "That's to pay for that hole in your window."

He said they'd taste better if you cooked them with onions, and he would have brought onions, too, but this year's crops hadn't made. The conductor thanked him, anyway.

And everyone left Worst Water Station happy. Except for Carl Woodward. The wind had blown down the telegraph wire, and no one had found the break yet, so that meant Carl Woodward could not telegraph his news to Denver City until the train reached Ellsworth.

CHAPTER 29

They arrived in Kansas City, Kansas, three hours behind schedule, but the conductor of the Missouri-Mississippi Express said he'd have them to St. Louis in seven hours, but he was wrong. They reached the depot in just under six hours and forty-seven minutes.

Of course, they had to wait two hours before enough men and equipment were found to move that flatcar to the St. Louis, Bloomington, and Chicago line, and then they had to wait till a section of track was repaired.

There were 297 miles to go. That's what the conductor told Nugget and Duncan.

He looked at his watch.

"We'll have you there in nine hours," he boasted. "One thirty-seven this afternoon or my name's not Jonas Casey."

Turns out, the man's name was Rafe Ellinwood, and they reached Chicago at five nineteen.

They saw little wildlife, but lots of fields of corn and wheat.

The delays were mostly waiting on side tracks to allow the trains that owned, and did not rent, the tracks they traveled, and it took two hours and fifty-three minutes to get out of Bloomington because of all the crowds that wanted to see the great treasure of zinc, and Nugget was generous. He gave them the same deal he had given the Hoisington bunch back at Worst Water Station, Kansas.

Duncan slept. He didn't remember falling asleep, and he jerked awake, startling Sara.

"Have we stopped?" he asked, and his hand found the butt of his .45.

"No." Sara yawned. "Just slowed to a crawl."

He frowned. They'd never get anywhere at this rate.

Duncan was sick of riding in trains, but the ride had been mostly smooth since they had gotten out of Kansas. When he looked outside, he saw no crops, no farms, but buildings. Homes and stores. Wagons and carts. Dirt and filth.

The conductor entered the coach, stopped long enough to have a drink of water from the dipper, wiped his mouth, pulled out his watch, and walked down the aisle, weaving as men and women did on moving trains, and stopped in front of Duncan.

"Fifteen minutes, Marshal. Fifteen minutes before we reach the Chicago station."

They were in Chicago.

They had made it. No robbery attempts. No derailments.

That's when the buildings suddenly stopped, and an odor filled the coach that was familiar to anyone who had ever driven longhorns or marshaled in cattle towns.

Cow dung.

Mrs. Clarke awakened, paled, held her breath, and turned to close the window.

That's when Duncan heard the first gunshot.

And Mrs. Clarke screamed.

Hitschmann and Webster came up quickly. Nugget

tried to find his weapon. His four guards thumbed back hammers.

Mrs. Clarke was on the floor, fighting to keep her son from climbing over her and onto the seat so he could see what was happening.

"Criminy!" one of Nugget's men yelled. "It's a madhouse out there!"

He saw the riders as he cocked the Schofield. Men wearing chaps, vests, hats—all rather new-looking—on fine horses. And behind them came a troop of cavalry, led by a man who looked just like George Armstrong Custer. The guidon was even that of Custer's. The soldiers behind them waved sabers or fired rifles. But . . . they were firing at . . .

. . . Cossacks?

And the Cossacks were being chased by . . .

. . . Indians!

Well, some of those might have been real Indians. The rider with the beaded buckskin britches probably wasn't. The black wig blew off his head, and the red paint on his arms didn't go all the way to his hands, and, riding as close to the tracks as he was on that fine Arabian stud, Duncan could make out the beard stubble on his face.

But most of those Indians—the ones riding like they had been riding all their lives—had to be real. Comanche maybe? No, no, those were Lakotas. Taller than Comanches, but just as ferocious, and just as marvelous riders as Comanches were. Maybe . . . just maybe . . . even a little bit better.

He wasn't sure about the Cossacks. And others appeared to be soldiers from other countries. England? France? Duncan wasn't sure, and, honestly, he didn't really care.

He looked for Ben Usher.

"Do you see Ben?" Sara asked.

"No." He smiled. "I doubt if Ben would do this—no matter how much Cody's paying him. Besides, Ben's quite the hand with a gun of any kind. And he can ride a horse." He shook his hand as one of the riders kept his horse rearing while waving his hat and yelling something nobody could hear above the din.

"But Ben can't ride like that."

And a clown rode a buffalo behind the Indians.

"I'll kill that devil before . . ." One of Nugget's men eared back the hammers on his double-barrel.

"No!" Duncan wasn't sure the man heard him, so he jerked the Schofield and fired. The weapon roared louder than a cannon in the confines of the coach, and the bullet ripped through the seat and just above the muzzle of the twelve-gauge.

The man yelped and swung the shotgun around, but the barrel caught the windowsill and he dropped the weapon.

He cursed, and started to grab the scattergun, but Nugget rose from his seat and pounded the top of the man's hand with the hilt of his big bowie knife.

"'Em ain't bandits, boy," Nugget said. He grinned.

Duncan let out a heavy sigh.

"Look!"

Little Joey Clarke had made it out of his mother's grasp and was sitting on his knees, and stuck his head, shoulders, and arms out of the window. He waved and hurrahed.

"It's Buffalo Bill, Mama. Look. It's Buffalo Bill Cody!"

Duncan ducked a bit and looked out the window. It took just a moment for him to find the rider, and Duncan had to grin.

Little Joey Clarke was right.

Nobody sat a horse like Bill Cody. And nobody could wear a hat that big or a vest that shined like Nugget's Liberty Bell of Zinc.

Buffalo Bill's Wild West show was out there. He tried to find Ben Usher, but had no luck.

"Why," Mrs. Clarke said, "they are all welcoming us to Chicago. Isn't this marvelous?"

Ben Usher, Duncan thought, would laugh till he cried when Duncan let him know how close Cody or some of his men came from getting shot at—and maybe hit.

And wouldn't Carl Woodward have enjoyed sending that piece of news to the *Times of the Rockies* and every other newspaper in the United States.

"Yippee!" Little Joey kept waving.

Duncan looked around. The two deputies were also leaning out of the windows, letting out whoops. Webster even drew his pistol and started firing rounds into the air.

That was fine for Buffalo Bill's troupe, but not for a deputy U.S. marshal. When Webster pulled himself back inside and started emptying the cylinder of empty cartridges, and began fishing out live rounds to reload, Duncan put his hand on the young man's shoulder.

"Let's not shoot that way, son." He nodded toward the riding cowboys and soldiers and Indians and Cossacks.

"They are shooting blanks, son. Those bullets you send in the air, well, they gotta come down somewhere. And there are a lot of folks in Chicago those bullets might hit."

"Gosh." Webster's face paled. "I never thought about that."

Duncan found a seat beside Sara. He put his arm around her, and she giggled.

"Isn't this something?"

Looking through the window, Duncan nodded.

He let out a sigh. They had made it to Chicago. No robberies. Just a little bit of gunplay. They had made it here safe and sound.

A band was playing somewhere, loud enough to be

heard over the squeaking, hissing, chugging, straining, coughing, and rumbling of the locomotives.

He had gotten that troublesome boulder of zinc out of Dead Broke. All he had to do was spend a couple weeks in Chicago, and then he could take Sara back to Dead Broke and enjoy a quiet, peaceful winter. He'd be playacting for a while, making a fool of himself. But he'd be with Ben Usher again.

Duncan had never taken a vacation in his life. But he would now. With Ben and Sara, maybe even Nugget.

This was going to be a lot of fun.

"Look!" Mrs. Clarke pointed out the window. "Look! Look, Joey. Look! Do you see? Do you see?"

Ducking a bit, Duncan saw it about the same time Little Joey did.

BUFFALO BILL'S WILD WEST & CONGRESS OF ROUGH RIDERS OF THE WORLD

An arrow—a giant arrow like one from the Northern Plains tribes—pointed the way.

"That's right," Duncan said. "The entrance is near the railroad stations."

The riders were slowing their mounts, now the train, moving at a slow crawl, passed men and women, old and young, children, young and into their teens. The men doffed their hats. Women and kids waved. The two deputy marshals, and even Nugget's ornery gunmen, waved back, calling out, "Howdy."

"Welcome to the greatest city in the world," a man on stilts said.

Something flashed. A photographer working his magic,

Duncan guessed, and the train's brakes squeaked. He steadied Sara with his left hand, and let his right grip the seat, just before the car jerked to a final stop.

The locomotives hissed.

Someone started singing:

> *Camptown ladies sing this song,*
> *Doo-dah, doo-dah.*
> *Camptown racetrack five miles long*
> *Oh, doo-dah day.*

"Auld Lang Syne" followed.

The conductor opened the door, removed his hat and said, "Welcome to Chicago, folks. Enjoy your stay."

"We plan to," one of Nugget's men said.

Duncan excused himself from Sara and walked to the deputies. "All right. We still have work to do. They say there's more than a million people living in this town, and I don't think all of them are that interested in seeing a Wild West show—but they might want a chunk of zinc."

He turned around and caught the attention of one of Nugget's guards. He didn't know where Nugget had disappeared to, but that was fine. The mayor could take care of himself.

He went back to Sara and said, "I've got work to do. See you at the hotel."

"All right," she whispered.

Duncan led the deputies and guards out the door and onto the flatcar. To his surprise, about a dozen Cossacks, four troopers, an Indian who wasn't a white man painted like an Indian, and General Custer himself, only he was bald and holding a long blond wig in his left hand, stood surrounding the covered six tons of zinc.

"Gentlemen," a voice called off to Duncan's right.

He turned to see William F. "Buffalo Bill" Cody, mounted on a dun stallion and sitting in a saddle that, considering all the silver embedded into the leather, had to weigh close to a hundred pounds.

"You are in my town, boys, and from what I've read in the newspapers, you've had quite a ride from Colorado to Illinois." He bowed slightly and returned his big Stetson to his head. "So, if you allow, my men will guard this treasure until Chicago's best policemen get through the crowd and take this to our grounds. And I will treat you to a splendid dinner and fine conversation at this city's best restaurant."

Sara had stepped outside.

Cody straightened and his eyes sparkled. "Indeed. You are my guests." He bowed again toward Sara. "And you will be my most special guest, my lady. I am William F. Cody, miss, and I am your most humble servant."

Duncan realized he was grinding his teeth again. And his fingers were balled into tight fists.

That Cody . . . he could be more troublesome than the devil.

Another man, wearing a fine black suit of broadcloth and a handsome Stetson, stepped onto the flatcar and took Sara by her right arm.

"Allow me," he said, "to be your protector for at least this night."

Duncan heard that—despite the noise of humanity and machines and animals all around him.

Ben Usher, he remembered suddenly, could be even a bigger pest than that scoundrel Buffalo Bill.

CHAPTER 30

Cody had closed the show early that afternoon, and he told Duncan that he would have to take out those losses from the salary he had promised. Then he laughed, but Duncan had read that gleam in the colonel's eye and figured he was joking—although part of that shimmer came from the whiskey on his breath.

He took the newcomers through the gate while there was still enough sunlight. Several men and women were walking around, picking up trash and putting the trash into bags.

The grounds stretched on for what seemed like forever, surrounded in the distance by the towering buildings of Chicago. Duncan smelled popped corn, fried beef, and scents that made his mouth water, but ones he could not recognize. He also smelled that pleasing aroma of horses. And cattle. Mounted Indians herded four massive buffalo toward a corral.

"How many acres?" Duncan asked.

"Twenty," Cody said.

"Fifteen," Ben Usher whispered.

Two armed Chicago policemen pulled back heavy canvas, and Cody led them into the giant grandstand.

"It'll hold twenty-five thousand," Cody said.

"Eighteen," Usher corrected in a voice only Duncan could hear.

"I realized that over the past, oh, five, six, seven years—maybe more—that I had been doing a great disservice to my American fans," Cody said, and he removed his big hat. "The Golden Jubilee for Queen Victoria in England. Giving that fine ol' gal—Vicky, I called her—a ride in the Deadwood stage. London. Manchester. Nottingham. Portsmouth. Sheffield. Liverpool. Antwerp. Brussels."

"Anywhere in France?" Sara asked. She had always wanted to see Paris.

"Never been to France, sweetheart," Cody said.

The publicity man walking next to Cody cleared his throat. "Marseille," he said.

Cody stopped and turned to the tall, pale man. "How's that?"

"We were in Marseille," the man said.

"When were we there?"

"Two weeks. December of '89."

Cody nodded. "Marseille. I thought that was in Italy."

"No, sir. It's in France. And we were in Lyon right before we went to Marseille."

"Lyon . . . that's in Italy, right?"

"No, sir."

"Portugal?"

"Lyon is in France, too."

Cody shrugged. "Lyon. Yes. That redhead with the beauty mark on her cheek." He touched his face near where the right side of his mustache curled upward. "She spoke Italian."

"Greek," the man said.

Cody nodded. "Berlin," he said. "Cologne." He turned to the publicity man. "That's Germany, right?"

"Yes, Colonel Cody. Germany. We were there three years ago."

"Anyway. The Scots saw us. So did the Spanish. Right?"

"Barcelona," the publicity man said. "Late December through mid-January of 1890."

Cody nodded. "We've even been to Canada. So all those foreigners have gotten to see my Wild West, yet I have been neglecting the people of my own country. Most of us in the West know what it has been like, but I realized those folks back in the East. Why, they've just read in newspapers and books about what all we've done for our country. They ought to see what it was like. And I'm showing it to them. And showing our history to folks all across the world who come to Chicago, thinking they'll just go to that circus about Columbus across the way. But when they enter the gates to my Wild West, they see history. Real history. For we show them the truth. No matter where they call home, they come to appreciate all that it took to conquer the American West. Even if they come from Luxembourg."

He turned to the publicity man. "We haven't been to Luxembourg, have we?"

"No, sir," the sweating man said. "But we will, sir. We will."

Laughing, Cody slapped the man on the back, almost knocking him to his knees. "You're a good man, Kinley."

"Kinlock," the man corrected.

But the colonel was moving on.

"From what I saw," Duncan said, "from the train coming in, you're showing more than just the American West, Colonel."

"That's a fact. We have Frenchies and Brits, Germans and Russians. Gauchos from Argentina. The Sixth Cavalry gave me twenty troopers, and I have lots of Indians." He pounded the tall Lakota's back. "Ain't that right, pardner."

The Sioux turned and looked down on Cody—and looking down on Buffalo Bill was hard for most men, tall as he was, but that Indian was a giant.

"You pay me to ride and fall down and get scalped. You don't pay me to knock me in the back."

Cody stopped, looked up into the Indian's dark eyes, and nodded. The Sioux looked big enough and tough enough to take down Cody, Usher, the soldier walking with them, and half of those men, women, and boys cleaning up the grounds.

He resumed the tour. "I want you to meet the gent who leads the cowboy band I've got going. Jim Swiney. He's a good ol' feller."

"Sweeney," the publicity man whispered. "William *Sweeney*."

Cody gave them tickets to the next day's first performance. He said he wanted them to see the show first, from the grandstands. He didn't give them reserved seats because, well, those cost extra, but he wanted them to see what the folks who paid to see his show got to see.

And, Duncan realized, it was something to see.

William Sweeney led the band to open *Buffalo Bill's Wild West* with "The Star-Spangled Banner." And before the crowd—there wasn't an empty seat in the whole arena, Duncan marveled—Cody came out, resplendent in his beaded buckskins and fine hat—on a prancing palomino stallion—followed by the "Rough Riders of the World," as the man speaking through the big horn told the cheering crowd.

The troopers from the Sixth Cavalry led the procession

behind Cody, followed by the Prince of Wales's lancers, Chasseurs from France . . . Cossacks . . . guards from Germany's Uhlan Regiment . . . then wild-riding gauchos from Argentina . . . Western cowboys . . . vaqueros from Mexico . . . cowgirls—at which the bruising-looking toughs sitting behind Sara and Duncan whistled so loud it hurt Duncan's ears. A mounted band of cowboys came next, followed by at least a hundred Sioux—led by that tall giant who didn't like being slapped hard in the back.

After they had circled around the massive grandstand and disappeared behind the curtain, the din subsided. The gent in the bowler then introduced Annie Oakley as the "celebrated sure shot." And she did not disappoint.

"For a little gal, she shoots almost as good as you," Nugget told Duncan.

"Better than me," Duncan said. When she punched a hole through the center of the ace of spades her husband held in his hand—shooting backward and sighting the rifle through the reflection of a mirror held in the hand by a young girl—Duncan was the first in his group to stand and cheer loudly.

The horse race came next, pitting a Texas cowpuncher on a dun gelding against one Cossack, a vaquero, a mean-looking Argentinian on a beautiful Arabian stallion, and that extraordinarily tall Sioux warrior, who looked practically comical on that small pinto pony he was riding.

A gunshot started the race, and it looked like pure bedlam.

The man speaking through the big horn announced while three cowboys carried the cowboy in the race whose horse stumbled and threw him over its head and into the dirt on the first turn that as soon as the horse manure and blood was shoveled away, the greatest Pony Express rider in the world would demonstrate the skills it took to deliver the mail in 1860 and 1861.

Then he cleared his throat after lowering the big horn, lifted it again to his lips, and said, "I beg your pardon, ladies and gentlemen, I meant to say 'the second greatest Pony Express rider' who ever lived." He waved his left arm, and continued, "For we all know who is the greatest Pony Express rider, the greatest Western hero, and the greatest showman in the world!"

He ripped off his hat, lowered the big horn, and shouted. "And here he is!"

Bill Cody trotted around the arena on another horse, waving his hat, and looking like the pure showman he was.

He disappeared behind a curtain after circling the arena, and as soon as he was out of sight, a wiry fellow galloped across the arena, jerked his pony to a stop, and slipped off the horse. Three other cowhands ran to the horse and rider.

"Marshal MacMicking?" Little Joey Clarke whispered.

"Yeah." Duncan was looking at the other side of the arena, anticipating the next so-called Pony Express rider.

"Isn't that Marshal Usher?"

Duncan turned. The young boy pointed at the man who had just galloped and now stood with the others beside the horse.

Sara had brought a small pair of binoculars and now looked intently.

Duncan squinted.

"Yeah," he said, and Sara nodded as she lowered the spyglasses in confirmation. "It sure looks like Ben."

"I didn't know Marshal Usher rode for the Pony Express," the boy said. "Wow! He's done everything."

Duncan cut off his laugh. "He has now."

"Here . . . comes . . . the . . . Pony . . . Express!" the

man yelled through the horn, and out rode another rider, galloping a bay horse across the arena.

The crowd cheered. Duncan and the others had to stand to see over bowlers and top hats and Stetsons and ladies' headwear. The cowboy band blared some tune that no one could recognize over the screams and shouts and cheers. The horse slid to a stop, two men grabbed the reins as the wiry fellow leaped out of the saddle, and jerked the mail sack, called a mochila, with him. That's where Ben Usher went to work, taking the mochila and dropping over the saddle just an instant before the rider leaped onto the horse, which bucked twice, then took off, raising dust, slapping his hat against the pony's side. The band hit the crescendo just as horse and rider disappeared.

"The Pony Express, ladies, gentlemen, children!" the announcer yelled.

Ben Usher swung onto the horse, and trotted off, doffing his hat as he passed the reserved seats in front of the grandstands where Duncan sat with his friends.

"That's a darn-tootin' good show!" Nugget bellowed.

Usher's eyes met Duncan's and both gunmen grinned. Usher shook his head as though he couldn't believe what was happening, put the hat back on his head, pulled it down tight, and kicked the pony into a slight lope. Then he was through the curtains, and the announcer was telling the crowd to get ready for the next act. And before Duncan could even catch his breath, a heavy wagon came into view, pulled by oxen, with two women, a boy and a girl, and two men walking alongside it.

Another wagon followed. Then two more.

The speaker started talking about the emigrant trails that led to Oregon, to California, across the Great Plains. He spoke of the dangers those brave pioneers faced.

Drought. Rattlesnakes. Mexican bandits. And the most aggressive warriors of all the Indian nations.

And then here rode those Sioux, whooping and firing arrows that lacked arrowheads over the wagons' canopies. The women screamed. The children hid underneath the wagons. The men held tightly on to the harnesses of oxen and mules to keep them from taking off at a run.

A woman, two rows down, screamed, "Oh, my Lord! Those poor little babies!"

A man in checkered pants cupped his hands over his mouth and yelled, "They'll be slaughtered by those merciless savages!"

"But," the man doing the announcing below thundered, "these brave emigrants will not be turned back. Not today. Not on this trail. For Buffalo Bill rides again!"

And Cody rode again, leading a band of twenty or more riders, cowboys mostly, but some dressed in buckskins, looking more like army scouts than waddies—one even wore a coonskin cap and had a beard that stretched almost to his gun belt. They fired their weapons into the air at first, shooting blanks, then lowered the barrels, aiming slightly at all those Indians. Duncan hoped they were blanks, anyway. Two Indians toppled off their mounts, but kept a firm grip on the hackamores to keep their mounts from racing away and maybe causing a horse wreck.

Two of the men standing next to a wagon wheel raced out, oblivious to the Indians riding around them, and waited for Cody to rein in his stallion, and then held the horse by the bridle as Cody slipped out of the saddle and drew a knife from his sheath. The knife's blade seemed to bend almost in half and wiggled a bit as he charged that tall Sioux, who produced a tomahawk.

They circled each other while the other heroes to the rescue fired blanks, and the other Indians dismounted and took seats on the ground while keeping their horses from ruining a good show.

A hush came out of the stands.

Duncan chuckled and shook his head.

The rubber knife hit the Indian's breastplate, and the man dropped the tomahawk, clasped his left hand over his heart, and sat down in the dirt, then fell onto his side. Cody bent down and ran the fake blade over the top of the Indian's black hair; when he rose, he held a black scalp, which he had pulled out of his shirtsleeve.

The ovation was louder than a cannon blast.

The band tried to play as loud as it could, but no one in the grandstands could hear a note. A boy a few seats down was jumping up and down, waving his little hat over his head. A young mother tried to keep her baby from squalling, but no one could hear the infant's cries. Duncan wasn't even sure if the mom could hear her little one.

A few Wild West operations had come to Durango back when Duncan was marshaling there, and he had seen other shows here and there—had even taken part in some dog-and-pony shows between jobs. He had seen theater in Chicago and New York, in San Francisco and Tombstone. He'd even seen Cody in a play in Kansas. He and Ben Usher. Well, Cody had said it was "a play." Duncan and Ben Usher said it was "absurd." Duncan had seen more circuses than he could count.

But he had never seen anything this . . . *amazing.*

He'd tip his hat to Buffalo Bill after the show.

Duncan glanced at the program he had been given. They were only five acts into the performance. Thirteen more to go. And then there still was that final salute and conclusion.

CHAPTER 31

Things kind of calmed down for a while. Syrians and Arabs came out on their horses, did their tricks, showed what they could do. The Indian young ones followed, illustrating the games they played. The man in the checkered pants a few rows down produced a flask and offered a sip to the white-haired fellow with a straw hat, who gladly took a pull and nodded his thanks.

Little Joey clapped and clapped.

Russian Cossacks rode out next, jumping their horses over hurdles, over each other. They almost rode as well as the Sioux. Then there was a short break, and a few minutes later, the voice through the horn bellowed that those in attendance were about to witness some of the greatest marksmanship ever presented by the man who had met many, and bested them all, the man that even Wild Bill Hickok—great friend to the amazing Buffalo Bill—had named "the best shot in not just the West, but the world."

Ben Usher rode out on what looked to be one of Buffalo Bill's horses to the center of the arena, dismounting with ease. It was hard to see because his shirt just sparkled, and Duncan had never known Usher to wear woolly chaps or a hat with a brim that big.

"He looks like some dude," Nugget said.

Duncan couldn't disagree.

"Not a dude. A clown. Like that drunk from that show that you run out of town a while back."

Even from these seats, Duncan knew that Usher wasn't carrying his .41-caliber Thunderer. He drew a Winchester from the saddle scabbard, worked the lever, and nodded at a woman wearing saloon tights that sparkled more than Usher's lavender shirt.

She tossed a bottle, Usher fired, the bottle shattered, and Duncan waited to hear pellet shots landing on the covered wagon a few yards away. But he couldn't. He could barely make out his own breathing with all the clapping going on throughout the grandstands and the reserved seats. Besides, there had been so much shooting, Duncan wasn't even certain that he could hear his own thoughts.

An idea came to him. Sell cotton wadding for the ears—especially for women and young kids. The couple of times he had tried buffalo hunting, the head shooter had advised him to use wadding. A Winchester rifle didn't make the same roar of a Sharps .50 caliber, but over a long period of time—and in an enclosed arena like this giant tent—even a derringer could damage someone's eardrums.

Johnny Baker came out next and showed his shooting. Then Usher and Baker fired their revolvers at a can, keeping the piece of tin bouncing across the dirt for twelve shots.

The crowd sang out praises and clapped till every hand had to hurt.

Annie Oakley came back, all three of them went to work, shooting cards and cigarettes, and even an arrow that one of the younger Sioux boys sent into the air.

After taking their bows, the three mounted horses, which were brought to them, and circled the arena, waving hats and smiling to those who had paid twenty-five cents or more to see the show.

The vaqueros from Mexico rode out next. Duncan had often thought, back when he cowboyed, and then when he arrested cowboys, that the Mexicans handled a lariat better than any Texas kid. Duncan liked this part of the show.

Twirling lassos did not make anywhere near the noise a Colt .45, Winchester .44-40, or Sharps Big Fifty made.

"What do you think?" Sara asked.

He turned and took her hand in his and gave it a gentle squeeze.

"I don't know what Cody's going to want me to do," he said with a smile, "but I sure can't do anything like I've seen so far."

"Oh, don't be silly," she said. "You're Duncan MacMicking. You can do anything when you set your mind to do it."

She leaned over and kissed him on the cheek.

"Gross," Little Joey said. "That's gross. Kissing's gross."

His mother smiled and tousled the boy's hair.

"You might not think so," Duncan said, "a few years down the trail."

"Gross."

Little Joey turned around and rose, clapping and yelling, "Bravo!" as one of the vaqueros kept jumping through a rope he kept spinning as two of his friends strummed guitars.

Women took over the next act—some in prairie dresses, some in saloon clothes, Indian girls in beaded buckskin of various colors—dancing first, then having a footrace that went about thirty yards. One of the Indian girls won that one. Next they raced on horseback, and the Comanche girl probably would have won had her horse not stumbled, and the Spanish girl—with hair blacker than any Duncan had seen—it was darker than the Sioux's or Comanche's—had not reined her dun up and checked to make sure the Comanche girl was all right.

The spectators cheered that sportsmanship, and the red-headed prairie gal trotted her horse back to make sure everyone was all right.

They did better on the footrace. The Spanish girl won, but then, Duncan figured she would. With those long legs. He tried not to stare at them too much, though. Sara was pulling for the Sioux girl, and she finished second. A distant second.

Cowboys rode out for the next part of the routine, and it was a wild one, because they drove out a bunch of wild ponies, lassoing them, then doing tricks, roping each other, then riding at a hard gallop across the arena, leaning from their saddles and snatching up whiskey bottles off the dirt.

Nugget leaped out of his chair. "Throw me that bottle and I'll pay you a dollar!"

The crowd laughed. The cowboy with the bottle couldn't hear, of course.

And Little Joey turned and told Nugget, "The bottle's empty, Mayor Nugget."

Even Nugget laughed. He reached over and patted the boy's head.

The soldiers from around the world took over the next act, and the announcer asked the crowd to be respectful, and to hold all applause till the last of Wales's Twelfth Lancers concluded the parade. The Sixth Cavalry boys started things, though their uniforms were dusty from riding to rescues earlier in the program and such, but they did just fine. So did King William II's Potsdamer Reds. They were all mighty fine, Nugget agreed, once the Twelfth Lancers finished its parade.

After the last of the soldiers were out of sight, the

announcer said it was time for . . . A drum started beating for the longest time. Before the announcer could speak, a stagecoach raced into the arena, and Little Joey leaped out of his seat and almost onto the fellow wearing the red bib-front shirt's back.

"The Deadwood stage!" But the announcer's shout and the crowd's ovation died quickly as twenty Indians—from Sioux, Comanche, Pawnee, and other nations—galloped after the big coach. The Indian boys—and two women— yipped and yelped and waved tomahawks and lances. The man in the duster riding shotgun fired one barrel, then another. One Indian leaped off the side of his horse—feigning death, but landing on his feet and not falling to the dirt and laying still until he was at least twenty yards out of the path of those galloping horses.

The warriors almost had the stagecoach. The shotgunner was lying atop the coach, playing dead, though one hand held tightly to the shotgun and the other, his right, had a much firmer grip on the railing atop the coach.

"Oh, no, they're all doomed!" a woman screamed from the reserved seats and fainted.

Duncan thought she was playacting. He realized she wasn't. He husband, or whoever he was, didn't appear to notice. He was waving his hat and screaming at the Indians and urging the driver of the coach to whip those horses into a lather.

"She's breathing!"

Duncan looked at Sara, who pointed at the woman. "She's not dead!" she yelled again. Then she took Duncan's right arm and pulled him closer to her.

"I might be scared, too, you know," she called out with a wonderful gleam in her eyes.

He pulled her close and let his left arm push her tightly against his body.

My, oh, my, he thought. *I might take a great liking to this show business thing.*

Mrs. Clarke let out a roaring, "Hurrah," when Buffalo Bill and his cowboys rode into the area. They quickly caught up with the Indians, some who pulled their mounts to a stop, stepped off into the sand, and carefully lay down. A few of the younger ones leaped off their galloping mounts and stumbled a few yards till they fell in a relatively safe patch of the arena. Buffalo Bill galloped close to the stagecoach, but he let one of his younger riders do the hard part. The kid leaped from the saddle and grabbed the railing. Luckily, the shotgunner playing dead was holding the railing on the opposite side of the coach.

Still, Duncan had to credit the boy's sand. He wouldn't be doing that for all the money in the till this evening. One slip, one bad fall, that boy could be crippled or dead. Instead, he used his feet to find holds in the open windows, and then he pulled himself onto the top of the coach, then moved to the driver, who was supposed to be dead now, but had kept a strong hold on the leather lines to that runaway team.

The Indians who weren't playing dead turned off to the side and galloped off. In retreat, Duncan assumed, since none of Cody's cowhands went after them. Cody held up his right hand, and let his left rein his horse to a stop.

And it was hard to hear just what the announcer was saying because of all the noise underneath the big tent, but the Deadwood stage—and this was one of the original coaches that had made those historic runs from Cheyenne to Deadwood back in 1875 and '76—was saved by none other than Buffalo Bill Cody, the greatest frontiersman in American history.

The younger Indian boys came out after the Deadwood stage had made a few laps around the arena. They got to race their horses for a while, while their parents came out quickly to set up teepees, and do some dances and sing some songs, and pretend to cook, and pretend to tan hides. Things like that. Probably, Duncan figured, to let all these people, who paid money to see this show, catch their breaths. He let out a little cough.

Probably to let all those cowboys and Sioux and trick riders and soldiers and sharpshooters to catch their breaths, too.

He pulled Sara closer. She giggled.

Then he felt the color leave his face and his heart start racing . . . or maybe even stop.

What the Sam Hill have I gotten myself into?

Buffalo Bill rode back. One of his cowhands tossed up plates and such, and Cody shot them with his pistol first, then his Winchester.

"Bet he's shooting shot and not bullets," one of the men below told his partner.

"Bet you couldn't hit 'em with a cannon firing grape-shot at point-blank range."

They both laughed, and then the one who had started the brief conversation pulled out a flask, opened it, took a sip, and handed it to his pard.

Cody took another ride around the arena, doffing his hat, smiling, and rode out of the arena, but only for a few minutes. Then he was back again, reining that high-stepping show horse to a stop in the center.

A young man ran over to him and handed him one of those big cones, which Cody raised to his mouth, then cleared his throat.

"Ladies and gentlemen, little boys and little girls, Americans and citizens of the world."

The crowd turned quiet, an unnerving quiet after all

the gunfire, hoofbeats, applause, screams, more gunfire, more gunfire, and plenty of deafening cheers.

"They gave me the name 'Buffalo Bill' for all those buffalo I killed. I killed them in the name of progress, in the name of survival, in the name of America. We wiped out the buffalo the way we wiped out the Indians. And sometimes I wish that I had never shot one of those big woolies because we almost killed them all off."

He bowed his head and lowered his hat. The moment of silence passed, and he let out a heavy sigh and raised his head. The hat came up and held.

"But, ladies and gentlemen, my friends from across the world . . . we did not succeed. And for that, we may thank God in heaven above."

That's when the big Sioux and one of those cowboys who had been riding, shooting, falling off his horse time and time again, only to get back up and ride and play dead again, rode into the arena. But they rode behind three massive shaggy buffalo.

The cowboys rode off, and the Indians came out, showing how they shot buffalo, though the arrows they fired as they rode around the behemoth shaggies didn't have points. Then some old buffalo hunters came out in their greasy clothes and big rifles and showed how they did their job that almost killed off the entire species. But they were shooting blanks.

And those magnificent big animals seemed bored by all the noise.

Finally, one of the younger men handed Buffalo Bill a freshly loaded Winchester, and Cody galloped his horse around the arena as the man with the big horn talked about Cody's big buffalo kills in Kansas, and how he became known to the West, and then all of America, and now all of the world as . . .

"Buffalo Bill Cody, the greatest showman on the face of the earth."

And Duncan thought he could hear Cody himself yell as he rode past:

"What do you think about that, Barnum?"

"What's so funny?" Sara asked.

He shook his head. "Nothing, honey. Nothing."

Cody levered the rifle as he rode, pushing the giant buffalo into a trot, and he fired, shooting blanks again, but keeping his rifle aimed well above the lumbering animals. They circled the arena twice, Cody firing a few more times, then reining the stallion to the stands, and stopping it as the crew guided those magnificent animals back to their pens, where they would be given plenty to eat, and get their fur combed good and neat for the evening show.

The announcer started talking about George Armstrong Custer and what happened in what's now the state of Montana, back in American's centennial year.

The man in the checkered britches shook his head and told his friend, "I like this circus a lot better when they show the 'Attack on the Settler's Cabin,' Ralphie, and not all this Custer stuff."

"Yep," his friend agreed. "Ask me and I'll tell you that yeller-haired glory hunter weren't nothin' but a dang-blamed Yankee who got what he deserved."

The man's Southern accent was obvious. Duncan looked around, waiting for someone who fought or whose daddy fought for the Union during the Civil War. But no one seemed to notice. Or maybe they didn't care. Or maybe . . . Duncan found his watch to check the time. Yeah, that was it. Everyone was too tired to do anything now. Or they were deaf. That theory sounded even more believable. Duncan tapped his head next to his right ear.

He was fine. He could hear.

"What on earth are you doing?" Sara asked.

He smiled at her. He heard that, too.

The announcer thanked the crowd for coming. He reminded them of the evening show. He told them that there was lots to see—and eat, including a fine restaurant on the grounds with prices for families and not robber barons—and that may God bless them, may God bless these United States of America, may God bless those who had come across the continent or oceans to see this show, and come back tomorrow and see it all again.

"My buttocks is raw."

Duncan quickly closed the door behind him.

Buffalo Bill stood in his office in the wagon, leaning against his desk, his chaps, britches, and underdrawers pulled all the way down to the floor, his boots tossed in the corner, his left hand pressing against the top of the desk, and his right holding a bottle of rye whiskey. Nate Salsbury had rolled up his sleeves and took another bottle of rye, and splashed the whiskey over his left hand, then his right, and then went to work patting down his partner's inner thighs.

"That burn?" Salsbury asked.

"I can't feel a thing below my third vertebrae." Cody took another pull from his bottle. He turned his head and nodded at Duncan. "I've rode forty, fifty, eighty miles in a day. Used to love sitting in a saddle more than courting a woman or making a fortune. Wait till you're my age, Mick. Just wait."

Duncan grinned. "I'm not that far behind you, pard."

"You're far enough." He held out the bottle, but Duncan shook his head.

"Where's that cute little gal you was with?" Cody asked.

Duncan frowned. "I don't think you're presentable at the moment, Colonel."

Salsbury must have hit the colonel with too much whiskey, because Cody let out a yip and a yell, followed by a fairly vile comment about his business partner's ancestry. Salsbury had met Cody in Brooklyn, back when Cody was performing in stupid plays about the Wild West, and Salsbury was troubadouring at a nearby opera house. Cody often said this whole Wild West gig was ol' Nate's idea.

The tall, slim, bearded man wiped his hands on a towel, and then poured more whiskey onto them, and moved up and down Cody's thighs. Cody took another pull.

"Don't get boiling drunk, Will," Salsbury told him. "You got an evening show. Remember?"

"You won't let me forget." He jerked when Salsbury's hands hit another tender spot.

When he was done with his stage-manager doctoring, Salsbury wiped his hands on a towel, and drank the last of the whiskey straight from the bottle, which he pitched into a trash bin, shattering more glass.

He smiled at Duncan. "What did you think?"

"You wowed everyone around me," Duncan said, and he was honest. "This is a big show."

"Big to run." Salsbury nodded. "And we don't have twenty acres here. We're talking to folks in Brooklyn about next summer. Ambrose Park. They say they can give us forty acres there. We'll have a grandstand with twenty thousand seats."

"If I ain't crippled by then," Cody said, and he looked at Salsbury. "Where's my pillow?"

"I'll find one that doesn't smell like whiskey and sweat." He nodded at Duncan, gave him a wink, and started to open the door, but it pulled open before his hand touched the knob.

Ben Usher walked in. Salsbury nodded at him, let Usher come in first, and then he walked out, shutting the door behind him.

"Whiskey?" Cody offered.

Usher shook his head. He smiled at Duncan. "Like the show?"

"Loved it." Duncan smiled at Cody. "Little Joey Clarke had a fine time. We all did. It must be something . . . being Buffalo Bill Cody to thousands of people, twice a day."

Cody finished his bottle and tossed it into the can.

"You'll find out tomorrow, son. That's what we're paying you for." He pulled his hat off his head and laid it on the seat of the chair. Then eased his whiskey-soaked buttocks onto that big hat, sighing as he sank into the chair.

Duncan was frowning now. "What do you mean?"

Usher chuckled, and Cody closed his eyes, leaning back, letting the whiskey work its magic on his buttocks and his thighs and his calves and his soul.

"Pay close attention to the evening show, ol' hoss," Cody said softly. "Because tomorrow . . . you're gonna be me."

CHAPTER 32

"What never you do," the Cossack told Duncan, "is take off hat."

"This hat barely fits me." Duncan looked at the clock on the wall of the wagon's office.

"Because of wig," the Cossack said. "Off hat, off wig come. Crowd get mad. Bad for all."

He tugged on the goatee. There was so much glue on it, he feared, when the goatee came off, it would take his jaw along. And had he known he was going to be Bill Cody's impersonator, he could have grown that short little beard. It might not have been as light or as gray as Cody's was getting, but it would have been his own. He was pretty sure, though, that Sara wouldn't have a thing to do with him if he grew a goatee. And the coloring they had put on Duncan's face might make him sneeze.

"Well?" Nate Salsbury stepped inside. He cocked his head left, then right. "I'll be! This might just work."

"Mebbe so," the Cossack said. "Drunk not. Mostly sober. Ride good. Shoot fine. Look like dance-hall girl, though. Cody. Cody look like man. Even when light make him look like . . . like . . ." He couldn't find the English word.

"The Fourth of July," Ben Usher said.

The Cossack nodded.

Usher walked from the wall and slapped Duncan's shoulder. "Just get 'er done, pard. Just get 'er done."

"You were marvelous," Sara told him in the wagon office after the afternoon show ended.

Duncan thought he had been shaking since he got out of that big tent. He felt pretty sure he was still shaking. That's why he had said no when Salsbury offered him a bottle of Cody's favorite whiskey.

"Natural-born showman," Ben Usher said. He took the bottle from Salsbury and had himself a healthy slug. "You might think of starting up your own show, hoss."

One of Cody's cowpunchers shook his head. "Last thing this country needs," he said, "is another one of these infernal things."

Duncan reached for the goatee and started to pull on it.

"Don't do that!" Sara interjected. "It'll have to go back on for the evening show."

So, instead, Duncan took the bottle Usher held out to him.

By the third day, Duncan started worrying. He still got a bad case of nerves that started as soon as he reached the showgrounds, and it didn't end until he rode out into the arena. After that, he just did what he had to do. It was sort of like stepping onto the street to meet a gunfighter. Only this was ten times worse. The worst that could happen in a gunfight was that you'd get killed. Here, you'd be a laughingstock. And with all those reporters coming in to write about *Buffalo Bill's Wild West and Congress of*

Rough Riders—from all over the world—being laughed at was a whole lot worse than getting yourself planted in some boot hill.

Cody dropped in on the third day, looking like a new man. His face was tan; he stood erect; he wore a tailored suit of black wool and a blue silk shirt with buttons of mother-of-pearl. His hat had just been cleaned, and you couldn't find anything sparkling about him other than his eyes.

He nodded at Cody, Salsbury, and Usher, and turned to the moneyman.

"How we doing?" he asked. A hint of fear accented his voice.

"Like hogs eating corn." The moneyman didn't even look up.

"But I saw folks surrounding that big zinc rock we brought in," Cody said.

"It is pretty." Salsbury nodded. "And big."

Cody frowned. Sighing, Salsbury ducked behind a rolltop desk and came up with a bottle of whiskey, which he held out to his partner.

But—to everyone's surprise—Cody shook his head. "The *Afternoon Daily Press* had something on the front page, saying how that Liberty Bell of Zinc was outdrawing me and the Columbus show across the alley."

"They have to pay you to see that big, beautiful boulder," Salsbury said. And opened the bottle and poured some whiskey down his throat.

"But are they still seein' me?"

"No," Duncan said. "They've been seeing *me*."

Cody dismissed that comment with a wave. "You know what I mean."

The moneyman sighed and stuck his pencil above his big ear. "There has been no significant increase in attendance," he said, "because there are no seats left to sell. And there has been no decrease because we have filled the arena for every performance."

"And if we haven't," Salsbury said, "someone paid for an empty seat."

"You're sure?"

The moneyman and Salsbury nodded.

"Maybe," Duncan said, unable to not sound as though he were pleading, "you'd like to see for yourself. From the center of the arena."

Cody seemed to be considering that, but sighed and looked at Duncan's goatee. "Get that gray out of that fake beard, son. You're playing Buffalo Bill Cody—not Methuselah."

Which made Duncan almost reach for the bottle, moving from hand to hand, himself. He probably would have, but the door opened, and Mrs. Clarke stumbled inside. She was paler than Duncan was just before he rode to the thunderous sound of cheers and applause and the cowboy band playing a brassy little tune.

Nugget and Sara came rushing in after her.

"By the eternal," the moneyman yelled, "I can't make an accurate tally with—"

"Shut up!" Cody roared, and it was he, that magnificent showman and protector of the fair and poor, who reached Mrs. Clarke first, steadying her and helping her up.

"It's . . . Joey," she sobbed.

Duncan shot Sara a glance just as Sara looked and found Duncan, and Sara was a sickening pale. Her eyes were wide, rimmed with tears.

Nugget said, "He's been took!" Then he let out a wail that sounded like an injured coyote. That stopped all the Indians practicing their singing and dancing out behind the wagon.

"What do you mean . . . *took*?" Duncan said.

With a trembling hand, Mrs. Clarke reached inside the pocket of her skirt and withdrew a crumpled letter, which was already stained with her tears. A lock of hair fell to the floor. Mrs. Clarke let out another cry as Sara reached down and picked it up, rising, placing it into the broken-hearted woman's hand. Turning to Duncan, Sara gave a slight nod.

That was Little Joey's hair. Same color, anyway.

He unfolded the badly used letter and read.

We have your boy.

He is all right for the time being.

If you wish to see your son alive, you will do EXACTLY as you are told. One mistake, and the boy will be feeding the fish at the bottom of Lake Michigan.

Do not alert the authorities. We have our own men who are Chicago coppers. We have men even more powerful than the police. We know EVERYTHING.

If you make one mistake, the boy dies.

If you do EXACTLY as we say, the boy will grow up to be an outstanding citizen and give you grandsons.

Two hours after tonight's show, you have no more than three men bring the Liberty Bell of Zinc to O'Malley's Docks at Michigan Street. How you get that big, beautiful thing is your business. But no more than three—UNARMED—men will bring the wagon to the docks. Once the barge is loaded and sailing off, you will return to your hotel room and wait. Your child WILL NOT BE RETURNED

until the barge has reached Blind River. Then your
boy will be safe.

We have no wish to harm a child. BUT
WE WILL.

DO EXACTLY AS YOU HAVE BEEN
INSTRUCTED.

If you think this is a joke, ask anyone in town if
they know Miles Sturgeon.

The last two words caused the moneyman to turn white.

"Heaven help that poor little kid," he whispered, and reached for the bottle that had been passed around.

"Who's this Miles Sturgeon?" Duncan asked.

"No one knows for sure. It's a nickname. Short for Whoever Crosses Him Will Be Feeding Miles of Sturgeon at the Bottom of Lake Michigan or Lake Huron." He crossed himself. "And Sometimes Lake Superior." He crossed himself again. "Or All Three Lakes."

Nugget bawled. "I don't wants nothin' to happen to Little Joey."

"Shut up," Usher barked, and looked hard at Duncan.

"Two hours," Duncan said. "After the show. That doesn't give us much time."

"After the show," Usher said. "This place will be crawling with so many people after the show, it'll take us a whole lot longer to get to O'Malley's Docks—bringing that six-ton rock—than two hours."

Salsbury took a long sip. "That's why they're doing this. Two hours." He nodded. "That'll keep Buffalo Bill from coming after them."

"Me?" Cody said.

Duncan turned to Nugget. "Mayor," he said, "we're going to have to borrow your rock."

Nugget nodded. "You gots it. I'd do anythin' for that good little reader of stories."

"I know." He turned to Usher. "You know where O'Malley's Docks are, I take it."

"I do. It's not the nicest part of Chicago, pardner."

"What I figured." He looked around. "Anybody have any idea what this Miles Sturgeon might look like?" He figured that was a wasted question, but he had to ask it.

Sara sighed. "They'll likely have someone in the stands. To make sure"—she nodded at Duncan—"that . . . you, Buffalo Bill, are in the show."

The moneyman said, "The show . . . the tickets have been sold. We have salaries to pay."

He kept right on talking, even though everyone else in the room felt the urge to slap the greedy punk.

"Yes," Salsbury said, and he looked at his partner. "The show has got—"

"Confound it!" Cody jabbed a finger at Salsbury. "I keep trying to tell you that it's not a *show*. It's a pageant of authentic, true-to-life American history."

Standing, he grabbed the hat off Duncan's head. "And I'll play myself again. I've been playing Buffalo Bill for nigh on thirty years. But you!" He stared hard at Duncan, then glared at Usher, and even frowned at Nugget. "You get that boy back—and that big rock. Give them villains what they deserve. You need any Indians to come along? They've been looking for a fight for years. I got Cossacks, too. And them Frenchies, well, they sure love a good duel."

CHAPTER 33

Johnny Baker could play himself and Ben Usher. Cody thought of that. The money counter and the rest of the troupe started working out other details, while Sara escorted Mrs. Clarke back to the hotel, and Duncan, Usher, and Nugget walked out of the wagon and toward the big rock that was still causing a whole lot of trouble.

"They'll likely have someone watching us . . . from the crowds." Usher spoke softly while they walked through the scores of people.

"That's how I figure it," Duncan said.

"Whatch y'all talkin' 'bout?" Nugget demanded.

"Don't talk so loud," Duncan snapped.

"Then don't talk like you's in church. Y'all knows my hearin' ain't good after all 'em dynamite blasts and cave-ins and such."

They stopped outside the big tent, which was nowhere near the size of Cody's monstrosity across the path. The citizens of Chicago—and across the world—were packing into this carnival for its last weeks in Chicago. Duncan knew he had some things going in his favor. First, Cody and his carpenters had managed a way to haul the Liberty Bell of Zinc from a secured warehouse after the show to a tent, where it remained while the grounds were open to the public. A special, heavy freight wagon, pulled by strong bull oxen, brought the giant gem from one place to the other. They even kept the team harnessed at the show because a lot of the kids wanted to pet them and laugh when they pooped. In fact, the children were much more interested in "those big cows" than they were in a "big sparklin' rock."

The sides of the wagon had been constructed with hinges and screws so that during the show, the sides could be let down, giving admirers a full view of those six tons. The sides were raised and latched shut for the six-block trip to the brick warehouse.

When Duncan had first seen what the police and the guards and Cody and the museum director were doing, he had questioned them.

"Why not leave the wagon here? Cody has security. A couple of guards is all you'd need."

The director and Cody, even the coppers, all chuckled.

"It'd save time, too, and there's always the danger of moving this big chunk from one place to another, over and over again."

The director then punched Cody in the arm.

"Am I missing something?" Duncan remembered asking. He was completely perplexed.

"Welcome," Cody had said, "to Chicago."

Duncan had just stared.

"Son," the kindly director then explained, "this way the Chicago Police Department gets to pay policemen to guard the treasure, and the policemen get light duty and get to hang out here at night, where they most likely won't get knifed, bludgeoned, kicked, spat on, or shot. The warehouse gets to charge Cody and the city rent, and four other policemen—two per shift—get to spend the night in an enclosed warehouse that is much warmer than standing on a sidewalk, with the winds whipping off Lake Michigan. And Cody gets free publicity. Have you seen how many people follow that wagon when it brings this beautiful work of God and nature from the warehouse to the back entrance? It's wonderful. Absolutely wonderful."

Usher had explained the other important details when they were back inside Cody's office in the wagon.

"What no one bothered to tell you about is the money that went to the museum and to the police department's bosses and to the owners of the warehouse and to the fellow that rents those oxen and then to people we don't even think about. You're not in Dead Broke, pardner. This is the big C. And that big C is for 'Corruption.'"

Then Cody had started chuckling before sliding a bottle of whiskey toward Duncan. "This city ain't got anythin' on any other place I've been. Brussels . . . Vienna . . . London . . . Montreal . . . Dusseldorf . . . Naples . . . Glasgow . . ." After that, Cody had taken a long pull from the bottle before laughing again. "You should have seen what all those fellas in Philadelphia wanted! And if you think the faro banks are crooked in Denver, try getting a Wild West going there!"

What they needed, Duncan figured, was some kind of distraction.

That's when Buffalo Bill Cody, who always came to the rescue (at least in *Buffalo Bill's Wild West* perform-ances, twice daily, Sundays included), did it again—just in the nick of time.

He rode up to the open tent on a high-prancing gray stallion, the sun reflecting off those jeweled studs in his shirt and beaded vest and that big silver buckle over his widening belly. Four band members followed, two on each side of the horses, and Buffalo Bill was saying something no one had ever heard him say in Chicago or at any other Wild West run.

"Free tickets, folks. Free tickets to this afternoon's performance."

The band members held out their fists, full of tickets—not for the reserved seats, of course, but the fifty- and twenty-five–cent ones.

He reined up the big horse, his face smiling, and Duncan thought he caught him winking at him. The families, the old men, the young men, the pretty women, the mothers, all those kids, rushed out of the gemstone's tent like stampeding cattle.

"There's still the guards," Duncan whispered.

"Not for long." Ben Usher grinned at Duncan and walked toward the wagon. He reached into his back pocket and pulled out more tickets. And those, Duncan knew, were for the reserved seats.

"We're taking the Liberty Bell of Zinc away early today, boys," Usher told them. "And these are from Buffalo Bill, himself, for your thanks."

"You mean," the fat copper with the brogue said, "we ain't got to stay for that night shift?"

"Nope." Duncan gave him a ticket. "But . . . you'll still get that extra pay."

The bruiser suddenly looked suspicious, and Duncan realized that Usher had overplayed his hand. But Usher figured that out just as quickly, and he came up with the perfect response.

"And if the captain or the commissioner object, you come see Buffalo Bill. And he'll make it all right with you."

"You sure about that?" the policeman asked.

"By thunder," Usher said, "you know how generous a man Bill Cody is!"

That might have been the only true statement Usher had made, and Duncan knew that Bill Cody would live up to Ben Usher's statement—if things came to that.

People raced after Buffalo Bill, cheering, holding up programs for him to sign, or hoping he would shake their hands.

Duncan looked around.

"We'd better work fast," he said.

Nugget didn't need any instructions. He dropped to the ground and started loosening the shackles on the oxen's legs, while Duncan and Usher raised the sides of the wagons and locked them in place. Then both lawmen jumped into the bed and began covering the massive rock with the canvas tarps, while Nugget dropped the shackles into the driver's box and climbed into the seat.

"I'll take the rear," Duncan said. He nodded. "You know the way. You get up there with Nugget."

Usher didn't object. He slipped around the covered piece of zinc, and the wagon moved. Slowly.

Very slowly.

The gate would be the first test, but Duncan let out a sigh of relief when he saw Nate Salsbury talking and gesturing at the guards and gate-minders and ticket-takers there. The rail was raised, and those coming into the Wild West grounds, and those leaving, all stepped aside. Some of them cheered. But most of them—especially the younger ones—ran past the oxen and the wagon and the three men.

And then they were away from the Wild West and entering something much wilder.

The streets of Chicago, clogged with humanity—the good, the bad, the worse, and the worst.

They bounced and rattled and had gotten past the railroad tracks and stations without much trouble, but as they crawled down a narrow street, Ben Usher turned around and motioned Duncan to come up to the front.

He moved safely. The wagon wasn't going fast enough to cause Duncan any serious injury if he fell out, and even Nugget could stop those oxen before a wheel ran over him, but Duncan didn't need any delays. He gripped the ropes around the canvas as he squeezed between the zinc and the sideboards, then let out his breath and moved to the center of the wagon and came forward. He saw the problem before he got to the driver's box.

The uniformed policeman with the thick gray beard stepped out, thumping a nightstick against his beefy leg, and raising his left hand and calling out. The Irish brogue was thick, but certainly understandable.

Duncan sighed. "Better stop, Nugget," he said.

"Why don't you just shoot 'em down?" Nugget whispered. "What I'd do. What we gots to do if we wanna save Little Joey."

"We start shooting, we won't get anywhere but to the gallows," Duncan said. "If we're lucky."

"He's right, Nugget," Usher whispered. "And we sure can't outrun them."

"Maybe they're honest men, like we is," Nugget said, and he pulled hard to stop the oxen.

There were four of them. The big graybeard and the one with the eye patch came around to Duncan's side. The little one walked up to the lead oxen and took hold of a harness. The fourth one walked to Nugget's side, but kept a good distance.

The sidewalks were crammed with people, but traffic on the street was slow. A few hacks and some freight wagons. One buggy. Fourteen bicycles. One rail-thin man with a beard longer and thicker and dirtier than Nugget's, and shirtless despite the cold, marched down the center of the street saying, or maybe he was, in an out-of-tune way, singing:

> *I tol' Mr. Lincoln not to go to no play.*
> *I tol' Mr. Lincoln not to go to no play.*
> *I tol' Mr. Lincoln not to go to no play.*

"Laddies," the man said. The chevrons said he was a sergeant, and he looked like one. "Ye be a mite far from yer Wild West."

"You're right, Sergeant," Duncan said. But he had no lie at the tip of his tongue.

The sergeant stepped back and tapped the canvas covering the boulder with that nightstick.

"And las' I heard, the warehouse where this big stone was spendin' the nights be a lot closer than ye be comin'."

Duncan nodded. "Right again, Sergeant."

The big man smiled behind his thick beard. "I recognize the daring Mr. Usher from when I happened to attend the World's Fair and Colonel Cody's fine, fine show, and I can guess that this gentleman driver, with a beard after mine own heart, be this Mayor Nugget I hear so much about. So you must be . . . ?"

"Mick MacMicking." Duncan's tongue always tripped when he had to say that name. Which is another reason he wished folks knew him just as Duncan.

The cop tapped his nightstick on the closest wheel.

"So . . . maybe now . . . that we know each other, me being Sergeant Aodhán Sorley O'Brien of County Clare, maybe now I can hear a bit of the God's honest truth from ye." The nightstick made a louder whack. "Or do I have to beat yer head in to convince you that I am not a bloody fool?"

"Tell 'em the truth," Nugget said. "Maybe these boys'll lend us a hand."

Nugget didn't say much that made sense, Duncan thought, but every now and then . . .

So Duncan sighed, and told the story. The sergeant stopped him by raising the nightstick high as soon as he mentioned Miles Sturgeon's name.

That name even caused the other policemen to take a few steps back. One of them spun around and studied all those pedestrians on the sidewalk and stared at the coachman driving an empty surrey.

"Sturgeon." The sergeant's face looked much paler. "Ye have proof of that, Mr. MacMicking?"

Sighing, Duncan reached inside his coat, found the papers in his pocket, and brought them out. A sudden blast of cold wind snatched two of them out of his hand, but one of the officers caught both of them with a leaping grab. Glancing at the papers Duncan had managed to keep, he let out a sigh of relief. The note from those kidnappers he still held, so he made sure the sergeant had a firm hold before he loosened his hold.

The sergeant handed the letters to the closest policeman, who brought the paper close and began.

"'We have your boy. He is all right for the time being.'"

He had just gotten to the part that said *Your child WILL NOT BE RETURNED until* . . . when he was interrupted by the young, thin policeman who had caught the other papers.

"Sarge."

"Hush!"

"Sarge." The officer stepped forward, holding out the papers. "You better read this one yourself."

The sergeant turned now, glaring, and barked, "It bloody better well be more important than a letter of ransom from Miles Sturgeon, Doherty, or you'll be gumming down your supper for the rest of your days."

He grabbed the papers, then whirled around and thrust them at the youngest of the officers. "See what this says, Pedley."

Pedley stopped when he read the name . . .

"Gennaro."

He paled. And it seemed like even people walking on the far sidewalk gasped, but that, Duncan guessed, was just another blast off Lake Michigan.

Slowly, the sergeant looked up. "You . . . you know . . . Gennaro . . . the Barber?"

Duncan felt confused. He shook his head. "I know . . . just met, actually . . . Gaudenzio. He's a barber. Gaudenzio." He had to fight to remember the last name. "Gaudenzio Giuffrida." He decided that Mick MacMicking wasn't that hard to say after all. "He just said if we needed anything while we're in Chicago, to look up his brother."

The sergeant held out his hand, gathered the papers held by the two policemen, and held them up to Duncan.

"If you're going to try to get that kid from Miles Sturgeon, you don't need us, Marshal. You need Gennaro the Barber. Gennaro 'the Barber' Giuffrida."

Duncan's eyes narrowed. Slowly, he took the papers and folded them again, returned them to his pocket. His mouth opened to ask, but the sergeant held up his nightstick, not threatening—in fact, the stick was shaking in his hands—and the sergeant waited several seconds, then breathed in, exhaled, and said, "Pedley, take these gents to . . ." He sighed. "No, Pedley, you're too young. You're too young to die. Die like that. I'll take them. You boys keep about a block behind us. And don't try to hide.

Hiding will get us all killed. But leave your clubs, cuffs, and pistols in that trash pile."

"What if someone sweeps it up?" Pedley asked.

"Since when has any trash on this side of town been swept up, Pedley?"

He turned, walked to the lead oxen, gripped the harness. "Come on," he told Duncan.

But the sergeant didn't sound overly enthusiastic.

CHAPTER 34

It didn't look like a barbershop. It looked like a two-story brick building—only Duncan couldn't find a window in the place. He thought he saw a door, but he couldn't be certain.

They had walked maybe ten blocks, and Chicago's blocks were long. The crowds had stopped two blocks back. This block smelled of dead fish . . . and maybe other things that were dead.

The sergeant turned around. "How many weapons do you have, Marshal?"

Duncan pushed back the tail of his coat, revealing the Schofield.

"That it?"

"That's it."

"Leave it." The sergeant began unbuckling his belts. "And if you're lying to me, it's your throat. So if you have a hideaway gun, a knife, anything, leave it with your partners."

Duncan stood, unbuckling the rig and handing it to Nugget, who was trembling.

"Now, you two," the policeman told Usher and Nugget, "just sit here. I know it's cold. But don't move this wagon.

Don't get off this wagon. Just sit here and try to keep warm. If you hear a scream, just sit here. If you hear a gunshot, just sit here. If that door opens, and a head or a finger gets tossed out, then you can leave. But not in a hurry. Just let these oxen go down to the corner, turn left, then turn left again, and head back to the Wild West grounds and don't tell nobody nothing. Pedley and the others'll meet you at the corner. They know, and you best remember, don't ever come back here."

He looked up. "You got that?"

Nugget nodded. "Can I go now?" he asked.

Usher sighed, reached over, and took the heavy leather lines from the mayor's trembling hands.

It was a door. Duncan had been right. And the door opened. And four thin men, with black hair and fast hands, waited as Sergeant Aodhán Sorley O'Brien and Duncan let two of them give them the most thorough and rough search Duncan had ever experienced.

To his surprise, once the door closed behind them, the hallway was lit well. The slim one found the papers and held them to the one who kept checking his fingernails. He smelled like he had just taken a bath after a fine haircut and fresh shave. Fingernails held up the papers and read all of them silently, then slid them smoothly into the inside pocket of his coat.

Fingernails nodded, turned, and walked down the hall. Duncan felt the shove, and he started following. He could hear the big sergeant's footsteps behind him. The other three came behind. He couldn't hear them at all.

Before reaching the hallway's end, Duncan heard the violin. It sounded beautiful. Then Fingernails stepped out of the hallway and into a beautiful room, maybe as wonderful as any Duncan had ever seen.

He looked at the ceiling and saw all the glass windows in the roof, and the lanterns that hung from beams. Incredible. Silver and gold. He saw the stage where the thin man played that violin, and he saw the woman in the lavender dress starting on the grand piano. And a fat man with a cello—well, Duncan thought it was a cello. He tried to remember if he had ever seen a cello, but that's what he always thought a cello looked like. And there was a fatter man plucking on the strings of that big bass.

And there . . . on a raised platform . . . were three barber's chairs—maybe the most beautiful barber chairs he had ever seen. They were empty. But behind the center chair stood a man. A big man. Enormous. Fat with huge jowls and a pencil-thin mustache. He was dark, with immaculate hair. He didn't look one thing like Gaudenzio Giuffrida, but Duncan knew that was Gaudenzio's brother, Gennaro. Gennaro "the Barber" Giuffrida.

Fingernails stopped at the edge of the platform and waited until the song stopped. He waited until the fat man stopped clapping. He waited until the fat man nodded, and only then did Fingernails step onto the raised floor and walk to the man behind the middle barber's chair. He whispered. The fat man kept his eyes on the band. Finally, Fingernails stepped back, and the fat man nodded.

Fingernails turned. The fat man looked at the band. He clapped his hands again. The members of the band bowed, even the one with the big bass. The fat man blew them all kisses, and then he moved to the front of the big chair and sat in it.

Fingernails stopped when he stood in front of Duncan. He said nothing, just nodded, made a quick motion with the pointer finger on his right hand, and turned around.

Duncan started, but a firm hand gripped his shoulder and jerked him around. The hand let go, but a finger pointed up, and Duncan understood. He removed his hat and walked after Fingernails. His shoulder hurt like blazes. For weeks, he'd have a bruise where that brute grabbed him.

He waited for Sergeant O'Brien to come after him, but heard only his own boots as they crossed the tiled floor.

Fingernails made one quick motion with his left hand.

Duncan figured that meant stop. So he stopped in front of the platform.

The paintings on the walls of this immense room—it covered the entire building, from wall to wall. The walls weren't brick, but immaculately carved wood. Duncan didn't know much about art, but these paintings had to be from masters. Mountains. Rivers. Villages from somewhere in Europe, he imagined. And the statues must have been centuries old. He thought he recognized some from the illustrated newspapers he had seen. He imagined Rome . . . London . . . Paris. And he had never smelled hair tonics so wonderful.

On the other hand, he thought:

There's a pretty good chance I'll be dead when I leave here.

The band members were leaving, not talking to each other, not even in whispers. They took their instruments with them—except for the piano—and Duncan heard them going up steps, but well out of view. He studied the ceiling again. It was a two-story building, but here, in this part, the ceiling wasn't that low. It towered above him—and did so for about half of the building's width. The other half held rooms on the second floor, he figured. He looked around, wondering if this place had a basement. It had to. Most buildings like this would.

Then he thought: *That's probably where they bury all the bodies.*

Fingernails was showing the big man the ransom note and the letter from that quiet little barber back in Dead Broke.

The big man rarely spoke, and when he did, he spoke in whispers. Even Fingernails spoke softly. The big man nodded a few times, whispered a question or two, nodded again, then shook his head, and finally said something. He sank back into the luxurious barber's chair, looking at the high ceiling and those large windows that let in much of Chicago's light.

Fingernails came straight to Duncan, stopping, and looking over Duncan's right shoulder at Sergeant O'Brien.

"Is he with you?"

Duncan didn't know how to answer. He didn't want to get a Chicago sergeant killed.

"I'm with him," O'Brien said.

Fingernails didn't look at O'Brien. His hard eyes didn't blink, just stared at Duncan, waiting.

"He's with me. He said I needed to see"—he tilted his chin toward the fat man in the big chair—"Mr. Giuffrida." He sure hoped he hadn't butchered that last name.

"And the two in the wagon?"

Duncan nodded. "Both are with me." He quickly added: "With *us.*"

"Friends?"

Duncan nodded again. "Friends. Old friends. New friend."

"What's in the back of that wagon?"

"The Liberty Bell of Zinc."

"That has been in all of the newspapers?"

Duncan said, "Yes."

"And the boy? What is he to you?"

"He's a friend."

"Does the boy have a mother?"

Duncan nodded again. "She's a friend, too." But this time, he added: "And so is her husband."

"Do you know Miles Sturgeon?"

He shook his head. "Never heard of him till he kidnapped my little friend."

"And you'd pay that much money to get that boy back?"

"That big rock," Duncan said, "isn't worth that much money. But I'd pay whatever anyone asked to get that boy back safe."

"And if you couldn't get that boy back safe?"

"I'm not letting that thought into my head."

"You should. Miles Sturgeon has no mercy."

Duncan nodded. "There are times when I lack it myself."

"This might be one of those times."

Duncan didn't bother with a response.

"How do you know Gaudenzio?"

"He opened a barbershop in Dead Broke, Colorado. That's where I live." He ran his hand over his face. "He's a good barber. A good man."

"You need a shave." He snapped his fingers and turned around. Duncan felt the shove in his back, and he followed Fingernails again. This time, he didn't stop at the podium. He stepped up and walked till he stood in front of the fat man in the center chair.

The fat man's left arm moved, and a big finger pointed. Fingernails turned and pointed to the open chair on Duncan's right. He walked to that chair, then climbed in.

If he weren't so tense, he could have fallen asleep in that soft, exquisitely cushioned chair—better than the best bed, even Sara's, that he'd ever slept in. But he didn't want to go to sleep. Not here. He might wake up dead.

The big man came out of the center chair. He walked

to the counter. A moment later, Duncan felt a hot towel on his face. Then someone started singing, and it took Duncan a minute to realize the voice was Fingernails's. He couldn't understand a word, but it sure sounded pretty.

The towel was removed, and before him stood the fat man, who was whipping a barber's whisk furiously, then spreading warm lather across his chin, neck, and cheeks. Someone took the bowl and the whisk, and Gennaro "the Barber" Giuffrida began slapping a new razor with a mother-of-pearl handle against the strap hanging from the back of the barber's chair. The fat left hand reached over and the fingers—big, thick, and gentle—smoothed Duncan's mustache.

"Beddu," the big man whispered. *"Molto carino."*

He seemed to be nodding with approval.

Then his right hand raised the razor, he made a sudden flick, and the blade opened. The barber's left hand came down to Duncan's head, and softly turned it. The razor came down. Duncan didn't even feel a thing.

The lotion stung just for a moment after the barber had finished the shave. The chair's back was raised, and the barber stood there alongside Fingernails and Sergeant O'Brien. Someone else must have turned Duncan's chair so that now he sat facing the fat barber, who was looking at his own immaculate fingernails. Duncan glanced at his hands. His fingernails were ragged and dirty, but, gosh, his cheeks and neck had never felt so clean.

The man spoke softly, mumbling. Even had he been speaking English, Duncan wouldn't have understood a single word. The barber sighed, then spoke again, words that remained incomprehensible.

"Don Giuffrida says," Fingernails translated, "that Miles Sturgeon is bad. Very bad. He lives because he has never done Don Giuffrida any harm."

"He hadn't done me any harm, either. We're willing to let him have that rock. We just want the boy back safe, and back to his mother and father."

The Barber spoke again. Fingernails nodded, then spoke to his boss, and the boss nodded and spoke again.

After clearing his throat, Fingernails said, "Giving Miles Sturgeon the big rock will not get this young boy back to his mother and father."

The Barber spoke again.

Fingernails said: "And you know that, as well as Don Giuffrida knows."

Duncan nodded. "Then we get the boy back safe another way."

The Barber sat up in his chair and leaned forward. *"Tu si assolutamenti sicuru?"*

"Don Giuffrida asks if you are certain, absolutely certain, about this?"

"That's why I'm here," Duncan said.

Fingernails did not have to translate. The fat man was out of the chair, and he walked over, grabbed the arm of the chair, and bent closer to Duncan. He spoke again, mumbling the words, before standing as upright as a man of his size could.

"Don Giuffrida asks if his brother is as fine a barber as Don Gennaro is?"

Duncan raised his right hand and brought it close to his cheek, but he didn't want to touch it because . . . well . . .

"Gaudenzio is the best barber ever to come to Colorado," he said, "but I've never had a shave this perfect in all my years."

The fat barber laughed—even before Fingernails translated, so the big Don must have understood English, at least some of the language. Then Don Gennaro Giuffrida turned, nodded, and walked to the end of the elevated floor, speaking orders (but not in English), moving his hands left and right. Men came out of the darkened hallway. They moved like ants, but they moved with a purpose, and they were pulling out revolvers, blackjacks, knives—one had two sawed-off shotguns hanging under his arms as he put on a big black frock coat—as they moved to another long hallway, one on the other side of the big brick building.

The fat man turned and spoke again.

Fingernails nodded.

"Then you and your friends in the wagon are invited to join us. *As are any other friends who are not in that wagon.*" His smile was brief. He knew about O'Brien's men following in the shadows. "Don Giuffrida will get that boy back. And Miles Sturgeon won't annoy anyone ever again after this night."

Fingernails snapped his fingers and started toward the door that Duncan and the others had come in through.

Duncan and Sergeant O'Brien, after letting out a long breath of something that wasn't quite relief—other than the relief of still being alive—followed.

CHAPTER 35

Outside, Don Giuffrida stopped at the rough sidewalk and whispered something to Fingernails. Or maybe it wasn't a whisper, Duncan thought. Maybe that's just how the fat man always talked. Fingernails nodded and walked to Sergeant O'Brien.

As they walked to the wagon, where Nugget sat shivering in the cold next to Ben Usher, Fingernails said, "Tell those two that if they touch their guns, they will be the third and fourth to die. You two"—he nodded at O'Brien and Duncan—"you will be the first."

"Keep your hands in plain sight." Duncan spoke just loud enough, and breathed a little easier when Nugget and Usher did as they were told. By the time Duncan and his party had come to the wagon, more men—they had to be Don Giuffrida's—were surrounding the big wagon.

The streets had been crowded up until they reached this block. Up until now, there hadn't been hardly anyone around except for Duncan and his volunteers. Now they were surrounded by more than a dozen men, and every one of them looked as though they would have sliced all of their throats just for a nickel.

"This is all you have?" Fingernails said with a mirthless laugh.

"They're good enough," Duncan said.

The wiry man then turned to the big sergeant, asking: "Where are your pals?"

O'Brien nodded down the street.

"How many?"

The big copper held up three fingers.

"Any good?"

O'Brien shrugged. "They always saddle me with the rookies."

Fingernails nodded slightly. "That's better then. Get them up here. But . . . if we see a weapon, we cut you to pieces." He turned to Duncan. "All of you to pieces. And remember: That boy Sturgeon has taken means nothing to Don Giuffrida. And that worthless piece of zinc?" He nodded at the covered massive boulder. "It means even less to Don Giuffrida."

The big sarge cupped his hands over his mouth and yelled, "Pedley! You rookies come out and keep your hands high. Walk slow. Real slow."

The three policemen came slowly, hands high: Pedley trembling, the tall one with the eye patch trying to look brave, the short one with the mustache looking left and right. They stopped just behind the freight wagon.

Fingernails nodded, and six of the swarthy men on the sidewalk came over and gave all those Chicago policemen a good patting down. One of them turned and nodded at the Don and Fingernails. Then those tough fellows stepped back.

"What time does Buffalo Bill's show end?" Fingernails asked.

Duncan found his watch, struck a match, and Fingernails struck a match—on one of his fingernails—and held it close to Duncan.

"Should be wrapping up in ten or fifteen minutes."

The match went out. Fingernails nodded.

"'Two hours after tonight's show, you have no more than three men bring the Liberty Bell of Zinc to O'Malley's Docks at Michigan Street,'" Fingernails said. "'How you get that big, beautiful thing is your business. But no more than three—*unarmed*—men will bring the wagon to the docks.'"

The sergeant shook his head. "You remembered that whole thing?"

"I remember everything," Fingernails said. He walked up to O'Brien's rookie coppers. "It doesn't say the three men can't be coppers. They'll do."

Duncan cleared his throat. He had a pretty good memory, too. "That note also says something about not alerting the authorities."

Three of the Don's men chuckled. Fingernails wasn't one of them, but he said, "Since when is a Chicago copper an *authority*?"

Ben Usher cleared his throat. "What are you thinking?"

Fingernails turned to reconsider Usher and must have seen something in Ben's eyes to give him the respect Usher deserved.

"We send these three coppers to O'Malley's Docks," Fingernails said. "Just like the letter says."

Duncan frowned.

The slight man smiled. "You do not wish to get that little boy back?"

"I wish to get Little Joey back alive. But I don't think this Sturgeon has any intention of letting the boy live once he gets that zinc."

Fingernails nodded. "You won't get the boy back alive." He smiled. "Unless we kill Miles Sturgeon and his men first."

"You think Joey's still alive?" Usher asked.

Don Giuffrida walked over and whispered something in his native tongue.

"Don Giuffrida," Fingernails said, "says that Sturgeon must keep the boy alive in case you or the child's mother or grandfather or this copper asks to see the boy first."

Duncan and Usher nodded, hoping that the big man was right.

"So what happens now?" Duncan asked.

"Three coppers." Fingernails nodded at the three un-armed students of Sergeant O'Brien. "They will take this wagon to O'Malley's Docks." He turned his head back to Duncan. "We"—he looked back at Usher and Nugget—"and these friends of yours." Then he grinned at the sergeant. "And this big mick. We will go to Chauncey's Fish House. That is where the boy is being held."

Usher cleared his throat. "How do you know that?"

"Because Don Giuffrida told me."

Usher shot Duncan a glance, then studied the fat man for a few seconds, and finally looked back at Fingernails. "If I remember that letter right," he said, "it also said that the boy dies if we make one mistake."

Don Giuffrida smiled. This time, he whispered something in English. "Then . . . make . . . no . . . mistake."

Pedley cleared his throat. "Sergeant, that letter also said something about knowing men more powerful than us policemen. It even said this Sturgeon has his own men who are . . . well . . . on the police force."

"Alas, laddie," the sergeant whispered, "that's true."

"'We know *everything*,'" Fingernails quoted.

The derringer appeared from out of nowhere in Fingernails's hand, and while the gunshot was hardly noticeable, the look on the face of that short policeman with the mustache would be ingrained in their minds for quite some time. The copper straightened, reached up, touched the little hole in the center of his head . . . right before his eyes rolled backward and he collapsed in a heap on the rough street.

The derringer vanished. Don Giuffrida walked over and kicked the dead man's left sole. He studied the corpse, frowning at his rough mustache and the stubble on his chin and cheeks—not a good shave at all—before turning around and pointing at one of his men.

That fellow moved quickly, unbuttoning his shirt, kicking off his shoes, and waiting while two other men began stripping the dead copper of his uniform.

"What time is it now?" Fingernails asked.

One of his own men got his watch out before Duncan could.

"We best start moving," Fingernails said. He asked Don Giuffrida something in that strange language. The big man smiled and answered, and Fingernails nodded.

He turned to the nearest swarthy man and pointed at the corpse that had been stripped to his winter underwear.

"You heard Don Giuffrida. Take this man to Lake Michigan and let him sleep with the sturgeon."

The wagon with the big piece of zinc went off with O'Brien's two coppers and one of Don Giuffrida's men in the dead corrupt policeman's uniform. About half of the other men in the shadows seemed to disappear. The rest stared at Fingernails and Don Giuffrida.

Fingernails walked up to Usher, O'Brien, Nugget, and Duncan.

"If you want out now, leave. Just don't whisper any word of what you have seen or heard or"—his head tilted in the direction of Lake Michigan—"you will sleep with the sturgeon, too."

"I ain't never gonna sleep ag'in," Nugget said, his voice higher than usual.

"You four and I," he said, "we will find the boy." He sighed. "It isn't as fun as killing, but Don Giuffrida insists that I help you."

"And . . . ?" Duncan nodded toward the fat man. "Don Giuffrida. . . what is his job?"

"The Don will look after us. As he always does. As any godfather does for his godchildren."

The Don stepped toward the men, starting with Fingernails. He mumbled a prayer in that melodic language, kissed his left cheek, then his right, whispered something else, and patted his shoulder before making the sign of the cross.

He blessed Ben Usher in a similar fashion, and then spoke to Duncan in a language that the lawman could not understand, but felt better after this prayer. Finally, he stopped in front of Nugget and put both fat hands on the wiry miner's bony shoulders.

"Are . . . you . . . ready?" the Don asked in heavily accented English.

"No." Nugget sobbed. "But it's fer Little Joey. So . . . I'll . . . try. . . ."

CHAPTER 36

Chauncey's Fish House sat in Chicago's South Side on the banks of Lake Michigan.

"Looks closed," Nugget whispered.

"It's always closed," Sergeant O'Brien said.

Lights along the harbor illuminated the front of the two-story structure and the cobblestone path that led from the street to the double front doors. Duncan shook his head.

"Whoever's in the house will see us once we step out of these shadows." He cut off the curse he really wanted to spit out.

Fingernails nodded. "That is true," he whispered.

"Can we slip around back?"

The man shrugged. He pointed farther south. "See the steeple? Turn there. Go through the graveyard and over the stone wall. Then you will step into Lake Michigan. Go out six feet. You wade slowly all the way until you see the big porch that overlooks the lake. That is where couples go to dine and watch the sailboats and barges and gulls—back when Chauncey had a fine place to eat."

"What's the best place to get into that building from the back?" Duncan asked.

The man let out a slight laugh. "After you wade through

Lake Michigan? Don't be absurd. It is almost November. Your lower legs will be frozen solid after one hundred yards."

Duncan swallowed another curse.

"Then how do we get inside to get Little Joey out safe and sound?"

"There is no safe way," Fingernails said.

Nugget grunted. "Why'd we have to wade through that icy water?" He jutted his dirty beard down the street. "Ain't 'em boats at that docks? Couldn't we just take one of 'em things and float on down, then stay in the shadows, just a-sneakin' along, till we reach the back of the house?"

Duncan waited for the objection, the sound reasoning, the laughing dismissal. But Fingers just stared at the old miner as though dumbfounded. He turned to one of his men, who shrugged.

"Well," he said at last. "Yeah. I guess . . . maybe . . ." He shrugged his shoulders. "I"—he tried to smile—"I don't swim."

Usher cleared his throat. "How do we get inside, once we're at the house?"

Fingernails recovered. "The boy is being held in an upstairs bedroom. That faces the lake."

"How do you know that?" Ben Usher sounded suspicious.

"Don Giuffrida told me."

"How did he know?" Duncan asked.

"Don Giuffrida knows everything."

Duncan looked at the house. "Three windows in front upstairs. You reckon there are three windows in the back?"

One of the ruffians cleared his throat. "Three windows. Three bedrooms. But back roof steep. Steep bad." He brought his fingers together on both hands and showed just how treacherous the climb up that roof was going to be. "Hard climb. Hard climb."

"If they hear us on that roof, they'll likely kill Little Joey." Duncan was trying to come up with a better plan.

"They won't hear you," Usher said. He pulled out his watch, but couldn't see it well enough to read the time. "We'll make a distraction out here. When you hear that ruckus, that's when you go into the windows and save Little Joey."

"How will you know when we're ready?"

"Telephone," Fingernails whispered.

"Huh?" Nugget said.

"Telephone." Ben Usher smiled. "Of course."

"Huh?" Nugget repeated.

"Mattia," Fingernails said, and began speaking in that lovely language to a slender man, except for his bulging arms that looked stronger than granite. Fingernails then snapped his fingers and pointed at two other men. Those men took off running, but scarcely making a sound, in the darkened boardwalk toward the dock.

"You and you." Fingernails pointed at Nugget and Duncan. "You will go with me. We will take the boat. Three windows. Three men. One room will have the boy." He turned toward the docks down the street. "Enzo will stay on the shore of the lake, near the docks, where the light is. No one will think anything of him—if they happen to see. Fishermen often wait here before leaving early to fish or throw corpses into the lake. When you are ready, you will strike a match. Enzo will see the match. Enzo will wave his hands to Marco. Marco will then wave his hands to you." He nodded at Usher. "And that's when—"

"I start the ball." Usher nodded back to him.

"Not quite," Fingernails said. "That is when Marco will telephone Chauncey's Fish House. When you"—he nodded at Nugget and Duncan—"hear the telephone ring and a man answer it, then we three will go through the windows and you . . ." Fingernails looked straight at Usher.

Usher repeated, "Start the ball."

My lower legs will be frozen solid after one hundred yards.

Duncan thought about saying those words, but he feared his lips were frozen shut. That Fingernails fellow had not been exaggerating as the rowboat drifted along Lake Michigan in a windy, frigid, miserable night. Even this close to shore, the wind blew brutally, and the waves often splashed into the craft, rocking it, especially now that Fingernails had turned the rudder and they moved faster to the shore. The boat hit ground, and Duncan, up front, jumped out, his feet feeling a quick numbness as his boots soaked up part of Lake Michigan. He did not bother trying to pull the boat to shore. He turned, extending his hand and helping Nugget out of the craft. Fingernails needed no help. They stayed in the shadows, waiting, looking at the darkened windows.

"Curtains," Fingernails whispered.

"For us," Nugget said.

"Hush," Duncan said. "Can't see a thing through those curtains. There won't be any light up there." He lifted his gaze, hoping to see some break in the clouds, but there was nothing.

"How we gonna get up there?" Nugget asked.

"Use the latticework as a ladder," Fingernails said. "We better go now."

"Latticework?" Duncan asked. He could hardly see a thing.

"Right side of the back porch." Fingernails shrugged. "I've eaten here."

Fingernails went first, moving like a cat. Duncan came up after Nugget, figuring he would have to push the man through some of the tougher parts, or catch him if he fell. But as long as he had been mining in Colorado's high country, Nugget moved like a mountain goat. He was on the roof long before Duncan made it.

The next climb, up the pitched roof to the three windows, proved tougher. But the shingles were firm, and as long as they stayed on hands and knees, scarcely making a sound, they had no problem—other than the frigid wind that seemed much colder higher up off the lakeshore.

Fingernails had the southernmost window, Nugget was near the middle one, and Duncan on the northern side. He stared, making out what he thought was a blanket for a curtain. He stood, holding on to the framework to keep his balance, and slowly swung his left leg toward the glass.

That's how he planned to make his play. Go in feetfirst, land on the floor. He thought he could see some light at the corner closest to him, so he stared at that light. It might help, he prayed. He didn't want to have to let his vision readjust to lantern or even electric lights, once he was in this bedroom.

He couldn't see Nugget. He couldn't see Fingernails, but he knew where both men were. He focused on Fingernails, waiting to see that match.

For five long minutes, it did not come.

The wind, he thought. *It's blowing out those matches.*

Then he saw something. It didn't last long, but it was there. If only Enzo had seen it.

Was Enzo waving his hands now to Marco? Was Marco signaling Ben?

He could feel his heart pounding. He held his breath. No one wanted to breathe on a miserably cold night like this one. He waited for that ring.

But it wasn't a telephone he heard. It was a gunshot, followed by a loud scream and then—Duncan thought the freezing wind had driven him insane—a trumpet sounding.

Usher was glad he brought gloves. Chicago had felt cold ever since he had arrived, but on this night, and this close to that big, frigid lake, he was freezing. But now he was ready. He thumbed back the repeating rifle's hammer and steadied his aim. Behind him, even as the wind picked up, he heard Marco pick up the telephone in the feedstore behind him. He wondered if Marco could teach him how to pick a lock that quick with just a hairpin.

"Operator," he heard Marco's voice, "would you please ring Chauncey's Fish House?"

That's when he lowered the hammer, and the barrel of the rifle, and looked to his left. A shot came from the street that intersected with the lakeshore road. He recognized the sounds of galloping horses . . . Why, that had to be a bugle.

The rider on a gray steed came into view. The Winchester the man held—the reins were in his teeth—spat flame and sent a leaden bullet crashing through one of the windows.

Another man on horseback followed the charging leader. Usher rose. The leader was Buffalo Bill Cody. The man behind him was . . . ? Usher had to squint.

A Cossack?

* * *

Duncan crashed through the window, just as he had planned, and felt some shards of glass cut his arms. The blanket hanging over the window like a curtain, luckily, fell off to the right—and the wall sconces weren't blinding. He hit the bed with his boots, bounced up just as the door opened to the hallway and a rough-looking man came in with a shotgun. The barrels blasted, but Duncan was bouncing off the bed and the buckshot tore into the wall. Up again toward the ceiling and the window—now letting in that frigid October wind—and the man with the shotgun looked up in disbelief. He tossed the shotgun to the rug on the floor and palmed a nickel-plated revolver.

But Duncan was coming back down now and had levered the rifle and took quick aim.

The man screamed as the bullet punched through his shoulder and sent him spinning in circles before he fell to his knees. By then, Duncan had bounced off that big bed, but this time went forward toward the wounded kidnapper. His boots hit the floor about the same time as the barrel of the Winchester slammed against the wounded man's skull and planted him unconscious next to the spittoon he had overturned.

Duncan bounced up, swinging the Winchester toward the open door. He heard a window crashing downstairs, gunshots, screams, the snorting of a horse, more gunfire, and then a foul word in Russian that one of the Cossacks had taught him.

The noise downstairs sounded like the reenactment of the Little Bighorn at *Buffalo Bill's Wild West*. But Duncan didn't care about that—not for the moment, anyway. He moved past the unconscious man and came through the door into the hallway—just as another man topped the stairs.

Duncan didn't have time to aim. He just touched the trigger and saw the man grab his left thigh and fall down those stairs. A noise to his left caught his attention, and he dropped to one knee while levering the rifle and aiming down the corridor.

This time, he didn't pull the trigger, recognizing Fingernails as he came through the far bedroom, dragging an unconscious man by his long, filthy hair. Fingernails held a revolver pointed right at Duncan, but he hadn't fired, either.

It was good, Duncan thought, to work with professionals.

Another noise sounded—and that one was a wild scream coming from the middle bedroom.

And then a shriek—"Look out!"—from inside that same room.

That was Little Joey Clarke!

Both men sprinted down the hallway. Fingernails was reaching for the doorknob just when the door flew off its hinges and a man in pinstripes came right with it, hitting the far wall and sliding to his left in an unconscious heap.

Fingernails nodded, and both men moved through the opening.

Duncan went low. He hit his knee and saw Nugget, pounding a bloodied man's head with a chamber pot, then kicking him to his side, then kicking him where it hurt, and then looking up, seeing Fingernails and Duncan, and then spinning around and yelling, "Is you all rights, Little Joey?"

Duncan's head whipped around. Off in the corner stood Little Joey Clarke, eyes and mouth wide open, looking directly at Nugget. The boy didn't answer. He might be in shock. But seeing Nugget, his hair and beard wild, blood leaking from a cut over his right eye and at the bridge of his nose, holding part of another man's scalp—Duncan spotted that one in a daybed, knocked cold—and another one against the far wall, trying to hold his teeth in his crimsoned mouth.

"Are you all right, Little Joey?" Duncan asked.

The boy just stared in silence at Nugget.

"Of course, he be all right." Nugget picked up a knife and a revolver. "But they ain't."

The sounds of more gunshots, screams, a trumpet, and at least one whinnying horse came from downstairs.

"And they's likely a passel of other vermin waitin' to see what Colorado justice looks like in this town." Nugget stormed out of the room, stopped, turned around, and beckoned Fingernails, Duncan, and the boy.

"C'mon. Let's go get 'em!"

But by the time they reached the stairwell, the Battle at Chauncey's Fish House was pretty much over.

Sara Cardiff feared the worst when she and Mrs. Clarke reached the steps to a restaurant that looked like it had been caught in a riot. Then she heard Little Joey's voice. Mrs. Clarke yelled her boy's name and raced inside.

When Sara stepped through the doorway, Ben Usher was walking through what once had been a large bay window that offered a good view of the street.

She saw Duncan standing at the foot of the stairs, talking to a handsome, and mysterious-looking, dark-skinned man. Buffalo Bill Cody sat in the saddle on his big gray, one leg hooked over the saddle horn, smiling, and nodding, and directing where the Cossacks and the Sioux should drag the unconscious. He kept yelling at several men who stood on their knees, their hands placed behind their heads, some of them white-faced, some crying, most of them whispering silent prayers.

"Where is that Miles Sturgeon? Where is he? If I don't

get an answer soon, I'm gonna show ever' last one of you how I took that first scalp for Custer!"

"Miles Sturgeon . . ." Everyone turned to what had been a real pretty set of double doors. A big man stepped inside. Four thinner, but deadlier-looking, men stood as close to the big man as possible. The fat man smoothed his perfect mustache. "He sleeps with the sturgeon," the fat man said.

Sara was guessing at maybe half the words the big man said. She moved a few steps toward him, mesmerized. Obese, he most certainly was. But he was handsome in his own way, mesmerizing. He looked ominously deadly, but all man.

"He will bother Chicago no more." He grabbed one of the wounded ruffians and jerked him to his feet. "Nor will you. Or any of Sturgeon's men."

Again, the words were jumbled, but that vicious-looking dark man standing next to Duncan later confirmed that is what the Don had said. "For if you are not out of Chicago by dawn, you will join Miles Sturgeon."

The deadly-looking man left Duncan's side and moved to the Don. They whispered something that sounded a bit like Italian, but not quite. Then the dark man with immaculate fingernails and a face that was incredible—though she'd never let Duncan know that—walked up to Duncan and Colonel Cody.

"You should take your boy, your friends, and go now," the man said in a wonderfully amazing accent.

A big cop came inside, looked around, removed his hat when he saw Sara and Mrs. Clarke, and walked to Duncan and the handsome dark-skinned man.

"O'Malley's Docks is burning to the bloody ground," the man said in an Irish brogue. He looked around the big room. "But it dunna look like this."

"Go," the handsome man said. "Go before Don Giuffrida forgets his kind heart."

"Let's go, Mommy," Little Joey said. "I want to tell you all about it!"

"Yes," Mrs. Clarke said, and led her son out into the cold night. "I want to hear all about it."

"The wagon's outside, ma'am," the Irish policeman said. "With that big thing of zinc. You all"—he waved his hand toward Nugget and Duncan and Usher—"take that back to your hotel."

"What about the police?" Duncan asked. "Shouldn't we wait to tell them what happened?"

Even the big Irish policeman laughed with the swarthy men.

"The police?" The handsome man with fingernails Sara would kill for just rolled his eyes. "In this part of town?"

CHAPTER 37

"I still can't believe it," Nate Salsbury complained as they walked out of Bigelow's Museum of America's Natural Wonders, Treasures, and Legends. "Not one word in any Chicago newspaper about what you said happened last night. Will, if you're pulling my leg . . ."

"Oh." Cody waved his hand and shook his head. "We'll be done with Chicago in a few days. We're moving on to Brooklyn to start the new year. And Brooklyn doesn't want to hear about anything that happened in Chicago."

Sara turned around and walked past Duncan and Usher to Nugget, whose head hung down as he stood on the sidewalk in front of the museum. Joey and Mrs. Clarke were beside Dead Broke's mayor.

"Don't be sad, Mayor Nugget," the young boy said.

Nugget wiped a tear and sniffed. "Ain't sad," he said softly. He hooked a thumb toward the museum's entrance. "That Bigger Low feller says I can come see my Liberty Bell of Zinc anytime I wanna."

"We better get back to work," Cody said. He looked at Duncan and Usher. "Y'all going back home now?"

Duncan nodded and held out his hand. "Reckon so. If

we wait much longer, we might not be able to get up that mountain till late spring."

"You, too, Ben?"

Usher smiled. "Reckon I learned I'm just not the showman type."

Duncan whispered: "I thought Dead Broke bored you, pardner."

Usher just chuckled. "After Chicago, Dead Broke seems exciting enough."

Cody and Salsbury shook hands with the two heroes.

"You can work with me in Brooklyn," Cody told them. "It's gonna be a crackerjack run."

"Why don't you brings your act to Dead Broke?" Nugget suggested.

"Mayor," Cody said with a wide smile, "I just might do that one of these days."

"Let me see if I can get you folks a hackney." Salsbury shook hands before walking up the street.

"Nugget?" Little Joey asked. "What you gonna do now?"

"Oh, I gots me a fine idear."

"Tell me!"

"Tell us," Sara said.

"Well, I still gots me that Diamond Nugget of Silver. And now I's gots my own museum in Chicago, where folks'll be seein' my Liberty Bell of Zinc. I'm thinkin', Joey, lead. All this gunfightin' and such has gotten me thinking that lead. Lead. The biggest, most magnificent discovery of lead ever made. And I'm gonna find it right where I found my other big rocks. Lead. Nugget's Leanin' Tower of Lead. Like that Leanin' Tower of Pistols Joey read me about."

"It's 'of Pisa,'" Joey told him.

Nugget didn't hear. "What do you think?"

"Gosh, Mayor Nugget," Joey said. "That'll be even more spectacular than anything anybody's ever seen on This Side Of The Slope."

Duncan turned to Usher, who was shaking his head.

When their eyes met, Usher hooked a thumb toward the mayor.

"Nugget's Leaning Tower of Lead." He laughed again. "That's a hoot, now, isn't it, pardner?"

Duncan just shook his head. "Pardner . . . I wouldn't bet against him."

**TURN THE PAGE
FOR AN EXCITING PREVIEW!
JOHNSTONE COUNTRY.
WHERE OLD ENEMIES UNITE . . .
TO FIGHT A BLOODIER KIND OF WAR.**

**Introducing Trace and Chaw: a pugnacious pair of
Civil War veterans who nearly killed each other in
battle—but lived to fight another day. Together . . .**

They met in a bloodbath. Two demons in uniform caught
in the middle of one hell of a war. Private Chaw, the
Rebel, liked chewing tobacco and fighting blue-bellied
Yanks. Private Trace, the Yankee, hated Southerners,
especially ornery cusses like Chaw.
But when the smoke cleared after
the Battle of Deadeye Gap, the Blue and the Gray
of their uniforms didn't matter anymore.
Both were stained blood red.
And both were the last men standing . . .

This was the beginning of a beautiful friendship.

Now that the war's over, Trace and Chaw travel the
West together, taking on odd jobs. They're handy with
six-guns and gut-shredders, fond of women and liquor,
and always ready to raise hell. Somehow, the unlikely
partnership works—until Trace and Chaw sign up with a
freighting company run by a beautiful woman.
Her company is caught in the crossfire of two rival
mine owners who want to control the freight routes.
Like it or not, Trace and Chaw are stuck
in the middle of another war.
And this one's going to be every bit as bloody—
and it might be their last. . . .

NATIONAL BESTSELLING AUTHORS
WILLIAM W. JOHNSTONE
and J.A. Johnstone

THE BEST OF ENEMIES
A Trace and Chaw Western

First in a New Series!

Live Free. Read Hard.
williamjohnstone.net
Visit us at kensingtonbooks.com

On sale now, wherever Pinnacle Books are sold.

CHAPTER 1

The first thing the man felt was heat, heat from the unforgiving sun baking down. By the time he came around, it had already reddened his upturned face and blistered his lips.

The next thing he noticed was yet more heat, but this time, it came from within himself, from below himself, as if from the earth on which he lay.

He forced his eyes open, just a crack at first. All he could see were stinging pinpricks of light through a gauze of pink that edged out to redness. Jagged, brittle snatches of memory drizzled back to him at the same time. And not a bit of it impressed him.

All this told him was that he had to be dead, given what he was recalling. He almost wished he had lost his ability to recall anything, so awful were the bits of memory, of what he had seen and lived through. Or had he?

Then sound flooded in, and became more pronounced. But at first, all he could hear was a whooshing and thudding.

With more effort than he bet he'd ever expended on anything in ages, the man lifted his head. It wobbled on its feeble stalk of a neck. He cracked his right eye wider than its slit and saw bright, warm light, and little else. How on earth did he get here? And where was "here"?

All he could recall was fighting. Seems that's all he'd done since he was born. What did that mean?

Notions, facts, or perhaps they were fabrications, he could not yet tell, flitted in and out of his mind. He gritted his teeth and fought to keep his eyes open. There, he looked down along the length of his body and saw himself, stretched out on his back in the sun. His clothes looked sodden, must be sweat.

And then, as if someone had clapped their hands and awakened him fully, he remembered who he was. And from that revelation, it was a short jump to how he got here. Wherever "here" was. He figured that in time, that, too, would come.

And then he remembered—the war. The war and the cursed Yankees who started it. And there he was, all laid out, baking in the sun, not certain how alive he was, or if he was on his way out. The latter possibility seemed the most likely, given the pain he felt, the light burning away at him, and the rush of memories flooding into his mind.

But right then, he figured he knew who he was, and that was pretty good. He was Private Chaw Dagworth, of the Army of the Confederate States of America.

He glanced down at himself again as he struggled to raise himself up onto an elbow. And if he was in the Confederate Army, then that meant his uniform would be gray. And if that was the case, why was it so sodden-looking? Ah, yes, the fighting. *The cursed, fool Big War Twixt the States a protracted fracas,* as his old colonel used to say, *caused by Yankee bellicosity.*

Chaw grunted and felt a stinging in various parts of his body that quickly gave way to lancing pains, as if someone were sliding knives in and out of his arms, his sides, his legs. What was happening? And then he knew that he wasn't seeing a sweaty uniform, he was seeing a blood-soaked uniform. And as soon as that dawned on him, the rest of his situation became as clear to him as a cool mountain stream.

As he shoved himself up, despite the constant throbbing all over his body, more memories came gushing on in. Uninvited, but there they were, anyway. . . .

His company had been taking a ridge, below which was a hollow, what was it called? Deadeye Gap, that's it. And then he'd seen a bluebelly and had taken off after him. That's right, that bluebelly and Chaw got into it pretty good. For a Yankee, the man was brute enough. Must have had Rebel bark somewhere in the woodpile.

In fact, Chaw recalled shouting that at the man as they tore into each other, each giving as good as they got. That comment sure got that bluebelly riled. That foul Yankee had called Chaw a slave trader and a child killer and all manner of raw names, none of which were true. Chaw found this humorous, considering the Yank was a foul traitor and a child killer and a secret slaver himself!

Of course, Chaw had no way of verifying such, but he didn't doubt that bluebelly was guilty of that and a whole lot more. He was a foul Yankee, after all, wasn't he? That alone was reason enough to pin the entire mess on him.

As he lay there, Chaw pulled in as much of a breath as he could—it wasn't a deep one, nor was it clear. Sounded to him as if he was breathing through a ragged pig's bladder. That reminded him of home at pig-killin' time, when the menfolk back home used to inflate and tie off the bladders for the kiddies to bat around.

None of that much mattered now. He was likely dying and would as likely never see his poor old family ever again. Not Ma, nor Pa, nor Jube, nor dear old Daisy the hound.

Chaw grunted and swung his gaze slowly over to his left. What he saw somehow did not surprise him, although it should have. But he reckoned some part of him knew what he would see before he looked there. And what he saw did not fill him with satisfaction, as he had expected it should. Nope, seeing that dead Yank, not but a few yards to his left, only made Chaw Dagworth feel almighty awful.

Even if the man was a foul Yankee, that carcass left Chaw hollowed out inside, even more than before. Because it only meant that, as bad as he felt, that Yank was worse off. For he was already dead.

And so, that meant that Chaw had given away his own life—and for a cause that had become so muddied and confused for him and most of his fellow Rebs, most had, at one time or another, considered running off in the night. Even though it meant risking getting shot in the back. And now, here he was, surely about to die himself, and that was a raw, hard thing to take.

The Yank, in Chaw's brief glimpse of the man, and then on repeated forced looks, appeared to be in particularly rough condition. The bluebelly, too, was sprawled out on his back, and he, too, was covered with what looked to be a whole lot of dried blood from gashes and rents in his once-blue uniform. He knew this because there were a few spots of blue wool still visible through the darkened blood.

Was this it, then? Nothing more than kill or be killed? How on earth, he wondered, would his death, or the death of that foul Yank beside him, be helpful to the cause of the South, or the cursed North, for that matter?

Chaw closed his eyes a moment and worked to breathe a bit more. And he came to the conclusion that there wasn't a single scrap of usefulness in his sacrificing himself for the dang cause. No, sir.

And then he heard a sound. From his left.

Chaw grunted and worked to angle his gaze back over in that direction. He blinked hard and opened his eyes again, forcing them wide. Couldn't be. He could swear he saw that foul Yank move!

Long before he opened his eyes, Private Fullcup Trace, of the Union Army, lay awake. Keeping his eyes closed on waking each morning was a lifelong habit, and something that, even in the much-abused state he knew his body to be in, he nonetheless maintained.

He found it beneficial to slowly, over the course of several minutes, allow himself to come around to full consciousness. In this way he could take account of who he was, what had happened to him, and where he was at that moment.

All of this came to him as he lay there, sipping air between parted lips. He knew who he was—Trace, he was called—for he became aware of such as if someone had whispered it to his mind.

But it also soon became obvious to him that his normal method of waking was not going to cut it this day. For memory reminded him in the harshest way just what it was that had landed him where he was, and in the state he suspected his body of being in.

First he felt a thudding building within him. It started down low, deep in his guts, and rose as if it were marching right into his chest, and on up his gullet. By the time it wormed its way into his mouth and nose, he had begun to ache all over.

And then, the memory of the events leading up to all of

this flooded into his mind. The lashing agonies that come with what surely were a thousand cuts, stabs, cracked ribs, broken fingers, and more thrummed with a sudden and searing pain over all his body. As bad as was that pain, it bowed down before the thudding of the cannonade playing out betwixt his ears.

With more effort than he felt capable of, Trace cracked open his eyes. The sunlight that had been there, awaiting this moment with supreme impatience, drove forward and inward. As Trace squeezed his eyes shut once more, although too late to avoid this fresh, raw wash of pain, it felt as if forge-fired daggers were jamming themselves like steel vipers into his skull.

An unbidden moan, low and fragile, was accompanied with a deluge of memories that flooded over him. And he knew without doubt where he was. The battle atop that cursed ridge above Deadeye Gap, it was called. They'd found that holdout Reb company they'd been chasing for weeks.

Those foolish graybacks fought like cornered lions, with claws out and fangs slashing, and with a hard pistoning of their gunfire that seemed to not let up. Trace recalled wondering out loud, with some of the other Union men, if maybe the Rebel soldiers truly didn't know that the war was all but over for them.

No, there hadn't been any surrender as such—at least, not yet. But it was bound to happen soon. That's what they had all thought going into the latest fracas with the elusive, dastardly Rebs. The enemy numbers were raggedy and slowly dwindling, but they nonetheless fought at every turn as if they were freshly minted men.

Trace groaned again as the rest of the preceding events came back to him. He recalled how he had made his way down past the far side of the battle, chasing after a pair of

Reb snipers. He knew from experience that they'd been looking to sneak up around to where the Northern Army was encamped. That would not stand.

Trace had gotten the drop on them, sure, but instead of letting him take them as his prisoners, they'd put up a fight. He'd expected that, anyway. He didn't recommend it to anyone, even a foul Rebel, but he could hardly blame them, now, could he?

As he fought, trading shots with the two snipers, Trace realized from the sounds of the battle above and behind him, atop that ridge, that the melee was not about to end in favor of these maddening Rebels and the rest of their Southern ilk.

He was all but through with these two, having pinned them pretty well, despite being a lone soldier against two men. He had the landscape to thank, in part, for that, too. He had been able to position himself behind a boulder the size of a wagon, while the two Rebs he'd been pursuing had found themselves at the bottom of a gully with nothing but knee-height rocks and crusty pines no thicker around than a man's arm.

Then he had touched finger to trigger and had been about ready to send those two Rebel curs barking to the netherworld. Despite how he felt about them and their cause, there was that flicker of a moment when he regretted ever being involved in this foul mess, to begin with.

It had less, far less, to do with the individual soldiers, no matter the side, than it had to do with the cause each side fought for. And for all that, he knew that all these deaths could be laid at the feet of the leaders on both sides for their failure to keep talking, keep shouting at each other across the negotiation tables.

Trace didn't care how angry they got or how many days or weeks or months or years it would have taken. All of it would have been breath and time well spent if it had saved a single life of one of the soldiers on either side. Instead, they had ended up fighting, either by choice or, as had proved the case, by force, to fight and die for their respective so-called causes.

And Trace knew he wasn't the only man in the Union Army who felt that way. And he had it on good authority that most Rebs felt the same darned way, too. Fat lot of good it had done any of them.

All of that flooded into and out of his mind in that whisper of a moment before he squeezed the trigger to take yet another Rebel man's life. And at that moment, a shot whipped by his head from behind him. It spun Trace's gaze hard over his right shoulder. At the same time, instinct drove him down to one knee.

There he spied yet another grayback. This one, however, wasn't oblivious like his fellows. Trace had, after all, gotten the upper hand on those two Rebs down in their gully, looking this way and that.

In recalling that day, however many days before, Trace now realized that moment could have well ended it all, and in eyeblink speed. But for some reason that crazed Rebel he'd seen over his shoulder, with his rifle aimed right at Trace's head, had decided not to shoot him.

What he did instead genuinely surprised Trace. The man had delivered that shot at him. And when he faced him, Trace saw that the Reb hadn't been far enough away to have missed him.

Why hadn't I heard the rascal sneaking on up behind me? thought Trace.

As if in answer to the question of "why" echoing in Trace's skull, the Reb who'd shot at him from behind, and who held a revolver aimed right at him—he must have used his rifle to deliver that first, too-close-to-have-missed shot—shouted from about sixty feet away.

The Reb eyed him down the short barrel and barked, "I am a son of the South and as such I am too proud to shoot a man in the back, even if he is a foul, yellow, bluebelly Yankee!"

By then, of course, Trace had his own gun aimed right at that Rebel's gut. He rose once more to a standing position. Behind and below his big boulder, he heard a voice shout to another, "Let's git gone back to the fight! That Yank's done for!"

That told Trace he didn't have much to worry about from those two. He could concentrate on dealing with this crazy Rebel. A man who had him dead to rights, but who made him turn to face him before he would shoot him was a crazy man. Or a man with a conscience.

Make that a Rebel with a conscience. He knew there were a good many of them because he'd learned a whole lot since he started in on this war, with all its marches and lousy, maggoty food, and surly officers and lack of leadership with brains.

He'd learned that most Rebs were just about the same as most Yanks. That was to say, they were all just men. Men with wives and children and parents and cousins and friends and homes and farms, all of it.

And now here was one who wanted to fight him, face-to-face, fair and square. *All right, then,* thought Trace. *Let's get to it.*

He rose back to standing height, keeping his rifle aimed at that man's chest, and said, "What's it going to be, Reb? We have each other square on!"

"Shut up and approach. We'll see how far you make it, you stinking Yank!"

And so they had advanced on each other, slow step by slow step, their respective barrels not faltering, their boot steps sure and well placed, their eyes never leaving the other's, their trigger fingers ready to dole out the last sound the other man would ever hear.

But neither man pulled a trigger. Neither man dared to be the first, apparently, for they each advanced and strode with caution and unwavering concentration right toward the other.

And then they were close enough to see the grime caked in the lines on their faces, to see that they each could use a real shave, a haircut, a month's worth of sleep, and the same of food.

"Enough!" growled Fullcup Trace, flinging away his rifle. He didn't care any longer.

They'd been staring each other down for long, long minutes, slowly circling, and the situation had grown more than tiresome. A vital need had grown in him that they fight like men, men who were unafraid to cower behind the false cowardice of a gun.

As Trace regarded the other man, the grayback sneered, and he, too, sent his own gun spinning to the dirt. That's when things really began to head off into an interesting direction.

Again, as if by mutual unspoken agreement, the two men each sneered, their lips pulled back over tight-set teeth. Their eyes narrowed and growls crawled up out of their throats.

Arms drew up fast and their hands sought each other with clawlike fingers, fingers that closed on the other, on arms and chests. They balled wool tunics and at the same time jerked the other man this way and that, hoping to gain the upper hand.

They each gave voice to deep rage that, while directed at the other man, really represented the anguish and frustration and fear and confusion they had each felt for the past couple of years of being forced to kill or be killed.

Propelled by a clot of such feelings that fueled their rage, the two men muckled onto each other, hard and fast; neither uttered any sounds that could be recognized as words. Instead, there were growls and barks and the utterances of seething anger.

They circled, breaking their holds, only to collide again; one arm grasped clothing or hair, it mattered not. The other was curled into a thick fist that drew back, then drove forward like a sledge wielded by a railway man.

Their blows staggered each other, sent blasts of starlight even during the day before the receiver's sweat-riddled eyes. The punches and cudgel-like shots staggered each other, and yet neither man relented. Once they had agreed to brawl it out, neither man gave the other a moment's peace. Legs kicked, circled around other legs, seeking to trip.

The Reb was able to use his momentum to drive the Yank backward once. One of the man's blue-clad legs lay pinned beneath him, and the Reb knew something had happened to that bent knee. It had not broken, for the man would have yipped like a kicked dog, but nonetheless he knew something very painful had overtaken the man.

He grinned, his gritted teeth stained yellow and gray, as if to match his uniform, and he used the moment's pain to his advantage, jamming his own knee into the Yank's midsection.

But his hubris at finding himself atop the other was short-lived, for he had lost, for a moment, his accounting of the Yank's left arm. And as the Reb bent low to deliver a pulled-back punch, he left his own right side exposed.

The desperate Yank's left fist slammed into the right side of the Reb's ribs with the force of a hickory log being jammed, butt end first, into the man's torso, with deadly, unexpected momentum.

The blow shoved any air the Reb had in his chest, up and out, in a rush that ended in a wheeze. The worst of it for the Reb was feeling the sickening, sharp, lancing pain deep inside. He'd been down that painful road before and knew he'd just received a broken rib or three from that foul Yank.

The Reb collapsed to his left, falling off the pinned Yank long enough that the man in blue could roll to his left. Again, as if by mutual consent, the two men rose to their knees, facing each other, panting their rasping breaths. Hatred, directed at each other, glowed through their narrowed eyes, their chests working like bellows.

The Yank put little weight on his bum knee, for it pained him already and he knew it was swelling. He bet that something inside, the stringy bits in a man's body that hold flesh to bone, had torn or separated somehow.

The Reb raised his left hand to rest against the right side of his rib cage. He knew it showed a weakness, a wound dealt by the Yank, but he had to do it. Trace probed gingerly and again could not help the sharp-dawn breath of limping forward. With the Reb sipping shallow breaths, they drove at the other. Now each was intent of furthering the damage he had already inflicted on the other man.

How long they fought, neither man knew. Not that either of them cared. The brawl had become far more than two enemies having it out to some sort of end. It was the long-pent result of years of hardship shoved on them each day by their superiors, by the weather, by other soldiers, by bad food and worse water, by unforgiving terrain, and by the long-forgotten reasons behind why each was told they must kill other men.

And so it went, for hours or days or weeks, neither man knew or cared. At some point, one of them, neither could recall later which, tugged free his knife barely an eyeblink's worth of time before the other did.

Thus the fight went on, continuing with each man guessing the move of the other, growl for growl, punch for punch, kick for kick, driving knee for driving knee, butting head for butting head, lunging, snapping teeth for the same. And now was the deadly promise of honed steel.

The appearance of blades in their scar-knuckled, brawl-reddened hands kindled in each man a renewed fire, a burning rage to kill, and to not be killed. It was no surprise to either man that his opponent wore a sheath knife on his belt. Most soldiers did, and frequently these tools were brought from home, cherished items that a man regarded with as much or more fondness than his gun.

A hip knife was perhaps a man's most relied-upon possession. It was a tool he used many times a day. Men shaved with them; used them to cut hair and trim beards; to skin, gut, and slice fresh-killed critters for the fry pan or pot, from turtles to swamp rats to rabbits, and more.

A big-bladed knife also could be used to split lengths of branch wood for kindling, for sharpening sticks, for cooking and hewing stakes for tents. And as long as a man had a whetstone in his possibles sack, it could also be used to dig a cathole in the steel-dulling earth, should a man care that much about covering his leavings with more than forest duff.

Occasionally, although the men agreed it was happening more and more as the war dragged on, these knives had begun to be used to defend one's life, and to attack a foe as well.

As each man, Trace and Chaw, lifted free his knife, a sneer rose unbidden on each face. Without warning, they rushed at each other, snarls of rage ripping from their mouths.

They fought with bedraggled bodies sporting bloodshot eyes, bruised and bloodied mouths from split lips and smacked noses, and sweat-plastered hair. They wore the grime of repeated slammings and rollings in the dust and churned soil of the small, scree-riddled plateau they each had been stomping and trampling and kicking and furrowing for hours.

They fought as beasts, coming together amid howls and clouds of dust, slashing and driving, peeling apart and wielding keen blades afresh with each parry and thrust. Over and over, they attacked, not seeming to lose the renewed, whetted appetite for blood they each shared.

Their thirst for killing clouded their usual individual sensibilities and they fought hard and viciously. They rarely fell apart without leaving hacked slices in the arms of woolen tunics, on through into the sweat-soaked underwear beneath, finally drawing blood in scarred skin befouled by war and hard living.

Cuts more than gashes, although there were plenty of those as well, covered each man's head, face, torso, arms, hips, backsides, and calves. It seemed to each man as if they were covered with the denizens of a huge hive of deadly hornets, for with every move they made, their bodies screamed from the constant, stinging pain of a thousand lacerations.

Over time, neither man knew how much, the welter of agony each found himself mired within began to take its due toll.

Each man, the Reb and the Yank, after hours of cutting and slashing, howling and colliding, clubbing and flailing at the other, hammer and tong, staggered backward.

Trace, the Yank, had no idea how he had managed to stay upright for so very long, as his knee had somehow endured far beyond ordinary pain.

When he had been able to steal a quick glance at himself, he had been shocked to see, through the slashed fabric of his trousers, that they were no longer showing any trace of blue. They were matted with a reddened black, and were sodden with sweat and blood. His own and that of the foul, determined Reb.

What had shocked him most was the size of his knee. It had swelled to what seemed the size of a man's head. The ragged trouser leg about it, although slashed, had also brought with it a cold dose of luck. The knee had been able to swell and not be constricted by the fabric itself, for good or ill.

The Reb, leaning against the boulder before which the Yank had begun the fight, felt his breath wheezing in and out of his damaged breadbasket and rib cage. He hated to admit it, but that Yank had delivered into his side one mighty wallop, a pummeling such that the Reb was certain he might never again breathe as a normal man.

That thought had been from who knew how long before. Before the brutality their knives had inflicted. Now the Reb was a gasping, wheezing mess.

It was all he could do, now that they had fallen back apart from each other once again, to maintain his tender hold on his knife. He glanced down at himself and saw nothing he recognized.

Not his right hand, nor the knife in its grasp. He knew there was a knife there somewhere, hidden under a thick, syrupy coating of red-black gore that streamed and sluiced in steady rivulets down his drooped arm. The hand and fingers were covered with their own slick gore, beneath which dozens of cuts screamed at once. As did his entire body.

Chaw glanced up once more, as he held his left hand to his right-side rib cage, the tenderest spot on his entire savaged form. "If I . . . look . . ."

He swallowed and licked his lips—his voice a cracked, croaking thing. My, how he longed for a long sip of cool, clear water. "If I looked as bad . . . as you . . . Yank . . . I'd up and die already."

The Yank regarded the Reb as he leaned against the trunk of a much-scuffed pine. What he wanted to say was: *Of course you would! You're a weak-kneed Rebel!* But what came out, between huffing gasps, was: "Could say the same . . . to you, Reb. . . ."

In all the time of that fight, neither man had done much more, soundwise, than to grunt and shout sounds that were not words. But they did not much care. But now, hearing their voices, after hearing nothing but raw animal sounds from themselves, surprised each of them.

It also seemed to trigger something within each of them once more, yet another animalistic lunge to satisfy the unreasoning rage each felt at nearly being killed by the other.

They bolted forward, once more as if they had nodded in agreement with one another, and yet they hadn't. This did not slow them down, but the wearing, atrophying pain of the protracted battle had shown its strain as each man shoved up and away from the only things that were really keeping them upright—the boulder and the tree.

They lurched forward, staggering and eyeing each other through blood-flecked eyelashes, blinking and wheezing, their knives held halfway up in weak grasps. Each man, with his eyes fixed on the other, advanced. Paltry, feeble step by lurching, halting step, they drew closer, slowly, grunting and wheezing, bleeding and groaning.

And, as had happened since they began their attempt at mutual destruction, they each faltered within ten feet of each other, and the last thing each man saw was the other, his sworn mortal foe, sagging and collapsing. Eyes rolled back in heads, knees buckled, heads sloped backward on their weak stalks as their bodies slowly sank to the churned, bloodied earth.

Each man sloped to the side, then flopped, sprawled flat on his back, but a couple of yards apart. Each still held his dagger in a death-clench grip, stiffened into place by the sticky, drying blood.

When Private Chaw Dagworth, of the Confederate Army, came to, and as he gazed on what he assumed was a dead Yank, not but a few feet to his right, a Yank he had apparently killed, the entirety of the brutal fight came back to him. And he did not feel one sliver of goodness about it, not one slender thread of pride or satisfaction in having laid low yet another Yankee soldier.

Instead, he thought about how evenly matched they had been. Too much so, it seemed, for it had been one heck of a fight. And as much as he had tried to outmaneuver that blue brute, the fellow had done the same to him, as if they were each reading the other man's thoughts.

How long had they fought? Had it been mere minutes? Hours? The way he looked and the way he felt, it surely must have been days, days in which neither man was aware of light or dark passing. When neither one broke away, despite the fact that they yearned for a drink of water so badly from their respective canteens.

But now, with the thought of water, the wetness of it

touching his lips, cooling his parched, burning throat, now all Chaw could think of was water, of getting a sweet, sweet drink into himself.

Where was his canteen?

He looked down at himself, but no, it was not strapped about his chest as usual. Nor was the rest of his gear. Where was it all?

And then he remembered—he had shed the canteen, the blanket roll, his pack, in the dried grasses at the base of the tree. That tree that somehow the Yank had ended up closer to than Chaw.

He glanced back that way, beyond the Yank, and Chaw saw he'd been wrong. For the man now looked not to be alive but dead. *Deader than dead,* as his old pap used to say. If he could only get on over there, past the Yank, over to the tree, where his gear still lay in a heap. Get to that canteen.

Then he saw what he had assumed was trickery of his eyes, that cursed Yank was moving again. Yes, he was alive! His chest was rising, falling, rising.

Chaw could not understand two things—how the man could possibly be alive, for Chaw had convinced himself that he alone had survived the awful fight. And the second thing he could not fathom was why he felt relief, immediate and flooding through his mind, as he saw that bluebelly breathe.

Hadn't he fought such men for years now? Hadn't he vowed over and over again that he would kill every Yankee he came across?

Chaw groaned and squeezed his eyes shut, then opened them again, the dried blood cracking slightly about them.

Back to the water, he thought. *Concentrate on getting water, or nobody, not you or the Yank, is going to live for much longer.*

And then Chaw had, what at that moment he knew, was the very best idea he had ever come upon in his whole life. He turned his head slowly, painfully, to the left and saw that massive boulder where the Yank had been standing when Chaw had first popped off that warning shot. And there, at the base, was the Yank's own gear pile. And among it, not but a few yards to Chaw's left, sat a canteen.

He grunted, trying to shove himself over onto his left side, pinioning himself from behind with his bloody right hand. That's when Chaw felt his knife still gripped tightly in his hand. He tried to let go of it, but it stayed there, attached somehow to his palm.

He raised it and saw that it was glued to his hand, and then he knew—it was blood, likely his own, thick and mostly dried, holding the knife there. The sight of it made his head and guts churn. He flopped back to the earth with a gasp from his wounded ribs, his wind pinched and painful.

Why hadn't he shot the cursed Yank when he had the chance? What stayed his hand? Surely, it wasn't just not wanting to shoot a Yank, even in the back. He'd done it a few times before. Yeah, it left a sour taste in his gut and mouth and mind for days after, but then he'd seen a new atrocity committed on a Reb by a Yank, and he'd gotten over it right quick.

A few feet away, Private Fullcup Trace, of the Union Army, managed a good few pulls of breath and worked at trying to open his eyes all the way. Something not unlike what a child felt when he awakened with eyes half-crusted shut following a night's sleep.

But this was different, and something he'd not felt before, not in all his adult years. He scrunched his eyes and worked his cheeks until whatever it was freed up a bit, enough for him to force, then pop open first one eye, and then the second.

He tried to raise a hand, but neither wanted to respond. And then, with a bit more concentrated effort, he was able to twitch life into first his left and then his right. But the left felt heavier. He gritted his teeth and forced his eyes open wide. It was a mighty effort and he didn't want to let his mind trail down the path of finding out why. Not yet. First he had to find out what that new sound was, off to his left.

Instinct told him to keep his movements as quiet as he could, but for all that, he grunted as he worked to raise himself up onto his left elbow. He looked down at his left side and saw that his hand, a blood-crusted claw, was curled tightly around what looked to be a knife. Yes, it was a knife, his hip dagger.

Trace looked at his fingers, but somehow could not make them do his bidding. He'd have to use his right hand, which seemed to be working all right. He again heard a sound from his left, and, reminded of why he had been roused in the first place, he looked over to the left.

The first thing he saw was the big boulder, and he recognized it as the one he'd been hiding behind . . . for some reason. What had it been? And then he saw a body before the rock, but it was moving, faced away from him, doing something. . . .

On seeing it, in a fingersnap of time, it all came back to him and Trace recalled everything that had happened. Chasing those two Rebs, pinning them down in the draw, then being jumped and surprised from behind as he hid by the boulder.

He'd spun and seen that Rebel. He was a tall, rugged-looking, scruffy, gray-clad fellow who'd gotten the drop on him. But instead of shooting to kill Trace, he'd missed him, missed him with intention.

It had made no sense to Trace then, and it still didn't. Despite the fact that the Reb had shouted something about how he'd not resort to shooting a man in the back, even if that man was a lousy Yank.

Trace almost grinned at the thought of him being referred to as "lousy." He reckoned he'd been called a whole lot of things in his life, but not quite that. And then . . . then they had fought. Oh, how they had fought.

Hammer and tong, as the old-timers used to say. Neither man had been willing to give in, let alone give up. It had been the hardest, rawest, most brutal fight of Trace's life.

A hawk's piercing call from high up sounded. Other than that, and the slight sounds the Reb was making— what was that fellow doing?—there was no other sound. Nothing. Not even battle noise. There should be that, at least. It was . . . Deadeye Gap, that's right.

Something seemed . . . not right. He should hear something, should feel something. But all he felt was . . . numb. As if he'd spent a week inside a whiskey bottle and still hadn't reached the bottom of the thing.

He looked around himself, down at his bloodied mess of a body, and saw his right leg, puffed at the knee. So much so, in fact, that it looked as though there were two limbs in that trouser leg. *If I'm that bad off, why can't I feel it?*

He squinted and tried to see what the Reb was up to, but the man was faced away from him, looking at the boulder, but doing something over there.

So why, thought Trace, *can't I feel something, anything at all, other than this fuzzy, sort-of numb sensation?* And then a thought came to him: *I must be dead. This must be what it's like to be gone. Or maybe in that limbo place, because I have not been sorted out yet by whoever was in charge up there. Or . . . no, can't be down there. Can it?*

I'm stuck in this middle layer of whatever this was, neither dead nor alive. He'd read about this, he thought, or maybe he was just recalling it from his gran's growled interpretations of the Bible. *Either way, here I am,* thought Trace. *Dead or dying.*

Had that Rebel bandit killed him? As bad as Trace was beginning to feel, it must be so. He must have been killed in the fight. He sure knew it was a fight for the ages. And yet, when a soldier is dead, or nearly so, what did that matter? *You might well have fought for some cause you believed in, sure, but when you're dead, what good is that cause to you?* Trace thought.

Heady stuff, he figured, but the upshot of it was that Trace was convinced, more and more, with each second that passed that he was sitting, or lying down, on Death's doorstep. And the Rebel?

Trace wagered that if he himself was dead, it stood to some sort of reason that his licks had laid the Reb low, too. But then why was that rascal here as well? Must be he had killed the Reb at the same time the Reb had done for him. Must be that one of his licks managed to find purchase on the Reb's body, a blow that surely had laid low the man.

As memory trickled, then flooded in, so had his begrudging admiration for the Rebel. As with most of his kind that Trace had come across, he was a scrapper.

"Hey!"

Trace jerked as if slapped. What had that been? Or who?

"Hey, you! Yank!"

Trace had heard that, hadn't he?

"Hey now, Yank!"

The voice had come from his left, He looked over that way once more and saw that the Reb was now facing him and looking his way. And he held a canteen below his lips.

At the thought of that word, Fullcup Trace felt a quick zing of something charge into him. Water. He would kill all over again for a drink of water.

"Yeah, I see you heard me."

Trace looked at the man once more. Was the Rebel smiling? Can a man smile when he's dead? Oh, but this felt all too confusing.

"You best do what I did and crawl on back there behind yourself. My pack's there, not but a few feet behind you, at that tree. Got a canteen there."

The words, somehow, leached through the gauzy, thick scrim that Trace felt covering over himself, and he knew that even if he was dead, he had to try to act on those words. They were important somehow. For they meant there was water at the end of them, and even if he was well and truly dead, which seemed pretty likely to him, he sure could use a drink of water.

"Wake up now, man, and go get that water. We ain't through tussling with each other yet."

Trace glanced once more at the Rebel to his left, then shifted his body such that he looked to his right instead. Sure, there was the tree, it was the tree the Rebel had been standing before when Trace had been tipped off by that shot that should have, by rights, killed him.

But it hadn't, and now here he was, and the Reb was telling him he needed to go get water. If Trace was understanding all this correctly, that meant the Reb was telling him to go get the Reb's water. And that sounded like a trap. A trick. Rebel treachery.

But then it occurred to Trace that the Reb was drinking water, and it was Trace's water. His very own canteen.

Why was he doing that? But did that mean that he trusted Trace? No, it only meant that he was thirsty.

All of this thinking amounted to nothing more than confusion for Trace. He glanced at the Reb's dropped gear at the base of that tree, not all that far from him, to the right, and he thought he could see the man's canteen. And the sight of it gave him an overwhelming urge for water.

He grunted and worked to flip himself over onto his right side. Even as he did this, he stuck his thick, swollen tongue slowly out of his mouth and touched his lips. He had to get to that canteen.

Ever since Fullcup Trace was a child, he could recall no time when he did not accomplish a thing once he set his sights on it. And that water waiting for him was no exception. He saw it and he wanted it and that was all there was to it. That, and crawling on over there.

In his mind, he was nearly there. But when he glanced quickly down at himself, he had only planted one elbow, his right, to the dusty earth. He still needed to get himself righted and angled so he could make it over there.

He squeezed his eyes shut and gritted his teeth and somehow he managed to get the top half of his body angled where it should be, aimed for that water. He made for it, somehow, and felt himself actually moving forward, slower, he was certain, than an ant. But then again, he was dead or nearly there, so why should he complain? He was moving pretty well for a dead man.

He almost laughed at this, but somehow he hadn't the strength. He moved forward with one elbow and then the forearm of his left arm. And there was that knife, still gripped in his locked fingers, and he couldn't figure out how to let go of it.

Maybe it was best he didn't. That Reb might be sneaking on over to ambush him at that moment!

Trace wondered about this and figured that as bad as that man looked, he wasn't going to move any faster than Trace. And besides, he was nearly to that water.

Then he felt something down low that he hadn't felt before. It was on his legs. *No, just the one leg, ah yes,* he thought. That swollen right leg. It was paining him something awful.

Could that be right? If he was on his way to death, just waiting for someone to tap him on the shoulder, would he be able to feel that pain?

As he crawled, now no more than a few feet from that water, that leg began to throb hard. He groaned again, and let himself do it. It was a sound, after all, and that might lead to him being able to say something. Or to shout, should he need to call for help from one of the boys. They'd take care of that Reb, and right quick, too.

Trace saw it now, just ahead of him, jumbled with a small pile of gear that looked a whole lot like his own. He spied a bedroll and a pack, and, leaning against the pack, a canteen, round and carved wood and bound with what looked like rawhide, tight and shrunk to fit. A strap handle of some sort of grimy cloth, knotted and looking as if it had been through a war.

At that thought, Trace did snort, just a bit. His lips split as he did so and he felt the stinging anew.

He brought his left hand up to grab that canteen, which sat right there before his face, but that blasted knife was still part of his hand. He shifted his weight over to the left elbow and reached with his crusted, filthy right hand.

It was a shaking thing that looked like it should be attached to some old dead man. But it did the job, after a couple of grabs, and he felt that canteen jostle, heard the water inside, felt the promising weight of it—it felt more than half full.

He drew it to his face and leaned it against his nose, while his fingers fumbled with the wooden bung. It was attached with a strip of string and he grunted and made a slight, squealing sound deep in his throat trying to get it dislodged.

When he finally was able to drizzle that soothing, although warm, liquid onto his lips and into his mouth, he nursed on it like a feeding piglet, and he didn't care who heard him. Never, never, never—and he could not be convinced otherwise—had anything in the history of the world tasted as good to anyone. Ever.

He sipped and slurped and guzzled, and although he knew he really should ration that precious stuff, somehow he could not make himself aware, could not make himself do the thing he knew he needed to do.

Which was to ease off on the water and . . .

"Take 'er easy, Yank, or you're liable to get a gut ache and throw it all up again. Then where will you be?"

Trace paused when the man first began to speak. It reminded him of what he had forgotten, namely that he was not alone. He angled himself to face the man, finding it easier to move and maneuver, now that he had been somewhat revived due to the water.

He saw that the Reb was still where he'd last seen him, over by the boulder. But now he was seated and leaning against it.

"Huh?" said Trace, surprised on hearing his own voice. "Huh?" he repeated, more to hear his voice falter. But at least he could still hear and feel.

All of his senses appeared to have been rejuvenated by the water. It was a lesson he'd long known, but as he'd experienced throughout life, it often paid to be reminded.

"I said to back off the water. Rest up!"

Trace let these words sink into his mind a moment, then said, "Why?"

"Got to take care of you. . . ."

"Why?"

The Reb chuckled. "So I can kill you fair and square, that's why!"

"Don't count on it, Reb."

And so it went, with each man resting and occasionally nibbling on the canteen of his enemy. Remembering, in their fatigue, to look across the few yards toward the other, taking stock and planning just how he would, with very little strength and a body sliced and stabbed and broken and bruised and aching, renew his attack. That was about all they had strength for.

This kept up for hours, and the sun began its descent.

"Reb!"

"Yeah?"

"You got food in this pack?"

"Not much. Hardtack. Coffee. You?"

"About the same. No coffee, though."

"Have at it, Yank."

"You, too, Reb."

Neither man did much more for long minutes as the shadows grew. Trace had been able to pry the fingers of his left hand from around the handle of his knife. He still couldn't flex them fully, but they were moving, bit by bit, a little better than they had been.

Then the Reb said, "If we built a fire, we could have ourselves coffee."

"I don't have any coffee," said the Yank.

"I do, like I said. In my pack. But no flint or steel."

"I have those."

"All right then," said the Reb. "Where?"

Silence, then Trace, the Yankee, said, "Best by that boulder where you are."

"Yeah. All right. Bring my gear?"

"I will," said Trace, trying to figure out how he was going to do that and get himself on over to the rock where the Reb sat with Trace's own gear. But he did it.

At the same time, the Reb managed to get himself up to his feet, although he leaned heavily on the rock, and worked to toe up tinder and duff from the ground.

The entire knobby plateau on which they sat was sparsely treed, mostly with low, stunty growth, but there was enough of that. There were also a few dropped branches, and a long, dead tree, brittle and dry. So finding fuel for the fire did not look to be a problem to two men used to scavenging for such on behalf of their respective outfits.

Trace managed to also get to his feet, although his swollen knee proved a painful hinderance to his being able to move any faster than a snail with no ambition. Still, he pressed on, dragging along with him the Reb's pack and canteen and blankets, as well as the man's rifle, lugged by its sling, so a return trip to the base of the tree would not be necessary.

Although they had spent the past few hours but twenty or so feet apart, the two men approached each other with slow caution and grim looks. Each once more held his knife, and Trace was relieved to see that the Reb looked about as bad as he did.

He'd wondered earlier, since the Reb was so chatty, at least compared with himself, that maybe the man wasn't as bad off as Trace felt.

He knew that wasn't a very charitable way to think, but after all, this was a man who was a member of a group he'd been told to hate, so much so that he must kill him. But at that moment, seeing the haggard Reb before him, a man who, when he'd had the opportunity to shoot Trace, had not done so, gave Trace a strange sense of calm and relief.

He knew then that, at least for the time being, however long that might be, they had reached a truce of sorts and would break bread and share coffee. After that . . . well, that was a bridge they would cross when they reached it.

Together they managed to kindle a fire and keep it fed. All the while, from opposite sides of the fire, the two men stole glances at each other, stern faces not slipping a bit.

They exchanged snatches of speech and answered the other's brief questions without much elaboration. Soon, it became apparent to each man that the other was tired. *Dog tired and bone weary,* as Chaw's old gramps used to say.

Darkness descended on them, and while they had dragged back to the fire enough snapped wood and half-rotted lengths and sticks and such, they knew they would be unable to keep it fed through the night.

Trace fought to keep his eyelids open. Finally, he sighed. "Am I safe?" There was a brief pause and he realized he had likely just awakened the Reb from a catnap.

"Safe? From me?" The Reb chuckled. "Yeah, I reckon. As long as I am from you."

"Yeah, okay. Truce for sleep."

"Truce for sleep. . . ."

our website at
...ngtonBooks.com
to ...n ... or our newsletters, read
more from your favorite authors, see
books by series, view reading group
guides, and more!

Become a Part of Our
Between the Chapters Book Club
Community and Join the Conversation

Betweenthechapters.net

Submit your book review for a chance to win exclusive
Between the Chapters swag you can't get anywhere else!
https://www.kensingtonbooks.com/pages/review/